GREATER *miracles*

OTHER BOOKS BY THE AUTHOR

For brief synopses of Mark's other books, a study guide,
an author profile, as well as an engaging conversation
with Mark about the writing of GREATER MIRACLES,
please go to the Extras section at the end of this book or
visit our website at: www.IFMedia.org/IFBooks.

GREATER *miracles*

MARK S HASKETT

IF BOOKS

Modesto, California

First Softcover Print Edition, March, 2017.
Second Print Edition, March, 2022.

Copyright ©2017, 2022 by Mark S. Haskett.
Published by IF BOOKS.

ISBN 978-0-9971259-6-2

Printed in the United States of America.

*IF Books and IF Media are subdivisions of
InnerFaith Resources, Modesto, California.*

CONTENTS

Premonition 1

1   Natalie / Gabriel's Need 5
2   Visalia / The Roofer 13
3   Leaving Again / Vincent 25
4   The Deer / Lieutenant Fiske 37
5   Arrival in Chiloquin 52
6   The Ammunition Plant / Lane 68
7   Gabriel's Dilemma / The Ranch . . . 84
8   House Rules / Gumbo 98
9   Back to the Ammo Plant 116
10   Corky Girls / Doyle 132
11   Gabriel's Miracle 155
12   Deputy Chino / The Legend 171
13   The Town Meeting 188
14   The Maqlaqs' Visit 206
15   Beatty / The Sermon 222
16   Jenna / The Accident 240
17   Gabriel's Confession 254
18   The Lockout / Sabotage 267
19   Richard / Vincent Returns 284
20   Fiske / Conspiracy 301
21   Inside the Ammo Plant 321
22   Endings 337
23   Beginnings 352

EXTRAS

Study Guide 370
About the Author 373
Author Interview 374
Other Books by the Author 380
Pages for Notes 381

Premonition

*N*o warning. *No screeching tires* to prepare those who hadn't seen it coming. Only the sudden, chest-thumping boom that sounded and felt more like an explosion than the impact of two vehicles.

Or, more precisely, big-rig and minivan.

Gabriel found himself outside almost against his will, slowly crossing the parking lot inside a swirling tunnel of people running, shouting, crying. He stopped beside the highway, tried to focus. The scene was even more gut-wrenching than he'd expected, ripping open his past, forcing him to gasp for breath before he could go any further. No sooner had he stepped off the curb than he was overcome with the urge to vomit. He fought it, swallowed, stumbled like a bleary-eyed drunk onto the pavement.

By the time he'd circled the minivan to locate the last of its ejected passengers, the victim's head and upper torso were concealed beneath a bright blue windbreaker. As Gabriel bent down to pull the bloodied polyester aside, one of the two men standing nearby spotted him.

"You don't wanna look under there, pal," he said, taking a sudden step back. It was clear *he* didn't want another look either.

Gabriel peeled away the windbreaker regardless, fought off the urge to retch a second time. The teen's gender was distinguishable only by her long auburn hair, now matted with blood, and the pubescent mounds beneath an inexplicably unsullied sweatshirt. The right side of her head and face were crushed, a split in her skull sprouting like a row of glistening cauliflower.

It was, Gabriel thought, the worst injury he'd encountered by far, bad enough to make him wonder if he'd finally run up against the limits of his unwelcome gift. He couldn't imagine putting all the pieces of this wreckage back together, not to mention what oozed from behind it. Then again, imagination played no part. Thinking only delayed what could not be stopped. Consciousness was constriction. If he added anything to the process, it was merely to submit, to abandon himself and his limited understanding and simply let that something *be*.

He drew a breath, ignored the heat beginning to flow into his hands, gave up control. Shutting out the sickened protests of the two bystanders, he began to push the girl's brain back inside her skull, felt the gelatinous lumps thickening, the jig-sawed bone knitting together beneath his fingers.

Her congealed blood was now liquid again, running like warm syrup, dripping off his wrists as he drew one hand down the nape of her neck, smearing across her shoulder blades when he reached inside her collar and down her spine. At the same time he slid his other hand up under her sweatshirt, across her chest, palm flat against her breastbone, riding over her ribcage and back onto her abdomen as if to ensure he hadn't missed anything.

It was just then that Gabriel heard another voice through another tunnel, shouting as the others had, vaguely sensed a hand grabbing hold of his own collar. Before he could react, his body was surging, reeling butt-first, the momentum carrying his shoulders and head in an arc that met the asphalt with a loud crack he heard rather than felt.

He wasn't sure he'd blacked out. But he soon became aware of a highway patrolman bending over him, indignant stare piercing through bronze Ray-Bans. An instant later the patrolman glanced away, his glower evaporating at whatever caught his eye. His head quickly rose out of view only to be replaced by that of the man who'd spoken to Gabriel earlier.

"You okay...? Hey, doc – whoever you are... you *okay?*"

Gabriel lifted himself enough to nod.

The man reached down, offered a hand. "The badge here didn't realize what you were doin' when he drove up." Then, lowering his voice: "Course, I didn't know what the hell you were doin' either..."

Gabriel dabbed at the back of his head, blinked, saw the teenager now being attended by two paramedics who'd arrived just after the patrolman.

"...an' for the life a'me, I *still* can't believe my eyes."

The man shook his head for added emphasis, looked up as another paramedic appeared from behind them, pushing a gurney with an oxygen tank.

"Anyways, looks like she's breathin' again. Could'a sworn she opened her one good eye just before you got decked."

It seemed so long ago now, the series of events precipitating his latest journey, that left him in the same sorry predicament prompting every other journey before this.

He had no inkling his life was about to change. Or change *back.* Not that it mattered. Much as he might wish otherwise, the watersheds in his life were never really under his control, though they *did* result from one of two recurring causes. Either he'd been exposed again – or rather his gift, his *burden,* had. Or else there was a woman involved. By the time he'd turned twenty-one, it had more often become a combination of both.

Like most of the women Gabriel Woods sought out – before Lane at least – this one was a waitress. She was also in possession of a simple, unpretentious beauty he would like to have enjoyed on a regular basis had his life been anything approaching normal. Although this, too, didn't matter: Fitness was more important than physical attraction.

Having learned from past mistakes, Gabriel made a few discreet inquiries into Natalie's background, as much as he could without seeming like some jilted lover who'd begun stalking her. A buffed-up busboy confessed he'd seen her several times working out at the Gold's Gym in Bakersfield. A fellow waitress was "kinda sure" she'd donated blood when the Grapevine Denny's sponsored a drive in support of the local Guard unit just back from Afghanistan. And when, during Gabriel's fifth visit to the restaurant – always making sure to sit in Natalie's section – she stopped at his booth and casually mentioned the "Making Plans for Life" class she'd begun at the Unity Fellowship in Arvin, he could hardly keep from proposing a weekend getaway, unbridled lust and all, right there at table twelve.

As far as he could determine, she was the model of health. Which meant there would be no repercussions.

And he, in turn, would be patient. As long as his lack of physical contact hadn't become a desperate need, and assuming his coworkers and acquaintances weren't on to him, he was content to let things unfold at their own pace. In fact, developing a new relationship gave his vagabond existence a semblance of stability, an excuse to pretend he was no different from the next guy – even though, to his serial regret, he knew he'd eventually skip town without so much as a scribbled note.

After three more visits in a single week, Natalie grew more curious, began to prop herself against the vinyl backrest across the aisle and chat for a minute or two. By the following week she was slipping into the booth alongside him for more extended conversations, as long as the dinner rush had abated and the manager was busy tallying up the day's receipts.

"You like the ocean?" Gabriel asked, almost out of the blue, on his eighth visit.

"Love it," she replied. "Family used to drive over to Morro Bay, or sometimes Pismo, practically every summer. 'Been a long time," she added wistfully.

"Wish I'd gotten a job over on the coast," he said, mirroring her mood. "But then, I might never've met you." He squinted at her with a sudden smile, pausing for effect, then popped the question he'd been waiting nearly a month to pose.

"Ever make love on the beach?"

The query caught Natalie off guard. It was a little more direct than his usual soft-sell, Gabriel had to admit. But his lingering, boyish grin and pale gray eyes put her at ease.

"Umm, no... can't say I have."

"Me neither." He gazed toward the interstate, the lights of passing motorists streaking the dust-glazed window. "All that sand for one thing." Another pause. "Nope. Just give me one of those cozy seaside cottages with a deck and a sliding glass door and a queen-size bed with a view a'the waves."

She gave him a sidelong glance as he continued to stare thoughtfully away, and almost as if he'd scripted it, she finally said, "I know a place just like that."

He got the company pickup and two-and-a-half days off on Natalie's next weekend – a Wednesday and Thursday, according to her posted work schedule – and called the motel she'd told him about just north of Morro Bay. Except for his remark about the beach, they hadn't brought up the subject of sex again. Nor had they so much as brushed up against each other on the two subsequent visits it took to confirm that, yes, they would indeed be going away together. Not so much for the beach, it was hoped, as the view from the Simmons Beautyrest.

Halfway to the coast, at the end of a meandering monologue about her father's preference for unfiltered Marlboros, Natalie reached over and stroked Gabriel's shoulder. It was as innocent as it was brief, but he felt a tiny charge. Both of them felt it. Even Gabriel assumed it was a natural reaction to their sudden self-consciousness at having touched for the very first time. That, and maybe the electricity generated by their unspoken agreement about what this getaway was really *for.*

There was even more electricity when, an hour later, they dropped their luggage just inside the door of the blue-and-white cottage that faced the beach, opened the drapes to an unobstructed view of wind-blown foam roiling fifty yards below, and could hardly pull off their clothes fast enough.

They ignored the view of the surf for a good two hours. Then, nearly exhausted, they slipped on swimsuits to go outside and sit on the deck. For another quarter hour they debated a stroll on the beach. But by the time they finally hopped off the deck, the ocean breeze had strengthened enough to strip foam from the wave tops and sting them with sand whipped up by passing joggers. It was precisely the excuse they needed to go back inside, shower off together, and ignore the view for the rest of the afternoon.

A persimmon sun was flattening itself against the horizon when they both admitted they were starving. Natalie remembered a corner cafe on the embarcadero across from Morro Rock where her family often celebrated her father's birthday, an event that always coincided with their summer vacations. They drove into town and found the cafe without any trouble, though the owners and the menu had changed five or six times in the eighteen years since Natalie wore pigtails.

The cafe was a 50's diner now, its quilted chrome just a bit too shiny to be convincing. Gabriel smiled when Natalie asked for the foot-long hot dog – "with tons of mayonnaise, please" – opting for the house special instead.

"Was chicken fried steak really that big an item in the Fifties?" he wondered aloud, after the waitress left with their order.

"Don't know. My dad could tell you... if he was still around."

And with that single comment she seemed to go inside herself. It was nearly a minute before she blinked several times and came back.

"He was down to half a lung before he died," she went on, "and even then he wouldn't quit. 'Course, heredity might've had something to do with it. In my case it's lymphoma."

Gabriel dropped his jaw, then his fork. "You mean you... *you* have cancer?"

"If you can believe those last two biopsies."

"Jesus," Gabriel said, but not for the reasons Natalie suspected.

"It's okay," she said, reaching across the table as if he were the one who needed comforting.

He recoiled before their hands met. She blinked again, sat back in the booth, palms up.

"See—? That's why I don't tell people. Like I'm communicable or something." She sighed, looked him up and down while he sat there stiffly, then glanced away with a shake of her head. "I figured one of the other waitresses told you, the way you always avoided touching me..."

Now Gabriel blinked. *Was he that obvious?*

"...but then I figured it must not bother you after all."

"It doesn't. I mean, the cancer doesn't..." He stopped, regrouped – *when could he stop lying?* – waited until she faced him again before leaning forward onto the chrome-rimmed tabletop. "I *want* to touch you, Natalie. I want to make love to you again... tonight."

And why not? The damage – or rather its opposite – had already been done. Like Midas turning dross into gold, Gabriel's touch brought its effect whether he intended it or not. Most often *despite* those intentions. And now, if anything, he needed to act as if nothing had happened, to give Natalie no reason to suspect his role when the inevitable questions began cropping up.

Their server reappeared in her pleated skirt and natty red scarf, paused while Gabriel withdrew his arms from the table before setting their plates down. Natalie nodded appreciatively as the perky novice smiled and bounced away, then returned her gaze to Gabriel.

He continued to stare back patiently, soft gray eyes an almost startling contrast to his sienna skin. There was the diagonal sheen of an inch-long scar above the bridge of his nose, but his face was otherwise flawless, lean and smooth and framed by thick, dark brown hair not quite long enough for a ponytail.

Maybe, as Natalie's thoughtful silence seemed to admit, Gabriel's reaction was only surprise and concern. Besides, they had another whole day and night to spend together. Why throw away what they both knew they'd come for, over what was probably a simple misunderstanding?

Gabriel was sure that's what she'd decided. He was even *more* certain once they'd returned to their beachfront cottage and Natalie was as unrestrained and exuberant on the sheets as she'd been before dinner.

Which is why her request to go back home the very next morning seemed so baffling.

The waves outside their cottage were glistening in the first light as Gabriel began to rouse. He found himself gazing at the ceiling while it brightened and darkened in tandem with the crashing surf, pondered why, finally theorized that the sunlight would reflect off the sparkling foam as each wave broke, then fade until the next wave crested. He laughed out loud to think he could be so clever this early in the morning, then quickly sobered when he realized Natalie wasn't lying beside him. Nor had she been for the few minutes he'd spent formulating his light-wave theory.

He leapt out of bed, found her on the deck sitting pensively in one of the chaise lounges where she couldn't be seen through the sliding glass. She didn't seem to notice when he first drew the door aside, then finally glanced over her shoulder with a distracted smile.

"Everything okay...?" he ventured.

"*Better* than okay."

He attempted his own awkward smile, but she'd already turned back toward the ocean.

"I mean, it's just so weird. Sometimes I can barely get out of bed in the morning. That's always my worst time. Before we came here I was worried what you'd think." She tossed an apologetic shrug. "It's like I get old and creaky during the night... and it takes an hour or two for me to limber up again. After that I'm usually fine for the rest of the day."

He closed the slider without comment, found himself clasping his arms against the chilly sea breeze, even as he noted the skimpy shorts and tank top she was wearing.

"But not this morning. God, I haven't felt this good since before I... I don't know—*years*. Even longer since I went jogging on the beach at daybreak."

She shook the sand from her hair in joyful disbelief, picked her cell phone off the deck before lifting herself from the chaise. "Gabriel, you're gonna think this is really stupid of me, but I just made an appointment with my oncologist for later this afternoon. I can't wait to see her face when she gets the results of my next test."

The drive back to Bakersfield wasn't the three-hour interrogation Gabriel had feared. Far from suspecting he had anything to do with what she called her "spiritual blessing," Natalie seemed content with her own ready-made explanation. After all, it was practically a mantra at the Fellowship in Arvin: *Expect a miracle.*

"I never gave up hope," she said as Morro Bay disappeared behind them. "*Never.* Not ten minutes before you picked me up yesterday, I did the meditation I learned there."

And for once, Gabriel thought, a person's religious beliefs actually worked in his favor.

Natalie was also content not to discuss her recovery any further. In fact she was silently serene for the rest of the trip, enjoying the warm wind riffling her hair as it came through the open window, watching the passing fields and terraced, newly-leafed vineyards with the grateful eye of one whose death sentence had just been commuted.

Gabriel was equally happy not to intrude on her thoughts. He needed time himself, beginning with the question of whether he could remain in Lamont any longer, close as it was to both Natalie's apartment in Bakersfield and the Denny's where she worked.

And for the fifteenth or twentieth time since it all began – actually, he'd stopped counting years ago – Gabriel understood that he'd be moving on. It was too risky to stay now. Lucky for him, Natalie had never asked for his address, so she probably wouldn't be appearing on the steps of his boarding-house anytime soon. But she had enough information to track him down if she had a mind to, or if her doctor might want a more rational explanation for Natalie's "miracle" than her mere expectation of one.

The logo of the construction company that employed Gabriel was emblazoned across the door of the pickup they'd been riding in; he couldn't be sure she'd noticed it when dropped her off. And he could only hope she hadn't seen the magnetic sign affixed to the pickup's tailgate, which bore not only the name of the subdivision where he'd pounded nails for the past five months, but his site supervisor's cell phone number.

In any case, if events unfolded as usual, no more than a week would pass before someone would start poking around and asking questions.

Someone always did.

2

V*isalia wasn't as far north* as he'd originally intended to go. As a rule, Gabriel put several hundred miles between his successive sojourns, if not more. Twice, in fact, he'd ended up going from one coast to the other. The first such cross-country trek took him from a tiny burg southeast of Everett, Washington to Uxbridge, Massachusetts. Only last year he'd traveled all the way from Comfort, North Carolina to Ocotillo, just north of the border between California and Mexico, taking three days and four different rigs.

He was never quite sure what made him stop. Sometimes it all came down to where he found work, or had a hunch he'd find it. More often it was a roll of the dice, the simple, unfounded hope that perhaps here he could lose himself, live at last in blessed anonymity, his healing touch given no cause for use.

To be exposed was to surrender control of his life. A single incident – even where the recipient promised to keep it a secret – inevitably led to another. In days, sometimes hours, word would spread... not far to begin with, since people wanted to confine their good fortune to family and friends. But the crowds would come nevertheless, gathering outside wherever he might be staying, clamoring for their own healing or bringing loved ones who needed his restorative touch: Babies with birth defects, children with inoperable brain tumors or holes in their hearts, adults with mental disorders, addictions, disfigurements from industrial accidents or war injuries.

He'd seen it all, needed only a few such experiences to realize that demand would always exceed supply, and because things got out of hand despite his best efforts to control them, his only escape was to, well, *escape.*

This time he packed up his mother's Bible and canvas duffle bag and hitched a ride into Oildale, avoiding all but the outskirts of Bakersfield. After wagging a thumb on the 99 onramp for only ten minutes, an Office Depot delivery van pulled over.

He hadn't bothered with goodbyes. Even the leathery spinster who had rented out the bedroom next to hers at the boardinghouse, who'd taken a special liking to him ever since she discovered the stash of canned goods he collected for the local food bank – even *she* wouldn't realize he was gone. At least not until she opened the envelope he'd tucked under her door. There was no point in making promises to stay in touch or drop a postcard from somewhere along the way. Better to make a clean break, leave no trail, paper or otherwise.

Earlier that afternoon, before he rolled the Grant Homes pickup to a stop beside the construction trailer at Camden Corners, he'd intended to simply walk away, leaving the keys in the ignition without even asking for his last week's wages. Unfortunately, his pot-bellied site supervisor, Lowell, hadn't gone home as early as usual. With the workday running 5 a.m. to 3 p.m. – and no one volunteering for overtime in the current heat wave – Lowell could generally be counted on to bail out before 2 o'clock. That was about the time the trailer's window-box air conditioner gave up the fight against an unremitting sun on a poorly-insulated tin roof.

But it was 3:30 and Lowell was still at his desk. He must have heard the pickup coming, because by the time Gabriel pushed the gearshift into park, Lowell was outside on the metal landing, leaning onto the handrail with a conspicuous smirk.

"Either you two didn't hit it off like you thought," he snickered, "or that beachfront love-nest got overrun with sand crabs. I hear they get pretty thick every spring."

Gabriel slammed the driver's door, reached into the back of the pickup for his duffle bag. "Or maybe we figured it couldn't get any better than the first night, so why even try?"

The smirk turned into pretended admiration. "So. You *do* play as hard as you work. I figured you for the type."

Lowell had also figured out what Gabriel was up to when, a week earlier, he'd stopped by the trailer to ask for the pickup and two days off. Loaning him the F-150 wasn't exactly company policy, but the jovial supervisor had never seen a man work so diligently, often through holidays and weekends, with nary a complaint. His lead framer was unusually quiet; he kept to himself, yes. But not in an anti-social way like some of the other laborers. And he could put up half again as many stud walls in a day as anyone else at the subdivision.

After four months on the job, Lowell often let Gabriel borrow the extra pickup at the end of the day, assuming correctly that he'd met someone. It hardly came as a shock when Gabriel offered to work overtime without the fifty percent bonus, in trade for a Wednesday through Friday leave of absence.

Gabriel slung his bag over his shoulder, walked to the metal stoop, reached up to hand Lowell the keys. "Mind if I take the rest of the time off you gave me?" he asked, offering no clue that he wouldn't be coming back at all.

As it turned out, the recently reborn town of Visalia was the Office Depot deliveryman's next stop. Just over an hour north of Bakersfield, the StepVan took the King's Canyon exit and headed east toward the Sierra Nevadas. Gabriel offered to buy dinner at a Carrows on the outskirts of town, but the dour deliveryman drove on, preferring to complete his next-to-last stop before taking a break.

Four miles further up the highway was a brand new Office Depot, the apparent anchor tenant in a still-unfinished shopping center. The retail plaza was surrounded on three sides by new housing tracts, one of which appeared to have broken ground only recently, spurred by a fresh infusion government-backed mortgage money. A half dozen concrete slabs had just been poured, forms still intact, cinderblock walls just beginning to rise behind them. Near the tract's flag-lined entrance, a gleaming aluminum trailer was draped with a colorful banner that announced, *Temporary Sales Office.*

When the deliveryman came back to start unloading cartons of manila envelopes, toner cartridges and desk chairs that would go on sale tomorrow at fifty percent off, his ride-along was nowhere to be seen.

Labor Day was only two weeks away when Gabriel began visiting the Carrows on the west edge of town. He'd thumbed a ride twice and even braved a city bus, what with the site supervisor being far less appreciative of Gabriel's framing talents than Lowell had been. A few weeks ago he'd tried softening up Hanshaw – better known as "Handjob" to his underlings – by working four straight overtime shifts. But when Gabriel requested use of the company car that weekend, he was told in no uncertain terms that the hybrid Lexus was strictly for taking prospective homebuyers around the jobsite, and never to ask for it again.

It was fortunate Gabriel wasn't especially needy, despite having had no contact with anyone since Natalie. And the need, even if he'd had it, wasn't about sex anyway. That may have been the icing; but it was the straightforward feel of another person's skin he lusted after. Simple human touch, without any miraculous consequences.

Over the past decade he'd learned to avoid the kinds of crowds where physical contact was likely, to wear long sleeves even in hot weather on the chance someone might brush up against him, to be ever vigilant. His ventures onto buses or into restaurants – navigating through any public place, for that matter – were always exercises in maintaining a safe distance, stepping aside when anyone might approach too closely, and occasionally twisting away from near collisions with a display of acrobatics that would make a contortionist proud.

In winter he was usually protected by thick jackets and extra layers of clothing, both his own and others'. But summers were high risk. Even the long-sleeved work shirts he continued to wear despite the heat couldn't insulate him from a bare shoulder or the innocent clutch of a child who might come up from behind.

Once, a two-year-old in leg braces bumped into him, then burst out crying when the power surged through her little body and made all that expensive hardware obsolete. Gabriel was lucky that time, even though the frightened mother was convinced he must've been up to no good.

Still, the feel of another's flesh couldn't be put off indefinitely. It was time to explore the usual options in advance of the inescapable need.

What was the Scouts' motto?

The Tuesday on which he'd planned his next after-hours foray to Carrows dawned with the kind of warm, breathless air virtually guaranteed to push daytime highs above the century mark. It was also the twenty-third straight day of work for most of the crew.

Sales at the subdivision had been brisk ever since new Fed policies returned market stability to pre-recession levels. The usual two-month lag between a customer's loan approval and finished home had slowly increased to well over twice that long and, in an effort to reduce the delay, Hanshaw had instituted a seven-day work week. A few hardy volunteers were putting in as much as thirty or forty hours overtime, Gabriel among them. With no days off to provide relief, some of the laborers were finding new and creative ways to break the monotony.

For the past few weeks, the roofing crew had begun to host an after-hours "shoot-out." Every three or four days – or whenever some lesser journeyman suspected that the reigning master was vulnerable – a contest would be announced. Word spread throughout the subdivision, and often into adjacent developments. Soon after the end of the shift a sizeable peanut gallery would assemble to cheer on the opponents. The roofer who could nail the most shingles on his assigned house in fifteen minutes, and still pass inspection, would take the kitty. As much as two or three thousand dollars in side bets might also change hands.

Arliss, as inebriated as he routinely kept himself, had never been beaten. Gabriel had watched from ground level during several previous contests, reluctantly admiring the ex-cowhand's confident, rapid-fire sweep that could nail down a line of cedar shingles as straight and neatly-spaced as those of his most sober workmates. Maybe the three or four six-packs of Bud Light he consumed daily actually helped.

But this particular Tuesday a recent hire – a fellow roofer with two years' experience named Brad – had also been watching Arliss work. He eventually convinced himself that the master had downed one six-pack too many. Just before 3 p.m., when even the most heat-tempered laborers had packed up their gear, the newcomer threw down the gauntlet and put a week's pay into the pot.

Arliss sized up his latest challenger, gazing across the chasm separating the two rooftops where they'd been working for the last two hours, and simply laughed. Then, moments later, he was standing over the front eaves, peering down at Gabriel where the latter had just finished cutting through a stack of lap siding.

"Lupé di'n already take off, did he?" Arliss queried, with a slur that appeared to validate his challenger's hopes.

Lupé was basically the jobsite gofer, keeping the entire crew stocked with nail strips, two-by-fours, electrical wire, cedar shingles – and in Arliss' case, cold bottles of Bud which he regularly brought up from a chest concealed in the back of his beat-up Ranchero. Everyone knew about the ice chest, including Hanshaw. But the site supervisor looked the other way, and his fellow laborers knew better than to raid his stash for fear of being pelted by a rainstorm of roofing nails.

At that moment the Ranchero fish-tailed around the corner three lots south, lumbered up the street and bounced into the packed-earth driveway destined to become concrete by this time next week. Lupé got out, immediately looked up at Arliss as if awaiting his bidding.

"New guy wants to donate a week's pay to my beer tab." Arliss gestured toward the neighboring rooftop, then peered down at the split cedar in the back of the Ranchero. "Give us three more bundles each, and bring me up another six-pack."

"We're all out."

Lupé offered an apologetic shrug. It was clear he wasn't referring to roofing materials.

"Well then, go get me some more," the master spat back, as if
Lupé should've known. Then, squinting at Gabriel: "Meantime, maybe
ol' sonny boy here'll do me the honors."

Gabriel looked back without moving. Much as he might admire
the man's skill, Arliss was one of the most obnoxious people he'd
ever run across. It wasn't just that he treated Lupé like his own
personal bitch. Pretty much *everyone* was two-legged livestock as
far as Arliss was concerned, and therefore equally subject to a rab-
bit punch or swift kick if they strayed within range.

As a result, Gabriel gave him plenty of room on the rare occasions they were simultaneously at ground level. Which gave Arliss
the impression Gabriel was afraid of him. Which, in turn, explained
why Arliss never called Gabriel by name. It was always "sonny boy"
or "wussy boy" or simply, "Hey, meat!"

If Gabriel hadn't learned the wisdom of avoiding potential con-
frontations long ago, he might've enjoyed the excuse to knock Arliss
on his ass. Only problem was, the physical contact would probably
end up restoring whatever remained of his liver. Far from teaching
Arliss a lesson, a good thrashing would probably extend his life by a
decade or two.

Even Gabriel's anger, it seemed, couldn't diminish the effects of
his touch. So he nodded back and dutifully unloaded six bundles of
cedar shingles from the Ranchero, then went off to find the forklift
while Lupé drove away to fetch more beer.

By the time the bundles were hoisted onto their respective patio
covers and the clock was ticking, there was still no one else around
to watch the contest. It was just as well for Brad. The fewer the
witnesses, the better. Because after a feverish five minutes it was
clear Arliss was nailing down a good thirty to forty percent more
cedar than his opponent.

Actually, the disparity wasn't that bad compared to some of Arliss'
previous challengers. On the other hand, it *did* give him time to
have a little fun at Brad's expense.

Lupé was just returning from his beer run when Arliss switched off his safety and began taking potshots. As he paused to lay out the next row of shingles, Arliss would playfully point his nail-gun in Brad's direction, sometimes making an effort to aim, sometimes not, then squeeze off a few rounds. "Hey there, pardner," he taunted, "I got more nails 'case you start runnin' low." And then he'd squeeze off a few more, cackling the whole time like a drunken sailor.

The roofing nails could easily penetrate heavy-gauge metal flashing at close range. Cedar shingles and pine one-by-sixes were like butter. But across the gulf between the two houses, the stubby nails quickly lost punch and landed harmlessly near Brad's work boots. Even so, the fact that Arliss had time for such sport was downright embarrassing, if not insulting. Brad mumbled a few epithets under his breath, couldn't resist popping a few back in retaliation. He wasn't going to win anyway.

Ten minutes into the contest, several of Brad's nails actually began to reach Arliss. A gentle breeze had come up, the wind catching the over-sized heads just enough to add a few feet to their range. Whatever the explanation, Arliss didn't like it. He flinched and swatted at the intermittent stings, swore loudly enough to be heard a block away, ducking his head down even as he continued to squeeze off a few of his own rounds now and then.

Gabriel exchanged glances with Lupé as he started up a ladder with the fresh six-pack, both of them trying hard not to laugh out loud, grinning with secret pleasure that the champ was no longer having quite so much fun. Nor was Arliss turning around to see where his latest barrage of nails was landing, or even if he was aiming anywhere near Brad's current location.

It was during this pause in their respective volleys that Lupé climbed onto the patio cover and approached Arliss from behind, still afraid to open his mouth for fear he would burst out laughing. It was also a mistake. Gabriel could kick himself for not seeing it coming.

Because all of a sudden Arliss swung his arm around like a desperado firing blindly at a posse in pursuit, quickly squeezing the trigger of his nail-gun once, twice, three times. It took him exactly that long to realize that the *pop-pop-pop* wasn't followed by the usual swish of air, but the solid thunk of galvanized iron driving into pine.

Or something strangely like it.

The first nail pierced Lupé's skull just above his right eyebrow, the second two inches higher and to the left. The third nail opened a gash across his temple, but failed to penetrate the bone. Mouth gaping, Lupé went backward stiff as a board without so much as a hand to break his fall. He bounced off the sloping roof, spinning in mid-air, dropped onto the hardpan below with a sickening crack. If the nails hadn't killed him, the fall surely did.

Brad hadn't seen the headshots if only because he was turned away to protect his own face. He spun just in time to see Lupé go over the eaves, winced at the sound of the impact, threw down his nail-gun and bolted for his ladder. He was back on the ground as Gabriel rounded the corner from the front yard.

Lupé lay face down between the two houses, his head wrenched unnaturally to one side. As Gabriel watched from a safe distance, Brad squatted down, probed for any sign of life. After several attempts he straightened, glanced up with a somber shake of his head.

"If there's a pulse," he said, "I sure as hell can't feel it."

He reached down again, placed his hands beneath Lupé's abdomen and carefully turned him over. Almost immediately he reeled back, scrambling to his feet, gasping at the sight of the two roofing nails embedded in Lupé's forehead. He hadn't known until just then what caused the fall, blinked in horror at his belated realization.

Above him, Arliss finally stuck his head out over the eaves, was now gazing down at the scene through bleary eyes.

"Must'a snuck up behind me. Is 'e... you know...?"

Gabriel broke in first, turning back to Brad. "Better get Hanshaw and call nine-one-one. I'll see what I can do before the ambulance gets here."

Brad continued to stare at the two nails, looked up at last with an expression conveying how foolish it was to think anything could help Lupé now. Then, with a searing scowl at Arliss, he took off between the bare, wood-framed houses, sprinting for the construction trailer four blocks north.

Gabriel waited for him to disappear, likewise glanced up only to see Arliss draw back out of sight. He knew he couldn't wait any longer, couldn't stand around and pretend there was nothing he could do until the paramedics arrived to pronounce Lupé dead. He shook his head as Brad had done, somberly, and for entirely different reasons.

Kneeling beside Lupé's body, he reached down to test each of the nails. They were both tight as screws, with only a thin, glistening outline of red surrounding the punctures. Gabriel slipped a chisel from his tool belt, worked the tip under the head of each nail, lifting them up just enough to get at them with pliers. It took all Gabriel's strength to twist the first one out. The second yielded a bit more easily.

There was no spurt of blood from either of the holes as Gabriel had hoped; that would've meant Lupé's heart was still pumping. Instead, the darkening blood merely rose, slowly, overflowing the two wounds just enough to spill into his left eye socket before trickling down his cheek.

Gabriel sighed, unbuttoned his sweat-stained work shirt, yanked it off to begin soaking up the pool from Lupé's eye. Tossing it aside, he closed his own eyes and began massaging Lupé's forehead, running his hands over the puncture wounds, all the while knowing his actions had no power in themselves. It was simply a ritual to keep him occupied, to prevent any thoughts from slowing down the process. Still, with every stroke the two holes seemed to close up a bit more, like spackle filling a sheetrock joint.

When all that remained were two shiny pink depressions, Gabriel rose, repositioned himself above Lupé's body and encircled his neck with both hands. He was mildly surprised to find that the jumble of disconnected vertebrae had yet to reassemble themselves, but quickly dismissed any doubt. That was the key: *Get out of the way.* Let it happen – as it did whenever someone might bump into him by accident.

Suddenly Lupé's chest rose. He let out a groan, low at first, then louder and thickening with obvious pain. A good sign, Gabriel allowed, considering the alternative.

He abruptly stood, breathing out a mixture of acceptance and sadness. He would be leaving again; the necessity of it wasn't even in question this time. He stared into the dusty light between the line of houses, knew he'd miss this place as much as Lamont, this next, missed opportunity to find normal, finally reached down to unbuckle his tool belt.

"Woods—?"

Gabriel swirled. *Hanshaw.* He looked past the supervisor for his Jeep, then thought, no, he could never have gotten here that fast, even with Brad running full-tilt to find him. He must've been making his rounds on foot and simply happened by.

How much had he seen?

"Paramedics on their way?" Gabriel asked, playing dumb.

"Para—" Hanshaw cut himself off, stepped sideways to get a better angle on the downed roofer. "What's going on? Wha'd you just do there—?"

"I sent Brad over to call for help," he said, parrying the question. "Didn't he tell you?"

Gabriel glanced down nervously, noted that Lupé was beginning to rouse. "He, uh, took a header off the roof during the... when he was lugging up another bundle for Arliss."

By this time Arliss had reappeared above them. The master was looking a bit nervous himself, though his expression quickly turned to amazement as Lupé groaned again and lifted a hand to his forehead.

"I'm guessing one of the metal tie-downs snapped, hit 'im across the face," Gabriel explained. "Must've knocked him cold. That's when he went over." He raised his gaze toward Arliss, who continued to stare, incredulous. "Isn't that right, Arliss...?"

Several seconds.

"*Arliss.* Isn't that right—?"

The ex-cowhand could spot an opportunity when it came along, even if it took a few more seconds to filter through the Bud-induced buzz. He finally pulled his eyes off Lupé, nodded at Hanshaw.

"Zackly what happened... like Woods said." It was the first time Arliss had called him by name. "Can't believe his neck ain't broke."

He blinked at Gabriel before returning his gaze to Lupé, still unable to comprehend, and despite what he'd just told his supervisor. Not that Gabriel was worried. Whatever the drunken roofer might say – now or later – would automatically be suspect. By tomorrow the whole incident would be lost in an alcoholic haze; it was Brad's testimony that would seal his fate.

Lupé's eyes parted, closed, then finally opened wide as if it was all coming back to him. He seemed to struggle for a moment, attempted to prop himself up on an elbow. Gabriel quickly stepped over, gently pushed his shoulder back down, met Lupé's eyes with urgency before turning back to Hanshaw.

"Even so, it'd prob'ly be a good idea to keep him quiet, call an ambulance, get 'im to the hospital for some X-rays. OSHA will be all over this if we don't go by the book, right?"

Maybe Hanshaw was buying it, maybe not. As he continued to peer back dubiously, the wail of a siren rose into the silence, echoing through the stud-lined walls of the half-built homes. Evidently Brad had called 9-1-1 himself, having found the trailer vacant. Gabriel suddenly wanted to be gone before the medics arrived, and definitely before Brad returned.

He removed his tool belt, set it down beside Lupé as though he might come back later to retrieve it. Then, turning, he noticed the two bloody roofing nails nearby, maintained his composure, casually pushed some loose dirt over them with the toe of his boot.

"And maybe I'd better go out and pull the tarp back over that ice chest nobody's supposed to know about. OSHA might take a dim view, 'case those paramedics mention it in their report."

His supervisor said nothing, hardly moved as Gabriel stepped around him and started for the driveway. Above them, from the rooftop, Arliss watched Gabriel reappear in the front yard and reach into Lupé's Ranchero, shutting the lid of his re-stocked ice chest before the ambulance could pull alongside.

He too said nothing, even when Gabriel kept right on going, crossing the street two houses down, eventually breaking into a lope just before he disappeared behind a Mayflower truck parked on the next block where a lucky family was now moving into their first home, preoccupied with their own small miracle.

3

*L*ane D'Arcy had heard whispers about a looming strike two weeks earlier, knew it was for all the wrong reasons but was privately jubilant nevertheless. The time had come for Chiloquin to reconsider where it was headed in this messed-up millennium – actually it was long overdue – and not merely because of what had happened to her.

Admittedly, the two years since her accident had given her the opportunity and the emotional distance to reflect on how quickly the town's new industry had usurped the rest of their economy. She understood how easily they'd all been taken in by prospects of a brighter future, and how tragic this more recent imposition of white culture had been for the local Native American population. But the fact was, she'd been won over just like all the others – even the Maqlaqs. Which is why, much as certain elements in the community might want her to take a public stand on the issue, she felt unworthy.

And it wasn't a question of how she'd been forced to make ends meet since her benefits had run out. She was basically the same person she'd always been – no wallflower, she; and certainly no standard-bearer for moral behavior, despite her parents' influence. She wasn't about to make excuses for what her life had become.

But aside from her end-of-the-month appearances outside the plant gates to solicit the company of a sympathetic friend or an old flame, she hadn't been near the assembly lines in well over eighteen months. She made no effort to keep up with plant politics. What she *did* know was acquired secondhand and mostly by accident.

Still, she found it mildly amusing to discover she knew more about conditions at the plant – and elsewhere in town – than almost anyone. Maybe it was because she had friends and lovers on both sides of the dispute. Or rather *all* sides. Maybe she had more power than she knew.

Or maybe not, Lane reassured herself, closing her eyes now, settling into the bucket seat, listening to the whine of the plant's automatic gate in the distance and the impatient gunning of car engines as the day shift expelled its first prospects.

Gabriel had taken a circuitous route back to the rooming house on the chance someone might be coming after him. Not that he expected someone *would*. Not right away.

After an incident like this, where several people were involved, witnesses almost always took time to search for a rational explanation first. Only when it became clear something out of the ordinary must have occurred – and it usually *did* become clear – only then would anyone come looking for him. And by that time Gabriel would be gone.

In this latest case, Lupé would no doubt be asked for his own version of what had happened. But having been knocked unconscious, the only thing anyone could be sure he'd seen were stars. Arliss, for his part, would either take the 5th, or take another cold one from Lupé's ice chest. More likely both. And Brad's claim about seeing the imbedded nails would be hard to accept with no one else's testimony to back him up.

After all, Lupé's injuries *might've* been caused by a metal binding strap breaking under the strain. The ties had been known to
snap before, and maybe this one had picked up some loose pebbles
from the patio cover before it lashed across his forehead. That might
account for the shiny depressions, or even the two round objects
Brad "mistook" for nail heads. The gash at Lupé's temple was perfectly consistent with the sharp metal edge of a strap. Either way,
Gabriel would be on the road before anyone thought to get his take
on the incident.

He'd almost finished packing, pausing now and again to peer
out the second-story window, when the old woman who gave him
room and board appeared in his doorway. His landlords – or more
accurately, land*ladies* – were almost always elderly women. For one
thing, the concept of a "boarding house" was simply foreign to most
people under seventy years of age. Perhaps it was a holdover from
the Great Depression. And it was women of that age whose hus-
bands had died, leaving them with a house too big to be used so
little, who thought of turning their unoccupied bedrooms into fur-
nished apartments for traveling salesmen and seasonal workers and
wayfarers like Gabriel.

At least that's how Mrs. Marple saw him – another habitual
wanderer, never putting down roots, stopping only so long as a temporary job might hold out, or hold his interest. She had no idea
there were other motives behind Gabriel's travels, only that he was
a decent, clean-cut young man who was still searching for something missing in his life; and among his quirks was a tendency to
become unusually nervous when other people came too close. That's
why he never sat at the table with her other boarders, preferring to
take his meals alone in his room – assuming he hadn't gone out for
a bite at one of the local coffee shops.

So she respected his space. Everybody had their own personal
idiosyncrasies, didn't they?

"I just hope the market for new homes isn't going sour again,"
she said, fumbling with the brown lunch sack she'd brought up.
"Much as I hate all those developers buying up good farmland, my
income depends on 'em. Social security hasn't been enough for years."

Gabriel knew that another of her boarders poured concrete at a competing subdivision. The man had mentioned how his work at this particular site was nearly finished, and that Kaufman & Broad was sending him to a new job in Redding next month.

"The greedy bastards let you go?"

Mrs. Marple suddenly frowned, holding out the paper sack. Gabriel couldn't help but smile as he accepted it. The old woman had spunk as well as business smarts. One more thing he'd miss.

"No. I quit, actually." And then, to reassure her: "If anything, the market's stronger than it was before the meltdown. I'm sure you'll fill the vacancy in no time."

"Oh, you're right about that. Got two more young men on my waiting list." She nodded toward the lunch sack. "There's a turkey sandwich, a banana, those corn chips you like with the sea salt... and one of my fudge brownies. I'm sorry you can't stay for supper."

"And I can't thank you enough for everything you've done, Miz Marple," he added, still smiling, stuffing another work shirt into his bulging duffle bag.

"So... what about all this?"

She waved a hand, frowned at the half dozen cartons of Del Monte green beans and canned potatoes he kept neatly stacked in the corner. He glanced away, offered an apologetic nod as he attempted with some difficulty to zip up his bag.

"Right. I, uh, put in a little extra with this month's rent, over there on the dresser. Maybe you can pay that kid to load it into his wagon, haul it down to the food bank for me... you know, the one with the arm...?"

She knew exactly. He was a thirteen-year-old from the next street over, eager and good-hearted despite a gimpy right arm he'd been saddled with since birth. He'd come to Gabriel's attention a month earlier, on a crisp Saturday morning after he knocked on Mrs. Marple's front screen and offered to mow her lawn for three dollars. Gabriel had agonized over the prospect of doing something for the boy; but that kind of naive benevolence is exactly what had first gotten him into trouble back in North Carolina.

"Next time I see him," she nodded.

And with that Gabriel slung the duffle bag over his shoulder as if to leave, then hesitated, pausing to watch Mrs. Marple cross the room to the dresser. An envelope with her name scrawled in pencil was tucked beneath a cut-glass jar brimming with hard candies. Each of her three other boarders had a similar jar on their dressers, checked every day to make sure they were full. Yet another holdover from the Depression. She stopped, reached almost reluctantly for the envelope.

With the old woman distracted, Gabriel stepped back to the nightstand. Next to the antique lamp was a dog-eared, white leatherette volume with a zipper around three sides and the words "Holy Bible" imprinted in peeling gold leaf on the cover. He picked it up, gently pulling the small brass cross to unzip the book's jacket, turning his shoulder so the old woman couldn't see the contents if she happened to look up.

A sense of calm fell over him as he opened it, as it always did. On the translucent flyleaf was the inscription he re-read every evening before turning out the lights. He ran a finger over the familiar, feminine strokes, uncertain whether he'd get another chance that night, then flipped back the first few pages. Past the preface and the table of contents and the words "In the beginning," all the remaining leaves had been glued together with wallpaper paste. A neat four-by-six-inch cavity had been cut out, not unlike Andy's Bible in *The Shawshank Redemption*, to hold the few valuables he kept.

Gabriel made sure they were all there: The brass pillbox from a great-great-grandfather who'd been a horse soldier after the Civil War; his mother's plain gold wedding band with its deep gouge on one side; a wrinkled snapshot of himself on his eighth birthday. There was the key to a safe deposit box at the Farmers & Merchants bank in Lawrence, Kansas, for which he'd paid ten years in advance six years ago; and of course the turquoise-studded money clip with the fifty- and hundred-dollar bills he kept in reserve for his next, inevitable move.

Caressing each of the items in turn, he suddenly became aware that Mrs. Marple was now facing him, holding up her own fistful of Franklins. Gabriel knew what was coming, quickly zipped up his Bible.

"Young man, this is three times what you owe me."

He shrugged. "Actually, it's twice what I owe you, plus another two hundred bucks to buy more canned goods for the food bank next week, and twenty more to pay the kid to deliver everything."

Gabriel knew she wasn't hurting financially, as were some of the landladies whose rooms he rented. But without his own home or any real social life, he always had far more money than he needed.

"And if you won't do this one last favor for your favorite tenant," he added with the boyish grin that melted spinsters and waitresses alike, "there's always your favorite charity."

She scowled again, in the same way his mother had – disapproving even as it conveyed her gratitude. Then, pointedly, she glanced down at the Bible in his left hand.

"You've always kept that book close by, haven't you, son?"

He lifted it, shoved it into a pocket on the side of the duffle bag. "It's gotten me through some tough times."

"I stopped reading it when Harold died," she said matter-of-factly. "Never did find much comfort in it."

Gabriel adjusted the shoulder strap, started for the door.

"Guess you get out what you put in."

Highway 99 seemed busier than usual, though no one was stopping. Picking up a ride out of Visalia had proven easy enough. Problem was, he hadn't taken the extra ten seconds to ask where the driver was headed; his only concern had been to leave town as soon as possible. When it turned out his ride would be continuing west to Coalinga, Gabriel quickly asked to be let out so he could hitch another – preferably one headed north.

Apparently, the connecting loop from 158 to northbound 99 was the wrong place to stick out a thumb. Even big-rigs could take the two-lane ramp at sixty miles an hour. Nor was there much of a shoulder where a kind-hearted trucker could pull over to begin with. So Gabriel ignored the "No Pedestrians" signs and the late afternoon heat, hoofed the half-mile up the incline and back down to the freeway. Ten minutes later he was walking backward just outside the shoulder stripe, facing the oncoming traffic, waving his thumb at everything that moved.

He'd backpedaled well over a mile before a Club Wagon with peeling paint and three seats full of Mexican farm workers slowed and pulled off the pavement about ten car-lengths past him. No doubt Gabriel's deep tan and dark brown hair had fooled the driver. It was not uncommon for migrants to thumb rides along country roads in the area, and sometimes find their next job that way. But trolling 99 was an invitation for the CHP to stop and demand a green card. And even if a valid work permit was produced, the officer was likely to write out a ticket that might cost four or five day's wages. The driver was only doing the foolish hitch-hiker a favor.

He evidently realized his mistake about the same time Gabriel finished counting nine heads through the smoked-glass windows. Not keen on the lack of elbow room, Gabriel stopped jogging toward the van just before it clunked into gear, lurched back into the slow lane and left him alone once again.

Another ten minutes had elapsed when a highway patrol cruiser sped by without stopping, lights flashing, presumably on its way to more important business. And it was almost a half hour before a drab, slate-gray eighteen-wheeler whined through its lower gearbox and finally came to a dust-swirled stop a quarter mile ahead. It was so far away, in fact, Gabriel couldn't be sure the driver had actually stopped for *him* – not until the passenger-side door was pushed open and left that way.

Gabriel picked up his pace, half running, half walking the four hundred yards, at the same time looking for any identifying graphics on the truck. Unlike the rolling billboards hawking local brand names like Foster Farms and Save Mart and Lagunitas Brewing, the rig now awaiting him was drab as a weathered barn, with no hint of company or contents. Its spotless chrome wheels suggested an independent operator, but the plates were government issue.

As Gabriel reached the rear of the trailer he slowed to a walk, giving himself a few moments to catch his breath. A raspy voice rose over the sound of gravel crunching beneath his work boots.

"That's okay – take your time. I got another fourteen hours to bring this load in."

Gabriel halted beside the open door, looked into the cab to find a grizzled old salt peering down at him, complete with white crew-cut hair and a bushy, gray moustache.

"Sorry," he shrugged, suddenly wondering if the man's remark wasn't meant as a joke after all. "For a minute I thought you'd stopped for somebody else up the road."

"Yeah, well, all the hardware stacked behind this flimsy sheet metal—" The trucker hooked a thumb at the cab wall behind him. "—not a good idea to slam on the brakes, know what I mean?"

Gabriel nodded despite *not* knowing, was about to ask what kind of hardware the trucker was hauling when he noticed the vinyl sticker in the lower right corner of his windshield: *No Riders.*

"Don't sweat it," the trucker said, following Gabriel's eyes. "Just gives me an excuse if I don't like your looks." He glanced down again, presumably finding nothing in Gabriel's appearance to cause concern. "So—you gonna stand out there in this god-awful heat or climb the hell in?"

Gabriel reached up for the handgrip, stopped, was more careful this time. "So where you headed?"

The white-haired salt looked him up and down, seemed to know his prospective ride-along wasn't exactly following an Auto Club triptick. "Like it matters?" he said, and pushed the gearshift forward.

"Vincent... call me Vincent," he'd said.

Gabriel wasn't certain it was his first name or last. What he *was* certain about was the trucker's motive for picking him up.

Over the past four hours Gabriel had been assaulted by more words than he'd processed during an entire summer building houses. Even the women he'd been with didn't go on this much. Of course, much of the time Gabriel spent with women was specifically for *not* talking. But the preliminaries to those rare occasions – the hours of personal probing and posturing and sometimes dancing around the subject of sex – didn't involve anywhere near the volume of verbiage the trucker had dished out with hardly a break.

In Vincent's case, most of his stories revolved around his Army logistics battalion, the focal point of which were his four consecutive tours of Viet Nam. And, he was careful to point out, he meant

"tour" quite literally. He'd gotten to know the country like the proverbial back-of-his-hand, hauling equipment and supplies from the
lush green mountains of the north to the patchwork paddies of the
south and everywhere in between. He'd also gotten to know the
people, for whom he developed great admiration and even love, despite his ongoing references to "the slants" and his strangely reverent descriptions of napalm bombings that wiped whole villages off
the map and laid waste countless acres of jungle.

During his years "in country" Vincent had survived three land
mines, enough sniper attacks and RPG assaults to know "just what
our kids went through in Taliban land," as he put it, along with a
mortar round that blew the trailer clean off the tractor he was driving between Da Nang and Khe San. "Damn lucky I was doing forty-
five clicks at the time and not forty," he laughed, "or the shell woulda
landed in my lap, not my backside."

It was such "legendary coolness under fire" – not *his* words, he
modestly recalled, but those penned by a journalist from *Stars and
Stripes* – that earned him the commendations he carried around
with him even to this day, including one from the President himself.
His reputation also won him a job with a major trucking company
after he'd been shipped stateside. It was the same one he worked for
now, close to four decades later.

"And what company would that be?" Gabriel inserted into an
uncharacteristic pause.

"U.S. government," Vincent replied. And for the first time he
refrained from providing any further details.

Gabriel raised an eyebrow but didn't press him. Maybe Vincent
was waiting for him to ask. The non-stop narrative, however, had
begun to fill up his brain. He wasn't used to all this listening and
nodding, or having to remain attentive in case a question about
Gabriel's own limited knowledge of that wasted war should come
his way. Besides which he hadn't had anything to eat since a twenty-
minute lunch break back in Visalia, and he was more than ready for
a sandwich and silence.

He reached down to the duffle bag he'd placed strategically between them on the bench seat, started to remove his paper sack
from the side pocket.

"Mind if I break for some chow?"

"Go right ahead." Then, as if suddenly aware he'd been bending his rider's ears for four hours straight, he glanced across the cab. "All that jawboning, I forgot to ask if you had anything to eat."

"No problem. All that jawboning, I forgot I was hungry."

He added a smile, finally succeeded in pulling out the nearly-flattened lunch sack, accidentally knocking loose the Bible he'd tucked into the pocket next to it. The zippered volume bounced off the vinyl and down onto the floorboard, landing just behind Vincent's pedal foot. The trucker reached down before Gabriel could react, lifted the book into the amber-colored glow now silhouetting the mountains west of Redding. The waning light caught the peeling gold leaf on the cover.

Vincent blinked with mild surprise, hesitated a bare instant before handing it back. Gabriel took it, watched warily as Vincent returned his gaze to the highway, waiting for the inevitable comment. This time it was a full minute in coming.

"You, uh, mentioned you worked in the building trade...?"

"Framing and finish work, mostly." By then Gabriel had managed to unfold the wax paper Mrs. Marple still preferred over Glad Wrap, found the sandwich she'd made only slightly thicker than the sliced meat inside. "You want half a' my turkey on whole wheat? Little worse for wear, but I'm sure it'll taste okay."

He could tell his attempt at changing the subject hadn't worked, silently berated himself for his carelessness. It was uncanny how his Bible never failed to elicit some kind of reaction from whoever might see it, most of which fell into one of three categories.

Some of his travel companions would appear downright uncomfortable once they spotted it. They might squirm in their seats, suddenly grow nervous or even freeze up as if the book was some kind of leather-bound talisman, as if it possessed magical powers to see into their hearts and expose all their evil deeds and dark secrets and now they were sitting naked in the driver's seat like Lady Godiva on her horse, only not as pretty.

Others would be uncomfortable not so much with the Bible itself, but with Gabriel, suspecting he must've had some secret agenda for thumbing a ride. He was now waiting for just the right moment to spring his trap, save their souls, bring them to Jesus, make them give up their booze and bad language and rest-stop blow jobs.

The third type of reaction, the one Gabriel hated most, occurred when a driver or fellow passenger glimpsed his Bible and took it as an invitation to talk religion for the rest of their trip. Several travelers from whom he'd accepted rides assumed he must be an itinerant preacher – maybe it was his longish hair and thoughtful demeanor – or at least a student at one of the sectarian colleges they may have passed. And despite all his efforts to set them straight, virtually everyone in this category would proceed to offer their personal views on the subject.

He'd heard so many testimonies, debated so many lame interpretations of Bible verses, listened to so many pitiful arguments to justify why people believed and behaved the way they did that he simply refused to be drawn into these discussions any longer. On his last cross-country journey, in fact, he denied owning the Bible or even knowing what tales it told, claiming he was only transporting the book from a dying aunt to a distant daughter-in-law who wanted it as a family heirloom. It didn't help.

Worse, some people wanted to make sure *he* was saved, reminding him that his mere possession of the Good Book was no guarantee. Surely they'd picked him up on the side of the road for just this reason. It was his lucky day, and the only way Gabriel could short-circuit a sermon on The Four Spiritual Laws was to convince his Mack truck missionary that, yes, he had indeed been dunked in The River Jordan and come up with a clean slate; and even though he still couldn't quote chapter and verse like some true believers, his soul was on the fast-track to heaven, praise the Lord.

And in an oddly reassuring way, he knew what he'd said was the gospel truth.

"I'll take a pass on the half-sandwich," he heard Vincent reply.

Gabriel turned, looked across the seat to find the trucker eyeing the various other items he'd pulled from his lunch sack.

"Had my big meal a' the day at the Grapevine a couple' hours before I picked you up. There's a Denny's on the east side a' the I-Five I usually stop at when I drive this route. Got a couple cute little waitresses there, humor me when I flirt with 'em."

Denny's... Jesus – *Natalie.* Gabriel hadn't thought of her in weeks, suddenly felt guilty again... guilty for *all* the women he'd left behind, though Natalie at least was better off for having crossed his path.

"Wouldn't mind your fudge brownie, though, assuming that's what it is."

Gabriel found himself shaking off the haze again. The day was obviously catching up with him, and not just from all the talking. He glanced at the dashboard clock: *8:57.* It had been almost eighteen hours since he'd heard his travel alarm go off, since he'd put in a full day's work and then some. Time to call it a night. He knew Vincent wouldn't be pleased to lose his captive audience.

"The brownie...?" he finally replied. "Sure, it's yours."

He set Mrs. Marple's handiwork – squashed as it was – on Vincent's side of the duffle bag, then turned back with a conspicuous yawn, stretching his arms forward.

"Come to think of it, I'm not as hungry as I am sleepy." Slouching in the seat, he propped his knees against the dash. "You gonna be okay if I catch a few winks?"

"Me?—hell, yes. I get tired, I'll wait for a straightaway and grab a few winks myself."

The trucker stared ahead, seemingly dead serious, then turned to break a grin.

"Truth is, I probably *could* do this route in my sleep. But I'll be fine. Didn't get up 'til just before twelve hundred hours. This here's the middle a'my day."

He reached under his seat for the stainless-steel thermos he kept there, unscrewed the cap with one hand and poured himself a cup of steaming coffee as if he'd done it a thousand times. Which he no doubt had. Then, elbow firmly on the wheel as he started up the grade to Shasta Dam, he began to unwrap the brownie with his opposite hand.

"Anyway, I loaded up on java when I stopped at the Grapevine. Ought'a be good for another twelve hours, minimum. We'll be there long before that."

Gabriel thought briefly about asking him where *there* was, but doubted he could stay awake for the full answer.

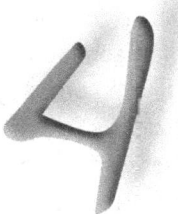

In fact, he'd managed not to stay awake for the next seven hours, despite the blow-out north of Weed, twenty miles up Highway 97 toward the Oregon border.

It wasn't serious. There was hardly more than a thump or two, followed by a minor pull to the right when the trailer settled an inch or two on that side. Vincent knew in an instant what had happened simply by the feel of it. One of the right-rear radials had lost a tread – damn Oriental tires; he wouldn't buy another set if they paid him. And as long as he kept his speed down, he could drive on to Dorris where he knew the manager at the S-turn BP well enough to haul him out of bed at three in the morning.

Vincent was only slightly annoyed when Gabriel slept through his cell-phone call to the gas station manager. But he could hardly believe it when his ride-along turned a shoulder, hunkered down against the passenger-side door frame and began to snore softly even as his Freightliner backed into the station's over-sized garage, staying there for the half hour it took to replace the defective rubber with a new Goodyear.

Still, Vincent was happy enough to be back on the road in under forty-five minutes. Unfortunately, he'd also driven for the previous hour at well below the speed limit, and now he was concerned he might not make his six-thirty deadline. And *that* meant he'd have less than the full hour required to unload his wares before the plant's day shift came on.

Goddam luck. He detested the mere thought of being late. Despite being shot at and practically blown off the road during every one of his four tours – not to mention four more decades behind the wheel – he hadn't missed a single scheduled delivery time. He doubted there was another driver in any company, military or otherwise, who came even close. And to hear some American servicemen these days whining about their overseas assignments, pleading to their congressmen to be brought home from Afghanistan or Raqqa or South Korea if they were kept a day past their enlistment... it turned his stomach.

So did the anti-war sentiment that had swept over the country of late – along with the whole goddam western world – despite the fanatics they were all up against. Maybe the administration lied in 2003 about their reasons for going to war, as they had in 1965. Maybe the intelligence corps and the CIA and the top brass were sheep, or simply idiots, and they didn't know the difference between a no-win situation and the peach fuzz on their chair-conditioned backsides. Then again, what in God's name do you do when you know the fix you're in isn't exactly what you planned on? And what the hell *can* you do, if what you're doing now is the only job you've ever known?

Vincent realized his mind was wandering. It had become tougher and tougher to be alone with himself. Which is why he often sought company during his trips, in spite of the sticker the U.S. Army slapped on his windshield. It wasn't that he'd begun to question what his life was about, what it was still about. And even if he *did* question it, he could always go to work for Yellow Freight Lines or USF, couldn't he? – or Sunkist for that matter. He could haul oranges rather than ordnance.

Or simply drive off the road and be done with it.

It was just before five when Gabriel's eyelids began to flutter.

"You always sleep like a dead man?" Vincent said when he'd finally lifted his face from the passenger-side window.

"Hardly ever." Gabriel blinked, rubbed his cheekbone where he'd peeled it from the glass, looked up with surprise to see a faint blush over the wooded mountains to the east. "You're kidding – it's *morning*?"

"See, I give myself at least ninety minutes, 'case I run into unexpected delays. We lost most a' that last night."

Gabriel sat upright. "What'd I miss?"

"Right rear tread came off. Got us some new rubber before we crossed the state line."

"Really... and I slept through the whole thing?"

"Deal is, the limit's only fifty-five on this highway," Vincent said, going right on. The lack of conscious company was obviously only one of the reasons he was in a foul mood. "Not exactly the best place to try an' make up for lost time. And now *this*..."

The trucker jutted a stubbled jaw toward the road ahead. Between successive rises in the pavement, wispy patches of ground fog brightened in the truck's high beams.

"Prob'ly get thicker before we get to Chiloquin. Don't matter if the daytime high hits ninety-five in this neck a' the woods, it's always cold and damp at night. But I gotta admit, this here's a little... unusual."

The truck bisected a chest-high blanket of fog, cab windows only a foot or so above the top of the gray-green layer, headlamps muted like the spotlight at the deep end of a dirty pool.

"*Chil*-oh-keen... sounds Indian." Gabriel rolled the syllables off his tongue once more, changing the accent. "Chee-loh-*keen*. And that's where we're headed?"

"Army munitions plant, a few miles beyond the main road through town."

Gabriel took his eyes off the fog, peered over at the trucker. "Munitions—? I thought you said we were carrying hardware."

"Euphemism." Vincent cast a deriding glance. "And here I thought you were smart enough to catch on. Proper term is *ordnance*, though most civilians don't know what that means either."

"What *does* it mean? What exactly are we hauling, anyway?"

He raised a brow thoughtfully as he went through the list. "Shell casings... tail-fin assemblies for mortars. Whole mess a' fuses. Those're the little babies can cause some excitement." There was almost a twinkle in his eye. "Doubt they'd go off unless some other truck crossed the center line and nailed us head on. And then we'd prob'ly be dead before any fireworks started."

Gabriel shifted uneasily, forced a chuckle at the trucker's dark humor, turned his gaze forward again. He could tell Vincent was gauging him from the corners of his eyes, clearly enjoying a little payback for the hours he'd spent with nobody to share his stories.

"Other problem is the deer. You heard the old saw about the dumb animals gettin' froze in your headlights...? Well, damn if it ain't true. Glare makes it hard for 'em to judge the speed and distance of oncoming traffic. Joke is, Highway Ninety-Seven is responsible for more venison than all the weekend warriors in the western states combined."

Vincent was on a roll now, back in the driver's seat in more ways than one. Gabriel found himself staring ahead, unblinking, afraid to take his eyes off the highway for even an instant. Which only fueled the trucker's enthusiasm.

"Must be hundreds of 'em up and down this corridor. *Thousands.* Bet I've seen three or four carcasses on the side a' the road every trip up here, and at least one family sedan or greenhorn freight jockey off in the trees as a result. You hit one just right—" Vincent lifted a hand from the steering wheel, thrust it forward in a broad, sweeping arc. "—and just like that you lose control. Not so serious if you're tooling along in your Suburban and all you're hauling are those new Calvin Kleins you just bought back in K Falls..."

He let the sentence hang there, unfinished, assumed Gabriel was smart enough for this one. And he was, to the point Gabriel actually felt reassured by Vincent's efforts to frighten him. After all, it wasn't as if they were risking their lives pulling a few tons of bomb parts in the trailer behind them. They hadn't blown themselves up for the last five hundred miles, had they?

Besides, their rig was only one of perhaps dozens of unmarked trucks – or fake pizza delivery vans, for all he knew – safely hauling explosives around the country on any given day. If the practice was all that dangerous, *Sixty Minutes* or *20/20* would've done an exposé on the issue by now, like all the hullaballoo about the railroad tank cars that carried crude oil and went off like A-bombs whenever they derailed, and then the industry...

Gabriel noticed Vincent stiffen behind the wheel even before he saw the buck himself.

The animal seemed to materialize out of nowhere, lifting its rack above the now unbroken ground fog like a hunter's trophy mounted to a black, featureless wall. Neither of them had seen the deer come out of the forest. It must have been concealed in the fog for the better part of a minute, head lowered, nose to the pavement, per-haps sniffing at something in the road.

The trucker knew it was futile to second-guess which way the buck might bolt, and sheer stupidity to try and swerve around him on the moist pavement. The best he could do was lay on the horn and apply his brakes firmly, without precipitating a skid.

The buck finally leapt, too late, for the line of trees on the east side of the road. The truck's right fender caught its hindquarters in mid-air, flipping the animal up and over the hood where it hit the support strut on the right edge of the windshield, ripping off the side mirror as it vanished in a blur of fur and hooves. Gabriel threw up his hands – too late to protect his face had the windshield actu-ally shattered. Instead, the passenger-side window took the brunt of the impact, the safety glass splitting cleanly down the center like two parts of a patio door, the broken pieces now overlapped and streaked with blood and fur.

The rig took another hundred and fifty yards to stop and pull onto the shoulder. Vincent immediately threw open his door and jumped from the cab, ran around to inspect the front-end damage. He winced, spat a few epithets in what may have been Vietnamese, glowered. The chrome radiator cowling and fender were badly mangled, right headlight smashed in, not to mention the crushed support strut and missing mirror.

None of which mattered to Gabriel. As Vincent continued to shake his head at the bent metal, Gabriel pushed his own door open, climbed down from the cab and began walking back in the direction of the buck.

Vincent didn't notice until he'd passed through the glow of the flashing tail lights.

"Hey! *Hey*—where you think you're goin'? I got a delivery in fifteen minutes, and ten more miles a' this soup to get through!"

Gabriel glanced back without stopping, his reply muted by the fog and the surrounding forest. "We can't just leave him there!"

"Oh yes we *can!*"

Vincent scowled, eyes narrowing as he watched Gabriel break into a lope, chest deep in the ground fog as if he were fording a stream. He huffed loud enough to convey his anger, lifted his eyes above his trailer. The blush in the early morning sky cast enough light to see color in the lodgepole pines on the west side of the road. In a few more minutes the sun would break over the lava buttes to the east, flooding the road with daylight. The fog would melt like spent steam above the lumber mill smokestacks up in Crescent, exposing the carcasses of all the deer killed that night. What was one more?

He lowered his gaze, raised his voice. "You got sixty seconds to get your ass back on my seat before I'm rollin'!" Then, stepping around to the driver's side, he quickly pulled himself up into the cab, took note of the glowing digits on the dashboard clock.

A hundred yards south, Gabriel was having difficulty locating the downed deer. He'd walked back and forth along the shoulder where he thought it should be, finally turned to look north as the truck continued to idle, trying to calculate the distance they might have traveled after impact. He decided he hadn't gone far enough, turned south again, jogged another thirty yards.

He'd just spotted the buck in a shallow gully beside the shoulder when he heard the big-rig grind into first gear. Gabriel spun around as the cab shuddered, strained against its heavy load and began to inch forward, passenger door still open wide. He considered running after it, decided not to, then, with a surge of adrenaline, thought about his duffle bag and the Bible with his mother's ring. At that moment an oblong shape rocketed from inside the cab, tumbling end-over-end before it disappeared into the blanket of fog.

At least Vincent hadn't left him without resources. Gabriel shook his head, watched for a few more moments as the truck picked up speed, turned back to the deer.

It was still alive, legs folded beneath its body as though resting, head upright, three of the five points on its right-side antlers snapped cleanly off. Oddly, though the buck appeared fully alert, it wasn't looking at Gabriel where he now stood on the shoulder, but past him, toward the center of the roadway. The animal continued to stare in that direction, even when the soft swooshing of an approaching car turned Gabriel's head to the south.

The top of the car – an SUV, he guessed – was visible just above the layer of gray, headlights glowing and diffused as if pushing a white fireball ahead of it. No wonder deer could become so easily mesmerized.

Luckily the driver had already seen Gabriel's torso over the ground fog. Mistaking him for another buck, the SUV veered into the southbound lane to give him as wide a berth as possible. Only when it passed did the driver's eyes meet Gabriel's, registering surprise that the looming shape belonged to another human being.

It was also in that instant the draft from the speeding car swept the fog aside long enough to reveal a second deer. Gabriel was momentarily startled by the ghostly form, and equally surprised it had lain, unseen, only a few feet away.

The deer, a white-tail doe, was sprawled lengthwise in the northbound lane, parallel to the center line, gashed and almost certainly torn up inside, but still in one piece. It occurred to Gabriel that the buck in the gully behind him had been attending to his wounded mate just before raising its antlers into Vincent's high beams. The doe had probably been hit by another vehicle some minutes before while attempting to cross the fog-bound highway.

From its position in the lane, and the tread marks on either side, it was clear Vincent had driven his rig directly over the smaller deer without knowing it, axles passing only inches over its rackless head, tires straddling its outstretched body. He hated to think what the animal might have looked like had Vincent turned even slightly from his path.

The sound of another approaching car pumped Gabriel with adrenaline once more. Without so much as a glance to see where it was, he reached into a newly-formed patch of fog, grabbed the doe by its bloodied forelegs and pulled, scrambling and stumbling backward toward the shoulder. The car whizzed by moments later in the opposite lane, heading south, fog lamps and side-panels a blur of yellow neon and metallic blue, its occupants aware of neither Gabriel nor the doe.

Or the buck.

As Gabriel finally reached the edge of the roadway, he slipped on the glossy wet border stripe, lost his grip on the doe's forelegs and tumbled butt-first into the gully, landing only inches from the larger animal. The buck was still in the same sitting position, and still staring not at him but his mate.

Gabriel pushed himself up, taking care not to make any sudden moves, turned just in time to see the doe lift its head. If the buck had been human, it might have done a double take. Instead it made a futile effort to get up, immediately crumpled, hind legs shattered and useless after the encounter with Vincent's fender.

The doe would recover; it was the buck who needed his attention now. Moving deliberately, Gabriel circled to his front, at the same time avoiding eye contact to let the buck know he meant no harm. For the first time the animal turned toward him, but Gabriel looked away and instead began to hum a lullaby he remembered his mother singing to him as a child. Admittedly, Gabriel had little experience with animals – though it was his best friend's lame horse that was first to benefit from his new-found talent – but he knew intuitively the sound of his voice would have a calming effect.

And it did, at least for a few seconds. Unfortunately, before Gabriel could get close enough to lay a hand on the wounded buck, a new sound began to compete with his lullaby. Yet another vehicle was approaching, this one unmistakably a big-rig, barreling north just as Vincent's had been minutes earlier, the flashback throwing the buck into a frenzy of fear for both himself and his mate.

Gabriel could hear the cracking of bones and cartilage as the buck attempted to stand once more. He threw himself at the animal's flank, narrowly avoiding an antler that ripped through his work shirt but only grazed his arm. He body-slammed the buck, hanging onto its thick fur while it struggled beneath him for several moments, then suddenly went limp. Immediately he pushed off, looked up to see the big-rig barreling through the remaining wisps of fog toward the doe, realized its hind legs were still sprawled out well into the roadway.

He scrambled up the embankment, work boots slipping on the matted pine needles, finally found traction. As he lunged for the forelegs again, the doe surprised him, rose up on all fours and bounded over his head, nimble as a gazelle. He ducked, turned to see it disappear into the shadows between the lodgepoles. A split-second later the big-rig blew by, shiny red fender close enough to touch, horn blaring as the driver belatedly spotted movement, its draft knocking Gabriel back into the gully.

And once again he was beside the buck. But this time the animal was standing, legs solid as tree trunks, looking down at him as he lay on his back. The buck seemed to acknowledge what Gabriel had done, paused long enough to lower his rack deferentially before likewise bounding into the forest.

Gabriel continued to lay there for some moments, breathing hard but satisfied, then at last sat up. As he struggled to one knee, he could make out a voice drifting down the road.

"Stay there!" the voice pleaded. "No—*please!* Don't try to get up!"

He sank back down, turned north to see the bright red big-rig pulled off not far from where Vincent had stopped. A woman in a leather vest and too-tight Levi's was running flat-out toward him in the dissipating mist.

"My husband's on the CB right now. Ambulance should be on its way any minute!" She was still running.

Gabriel slumped, turned away to hide a smile. Apparently the husband-wife team in the big-rig thought they'd hit *him*, not the deer. He looked up again, flashed on the memory of another driving duo he'd hitched a ride with years ago, remembered that the seating and the conversation were too close for comfort and he'd asked to be let off in the next town.

"How bad you hurt?"

The woman slowed to a walk about twenty yards away, then abruptly stopped when Gabriel stood to face her.

"Oh my God!" she gasped before he could answer, clasping her face with both hands.

Even in the spare morning light, Gabriel could see the glint of tears welling in her eyes. Her reaction baffled him – until it dawned on him precisely where she was staring. He nodded without even bothering to glance down, imagined how he must look with his work shirt soaked in blood, left sleeve ripped from elbow to shoulder, still more of the shiny crimson smeared across his hands and wrists.

"No, no—I'm fine," he said, now as desperate to calm the woman as he was the buck. "This isn't my own blood. Hell—you missed me by a mile!"

The sight was still too overwhelming. Behind her, the other half of the team had jumped from their truck, was now jogging down the highway toward them, one hand on his Stetson. A pair of cars passed on either side, both slowing to see what had happened, one of them pulling onto the opposite shoulder while the driver rolled down his window to offer assistance. Gabriel was suddenly feeling claustrophobic.

"Everything's okay—really." He raised his voice loud enough for both the husband and the Good Samaritan across the road. "I had to pull a buck off the highway so no one else'd run over him in the fog. You know, maybe lose control." He finally glanced down at himself, shrugged as if to minimize it all. "Carcass was a real mess. Prob'ly take a few pints a'Clorox to get *this* out."

The southbound car pulled back onto the highway, its driver now reassured – or else disappointed – that this was no emergency. The husband, meanwhile, came to a halt beside his leather-vested spouse, who finally lowered her hands but couldn't yet take her eyes off all the blood.

"Turns out the only ambulance was on a run down to the Indian casino," the husband said between breaths. "They won't be here for another twenty minutes or so. Thank God we don't need 'em." He squinted, just as struck by the bloodied work shirt. "Jee-*zus*—you sure you're okay?"

Gabriel nodded, climbed the embankment. "About that ambulance...? Better call him off so he doesn't break any speed limits tryin' to get here."

"Yeah, good idea..." The husband started back for their truck, hesitated. "Where *is* it, anyway?"

"Where's what?"

"The carcass."

Gabriel blinked, flustered, recovered quickly. "Back in the trees. Wouldn't want any kids to see Bambi all mangled like that." Then, pointing up the road: "I think I left my duffle bag up there where your rig's parked. You didn't feel any thumps when you pulled off the road, did'ja?"

The pair followed him back up the highway to their truck, eventually leaving him alone to search the embankment, but only after another round of questioning. The wife still seemed more concerned than suspicious. But Gabriel knew the husband doubted his story about dragging the carcass into the forest. He wondered aloud how Gabriel came to be there in the first place. "You come out here all by yourself for a mornin' stroll or somethin'?" he said with a sidelong glance.

When Gabriel truthfully explained that he'd been hitchhiking and asked to be let out there, the Stetson-topped trucker only glanced back to the treeline where they'd found him, perhaps marking the spot. And when their big-rig rumbled by, heading north once more, Gabriel wasn't surprised to see the husband peering at him through the window as if he were an escaped convict, raising the handset of his CB radio like he'd already made contact with the local police.

Gabriel couldn't hear what the trucker was saying, of course. He only knew he could use another ride – and fast. But not before finding his duffle bag. And not without slipping on another shirt.

The canvas bag turned up five minutes later and another twenty-five yards north, partially obscured by a cluster of pine saplings that had sprouted on the otherwise denuded embankment. Obviously the maintenance crews hadn't cleared the new growth since spring.

He knelt, quickly unzipped the duffle bag, found a clean work shirt on top and began to pull it out when it hit him: His Bible wasn't in the side pocket where it was supposed to be. He stood, scanned the area behind the saplings again. The book could easily have popped out in mid-air when Vincent hurled it from the cab. Gabriel told himself that's what happened, resisted any other explanation until a mental snapshot of the cab's interior came to mind, in the instant just before they hit the buck.

Damn.

He remembered seeing the Bible out of the corner of his eye, sailing off the bench seat from where he'd set it down the previous evening, after Vincent handed it back to him. He'd fallen asleep before tucking it back into his duffle bag, leaving the book exposed, next to his hip pocket. Gabriel hadn't been awake for fifteen minutes before Vincent hit the brakes and they'd collided with the buck.

Chances were, his Bible was still on the floorboard of the truck where it had fallen. Vincent probably drove off without even realizing it was there, inadvertently taking the few belongings Gabriel cared about. *Plus* thirty-three hundred dollars in cash, some of which he was sure to need by that afternoon, if not sooner.

Which is why Gabriel was staring desperately up the highway, wondering how much farther it was to the town with the Indian-sounding name, wondering if he could catch up with Vincent before he finished unloading his wares at the munitions factory.

And utterly oblivious to the fact that someone was coming up from behind him.

"Drop the bag—now!"

Gabriel glanced over his shoulder. A patrolman in a brown shirt and matching red-striped pants had planted himself two car-lengths away, flat-brimmed hat cutting a diagonal line against the brightening sky, his service revolver drawn and pointed at Gabriel's chest.

"*Drop it!* And keep your hands where I can see 'em." He waited until Gabriel complied. "Now turn all the way around... slowly."

Gabriel obliged once more, holding both hands away from his sides, trying to ignore a passing Jeep Wagoneer full of gape-mouthed rubberneckers. Beyond the lawman, perhaps fifty yards further south, a brown-and-white Blazer – not one of the white Crown Victorias driven by the OHP – was parked almost perpendicular to the highway. Its lights were still flashing, front tires on the embankment, blunt rear end jutting a good foot into the north-bound lane. Evidently the officer had been driving south when he spotted Gabriel kneeling over his duffle bag, then made a hasty, if somewhat incomplete, U-turn.

Gabriel couldn't be certain whether it was the blood on his shirt that first caught the patrolman's eye, or if the trucker in the Stetson had indeed broadcast his description over police band. He assumed it was the latter. Either way, Gabriel couldn't believe he'd neither seen nor heard the Blazer drive up. Not that it would've made any difference.

"What's the problem, officer?" he said, casually as he could.

The patrolman squinted, turned up a sardonic grin as if Gabriel should know better than to toy with him. "Problem—? Why don't you tell *me*." He motioned with his gun, indicating the front of Gabriel's shirt.

Gabriel squinted back, now beginning to understand. Ever since the husband-wife team pulled over, his only concern had been to keep his identity and his abilities secret. But this was turning into something else entirely.

"Look, I think somebody's gotten the wrong impression here. The trucker I hitched a ride with last night?—he hit a deer coming through here in the fog. Actually, there was a pair of 'em. We pulled over... and then the guy ditches me when I go back to see if there was anything I could do."

"*Do?* What?—like you're Starman or something?"

Gabriel cocked his head, taken aback by the quip, remembered only too well the cult favorite about the stranded alien in a human body and the deer his character had brought back to life. Not long after Gabriel was orphaned, his best friend's mother had rented the video, hoping the parable of loss and recovery might help him process his own grief. The film had been something of a lifesaver for Gabriel, giving him both someone to identify with and, later, the encouragement to strike out on his own journey. Strange the officer should bring it up now. Stranger still that he assumed Gabriel would understand the reference.

Perhaps Gabriel's identity *was* at issue.

"No," he replied firmly. "I just didn't think it was right to leave him there on the road, not to mention it's dangerous. So I dragged both of 'em off, which is how my shirt ends up with blood all over it." He paused again, brightened with another thought. "That *is* the law, isn't it? I mean, it's a person's duty to move an animal off the highway if you hit one, right?"

The patrolman was silent for a few moments.

"Show me."

Ten minutes later they'd retraced the same hundred-and-fifty yards Gabriel had walked twice before – the patrolman up on the shoulder of the road with his revolver, Gabriel down in the gully with neither his duffle bag nor his Bible. The present exercise, he knew, was futile. There would be no deer, nothing to verify his story. Then again, there was no evidence to disprove it, either. So maybe there was hope, after all: *Innocent until proven guilty.*

The patrolman found the spot before Gabriel did. What little blood the buck had left while resting in the gully had apparently disappeared into the damp pine needles. But the pavement where the doe had lain was a pool of thick, shiny maroon, despite the fresh tread marks that ran through it and already carried much of it away.

"Here," the patrolman said.

Gabriel turned, was surprised to see a pair of handcuffs flying through the air toward him. He reached out, snagged them instinctively, the way he might catch a hammer or box of finish nails tossed his way by a fellow framer.

The patrolman pointed again with the barrel of his gun. "Slip it over one wrist and cinch it up tight. Then put your hands behind you and do the other."

Gabriel scowled, looked up. "You're kidding, right?"

"You don't want *me* to put 'em on you. Trust me on that."

For the first time Gabriel felt a twinge of fear in the other man's presence. Essentially he and this unidentified patrolman were on this road together, miles from anything or anyone else. While the fog had pretty much evaporated, there was still very little traffic, and a minute or more might pass with no vehicles in sight. Gabriel could see the steely gaze and hard lines of his face, could tell by his demeanor he'd probably pulled over scores of speeding cars and drunken drivers and assorted vagrants, and he knew how to handle them without any back-up. He was mid-forties, Gabriel guessed, and still on the job. Had to be good at it.

"Alright, look—I'm putting them on...' Gabriel slipped one of the steel bracelets over his left wrist, tightened it, glanced up again. "...I just wish I knew why."

The lawman peered silently for several seconds – again the steely gaze – then looked away at the pool of blood. He followed the smear from the center of the lane to the shoulder, searched with his eyes for more blood on the embankment. saw none.

"You say you *dragged* the deer back in the woods?"

It was obvious where he was going.

"I, uh, carried it, actually. That's why there's no—"

"You picked up a three, four-hundred pound buck by yourself?"

"It was a doe. Small one, less than I weigh."

It *could've* been true, Gabriel thought.

"But you said the rig you were riding in... it hit a buck?"

"The buck was thrown off the road, over here somewhere." He pulled a hand from behind him before he'd closed the second cuff, gestured at the matted pine needles where it had likely lain. "The doe was up there, on the highway. Maybe somebody else—"

"So, then, you *dragged* the buck." the patrolman said, conspicuously eyeing the area Gabriel indicated. Equally conspicuous was the complete absence of drag marks or crumbled dirt along the knee-high ridge where the gully met the line of trees, over which Gabriel would've had to pull four hundred pounds of dead weight.

The patrolman nodded to himself, then glanced back at Gabriel.

"You get that other cuff on and sit your ass on the ground there. I'm goin' back in these trees, and if I don't find two dead animals, you an' me are takin' a little ride."

If the patrolman suspected that Gabriel had actually murdered someone, then hidden the body in the forest, he wasn't letting on. What he *was* doing, as Gabriel sat handcuffed in the gully, was poking around among the lodgepoles nearby, never losing sight of him for more than a few seconds, scribbling now and then on a memo pad he'd pull from his breast pocket not unlike Natalie taking lunch orders at Denny's.

After twenty minutes of poking and scribbling, he emerged from the trees with a rusty pick-axe whose deteriorating wooden handle looked as if it had lain in the forest for a decade or two. It wasn't immediately clear whether the patrolman considered it as evidence, or he was simply removing trash.

"So that's what I used to bury the bodies, right?" Gabriel offered a crooked smile, uncrossed his legs and attempted with some effort to stand, unable to use his hands for balance.

The patrolman ignored both his implication and the humor.

"Did I say you could get up?"

Gabriel hesitated, started to lower himself.

"No—go on. We're headin' back to the car anyway." Slipping the notepad into his pocket, he stood the pick-axe handle-up on the side of the road, reached down to a small leather pouch on his belt. "This'll just take a minute." Lifting the flap, he withdrew a two-inch glass vial, checked for traffic and stepped onto the pavement where the doe's blood was now congealed like raspberry Jello. He quickly bent over, scooped a small amount. capped the vial and returned for the pick-axe.

Gabriel shook his head. Surely the patrolman knew it would only turn out to be deer's blood. On the other hand there was so much of the sticky substance on the highway it seemed highly doubtful the doe could have survived. And without a carcass, Gabriel had to admit, it was more than a little suspicious.

The patrolman grabbed the axe, gestured. They began walking back toward his car, its flashing lights less glaring in the bright morning sun. The fog had vanished completely, but so had most of the hour since Vincent chucked Gabriel's duffle bag through the window of his Freightliner and left him to his fate.

"Mind if I make a suggestion?" Gabriel glanced back at the patrolman shadowing him; no reply. "A couple of phone calls and you might be able to clear this whole thing up. The trucker I was riding with?—he told me he was making a delivery in Chiloquin, said there's an ammo plant there...?"

Still no response.

"Anyhow, you call from your car, you might be able to catch 'im. Ask him about the guy he picked up last night, name'a Gabriel Woods. He'll back up what I told you."

"Yeah?—can he also tell me where the hell I can find your two dead white-tails?"

They were nearing the patrol car. Gabriel could see his duffle bag sitting on the embankment beside the right front tire where the patrolman had dropped it earlier.

"Look, officer, I can't tell you where the deer went. I don't know— maybe somebody saw where I dragged 'em when they were driving by, and then they go back, haul 'em off while I'm up here trying to collect my stuff."

Gabriel stopped beside the car, nodded at his bag, turned to face the patrolman as he approached. His service revolver was holstered, but he looked no less menacing with the pick-axe in hand. He continued to stare. Gabriel shrugged, took the offensive.

"Road kill isn't all that different from a deer brought down with a rifle, is it? I mean, a fresh carcass is just as good as some buck your average hunter ropes onto his hood, then drives home with after a day or two drinking beer with his buddies."

The patrolman squinted, allowed a brief nod. "I'll give you that. Matter a'fact, S-O-P is to call highway maintenance 'soon as we spot one by the road."

He motioned for Gabriel to step back, opened both the car's right-side doors before going on. "They dispatch a van to pick up the carcass, take it to a butcher up in LaPine who prepares it for the state prison north a' Bend. Prob'ly fresher than the venison they put out every so often at the Food Mart. 'Course," he added, "that's assuming one of our locals doesn't make off with the kill before O-T-C gets there."

Gabriel nodded back gratefully. It was the first time the patrolman had said anything remotely in his favor.

"So, you'll call the ammo plant?"

The patrolman threw the pick-axe onto the front floorboard, stepped past Gabriel to grab his duffle bag, tossed it onto the front seat.

"Yeah, I'll make a call on the way in. Meantime you think up a good explanation why there's no drag marks from the road to the trees. And then maybe you can tell me why there's no drag marks from the trees to the road, either... assuming you're right about someone hauling off the deer."

Gabriel could only stare in silence. The patrolman peered back, obviously pleased with himself, suddenly grabbed Gabriel's arm before he could react.

"You see my point, then," he said, yanking his suspect toward the back seat, pressing his head down, waiting just long enough for his legs to clear before slamming the car door.

They were less than five miles south of Chiloquin by the time he finally called the munitions plant. The first thing he'd done, in keeping with standard procedure, was report back to the station. And then he listened to the dispatcher – a delicate-voiced female barely out of her teens, Gabriel guessed – while she lambasted him over the car radio for staying out of contact so long.

"You bad to me, Lieutentant Fiske," her voice whined in accented English. "Why you keep doing this? I'm 'bout to send Buddy down to find you."

Gabriel suddenly realized the patrolman was more than some run-of-the-mill beat cop. It was also then that he noticed an embroidered patch, below the Stars-and-Stripes sewn onto his right sleeve. The circular emblem featured a sunburst design in the center of which stood a bison, similar to the profile on a buffalo nickel. Arcing around it were the words, *Department of the Interior: Bureau of Indian Affairs.*

The patrolman raised the handset. "Yeah? So why *didn't* you?"

"Cause he up in Beaver Marsh talkin' to some Bustin rancher who tell him one of our people take his firewood las' night."

Dead air for several seconds. Gabriel smiled despite himself. Clearly, he wasn't the only person to receive the silent treatment.

"Lieutenant? You say the murder suspect in custody now?"

"No, I *didn't* say that, Mel…" Fiske glanced in the rearview mirror as Gabriel's smile abruptly faded. "…And let's not call this a murder investigation just yet. At this point I'm bringing him in on a suspicious activities charge… maybe unlawful trespass."

"*Trespass?*" Gabriel echoed from the rear seat.

Fiske lowered his mike. "Maybe you didn't know it, but if you left the public roadway and stepped into the forest back there like you said?—you were trespassing on federally-protected Indian land. Good fall-back in case I can't make the other charge stick."

If the lines around his eyes were any indication, Fiske appeared to be grinning. Gabriel shook his head, looked away from the rearview mirror, tried to get comfortable despite the cuffs now cutting into his wrists behind him. Then, leaning conspicuously forward against the mesh between the seats, he met Fiske's eyes again.

The Lieutenant nodded reluctantly, raised the handset again. "Hey, Melody, patch me through to Colonel Halvorsen over at the plant, would'ja? His cell phone."

"I try, but he might not pick up. Shift change." Again there was no reply. Finally: "Okay, it ringing."

There was a click as the dispatcher hung up. The monotone pulses went on for a good twenty seconds before a new voice crackled impatiently over the speaker.

"Got a new crew coming on-line here—who's this?"

"Sorry to bother you right now, Jack. It's Fiske. Got somebody in my back seat, says he was riding with one'a your transport guys earlier this morning—"

"Vincent," Gabriel added through the steel barrier. "Don't know if it was his first name or last."

"You copy that?" Fiske said, flashing a disapproving look.

"Yeah. Got in a little after six-thirty, the ol' cuss. Not exactly in the sunniest mood. Pulled out ten, fifteen minutes ago."

Gabriel swore under his breath. Fiske lowered the mike thoughtfully, raised it once more.

"He say anything about what it was ruffled his feathers?"

"All I know is, he was five minutes late for the first time I can remember. That might've had something to do with it."

"Ask him if the front of his truck was damaged," Gabriel broke in.

Fiske paused long enough to draw more impatience from the man on the other end.

"So, is that all, Lieutenant?"

"Just one more thing…"

Fiske glanced in the rearview mirror, turned briefly to gaze out over the passing landscape. The forest along the highway had thinned to a mixture of lodgepole pines and quaking aspen. Through the tree trunks an occasional clearing showed signs of grazing cattle, fields of alfalfa, the sparkle of flowing water.

"You see any evidence he might've hit a deer this morning?"

"I saw the left side of his rig in the monitor as he was circling 'round to the loading dock, that's all." A few moments. "Look, we're still doing shift logs here. I can ask the dock crew, maybe try to raise

Vincent on his CB, but it'll be a while before I get to it."

"No big deal, Jack. Not a priority." Fiske glanced in the mirror again, caught Gabriel rolling his eyes. "Apologies for the timing."

The Lieutenant replaced his mike on the dash. The brown-and-white Blazer passed an intersection with a narrow two-lane road, a no-name gas station on the northeast corner with a poorly-lettered sign hawking propane. A minute later the car began to slow. Ahead was an off-ramp that curved gently to the right, dropping into a wooded ravine where another, wider two-lane road passed beneath 97, heading easterly. Fiske glanced back with another pasted-on grin.

"Welcome to Chiloquin."

The entire police department, Gabriel soon found, consisted of three men and two women. The dispatcher, Melody, turned out to be a heavy-set, fiftyish Indian woman with a child-like voice he still found hard to connect with her body, even when he watched her speak.

"So, this really... *him?*" she said, eyebrows raised, when Fiske escorted his suspect past her desk.

Gabriel was convinced she was about to say *murderer,* but deferred to Fiske's earlier request when he sent a stern look.

The two other male officers – also native Chiloquin – viewed Gabriel with similar guilty-until-proven-innocent suspicion, salted with anticipation that the department might have something more exciting than stolen firewood to occupy their time. The lankier of the two men, sporting a brass I.D. tag inscribed with *Buddy,* had apparently hurried back from Beaver Marsh just to see their suspect brought in. Judging by his reaction when Fiske marched Gabriel through the front door, the blood-soaked work shirt was everything he could have hoped for.

The lanky deputy was somewhat less excited when Fiske took off their suspect's handcuffs, then directed him to remove Gabriel's work shirt and drive it up to the county medical examiner in Chemult, along with the blood sample he'd taken from the pavement. The hesitation sparked by Buddy's obvious disappointment gave Gabriel just enough time to take the initiative.

"No, no, that's okay. I'll do it myself."

Stepping backwards out of reach, he began stripping off his shirt, preempting any further contact. Fiske's manhandling of him had already done *some*thing, Gabriel suspected, though the Lieutenant appeared none the wiser. Either way, Gabriel was feeling claustrophobic again. Being in a situation where others were almost certain to touch him – and where he was helpless to prevent it – had always been his worst nightmare. Two buttons went flying as he peeled the shirt from his chest, yanked his arms from the sleeves and tossed it to Buddy like it was infested with plague.

An uneasy silence followed while the three policemen exchanged surprised glances, wondering at Gabriel's almost theatrical display – *and* at his obvious discomfort with their proximity. Gabriel shrugged in response, was startled to note that Fiske had slipped the safety strap off his revolver, leaving a hand hovering over his holster even now.

"Go on then," Fiske finally said to Buddy, nodding at the small vial on the front counter. "And Mel, you call Chemult. Tell 'em I need a report *today*. If Shirley tells you the M.E. is gone fishing again, find out where the hell he is, 'cause Buddy's gonna go out there and haul his ass back to the lab."

Buddy frowned, but started obediently toward the vial and the front door. Gabriel watched him pass, eyes following him warily before abruptly coming to rest on a fourth, female member of the department. He blinked, stared. Either Gabriel hadn't noticed her earlier, or she'd just appeared in the doorway to an adjoining corridor. The woman was staring with similar wonder at *him*, though apparently less from his recent display than his bare, blood-smeared torso.

"You think we could find another shirt for our guest, Lieutenant?" she said, dropping her gaze momentarily before looking back at Fiske.

She too was a member of the local Indian population, Gabriel surmised, lustrous dark hair cropped shoulder length, three strings of multi-colored beads woven into the tresses at her left temple. She looked almost buxom in her crisp, tan uniform. Without knowing why, he felt reassured by the sight of her.

"I just put fresh sheets on the mattress, 'case he spends the night."

And just like that his reassurance dissolved. Gabriel glanced at Fiske, all the more uncomfortable at the prospect of being in custody that long. The Lieutenant scowled at his female deputy a few more moments, then stepped back to the counter where he'd dropped Gabriel's duffle bag.

He unzipped it, found another work shirt on top, shook it out. After checking the breast pockets to ensure they were empty, he rolled it into a loose ball and tossed it to Gabriel, then turned back to the canvas bag to begin searching its contents.

Gabriel knew he'd find nothing important or incriminating, allowed himself to scan the room more deliberately while he put on the fresh shirt.

In contrast to the building's nondescript metal exterior, the office was tastefully appointed, its side walls paneled with knotty pine. A pair of colorful Indian blankets were draped against the back wall, along with some sort of deerskin vestment featuring delicate beadwork. On either side of the smoked-glass doors in front were a sand painting of Crater Lake and a framed poster promoting what appeared to be a tribal pow-wow. A collection of woven baskets and decorative earthenware pots was neatly arranged at the far end of the front counter, spilling down a tiered display table onto the floor and along the base of one of the paneled walls. It was a veritable museum of Indian artifacts.

Gabriel's eyes completed the circuit, returned again to the female deputy. He was mildly surprised to find her still staring at him, eyes now locking with his, almost searchingly. Gabriel returned a questioning look, started to say something when she cut him off.

"It *was* a deer," she said matter-of-factly. "No—*two* deer... mates." She continued to hold his eyes as he tried to conceal even more surprise. "They ran off before anyone else stopped."

There was another period of silence before Fiske finally let out a laugh, shaking his head as he began stuffing Gabriel's belongings back into his duffle bag.

"Sorry, Chino, you got smoke-signals in your eyes on this one. Nobody – human *or* deer – could survive the loss a'blood I saw out there on that highway. I mean, I know your people still like to believe in miracles and all that, but let's get real here..."

Gabriel blinked again, broke eye contact with the policewoman, forced himself to look away at Fiske as he finished repacking the bag, leaving only his scuffed brown wallet atop the counter. Gabriel hadn't carried the wallet in years, leaving it to gather lint at the bottom of his duffle bag, pulling out the driver's license it contained only when a prospective employer insisted on some kind of formal identification. Such an event was rare, of course, since most site supervisors were more interested in his skills than his identity. He could've told them he was Mother Theresa and they'd have gladly signed him on by that name.

"This really you?"

Fiske slipped his license from beneath the yellowing plastic window, held up the card, glancing from the photo to Gabriel and back again. The card featured a much younger version, hair still close cropped and neatly combed, hopeful expression oblivious to a future that would soon begin to suffocate him.

Gabriel nodded. Fiske squinted.

"You realize this expired eight years ago."

"Don't drive anymore. I get free rides from truckers hauling bombshells."

The Lieutenant ignored the quip and the snicker from his remaining male deputy.

"Raphael Gabriel Woods... you go by your middle name, do you?"

"No law against it, is there?"

Fiske cast a dark glance, but chose to ignore this too.

"Salem, Virginia... seems you're a long way from home. That where you're from?"

"Originally."

"And now—?"

Gabriel paused to scratch behind an ear. "Various places. I work in construction... wherever the jobs are."

"And if you can't find steady work, maybe you'll take an odd job here and there...?" Fiske continued to build his case, if only in his own mind. He lifted the empty wallet, opened the money pouch wide for everyone to see. "Looks like you might be in a position to consider just about anything right now."

"Actually, I got some money tucked away in my Bible. Thing is, it's still in the cab of the truck I was riding in, you know, the one that hit the deer...? And if you'd just give me a chance to—"

"Only thing I'm gonna give *you* right now is some quiet time, courtesy a'the Chiloquin Hilton. Maybe you can try and get your story straight... two, three hours, I figure. That's how long it'll take Buddy to run those blood samples up to the M.E. and confirm—" He sent a glance at Deputy Chino before continuing. "—*officially*, if the part about the deer checks out. An' even if it does, you've still got more holes in your story than a jackrabbit full'a buckshot."

The report from Chemult was over seven hours in coming. It arrived in the form of a faxed, hand-written note, and fell over the Chiloquin PD-slash-BIA District Office like a proverbial wet blanket. An Indian one at that.

The county medical examiner hadn't taken the time to identify precisely what kind of animal the blood had come from. But he *had* determined conclusively that neither the congealed sample in the vial, nor any of several specimens scraped from Gabriel's shirt, were of human origin. In short, whatever else the investigation of Gabriel's alleged "crime" might be about, it was no longer a homicide.

By the time the note sliced itself off the antiquated fax machine's paper roll, Fiske had already given up the idea of pressing an unlawful trespass charge. Other than Gabriel's own admission about going into the forest, there was no corroborating evidence, nor any indication of wrongdoing – intentional or otherwise. The local bleeding-heart magistrate would call Gabriel's trespass a simple mistake bearing no consequences for either the indigenous population or the public at large, and proceed to gavel Fiske out of his courtroom. And Woods' inability to explain how a mortally-wounded animal could disappear without a trace was not by itself sufficient to hold him.

Still, Fiske had considered keeping Gabriel on ice for a day or two longer, with the hope some other crime might be reported, or some new witness might turn up. He'd heard of ritual animal sacrifices – quite messy and quite illegal under Oregon law – allegedly conducted by the Rajneesh followers who'd moved into the Prineville area years ago and taken over that county's government for a short time. Fiske couldn't recall any cult activity or Satanic rituals over the last decade, at least locally. But he continued to believe in his gut that Raphael Gabriel Woods – or whoever this unlikely vagabond really was – was hiding something. And he wanted, *needed*, to find out what it was.

Earlier in the day, before Buddy had returned from his two-hour run up to Chemult and back, Fiske put his other deputy on the computer to find out if their suspect had any outstanding warrants. No such luck. In fact, Deputy Trueblood not only found no criminal history, but little history of any kind. Other than a Certificate of Live Birth confirming the earthly existence of one Raphael Gabriel Woods, born to an unwed – and now deceased – mother in Salem Virginia some twenty-seven years ago, there were no records. Nothing. Based on the combined resources of the world wide web, from government files to credit reporting agencies to Interpol itself, Gabriel was a virtual non-entity.

Of course, the lack of a digital identity was hardly uncommon. Millions of people lived out their lives beneath the radar screens of modern technology. Some were no doubt illegal aliens – seasonal migrant workers, ranch hands and day laborers; Oregon had more than its share, as did its neighbor to the south. But many ordinary citizens were likewise invisible, electronically speaking. Gabriel could easily be one of them.

Around 10:45 that morning, Gabriel pounded on the door of the sound-proofed cell at the far end of their "guest wing," eventually attracting Deputy Trueblood's attention to tell him he hadn't had anything to eat since noon the previous day. The opportunity to serve Gabriel a meal gave Fiske an idea. Along with the microwaved beef stew, stale coffee and two slices of bread from the loaf Melody found in the break-room fridge, Fiske would send in Deputy Chino.

Gabriel squinted with mild curiosity when her face appeared in the foot-square window of the cell door, her eyes scanning the room.

Sitting cross-legged atop the military-style bunk opposite the door, he watched with growing curiosity as the door finally opened and the deputy stepped inside, carrying a lunch tray which she handed to him without taking her eyes off his. Then she backtracked, halted beside the stainless-steel sink bolted to the adjoining wall, leaned casually against its rim with arms folded.

He nodded his thanks, glanced down at the styrofoam cup of beef stew, picked up the plastic spoon to sample a bite.

"Little too much salt for my taste," he said after a few lip-smacks, "but it'll do."

Deputy Chino said nothing – rather Fiske-like, Gabriel thought. He scooped several more mouthfuls, aware she was staring at him the whole time, finally waved the spoon at his surroundings.

"Accommodations are nice. First jail cell I've ever been in, tell you the truth. Guess I was expecting rusty iron bars, maybe some peeling cinderblock—"

"Lieutenant Fiske sent me to see if I could get a better read on you," she broke in, glancing briefly toward the wire-mesh window. "I haven't told him what I already know."

Gabriel lowered the spoon. "And what exactly *do* you know?"

"What *am* I—that's what you should be asking. Aren't you just a little curious how I knew about the deer?" She unfolded her arms, pushed away from the sink. "What *you* are—now that's my question. All the Lieutenant cares about is finding something he can use to keep you locked up. I'm not clear yet why it's so important to him."

Gabriel's frown deepened. "Look, I'm a little confused here. Just exactly who's team are you *on?*"

"I'm only trying to protect you. You have..." She peered thoughtfully, stepped over to the foot of his bed. "...stronger medicine than I have. *Much* stronger." She lowered herself, raised an eyebrow when Gabriel abruptly placed the lunch tray down on the gray woolen blanket between them, as if defining a boundary. "I think it's good medicine. But I'm not always right."

Gabriel jabbed his spoon into what remained of the beef stew, sat back, blew out a puzzled breath.

"You know, I'd like to finish this gourmet meal you guys've cooked

up for me. I mean, I really *am* hungry. But, sure, I'll take the bait."
Gabriel cocked his head, peered back at her. "What *are* you?"

"In your language, I would be called an intuitive." She answered
immediately, then lowered her voice. "It's not something I was taught.
I've been this way since I was small, and I accepted my gift. But I
am, unfortunately, also a woman." She squared herself, looked up.
"Among the Maqlaq, if I were born into a man's body, I would be the
shaman."

"You mean, like a medicine man?" Gabriel nodded. "So that's
your medicine?—finding out if your Lieutenant's latest collar is really telling the truth? Reading their minds so he can—"

Chino bristled. "I don't read minds. I get a feeling, and sometimes a vision. And as far as Lieutenant Fiske is concerned, he hired
me because he thought I made a pretty little addition to all the other
native handiwork on display out there, and he knew I needed a job
just like most of us do." She sent another glance toward the door,
shook her head. "He almost fired me when I cut my hair... said I
didn't look Indian anymore. More like a damn Mexican. Those were
his words."

Gabriel shrugged apologetically, even if he was no less confused.
Why was she telling him this?

"Chino... Spanish, isn't it?"

"You'll find lots of Indians with Hispanic names. 'Specially down
in Arizona, New Mexico—"

"That where you're from?"

"No, my people are from south of Klamath, closer to Shasta.
Maqlaq, pronounced like the shoes...? Early traders who came here
were Spanish, thought we were all Chinese when they first saw us.
Chino means Chinese."

She allowed a laugh, then quickly sobered, aware that the conversation had begun to focus more on her than him. Gabriel offered
a smile, helped her get back on track.

"So the Lieutenant, he wants to use your... medicine... to find
out whatever you can about me, right?"

"He thinks I'm good at getting people to talk. Which I am."

She squared her shoulders, demeanor defensive once more. It
was possible, Gabriel thought, she and her commanding officer

weren't on the same team.

"Buddy and Trueblood both told him I can see things, but he doesn't believe it. Doesn't matter if I helped solve a few cases this way, all he can do is make jokes." She turned back, fixed her eyes on Gabriel. "I'm not going to tell him. I just want to know for myself."

A few seconds, then: "You mean, who am I?"

"No. I mean, what *are* you?"

Gabriel nodded, thought for several moments, picked up his spoon and shoveled another scoop of the lukewarm stew before an answer came to him.

"A medicine man... who doesn't accept his so-called gift."

The deputy returned to tell Fiske that, in all honesty, she could find nothing new.

She'd already suspected some special power in Gabriel; she knew as much even before Fiske had deposited him in the holding cell. And since she'd failed to uncover anything more during her lunchtime interrogation, she wasn't lying. Technically.

Which didn't make her report any less disappointing. Nor was Fiske happy when the fax arrived from Chemult. The bottom line was, he had no legal grounds for keeping Woods in custody any longer. If the trucker he'd hitched a ride with turned out to have a different story, Fiske might have some justification for not releasing him. But three hours earlier, Halvorsen had phoned from the ammo plant to report that dock workers had indeed seen damage to the front of Vincent's truck, consistent with his having hit a deer. As recently as twenty minutes ago, however, he also called to admit that he hadn't been able to raise Vincent on either his CB or his cell phone, so the story couldn't be confirmed.

"Sometimes the old fart turns off everything and pulls off at a rest stop to catch some winks," the plant manager explained. "And sometimes he drives up the road to Laney's place, spends the morning on her living room sofa. That is, assuming she's not..." There was a brief pause while Halvorsen selected the right word. "...*entertaining* any other guests. You know Lane doesn't have a phone, so I left a message at the Vernon plant in L.A., told 'em to call me when Vincent reports for the next shipment."

"When's that?" Fiske had asked.

"Not until Saturday noon, which puts him here on Sunday morning. And if there's a damn sick-out next week, I may just cancel *all* the deliveries for the duration."

It was shortly after Halvorsen's second call when Fiske unlocked Gabriel's cell door, pulled it open and stood stone-faced in the hallway. "Your things are on the front counter," he said without further explanation or apology.

Gabriel stepped out past him, careful to maintain a safe margin as they walked up the corridor and started back through the office, glancing around to find only Melody at her desk. Presumably the three deputies were back on their respective beats, searching for stolen firewood. Gabriel found himself strangely saddened at having missed Deputy Chino, began to formulate how he might ask the Lieutenant where she was without raising any suspicions.

"I don't know if you were just passing through," Fiske said, interrupting Gabriel's thoughts. "But if you were hoping to find some work in construction, Chiloquin's the last place you'd want to look." He paused while Gabriel reached for his duffle bag, apparently searching the contents to make sure his wallet had been returned, even if it was devoid of currency. "Only game in town, other than the *Kla-Mo-Ya* casino twenty minutes south, is the ammunition plant. And you're not about to find work there either, since we got ourselves a little labor dispute goin' on. 'Least the threat a'one. Wouldn't want to see you get mixed up in that."

Fiske suddenly glanced away as if reconsidering; maybe he *would,* come to think of it.

"Anyway, it's your call. I can give you a lift out to the plant. Or I can drive you up to the Amtrak station in Chemult so you can keep lookin' for work someplace else." He pasted another insincere grin. "Hell, we could even swing by the M.E.'s office up there, maybe get your shirt back." Then, just as quickly, his face turned stony again.

"Don't figure you'll ever get out those blood stains, though."

Gabriel wasn't sure how to reply. Or whether he should.

"Well, since I don't have any money for a train ticket to go *some-place else*—" He accented Fiske's words, perhaps overmuch. "—it looks like I'm stuck here for a while."

Fiske leaned an elbow on the counter as Gabriel zipped up his bag and started to turn, pushed his face so close that Gabriel had to draw back to focus.

"You haven't gotten enough of me yet? Just hang around a few more days and give me another chance to pick you up. Vagrancy is a term I'm pretty much free to define any damn way I like."

Gabriel was the first to blink. He pulled away, turned to meet the dispatcher's look of genuine concern, slung the canvas strap over his shoulder and headed for the front door without so much as a backward glance.

*T*he **U.S. Army Ammunition Plant** was two miles from town, just off the road that ran north through Chiloquin, then arched gently eastward over the top of an ancient lava flow before dropping alongside the Sprague River. Gabriel would not find the plant for another hour and a half. Then again, the "lift" Fiske had offered was never really an option.

Sensing the Lieutenant's eyes drilling the back of his head, Gabriel made a hasty departure from the police station, setting off in the direction of Highway 97 to give Fiske the impression he was indeed leaving the area for greener pastures. In less than ten minutes, however, with the beige metal building no longer visible through the stands of aspen, Gabriel found an old railbed he correctly deduced would lead him into town. He followed the tracks as they paralleled what appeared to be a private airstrip, then curved east over a rusting iron bridge into downtown Chiloquin.

Although "downtown" was perhaps too generous a word.

Chiloquin's economic hub was all of four blocks long, lined mostly with clapboard buildings reminiscent of an Alaskan trading post. The combined city-hall-and-chamber-of-commerce on Second Street was located in what was once a modest one-bedroom house. A block over, the local Family Supermarket and True Value hardware store attracted most of the foot traffic in town, which wasn't much.

Just up the street, a metal-and-stucco social services center had been completed only recently, the architect's sign still posted in a barren flowerbed. Its drab exterior was brightened only by the colorful mural decorating one wall of a warehouse directly across the parking lot. Both seemed incongruous among the other, rough-sawn wood structures.

Of the town's few brick buildings, a former Masonic Lodge, complete with its ruler-and-compass emblem and a dedication date of 1907, now appeared to be the local watering hole. Sitting at the corner of First and Yahooskin, its yellowing white-plastic sign was hand-lettered with the unlikely name of *Corky and Corky Girls*.

Gabriel went inside, stepped to the brass rail and asked the barkeep how he might find the ammunition plant. The fair-haired proprietor stared for some moments like it was a stupid question. "Go back outside," he replied at last, "find what passes around here for asphalt and follow it out of town for a couple miles. Sure hope you're not lookin' for work."

On the next corner north was another no-name gas station that also sold propane, where Gabriel tried for the next half hour to hitch a ride. Unfortunately, nearly all of the dozen cars he spied were going in the wrong direction, and the one that wasn't stopped only because the driver was lost.

The stocky station attendant finally took pity, trudged out to the curb and stood a few feet away, folding his arms as if to survey the streets and join in Gabriel's vigil. After a minute or so, he took a step closer, confided that traffic wouldn't be headed east for another hour or so when the next shift change at the ammo plant was scheduled. But there was a new rail spur off the Southern Pacific mainline, he said proudly, just above the intersection of Sprague River Road and Pine Ridge. It ran in an almost straight line to the factory.

"You willing to hoof it," he added, "you prob'ly be there in twenty, thirty minutes. Pretty country, too. Just keep your eyes peeled for the switcher. Hauls a few freight cars back to the main 'bout this time every day."

Gabriel thanked the man, looked to the northwest where the town's outskirts were bisected by parallel rail tracks and a slow-moving, rock-strewn river. Beyond it was a line of aspen where he guessed the police station was hidden, probably midway between the town and the state highway. He turned back.

"Anybody ever get arrested for walking along the tracks?"

The attendant waved the query aside with a grease-stained hand. "Naw. Half the young ones on the rez hike to The Buttes up that way. Prob'ly run into some. You do, tell 'em Jimmy Two Feathers says hi."

Gabriel ran into neither the youthful hikers nor the switcher the attendant had warned him about. But it was a pretty hike. Among the rolling, sparsely-wooded hills were swaths of farmland and pasture the color of amber, reminiscent of the countryside where he'd grown up. Everything was green and amber, like colors straight from jars of schoolhouse tempera, unvarying but for the deeper red lava rock of the distant buttes.

Not many cinder cones in Virginia, Gabriel mused. Still, it was all so familiar somehow. He could live in this place, even if it would last for no more than the usual few months, or half a year if he was lucky.

The track rose into a narrow cut made in the lava ridge north of Chiloquin, then began a leisurely descent into a broad river valley. After another mile or so the rails curved a few degrees to the right, the surrounding trees falling away on either side, offering an unbroken panorama nearly the full length of the valley. And there, in the center of an otherwise glorious vista, was the ammunition plant.

It was in plain view for the last half mile of his trek, looming larger with every step, sprawling over what must have been six or seven football fields. Its corrugated tin roof rose perhaps three stories in a coarse saw-tooth pattern, spiked by oddly-shaped vents and air-conditioning compressors. The long expanse of ochre siding was no doubt chosen to blend with the terrain, Gabriel figured; but even the most complementary color couldn't prevent it from looking horribly out of place.

In fact, the closer he got, the more of an eyesore it became. Tall, chain-link fencing ran the entire perimeter, rising from a low concrete wall, razor-wire coiled menacingly on top. The fence enclosed a red-asphalt parking lot with perhaps forty or fifty cars. On the side facing what was presumably the road from Chiloquin, a half-dozen freeway dividers had been spaced diagonally on alternate sides of the entry drive, requiring an approaching vehicle to undertake a series of S-turns. Behind the rolling gate was the kind of guard booth typical of a military installation.

The rail spur curved beneath another fortified gate in the rear, then straightened out alongside a long, concrete dock lined with metal roll-up doors. The switcher was still there, with three unassuming, graffiti-tagged boxcars coupled behind it. Nearby were a trio of loading bays for trucks, through which Vincent must have long since emptied his "hardware." Maybe he was back on the road now, or sleeping in one of the fleabag motels Gabriel had seen just north of Klamath Falls, with the words *Truckers Welcomb* and *Hourly Raites Avalible* misspelled on gaudy, back-lit message boards.

He stepped from the tracks, down the gravel embankment, following the chain-link toward the main entrance. A pair of uniformed guards came into view, standing beside the booth, one of whom sported binoculars with which he'd evidently been keeping an eye on Gabriel ever since he'd descended the railbed. The second guard reached into the booth as he rounded the northwest corner of the perimeter fence, withdrew a telephone handset trailing a long cord, spoke briefly before hanging up.

A minute later Gabriel halted beside the mechanized gate.

"Guess you didn't notice the signs," the guard with the binoculars said in lieu of a greeting.

Gabriel frowned, noticing for the first time the M-14 strapped at his side, then stepped back to scan the fence. He squinted, finally focused on one of the metal rectangles affixed every twenty yards or so, a good ten feet above eye level. *DO NOT CROSS THE YELLOW LINE!* the sign warned in urgent block letters, followed by the smaller, lower-case words, *or you risk being fired upon.* Gabriel looked behind him, blinked at the ill-defined, spray-painted line in the lava rock which bordered the fence, slowly lifted his hands as if to signal that he posed no threat and was sorry for his mistake.

"You can search my bag if you like," he added with a submissive shrug.

The second guard stepped past his armed companion. "No need. You're here to see the plant manager?"

Gabriel concealed surprise. *Had they been expecting him?*

"His name Jack, by any chance?"

"Colonel Halvorsen to us. Problem is, we got another shift change comin' up in just about—" He glanced back at a large clock inside the guard booth. "—four more minutes. Maybe if you'd been here, say, an hour ago..."

The guard donned a cordial, almost apologetic smile, then suddenly peered past Gabriel where a small sedan was just now pulling off the highway east of the approach road, kicking up a cloud of mauve-colored dust. Gabriel followed his gaze, spied two other cars already parked on the shoulder to the west, their drivers visible through the windows – perhaps wives or girlfriends who'd come to pick up their hard-working mates. If Chiloquin was as poor as it looked, there were plenty of single-car families around.

"That's okay," Gabriel said, drawing back the guard's attention. "I can wait."

"Look, here's the bottom line," the guard with the automatic rifle broke in, less cordially, "the Colonel's too busy to see anybody for the rest of the day."

Gabriel squinted. "*Any*body? Or me in particular?"

"Mister, ah, *Woods,* isn't it?"

It was the second guard again. And again Gabriel tried not to show his surprise. Clearly they *had* been expecting him.

"You're lookin' for a certain trucker, right?"

"Yeah. Older guy named Vincent. I'm not sure if it's his first—"

"I can't tell you where he is between runs," the guard went on. "Management doesn't give us that info. But the weekly schedule shows him coming back Sunday morning. If he's not here by six-thirty, sharp, it prob'ly means the world's about to end."

Gabriel allowed a smile, nodded, glanced away as he ran the numbers. Sunday was three days away. He had four dollar bills in his right front pocket which had somehow eluded detection by Fiske and his cohorts, and which he'd only rediscovered during his railbed hike out to the ammo plant. He'd need a motel or some other place to stay for the next three nights – not to mention food – until Vincent returned. So, allowing himself a buck thirty-three per day…

"Listen, you guys. This can't be such a big deal. I'm sure you've got a dispatcher, or some supervisor who can get in touch—"

"Sorry—" The rifleman broke in again. It was beginning to feel like good cop, bad cop. "—but my buddy here already gave you more than he should. It's time for you to take another hike."

Gabriel considered protesting once more, thought better of it, nodded. "Okay, fine. I appreciate the tip."

As the last few words left his lips, a whistle began to blow, faintly at first – maybe the switcher pulling away from the loading dock? – then steadily increasing in volume until it was shrieking like a jet fighter on after-burners. Gabriel looked away, spotted a blast of steam venting from the signal horn atop the roof. His unspoken question caught the second guard's eye.

"Gotta be loud enough to hear over the machinery noise in there," the soldier yelled over the din, "but you don't wanna start out full-blast when people are hand-packing live grenades." The whistle faded; the guard sent an almost neighborly smile.

Beyond him, a pair of doors in the expanse of metal siding burst open. A lone worker in olive fatigues emerged, then two more, heading for their cars in a separately-fenced area across the lot. Gabriel nodded back at the guard, blew out a frustrated breath, took a few steps toward the roll-away gate. Maybe he could at least catch a ride back into town.

"No can do," the first guard said. "Can't be anybody near the gate when I open it. You'll need to walk back up the road there, where the others are waiting." He yanked his shoulder strap to bring the M-14 to the front, used the barrel to point past the freeway dividers at the three parked cars.

It is a military installation, Gabriel thought. No use arguing.

He glanced from one guard to the other, both of them waiting impatiently for him to comply, then turned and started up the entrance drive, trudging past the concrete barriers. Only when he'd passed the third barrier did he hear the mechanized whirring of the gate.

The first two cars sped through the S-curves almost before Gabriel could get his thumb out. He shrugged, looked back at the plant, could see a few more workers spilling from the double doors, but no other cars backing from their spaces.

He headed for the highway. The three cars waiting on the shoulder were equally silent. As Gabriel neared them he could make out a dark-haired woman, perhaps late twenties and part Indian, sitting behind the wheel of a Chevy pickup – over half the vehicles in these parts were pickups – with two chubby pre-school boys fidgeting on the seat beside her. On his side of the entrance drive was a dented Toyota with a woman who was perhaps a decade older than the other woman, though easier to look at in her strapless top and bottle-blonde hair now ablaze in the afternoon sun.

The woman also seemed to be following him closely with her gaze, arm slung over the seatback as she peered through her rear window. When she was sure she'd caught his eye, she tilted her head to one side, ran fingers through her sun-drenched hair and bestowed what was clearly meant as more than a neighborly smile.

Gabriel felt himself blush, immediately crossed to the west side of the entrance drive. He stopped near the pickup and the fidgeting children, felt even more self-conscious when the two kids poked their heads out the side window, picked their noses and stared at him like they were watching chimps at the zoo. He waved and said hello as if that might satisfy their curiosity, and, when it didn't, walked on past them to where the third car was parked.

This one was a vintage Mustang, Gabriel noted with satisfaction, not unlike the '65 in which he'd first learned to drive back in Virginia, owned by the parents of the friend whose filly he'd saved. The lone occupant was visible through the windshield only in silhouette, staring straight ahead as she listened to the car radio. Her hair hung loosely around her face, swaying slightly as she rocked to the music, shoulder length but shorter on top, either punk-style, badly cut, or both.

Suddenly car engines gunned behind the chain-link. He swirled, saw a pair of vehicles moving at the far end of the lot. Gabriel wasn't going to miss these two. He stepped between the Mustang and the pickup, crossed the highway and positioned himself on the opposite shoulder where it would be easy for a vehicle to pull off.

The two cars – a late-model Bronco and another dirt-encrusted pickup – roared bumper-to-bumper through the barriers and bounced onto the road toward Chiloquin. Tires squealing, they must've been doing forty as they passed him, continuing to acceler-ate all the while, the pickup eating the Bronco's exhaust but jockey-ing to pass. Gabriel watched dumbfounded as they headed into a curve a quarter-mile down the road, now side by side. *Lunacy.* Then again, maybe that's what handling high explosives all day did to you.

And maybe standing on the other side of the road wasn't such a good idea after all, assuming everyone else was going to come out pedal to metal. He spotted a few more cars in the distance as they moved through the lot, started jogging back across the center line, heading once more for the opening between the Chevy and the Mus-tang. Then, suddenly, he slowed, looked through the driver's win-dow to get a better look at the punk-cut driver.

She too was light-haired – naturally so, he guessed – with fair skin and eyes whose color he could not discern in the shadows. She cast a glance his way as he approached, but quickly turned forward again to gaze through the windshield, holding steady even when he passed through her field of vision. By that time a Volkswagen van had come through the gate, Gabriel's own gaze locked on the van as it wound up the drive, then stopped at the edge of the highway.

He pivoted around the back of the pickup, started toward the van when a passenger got out and began loping his way. Gabriel immediately halted, assumed the lightly-bearded young man was coming over to say something. Maybe the more helpful of the two guards had tipped him off about Gabriel's needing a ride. Or maybe there was some additional information about Vincent he wanted to pass on.

An instant later it dawned on him that the young man was sim-ply being dropped off by one of his buddies, and now he was run-ning over to join his wife and kids in the pickup. Instead of going straight to the driver's side, he flung open the passenger-side door, the two boys practically tumbling out, chattering with delight as they threw their arms around his neck, both holding on for dear life while he spun them around.

Gabriel backed away to give them space, cursing his foolish assumption, then noticed too late that the Volkswagen van – now followed by another car – had begun to sputter out onto the highway. He turned, bolted around the back of the pickup, bumping into the front of the Mustang as he ran out into the eastbound lane, waving his arms in an attempt to flag down either of the departing vehicles.

They'd already passed him. He lowered his arms, huffing as he returned to the shoulder, realized as the sound of their engines faded that there was no longer any music emerging from the Mustang.

"You wanna keep your dukes off my car? It's a classic, 'case you didn't notice."

It was the punk-haired driver, her voice animated but muffled behind the windshield. Gabriel halted directly in front of the car, squinted through the glass as she flashed an ironic smile, then lifted her chin to gaze down the long hood at where he'd bumped into it.

"You can tell I keep this baby in mint condition."

Gabriel was grateful for the humor, walked around the front end to admire the pock-marked sheet metal, nodded approvingly at the gray primer that had been sprayed over the sky blue metallic paint where some previous body work had been done. He surveyed the rest of the car, taking conspicuous notice of several areas on the roof and right rear fender where dents had been filled in with mastic, more of the flat gray paint sprayed across it.

"Yeah, I can see that..." Still nodding, he leaned down to look through the passenger-side window. "My apologies for any fingerprints I might've gotten on that mirror finish."

A door slammed. Gabriel looked up to see the father settling into the cab of the neighboring pickup, the two boys still wrapped around his neck, his wife leaning across the seat to fix a passionate kiss as if they weren't even there. It went on long enough to make the children wrinkle their noses and push her away. The lovebirds straightened in their seats, laughed.

"Touching scene, isn't it?"

Gabriel leaned back down to peer into the Mustang.

"Scuse me—?"

"The happy family..." The woman was staring forward again, with a look both wistful and dubious. "Almost married Richard a few years ago. Good thing I said no, the way things turned out."

Gabriel wasn't sure he belonged in this conversation, but there were no more cars coming out for the time being.

"You mean that guy in the make-out session proposed to you?"

"Gold ring, bended knee... whole nine yards. Couldn't wait to start a family. Now he's got one ready-made."

The Chevy's engine turned over, revved, clunked into gear. It occurred to Gabriel he might still have time to run over and ask the happy family for a ride; maybe he could climb into the cargo bed without having to squeeze inside with them. But instead of raking the wheels for a U-turn back toward Chiloquin, the wife simply drove the pickup straight forward, cut diagonally across the top of the entrance drive and up onto the highway, heading due east.

He winced, looked back at the parking lot. People were still coming through the double doors, but once again no cars were moving. Gabriel shrugged, leaned casually into the open window of the Mustang. As long as she was opening herself up like this, the least he could do was act interested.

"So maybe you just weren't ready yet. Or maybe you're not the marrying type. Some people are better off single, you know." He should have stopped himself, but didn't. "And anyway, I'd say the guy was much too young for you."

The woman turned, fixed a glare right between his eyes.

"Nice. And just how much older *do* I look?"

Place foot firmly in mouth. Bite down.

"I didn't mean—" Gabriel pushed off the door, started to raise his hands in apology. His duffle bag slipped from his shoulder, thumped onto the gravel. "I mean I wasn't implying—"

She suddenly squinted, cut him off. "I don't recognize you, do I? You're not from around here."

Gabriel frowned, paused, reached down for the bag. "Nope. Just passin' through, as the saying goes. I had a little..." He hesitated again, mulled how best to gloss over the gory details. "...an unfortunate encounter with a couple' deer back on Ninety-Seven. Looks like I gotta stay around for a while, take care of a few things before

I can move on."

"So what are you doing out here? Not looking for a job, I take it."

It was the second such comment in as many hours. He considered asking her about it, decided whatever economic woes there were didn't concern him. And besides, he could hear engines starting up in the lot.

"Uh, no, I was just looking for—"

"So you're without any wheels for the time being." She cut him off again, pressing on with her line of thought. "And you prob'ly need a place to stay. Am I right?"

"Well, yeah, as a matter of fact."

Another pickup approached the gate, followed by a soft-top Jeep and a small import.

"You got any money?"

He turned back distractedly. "Money?—yeah, plenty. In my Bible."

The woman sent a scowl out the passenger-side window, mouthed the word *Bible* to herself, though Gabriel was once again staring toward the gate.

"Well then—get in."

Gabriel had already taken a step toward the oncoming pickup before her words sunk in. He did a quick double-take, bent down with his own questioning look.

"Get *in*," she repeated. "You can stay with me."

He still wasn't sure he'd heard her correctly. "Aren't you, uh, waiting for somebody?"

"Not if you're going to get in." She enunciated each word as if talking to a four-year-old, waited a few more seconds. "Look, either you get in, or you step across the road there so my friends won't think I've already got company."

Gabriel frowned, more confused than ever, glanced across the drive where the other car was parked. The bottle-blonde was now stroking her long hair for the trio of vehicles currently winding through the concrete.

Suddenly Gabriel's shoulders went slack, eyes blinking in realization. The woman in the Mustang must've read his mind.

"And if you think for one second what I *think* you're thinking...?"

Her voice rose with indignation. "You can just walk over to that Corolla right now and take your chances with Pamela."

The pickup and Jeep turned onto the highway – one right, one left – without stopping. The smaller car halted, backed up, pulled onto the shoulder alongside the Toycta. Even if he'd *wanted* to take his chances with Pamela, it no longer mattered. Gabriel concealed a grin, turned back to the Mustang, expecting its occupant to see the irony as he exercised his only remaining option. But when he started to open the door, she simply slung her legs over the floor-mounted gearshift and said, "Uh, uh—*you're* driving."

Gabriel froze, not certain whether to stare at the taut thighs that revealed themselves as she lifted herself into the passenger seat, or at the eyes that caught his for an instant just before she settled back down. It wasn't so much the crystaline green he could see now; it was the whites. Despite the slight puffiness encircling them – like she might've been crying earlier – the whites of her eyes were flawless. Almost luminous.

He forced himself not to stare – although she didn't appear to mind it – pushed the passenger door shut again, then obediently stepped around to the other side. Tossing his bag onto the hump between the seats, he got behind the wheel, took a deep breath and... suddenly remembered he had no driver's license. A current one, anyway.

Not that it had stopped him before. But getting caught this time would be all Fiske needed to throw him back in the Chiloquin clink.

His punk-cut benefactress broke in before he could make any excuses.

"I'm Laney," she said pertly. "Keys are in the ignition."

Her ranch was just north of the river, about eight miles up the highway. They would come to a bridge, she explained. Then, a quarter mile farther on the left, he'd see a bare dirt driveway with a mailbox painted to look like a spotted pony.

He hadn't driven a car since the trip back from Morro Bay with Natalie. The new F-150 with the Grant Homes logo had some pep, too, but not like this. The old Mustang was as responsive as it was powerful, despite its work-in-progress appearance. In fact, without even trying, he'd spun the tires as they pulled away, the two of them pressed back into their buckets when the rubber grabbed the pavement. Gabriel found himself looking nervously into the rear-view mirror as much as the road ahead, relaxing only when the ammo plant disappeared behind them and there was still no patrol car in sight.

"Nice acceleration," he said at last, glancing at the car's owner, secretly amused to find her gripping the edges of her seat.

"Yeah, and at this rate we'll be home in about thirty more seconds." She flashed a chastising look before turning to stare out the side window. "Might wanna slow down and enjoy the scenery, you know? Beautiful out here in the late afternoon, sun on the buttes an' all."

"Sorry."

Gabriel let up on the pedal, stole another glance. He hadn't meant to frighten her – or offend her with his earlier comment about her ex-boyfriend. But he could tell, sitting next to her now, that she *was* quite a few years older than her erstwhile suitor – late thirties if he wasn't mistaken – a few character lines etched at the corners of her eyes and mouth, a little more padding beneath her jawline despite a strong chin. Not to mention the puffiness around her eyes.

"And I'm sorry, what I said before—"

"You mean about Richard looking half my age?"

He blew air between his lips. "More like, I don't know—two, three years younger. If that."

She knew he was giving her the benefit of the doubt, turned partway with an appreciative, even if dubious, look.

"That's sweet... um... uh..."

"Gabriel. Gabriel Woods."

"Gabriel..." She nodded thoughtfully. "Old Testament. Mine's from the New."

He raised an eyebrow. "Laney's a biblical name?"

"In a roundabout way. Short for Magdalene, or Magda*lane*... you know, the other Mary?" She cast an ironic smile. "My parents gave me the name for the sole reason they wanted to call me Maggie.

Just *loved* the name Maggie... which I absolutely hated, even as a kid. Old ladies are called Maggie, not sweet little girls." She paused to correct herself. "*Little* girls, anyway. So on my first day of kindergarten I told the teacher my name was Lane D'Arcy, not whatever they must've printed in her roll book by mistake. My friends've called me Laney ever since."

She turned back toward him, modestly lowering her eyes as if to say he could be her friend, too. He thought it almost quaint, nodded back; and it was then she told him to watch for the bridge and the spotted-pony mailbox, and turned once more to stare out the window.

He followed her gaze to the line of lava buttes on the horizon, deep red rising from deep green. In less than a minute two bands of lighter green and gold appeared among the darker lodgepole pines, coming up fast, aspen and birch on either side of a gently-sloping riverbed. Gabriel shifted his eyes from the river to the bridge ahead, from the bridge to Lane, watching her as the car started across the span, tires thumping on the expansion joints, springs rocking gently in the shallow depressions between them.

Suddenly she jerked as if waking from a daydream, turned in her seat to look back at the river, then forward again.

"That was the Sprague. Now look for my pony—*there...* up there on the left." She spoke almost breathlessly, pointed, then lowered her hand to the dashboard as if bracing herself for the turn. "I'd like to stop and get my mail before we go on to the house, if that's okay."

"Your wish, my command.""

"Really. Well in that case, plan on doing the dishes tonight before you take out the..."

Her voice trailed off as the Mustang stumbled over the broken pavement where the road met her dirt driveway, tires immediately losing traction in the inch-thick dust covering its washboard surface. The car skidded diagonally as it came to a halt, the black-and-tan mailbox not three feet from the front bumper, a dense cloud of silt billowing around it.

"Whoa," Gabriel said with relief, "you might'a warned me about this powder." He exhaled, nodded toward the cylindrical mailbox affixed with a horse head and three wooden legs. "We almost took off one of Trigger's *front* legs, too."

"You mess with any a'my horses and you won't be invited back." She pulled up on the door handle, coughed from the dust still swirling around the car, but stepped out anyway. "Jeez, Gabe, I can't begin to see through all this. Can you make it out from where you're sitting?"

He smiled, played along. Besides, no one had called him Gabe in years.

"One step past the front end, and two to the right. At least I *think* that's where it is."

She too played along, closing the car door and marching out past the right fender, then taking two steps sideways like a wooden marionette before stopping directly in front of the mailbox. Gabriel had to chuckle when she reached out to either side, pretending she still couldn't see through all the dust, her hands eventually finding it only inches from the waistline of her dress. Then she yanked the straw-maned horse head to draw back the cover, removed a few envelopes along with the usual fistful of junk mail.

"I don't understand why they keep sending me this stuff," Gabriel could hear her say, more to herself than him, "when they know I won't read it."

Starting back for the car, she began sorting the pieces, letters on top, catalogs on the bottom. Maybe it was because she wasn't watching where she was going, Gabriel thought; but an instant later she slammed an upper thigh into the fender.

Hard.

So much so that one of the letters jumped from her hands, sailing in a lazy spiral before it plopped onto the silt-covered hood just in front of the windshield, in a straight line between them. Lane seemed to stiffen, glanced up briefly to where Gabriel waited behind the wheel, then looked down at the offending envelope.

Except that she *wasn't* looking at it. Not directly.

Her gaze, Gabriel now realized with fearful certainty, was a good four inches off the mark. And when she swept her right hand across the hood to pick it up, her fingers caught only a corner, spinning the letter into the windshield wiper so that she had to fumble for several more seconds before locating it again.

She finally pried it loose, straightened, tucked it back into the clutch of papers in her left hand as though nothing unusual had happened, stepped back to the car door. Gabriel said nothing, watching for further confirmation – as if he needed any – noting how she trailed her right forefinger lightly across the top of the door before grabbing the handle, how she lowered herself a bit too carefully into her bucket seat and turned briefly with a glance that didn't even try to meet his eyes, how she seemed to gaze blankly through the windshield without focusing on anything in particular.

As she was doing now.

"About forty yards up you'll follow the curve around to the left, through those trees," she said, gesturing ahead. "Then there's a meadow and the farmhouse on the right."

Gabriel let the engine idle for a few more seconds, was glad for his duffle bag on the hump between them, kept a wary eye on her hands nevertheless. Only when she was completely settled did he reach over to slip the T-bar back into drive.

"So... when, exactly, were you going to tell me?"

*S**he didn't reply, wouldn't speak*** another word until Gabriel pulled the car onto the parking strip alongside her porch.

While the rough-textured concrete appeared to be a recent addition – no oil stains or noticeable cracks – the clapboard house appeared less pristine, probably built in the twenties or thirties as part of a working ranch, judging by the barn and two neighboring corrals. A few posts in the porch railing were split or broken, the screen door torn just above the kick plate. An upstairs window was cracked from top to bottom, the metal flashing above it virtually stripped of the ivory paint once coating it. Paint was also peeling from the tongue-and-groove siding in several places, mostly near ground level where decades of winter snow had no doubt piled up against the house and melted the following spring.

It was all mostly cosmetic at this point, and nothing a handyman couldn't fix in a few weekends. But if you couldn't see the defects to begin with, what was the hurry?

Once again Lane seemed to read his mind.

"I know it won't win any House Beautiful awards, but I try to keep it from falling down around me... with a little help from my friends."

Gabriel turned off the ignition, leaned back against the door panel. As much as she might've wanted to ignore his earlier question, he was still waiting for an answer. She knew it, tossed a rueful glance his way, released an unexpectedly nervous sigh.

"Okay—you're right. It wasn't exactly fair. False advertising, if nothing else." She forced a laugh, played with the shaggy, strawberry-blonde tresses behind one ear before turning away again. "But it's like, I haven't tried to fool anybody in a long time and you're the first man in six months who didn't know about my... who wasn't aware I can't see. And I just, I wanted to remember what it felt like to be treated like a normal person. Even for a little while."

Gabriel nodded to himself. He, of all people, could sympathize with her desire to feel normal. For the few weeks he was foolish enough not to conceal his new ability, nary a soul treated him as they had before the wreck. Even Gabriel's best friend began to act increasingly uncomfortable in his presence, eventually shunning him entirely. And complete strangers – people who'd heard the rumors and drove from nearby towns to meet the young miracle man – were soon convinced he was either a child saint or the future Antichrist. Neither faction would leave him alone.

Lane turned back, now waiting for him to answer, raising her eyes not quite in line with his. Gabriel found that if he moved his head just slightly, he could connect with her gaze and pretend she was actually seeing him. He still found it hard to believe she couldn't.

"Why would I treat you differently just because you're blind?"

"Blind..." She seemed to mull over the word as if considering each of its politically-correct alternatives. "Oh, I don't know. Why are you sitting all scrunched up against the car door there, like you're afraid you might catch something?"

It was the usual reaction to *his* reaction whenever he felt cornered. But unlike other people who could see him, who could actually watch him draw back in fear, Lane had somehow *sensed* his distress.

Without realizing it, Gabriel had gone so far as to wrap his left hand around the Mustang's door handle, preparing for a hasty exit should it become necessary. He slowly loosened his grip, hoped she couldn't hear his clammy fingers unfurling from the chrome. He knew the cliché about blind people compensating with a heightened sense of hearing. Maybe it was true.

"I've never been real comfortable around women, that's all," he said at last, lying only by not including the male gender. Then, in the next instant, both the predicament he now faced, and a possible solution to it, suddenly came to mind: *How could he possibly stay in the same house with a blind woman for the next three days, and not blow his cover?*

"Tell you the truth," he went on, "I have this, uh... problem with being touched. It all started when I was sixteen, seventeen. Or I don't know—" He was winging it now, the solution revealing itself only as the words left his lips. "—maybe it goes back even earlier, to my childhood. Some incident I've forgotten, maybe, or repressed. And now it's like a—what do they call it?—a phobia or something."

"That so?"

Lane seemed to be staring through him now. He leaned forward a bit, moved out of her line of sight.

"Or maybe the girls have been chasing you ever since you were a cute little kid, and you never learned to enjoy all that pawing and grabbing—am I right?"

She gave an impish grin, casually threw a palm out as if inviting his response. Gabriel saw only the blur of her hand, immediately flinched, the back of his head knocking into the window glass. Lane raised her eyebrows, shifted her body in the bucket seat to face him squarely.

"Jesus, Gabe. You really *do* have a problem, don't you?" Then, in the space of a few wide-eyed blinks, her amazement morphed into amusement. "Well now, maybe that's something we'll just hafta work on while you're here."

Gabriel tensed, tightened his grip around the door handle all the more until she finally reached for her own.

"Come on, I'll show you around," she said as the door popped open. "You want the ten-dollar tour, or just a sneak peek?"

It would turn out to be the sneak peek. No sooner had the screen door thumped behind them than Lane announced dinner would be ready in thirty minutes. Earlier, she explained, before a friend had driven both her and the Mustang to the ammo plant, she'd cut up some chicken, thrown in some wild rice saved from last night's meal and left it all simmering on the stove. The aroma wafting from the kitchen told her the stew was almost ready – *and* reminded her she hadn't eaten since her usual breakfast of yogurt and toast.

"You gonna be hungry by then?" she asked, stopping in the center of a living room that seemed glaringly old-fashioned for her tastes, despite the little he knew of her.

"Oh, yeah—I could definitely eat..." It was just over four hours since Gabriel had polished off his cell-block serving of Dinty Moore, but the one meal barely made up for the two he'd missed. "Can I help you with anything?"

"Nope. I picked some fresh veggies before we left. Just take a moment to slice-n'-dice and throw 'em in with the chicken."

With that she turned, confidently crossed the room toward an adjoining hallway where a post-and-rail staircase rose to the second floor. Gabriel looked past her, noted the dozen or so photographs on the wall opposite the stairs. Beyond them was another doorway to a kitchen radiant with late afternoon sun. He watched as Lane slowed only slightly to brush her fingers against the stairway's anchor post, then, centering herself, began whistling her way down the hall like a dolphin on sonar.

When I'm Sixty-Four...

Gabriel nodded with admiration, could tell she must've had plenty of time to accustom herself to her handicap, figured she'd probably fixed more meals sightless than he'd prepared with two perfectly good eyes. He decided against following her, took a moment to glance around the living room instead.

It was more like the parlors of an earlier century: Flocked wallpaper adorned with stripes and intertwining grape leaves, a spinet piano with a small bust of Mozart on top, a bay window swathed in satin and gauze. In front of the window was a floral brocade sofa supported by ball-and-claw legs, complete with matching coffee table and an end-table featuring a Tiffany lamp that may have been the genuine article.

In a niche to the left of the tile entry where Gabriel stood was an ornate oval mirror, centered above an equally ornate credenza. Atop it were a pewter vase with an arrangement of dried wildflowers, a marble statuette of a scantily-dressed angel that would've made most Bible scholars blush, and an Indian basket not unlike the ones he'd seen at the Chiloquin police station. With the exception of the basket – which seemed suspiciously out of place among the art deco fixtures – it might have been the living room of half the boarding houses he'd stayed in over the past ten years. He felt right at home, inasmuch as he ever could.

"Just put your stuff down anywhere. We'll figure out sleeping arrangements later..."

Her voice echoed down the hallway, catching Gabriel the instant he'd started to slip off the shoulder strap of his duffle bag. *As if one "intuitive" wasn't enough for one day,* he thought. It was almost scary.

"...And the bathroom's down the hall on the left, in case you were wondering."

For once she was wrong. But he was curious about the Indian basket. Taking a step closer to it, he could make out a ten-dollar bill inside, folded loosely in half, along with a few other crumpled greenbacks.

"And the woven basket over there by the mirror?... you see it?"

She'd done it again. He shook his head, then, dropping his duffle bag beside the credenza, peered inside the basket, quickly counted twenty-six dollars, perhaps thirty if one of the wadded up bills was a five.

"Yeah, I see it."

Turning, he crossed the living room, began padding slowly down the hall toward the kitchen as Lane continued.

"I'm only gonna say this once, since this is your first visit. And then we won't mention it again—ever. One'a my house rules."

Gabriel absently pushed both hands into his pockets, winced

as the fingers of his right hand slid past the four one-dollar bills comprising the sum total of his bankroll. He might not be able to read anyone's mind, but he could guess where Lane was going.

"Thing is," she went on, "it's not exactly a bed-and-breakfast I'm running here. Not that formal. And even if it was, I wouldn't expect the kind of money they ask for over in Grants Pass or Medford, or 'specially Ashland."

About halfway down the hall Gabriel could see Lane come into view, her back turned, standing over a cutting board she'd placed next to the sink. She was chopping celery like a master chef, eight-inch blade gliding past her fingernails as she held down three stalks side-by-side, taking off perfect quarter-inch crescents in rapid succession.

On the far wall was a porcelain-and-cast-iron stove, a large pot steaming over one of its gas burners. Evidently she'd already sliced up some carrots and swept the pieces from cutting board to pot, a few of them missing their target. Several of the small orange circles littered the stovetop, though he could see none on the faded yellow linoleum.

"It's criminal, what they get for an eight-by-ten bedroom in one of those remodeled Victorians up past Lithia Park..." Her voice was raised, as if Gabriel was still in the living room. "...'cause a'the Shakespeare festival they have every summer—you know the one? People down from Portland and Seattle with money to burn. I swear to God I could make
a fortune with a farmhouse like this if it was on the other side of the Cascades... fixed up a little, maybe."

She finished slicing the celery, brushed the pieces into a small mound on her cutting board, promptly scooped them between cupped palms and carried them to the stove. Two pieces escaped, skittered under the butcher-block dinette in the middle of the room.

"Anyhow, I've still got bills to pay and food to buy, even if I do have my garden. My friends know I run a little short toward the end of the month, so if you'd like to make a contribution toward my household expenses and the cook's retirement account, well, that's what the basket's for."

She stirred the pot with a wooden spoon, set it down, stepped back to her cutting board to retrieve the knife. Gabriel was now in the kitchen doorway, arms folded, leaning against the doorjamb. Perhaps it was the soft sigh of regret that issued from his lips, or the rustle of cotton as his work shirt scraped against the chipped molding. Either way, she hadn't known he was so close, admitted her inattention with a quick gasp and jerk of her head.

Gabriel unfolded his arms, straightened.

"Sorry. I didn't mean to sneak up on you. I hate it when people do that to me. *Hate* it."

She breathed out, turned back to the lone bell pepper that remained.

"A symptom of your so-called problem with being touched?"

"Yeah... " He didn't appreciate her less-than-subtle jibe. "...and I'd rather not talk about it, if it's all the same to you."

Her knife halted its downward trajectory. She raised her head, equally surprised by his response, but said nothing.

To Gabriel, it appeared almost as though she'd paused to stare out the kitchen window, over the sink to her right. Through the dust-streaked panes he could see part of the barn and, off to the left, a stand of lodgepole pines. The setting sun had gilded the treetops with a metallic, weathered-copper green, their shadows stretching across the neighboring meadow only to rise again on the barn's faded red siding.

He couldn't put it off any longer.

"Lane... about your basket out there—"

"*No!*" She swirled, waved the knife. "I explained once, and that's the end of it. You decide the amount. I say any more, I'm no different than Pamela."

She turned her back again, resumed work on the bell pepper, chopping it cleanly in half, stripping the seeds with sudden determination.

"Speaking of which, I'm *not* Pamela, so don't just go off and assume my letting you stay here overnight means anything special—"

"I wasn't expecting—"

"—and if I've been known to allow a few of houseguests in my bed on occasion, well, chances are I was already sleeping with them even *before* the accident. Except when I—"

"Remember? I have this problem—"

"—was with Richard. Any money they leave in the basket is only because they understand how hard things've been—"

"—with being touched...?"

"—for me, and they're... only..."

Her words trailed off, Gabriel's gentle persistence finally breaking through her rant. She let her shoulders sag, dropped her head as if looking down at the bell pepper, now sliced into thin, perfect strips.

"Now ain't that a hoot. And *I* was the one who just brought it up again. Talk about dumb."

"It's not dumb, Lane. Look, to tell you the truth—"

"Stop right there."

She spun around once more, knife blade catching the sunlight, her eyes peering through him just as they had earlier. Gabriel took a breath, prepared for the rant to resume.

"That's the second time you said it."

"Said what?"

"To tell you the truth. You said it in the car, and again just now."

Gabriel frowned, couldn't see her point. "Yeah... so?"

"So, don't *ever* start off a sentence like that. Dead giveaway the next line's a big fat lie." She turned back, picked up the cutting board and marched to the stove. "I can't tell you how many times I've listened to some doctor or claims adjuster or company mucky-muck roll out those same words, and not a thing any one of 'em said turned out to be true. So please—" She cleared the cutting board in a single stroke, glanced back over her shoulder. "—don't say you're gonna tell me the truth. Just *tell* me the goddam truth, okay?"

He still couldn't figure out the connection. But he was absolutely certain that, behind her latest tirade, there was another story having nothing to do with the basket, at least not directly, and he wasn't about to get into it over a boiling cauldron of chicken soup, presided over by a knife-wielding woman who hadn't eaten since dawn.

He also knew that right now was probably not the best time to confess his poverty, even if he could convince Lane the condition was only temporary. Best to wait until after they'd eaten. And if she decided to kick him out at that point, at least the four bucks in his pocket would help pay for his supper.

"So, you ready for that quick look around?" she said, perky as before. "Gotta let this simmer for another fifteen, twenty minutes."

And that was another thing he couldn't fathom. Lane seemed to go from cold to hot – and back again – in the time it took to stir the pot, put the cast-iron cover back on and flash those iridescent whites.

He watched as she circled the butcher-block table and started for the back corner of the kitchen. Then, puzzled, he took two steps into the room, noticed for the first time a screened-in porch that had been blocked from view by an oak Hoosier next to the door-jamb. She opened the half-glass door to the porch, paused expectantly.

"You coming?"

"Uh, sure. Just let me pick up a couple' pieces of celery here."

He pulled back a chair, bent to reach under the table.

"Oh, those..." Lane said evenly. "You'll find two more over by the stove, next to the cabinet where I keep my pots and pans. Guess you didn't notice when you were sneaking up on me."

The air had grown surprisingly chilly, despite another hour of daylight, and despite the fact that autumn had officially begun only a week ago. He remembered Vincent's comment about Chiloquin being colder and damper than most other towns along 97. If Gabriel ended up finding work nearby – or anywhere in Oregon, for that matter – he'd need a new jacket soon.

His last warm coat had been donated to the Body of Christ Clothes Closet back in Lamont – when was it? – sometime in February or March. Over the years he'd learned to travel light, and the fleeced-lined jacket from the L.L. Bean factory outlet was too bulky to fit in his duffle bag along with his other clothing. He used the same excuse, in fact, to justify buying a whole new wardrobe every year whether he needed it or not – one of the few self-indulgent expenditures he allowed himself. As a result he would give his previous wardrobe away. Even the smallest towns where he took up residence had their homeless shelters. And there were plenty of less fortunate people – maybe others who moved from place to place as he did – who could use his cast-offs.

By the time Gabriel stepped off the back porch and out of his reverie, Lane was standing beside the barn doors, arms akimbo. He hadn't actually seen her cross the open ground between the house and the barn – she'd gone out the back door while he was still picking celery off the linoleum. But she couldn't have reached the barn that fast if she'd been walking the least bit tentatively. More like racing. She clearly knew every inch of her ranch's geography, inside *and* out.

"Speed it up, would'ja? I wanna show you my pride and joy while it's still light."

She waved for him to catch up, reached for the edge of the wood plank door, then disappeared into the quiet darkness of the barn. He hurried across the packed dirt after her, came to an immediate halt just inside the doorway.

Even with a dust-speckled sunbeam streaking in through a window over the loft, even with the rectangle of light outlining a second set of doors at the opposite end of the barn, Gabriel could barely see. He waited for his eyes to adjust, at the same time marveling how Lane could move through her permanent darkness with such ease, finally heard the rustle of animal hooves to his left. He squinted, could just make out Lane's cotton-print dress as she bent down beside one of several stalls running the length of the barn. She was stroking the muzzle of a young colt, its head straining between the pine rails. She looked up as Gabriel finally approached, grinned like a proud mother.

"Two weeks old today and healthy as a—" Lane chuckled at her own incipient pun. "—well, as a *horse*. Named him Fabian, after the Fifties singer. Isn't he beautiful?"

He came to within a few feet, halted once more.

"Oh, come on." She waved again, straightened. "I need to fill their troughs. Go ahead—he loves attention."

Gabriel looked after her as she stepped away, spotted the glint of water in a bucket near the doors at the other end. Above it, a spigot gleamed in a sliver of light, a coil of hose draped over the spike on a nearby post. With Lane thus occupied, he walked over to the stall, smiled to see the colt raising its nose toward him. He responded by holding out his hand in the manner he'd learned years ago when his best friend showed him – palm open, fingers out flat and squeezed together so they wouldn't be mistaken for carrot sticks or lumps of maple sugar – or, more likely at this tender age, mother's nipple.

The colt pressed his velveteen muzzle into Gabriel's hand, nudging it as if to keep it moving, whinnying his excitement. Gabriel obliged, running his hand up and down his nape, past his withers and across the vale of his back to his hindquarters. Despite the meager light he could see faint splotches, some lighter, some darker than the caramel-colored background.

"Can you tell what breed he is?"

The query wafted past the pine railings right on cue. Gabriel turned to see Lane lifting the hose off its hanger two or three loops at a time, dust clouds rising as the rubber thumped onto the bare dirt floor.

"Appaloosa, looks like. You need any help with that?"

"No, thanks." She was practically beaming. "So, you know horses, do you?"

"I know a spotted rump when I see one. I know Appaloosas came from Oregon, originally. Bred by Indians somewhere up north, weren't they?"

"How d'ya like that?—and a history buff to boot." She turned the spigot, picked up the nozzle. "Nez Percé. Before they were forced off their tribal lands."

She started dragging the hose back toward him, water spurting from the nozzle in fits and starts, finally emerging in a steady stream by the time she reached the neighboring stall. It was then Gabriel stepped aside to make room for her – and a moment later when he caught sight of a much larger shape moving in the shadows to his right.

He reacted with a sudden backward step, his surprise startling the colt, which in turn brought another flurry of movement from the shadows.

"Whoa, Tina," Lane said calmly. "Whoa, girl." She stopped at the rail, made a series of sloughing noises with the inside of her cheek that seemed to reassure the animal, then lowered the hose to a metal trough just inside the stall. "Your baby's just fine."

Of course. Gabriel hadn't even thought to ask where the colt's mother was. And with his eyes only now accustomed to the darkened interior, he hadn't seen the mare standing at the back of the adjacent stall. He took a few steps closer, peered over the railing. He could tell the mare was favoring her left foreleg, resting uneasily on the other three, leaning against the back of the stall as if she needed the barn's heavy wooden beams to help support her.

"Is she... okay?"

Lane's reply was so long in coming that Gabriel had to turn his head. Dim as it was, he could see the pain twisting her face.

"She went lame, thanks to me... only last week." Another pause. "Took her until then to get her strength back after she gave birth. And then she was so... full of energy."

The metal trough began to overflow, water trickling onto the hay around it like rain from a rooftop. Even Gabriel could hear the pattering. Oddly, it took a few seconds for Lane to react. At last she lifted the hose, moved it to the smaller galvanized tub in the colt's stall.

"I hadn't taken her out of the corrals since we confirmed she was pregnant. She was trying to tell me the whole time not to go that way, but I rode her straight through a colony of Belding ground squirrels at full gallop."

"You mean—" He had the sense not to go on. Lane was obviously suffering enough, hardly needed anyone else to lay on the guilt. If anything, Gabriel had to admire that she'd climbed into the saddle to begin with, sightless as she was.

"The Maqlaq whose stallion was the sire?—he came by to check on Fabian, found me and Tina out in the meadow. I don't know how he managed to get her back to the barn. He felt each one of her legs, said the right front was broken in three places. Then he put on a splint even though he was sure it would never mend. He told me the most humane thing to do would be..." Lane's cheeks were glistening now. "But I couldn't. I can't put her down. Not yet. Fabian needs his mother's—"

Again she broke off. Gabriel wished he could reach out, wished his touch were no different than anyone else's: Just the simple caress of a human hand, just when it was needed. That could be a miracle all by itself. Just that.

But maybe he could comfort her some other way.

"I see you keep them in separate stalls," he said, stoic as he could manage, trying to change the subject without being too obvious. "How do you actually... how does Fabian get fed?"

She seemed to appreciate his attempt, wiped her eyes.

"I try to take him into her stall two, three times a day. Any more and Tina gets completely worn out. Practically has to fight him off sometimes, he wants to play so bad." Lane nodded affectionately toward the colt, tried to smile. "I started giving him goat's milk in a bottle, to supplement Tina's. And Buddy makes up this mush of oatmeal and apples—"

"Buddy—? You mean Buddy from the police station?"

He wanted to suck the words back in the moment they'd escaped. Lane sent an odd look, tilted her head.

"He's the one who has the stud service. How do you know Buddy?"

Gabriel shrugged, trying to pull an answer from the proverbial hat, suddenly noticed the colt's tub was nearly full.

"Wait a minute. I'd better go shut off the water before you soak the place again."

He quickly stepped around her, headed for the spigot, hoping to concoct a likely story by the time he reached it. On the other hand, if Buddy was a friend of Lane's, there wasn't much use in lying.

"I don't exactly *know* him. He, uh, got involved after my little mishap on the highway this morning."

"When you hit the deer?"

The handle squeaked beneath Gabriel's hand. Lane waited until the water stopped flowing, then started back with the hose.

"Well—" He bit his tongue before the phrase *To tell you the truth* emerged, figured she probably heard it coming anyway. "—it wasn't Buddy who first arrived on the scene. I only met him after his boss gave me a lift back into town. A Lieutenant—"

"*Fiske*—?" Lane followed the name with a deprecating hiss. "Now *there's* a real piece a'work."

She halted beside the last stall, felt for the gate latch, took two steps perpendicular to the rail and reached out for the railroad spike driven into the post directly to her left. As Gabriel gave her room, she began to wind the hose over the spike in neat loops, like a journeyman electrician coiling his cord at the end of the day.

"Locals think of him as our police chief, but he actually draws his salary from the B.I.A., 'you believe that—? Only thing he really likes about Native Americans is their beadwork and their baskets, and they put him in charge of the regional Bureau of Indian Affairs."

She hung the last loop, turned with a scowl, anger replacing her earlier regret. That was *some* consolation, at least. Gabriel had dried Lane's tears after all, even if not in the way he'd intended.

"Anyway, stew's gotta be done by now," she said, starting back for the barn doors. "Mind if we finish up our tour in the morning?"

"*He went home with who?*"

Fiske could hardly believe his ears.

"Lane D'Arcy," Halvorsen repeated. The plant manager paused to look up at the illuminated display board showing which lines were currently active, quickly switched the phone from one ear to the other. "You remember—she's the woman who lost—"

"Don't mock me, Jack," Fiske broke in. "I know who the hell she is. I just can't understand *why*."

"What's the mystery? He needs a place to stay, and she needs the money."

"That's just it," Fiske said. "He *has* no money to give her. I patted him down myself before I..." He stopped, pursed his lips as though recalling a detail of this morning's incident he'd ignored at the time, vowing to analyze it later. "Huh. I had the weirdest feeling below my ribs, thought maybe I'd inhaled some dried blood, or something off his jeans..."

He trailed off again, could sense Halvorsen's impatience. "Anyhow, no money clip. Nothing in his belt. Wasn't even carrying a wallet—found that in his bag without a plug nickel inside. Not even a credit card."

"Then maybe he's telling the truth."

"Truth—? This guy's more evasive than the bookkeeper at the Kla-Mo-Yah casino." Fiske turned as Deputy Chino rose from her desk and started for the front doors, watched the fabric across her buttocks shift in alternating diagonal folds as she walked – right, left, right, left. "And even if he's right about Vincent driving off with all his cash, he's still hiding something. You ask me, he didn't end up here by accident."

And admittedly, that was the thought most unsettling to Halvorsen.

"Maybe it's no accident he went home with Laney, then."

"How so?"

"Just thinkin' out loud here, but wasn't it Lane D'Arcy who first raised the flag about the plant reverting to civilian use?"

A pause, then: "And you think Woods is connected somehow...?"

"Well, we know the Maqlaqs have been getting advice from union activists—on the sly. They know it's illegal to organize in any formal way, much less go out on strike. My hunch is, they're more interested in working conditions than Lane's latest scheme to change the world."

Halvorsen glanced up at the display board again, noticed the annealing bay go off line six minutes early, swore under his breath before going on. "She's never gotten far with the tribal council, what my sources tell me. But the town meeting tomorrow is for rank and file, and word on the street is, she'll be there."

"And she *does* have an axe to grind," Fiske added. It was obvious the wheels were turning full-tilt now. 'You think she'd bring in somebody to help make her case?"

"If she did," Halvorsen replied, "she sure as hell wouldn't be so obvious about it."

"Or maybe that's the ploy."

"Say again—?"

"Make a big entrance. Attract a lot of attention with something totally unrelated to what you're really there for. Then, once you're cleared, nobody pays attention anymore."

Halvorsen huffed into the handset. "I don' know... getting picked up on the highway with blood all over you is a pretty extreme way to make an entrance."

"Yeah, but the fact is, now he's settled in at the D'Arcy ranch, and meanwhile you're thinking he's here only because he's waiting for some truck driver, the same weekend it just so happens there's a town meeting to discuss labor issues at a government facility. Coincidence...?"

It was a stretch, admittedly. And Fiske could pretty much be counted on to see a conspiracy even when there wasn't any. Halvorsen knew the Bureau chief had a tendency to frame events in the most cynical, if not paranoid, terms – more so than could be explained by the compound effects of daily dealings with drunks, petty thieves and malingerers.

He, on the other hand, was a military man. As such, it was his job to consider every possible tactic a foe might use – whether home-grown terrorist or union activist. Creating a diversion was a tried and true method. Halvorsen couldn't discount it completely.

Neither could he let all the hard work he'd accomplished over the past decade be threatened. If Fiske often lost sight of the welfare of his charges, *he* hadn't. The ammunition plant had been a boon to the local economy, if not its salvation.

Chiloquin's lumber industry had long since vanished, after all, losing out to better-positioned mills in Klamath Falls, Bend and the Willamette Valley. Local agriculture and cattle-ranching weren't making anybody rich either, whether white farmer or Maqlaq rancher. And if the twenty-year-old Indian casino might provide a few dozen minimum-wage jobs, it was even more likely to line the pockets of tribal big-wigs and the Eastern corporations who'd rushed in with the start-up funds.

The munitions factory, in contrast, meant steady paychecks for hundreds of otherwise poverty-stricken families, even if the work schedule waxed and waned with America's changing defense posture. Fortunately, thanks to the ongoing War on Terrorism and the more recent campaigns against ISIS, things looked rosy for years to come.

In fact, with the exception of the mid-90s slowdown, things had been rosy right from the start. Following the first invasion of Iraq, during which Halvorsen had been a decorated logistics officer, it became evident to the government that the U.S. Army needed to diversify its suppliers of ordnance. Since World War Two, the military had relied primarily on only one provider of gravity munitions – the plant in McAlester, Oklahoma. True, there were numerous suppliers of the various components to make them. Vincent's pick-up and delivery route included two such factories in California alone: Masotech's plant near Los Angeles, and the U.S. Army's on-again-off-again Riverbank plant an hour south of Sacramento.

But having only one "packing plant" where those components were finally assembled and temporarily stored made the munitions supply chain vulnerable – especially in a world where a single devastating terrorist strike was always a threat. The powers-that-be decided it would be advisable to build several smaller assembly plants in isolated, defensible areas, thereby spreading the risk.

Halvorsen was familiar with the operation in McAlester, and knew local Native Americans had been some of its most diligent – and trouble-free – workers. After being assigned to one of the site search teams following Desert Storm, he uncovered an existing manufacturing facility in southern Oregon. The plant had once served as a lumber mill, and later as a farm machinery fabrication plant, but by 1992 it was largely vacant. Still, it had excellent railroad access and, better yet, a sizeable out-of-work population of Klamath Indians – *Maqlaq* in their native language – living within a forty mile radius.

Captain Halvorsen was promoted to colonel and made manager of the new Chiloquin Army Ammunition Plant. He not only presided over a full-scale overhaul of the previous facility, but a two-fold increase over its original size. He also became something of a hero to the locals. That is, until the mid-nineties slowdown tarnished his reputation.

Not that it was Halvorsen's fault. President Clinton's so-called "peace dividend" suppressed demand for conventional munitions to the point that seven of the twelve assembly lines had to be put in mothballs. Soon after, in accordance with the Armament Retooling and Manufacturing Support Act, half of the Chiloquin plant was opened to civilian use. And even though tenants could be asked to vacate their new digs with only thirty days' notice, companies from as far away as Tacoma jumped at the chance to take over portions of the industrial facility for little more than the cost of utilities.

Halvorsen did his best to keep the Maqlaqs on the payroll, converting full-time jobs into part-time and, when even those were lost, finding alternate positions whenever possible. Still, personal income took a major hit. Production of roofing tile and build-it-yourself storage sheds didn't merit the level of pay commanded by assembly of fragmentation grenades and 105mm tank rounds.

So the locals were initially pleased when world tensions in the late 90s began to ratchet up orders of munitions. By 9/11 and Afghanistan, the civilian companies were moving out and the ammo plant was well on its way to restoring all twelve assembly lines at three shifts a day. Trouble was, in little more than a year, the usually tolerant Maqlaqs had grown increasingly unhappy with the extra hours, especially in view of no pay increases and no comp time.

And as diligent as the Maqlaqs might be when they were on the job, most of them didn't regard their eight hour shifts as the focal point of their lives. It had long been part of the native culture to work just enough to get by, just enough to put food on the table – not out of any inherent laziness but because there were more important things in life. Furthermore, most of the Maqlaqs also maintained some working relationship to the land, even if it would never make them a decent living. They fished and hunted. They made handicrafts. They raised horses and cattle and grew the hay to feed them.

So what was the point of overtime if your rent was already paid and the children were sufficiently fed? And if the white employees were eager to work a few extra shifts each week because there was always the possibility of a future slow-down, native wisdom encouraged them to live more fully in the present and trust tomorrow to take care of itself.

Halvorsen might not agree with their attitude, but in a way he had to be grateful. It was such "wisdom" that enabled him to keep wages from becoming an issue when other sectors of the workforce were demanding raises. And workers were *getting* those raises – even in a lukewarm economy – largely because labor unions in this state still had clout. The mere possibility Gabriel Woods was more than he seemed was enough to make Halvorsen nervous.

"Any way you can keep Woods under surveillance?" he asked the Lieutenant.

"Well, Lane's house is a good hundred-and-fifty yards off the highway. I can't exactly drive a patrol car up her drive and set up a dish." Fiske allowed a laugh. "The one time I went out there unannounced, she was already outside to greet me. I swear she could hear my tires go from asphalt to dirt."

"Then what about Buddy? It was his stud did the honors for Lane's mare, wasn't it? Maybe he could drop in without raising any suspicions."

"It's an idea," Fiske admitted after a moment's thought, "though I haven't been all that sure of Buddy lately..."

"What do you mean, *sure of?*"

Fiske scratched his jaw with the phone. "I dunno. I'm inclined to think *all* my Indians are sympathetic to this sick-out." Another pause. "If anybody, I might send Chino to pay a visit. She couldn't get anything out of Woods before, but I caught 'im giving her the eye once or twice. 'Sides, she's closer in age, maybe a few years younger."

He might have added, *not a decade older like Lane.* But even if there was no love lost between him and Lane D'Arcy, Fiske wasn't about to make any unkind remarks. Not with Halvorsen on the other end of the line. And not after what Lane had been through over the past two years. He didn't want anyone to think he was heartless, for Chrissake.

"Prob'ly use that to my advantage if I can get Chino to cooperate," Fiske said at last. "I'll let you know if she finds out anything."

Lane's chicken gumbo – a recipe passed down "from the French side of the family," she'd said – was as good as any home-cooked meal Gabriel could recall. Of course, most of the meals he'd had over the last several years qualified as "home-cooked," technically speaking. But boarding house fare tended to be heavy and unimaginative. Meat and potatoes were standard, even if the preparation varied, and were usually accompanied by peas and carrots or lima beans. Gabriel would often develop a craving for a Cobb salad with vinaigrette, or maybe a cheese omelet at dinnertime. Anything to break the routine.

He sometimes wondered whether it was actually his culinary cravings that drove his preference for the female companionship he intermittently sought. Was it because waitresses were so easily accessible – and occasionally willing – or because he couldn't go another day without the Fresh Veggie Platter or the Country Scramble Lite?

The dinner conversation had likewise been on the "lite" side. Lane had insisted on hearing about *him*, so he gave her the bare bones bio, filling in as few details as possible: Raised by a mother who wanted him to attend seminary but died the year before he was old enough to apply; forced by "circumstances" to go out looking for work, and eventually finding it in a series of odd jobs for a contractor in Florida who built pool-side cabanas; then forced by "other circumstances" to look for work elsewhere. And elsewhere. *And elsewhere...*

He successfully distracted Lane from more sensitive areas by peppering his biography with descriptions of the various construction jobs he'd had, the differences in building codes between South and West, and the vicarious satisfactions of watching young families move into their new homes. He also painted some verbal portraits of the more interesting people he'd run across in the course of his travels – much to Lane's delight, he thought – like the beer-guzzling roofer in Visalia, or the one-armed cabinet maker in Twin Falls who taught him how to set a finish nail and pound it flush with one hand. Despite knowing Lane for less than three hours, Gabriel was certain she too would be among the cast of "interesting characters" he would remember fondly as he continued his journeys.

"So the bottom line," Lane said, lifting one edge of her bowl to capture the last spoonful of gumbo, "is that you're still, what?... searching?"

What I'm searching for, Gabriel wished he could say, *is a way to tell you I have all of four dollars in my pocket.* Instead he lied. "It's kind of in my blood now. I'm not sure I could ever settle down."

She nodded somberly, as if she had reason to be disappointed. Then: "Want seconds?"

"No, no. That was plenty. Should hold me for the night."

"Then we can prob'ly save the rest for Saturday lunch. If you don't mind leftovers."

"Are you kidding—? I'll plan my day around it."

She smiled at the compliment, then suddenly scowled.

"Oh, wait—we won't *be* here for lunch on Saturday." She looked across the butcher-block table, her gaze just missing his. "You want another chance to lay some rubber with that four-barrel pony out front?"

"Sure." *Assuming you haven't kicked me out.* "Where we goin'?"

"Beatty—southeast of here. You take the back road to Klamath Falls, then hang a left at the junction with 140. Little over an hour away. Maybe *half* an hour the way you drive. It's where my, umm... my parents live."

Gabriel stared at her, found her hesitation curious. He waited for her to go on, finally filled in the silence with a question.

"Special occasion?"

"No. They let me... I try to visit them once a month, usually go to the early service so the rest of the day is open. We'll need to be out the door by eight to get there on time."

"Services... on Saturday? Are you—" He pictured her living room, couldn't remember seeing a menorah on the piano or credenza; and there were no Sabbath candlesticks on the kitchen shelf where she kept a *You Are Special Today* plate. "—Jewish?"

"Did my blonde locks give me away?" She smiled again, struck a playful pose as she primped her hair and fluttered her lashes. "No, actually—Seventh Day Adventist. Easy to get us confused. We do the worship thing on Saturdays, too. Aren't supposed to eat bacon, and I'll bet the farm we have just as many rules about how to be a good person as Jewish people do, except—oops, *sor-ree*—we aren't allowed to *make* bets."

Her borderline tongue-in-cheek quickly turned serious. "Guess you could say I prefer to operate on faith. Not much interested in following the rules anymore."

Faith versus rules. Gabriel had heard the distinction made more than once during his travels: Judaism was a religion of rules and ritual, Christianity of simple faith and love. People who'd seen him toting his Bible – and couldn't help "sharing" their own views on the subject – often made the same claim at some point. "Law versus Spirit" was how most put it, usually implying the superiority of the latter. No need for rules.

He left such claims unchallenged until the time he took up residence in a boarding house run by an elderly Jewish couple. It was one of the rare instances where the husband was still alive. Gabriel had lived there for almost a month before he found out the couple's affiliation. Both were observant but unobtrusive, reciting their daily prayers and blessings before meals in private. A notice was thumb-tacked to the entry hall bulletin board saying they would perform no chores of any kind between sundown Friday and Saturday night. Guests were asked to prepare their own meals and otherwise fend for themselves during the interim. "It's our day off," they would say cheerily, attaching no religious significance.

But Gabriel knew otherwise, and he was impressed by the quiet way they handled problems and forgave boarders who were late on rent; in their regular donations of food to the local homeless shelter – a habit he'd picked up from them; and how they always judged a person by what they *did,* rather than said.

One evening after his two fellow boarders had gone to bed, Gabriel stayed downstairs with Morrie, the husband, to watch some portly-but-popular evangelist debate fellow celebs during a now-defunct, late-night talk show. *Politically Incorrect,* if his memory served. The mega-church pastor was decrying the "legalism" Christians could dispense with, since they alone were saved and had Jesus' love in their hearts. Morrie suddenly turned down the TV and turned to Gabriel.

"Say you're the Messiah," he said, as if he were part of the tele-vised panel, "and you've finally come down to make heaven-on-earth. The Holy One tells you to pick a dozen disciples to help you out, but you can choose from only one of the two groups he brings you. One group is made up of people who claim to believe in you, who sing your praises, maybe put a few dollars in the plate when it comes down the pew. The other group includes people who don't even know you, or think you're a figment of somebody's imagination... also maybe a few Buddhists and Muslims and ACLU members..."

With this Morrie, grabbed his forehead, laughed out loud, finally pointed for emphasis.

"...*But*, they all have a record for doing nice things for other people, some they've never even met, and usually without even being asked. So, Mister Messiah—which group do you pick?"

Gabriel squinted back at the balding man in the gray sweater-vest, jumping ahead to what he assumed was the lesson of his parable.

"So what you're saying is, faith isn't really faith unless it results in good works."

"What I'm saying is, good works *is* faith."

"*Gabriel—?*"

"Huh?"

"Did you even *hear* me?—I just asked if I offended you or something." Lane waited; no response. "You know—what I said about Seventh Day Adventists being like Jews...?"

It dawned on him that he *hadn't* heard her. And the fact that he'd been so lost in thought, with Lane only an arm's length away, gave him pause. What if she'd reached out across the table to touch his hand? Or gotten up with her empty soup bowl and brushed against him on her way back to the sink? He'd be forced to leave long before Vincent would return.

"For all I know," she went on, unaware of his sudden distress, "*you* could be Jewish. Not that it would make any difference."

"No, you didn't offend me, first of all. And second..." Gabriel lifted a hand to his jaw, nodded as though acknowledging it for the first time. "...I'm not sure *what* to call myself anymore. Not that it would make any difference."

"Well—there's a topic for further discussion. But right now," she said, scooting her chair back from the table, "I'm going upstairs to freshen up. And you're gonna do the dishes like you promised."

He was grateful she'd dropped the subject, mildly surprised she thought it was worth bringing up at a later time.

"Consider it done. But Lane—"

"*Laney*... if you intend to spend the night here."

He waited as she paused, placing a hand delicately on the door-jamb that framed the hallway, finally turned to face him.

"Laney... I still need to talk to you about something. Maybe when you come back down...?"

"Sure." She cocked her head, her interest now piqued. "Can you give me a hint?"

"It's about... my Bible."

She wondered at first whether she'd opened up a can of worms by allowing religion into their conversation, hoped she hadn't ru-ined whatever intimacy might be over the horizon.

Of course, she had no expectations. She hadn't been with a man for months, in *that* way at least, found she didn't crave it nearly so much anymore, ever since she'd decided not to let her blindness stop her from doing the things she loved. The sex had only been a phase, a reaching out to confirm that even if she could no longer *see* the world, she could still feel it.

And what she'd inadvertently, stupidly told Gabriel was true enough: The men she'd slept with since the accident had all been lovers at some point in her checkered, indecisive past, and she still considered most of them friends. All were single but one, and *his* marriage had been in trouble long before she'd contributed to its demise. As it turned out, Doyle needed help more than she did. Which was good for her to know, actually. There were worse ways of being blind than losing your eyesight.

It was also true that Gabriel was the first man she'd met in a long, long time – in Chiloquin, anyway. About a year into her sight-lessness, after she'd settled down somewhat, her parents began to introduce her to eligible bachelors during her monthly visits to Beatty. They were church members mostly, and all had obviously been prepped about her accident, though none were quite ready for her say-what's-on-your-mind manner, or the anger always simmering just beneath the surface.

So the prospect of a new man in her life, even someone "just passing through," was strangely invigorating. And Gabriel *had* assured her his quip about his Bible had little to do with religion. When she pressed him, he simply said, "We'll talk about it later." Things could still get interesting.

She finished her shower – just a rinse, really; she was worried about using up all the hot water – then slipped into a caftan that was neither too suggestive nor too modest. Walking out of her bedroom, she halted at the top of the stairs, listened. She couldn't hear water running in the kitchen, wasn't sure if that meant Gabriel had already finished the dishes, or he'd gone outside, or maybe he was waiting for her in the living room. Funny, she couldn't tell *where* he was.

She shook it off, started down the stairs, halted once more. For a moment she considered going back to brush on a hint of rouge – the only make-up she still bothered with – or maybe a spritz or two of *Obsession*, but decided against either. After all, this wasn't about romance, it was about...

...It was about...

...Inviting a complete stranger to stay overnight in the same house!

About bringing home someone she didn't know from Adam, and nobody in town or at the plant could vouch for either. It was entirely possible no one even noticed him driving off with her, and he therefore wouldn't be a suspect if anything should happen to her.

For the first time she felt vulnerable, considered how naive she'd been to think the sound of a man's voice was enough to go on, how foolish it was to have invited this particular man into her home, this stranger she'd picked up as if she were some street-corner trollop. She was worse than Pamela. This man who called himself Gabriel could be one of those seemingly innocent, doe-eyed, maybe even handsome types people read about in the tabloids, who sweet-talk their way into victims' lives and end up sawing them into little pieces before burying them in their own backyard.

Or maybe he *wasn't* handsome. How could she tell? He might be covered with boils and scabs for all she knew. And the fact he'd made a special point about her not touching him... what was *that*

about? What kind of nut case had she let in? All she could do now
was—

"Lane—?"

Gabriel took a step into the hallway, looked up to find Lane near
the top of the stairs, gripping the rail, her knuckles almost white,
though he couldn't yet see her face from where he stood.

"Are you okay...?"

It was after her second failure to respond, after he'd walked far
enough into the hallway to see the fear wrenching her face, when he
bolted for the stairs and started up.

"Don't—! Don't you touch me!"

She released her white-knuckle hold on the railing, pushed both
palms out imploringly. Gabriel immediately stopped, knew he would
have caught himself anyway, squinted up as the irony of her request sunk in.

"I'm the one who didn't want you to touch *me*, remember?"

It was clearly lost on her.

"But why—? *Why* won't you let me touch you, Gabriel?" She
took another breath before admitting her suspicion. "What are you...
hiding?"

What he first thought might be some surge of physical pain, or
the resurfacing of some paralyzing memory, he now recognized as
fear.

Of him.

"No, Lane. You can't really be thinking... I mean, I'm not going
to hurt you—"

"Oh my *God!*"

Both hands rose to her mouth. Evidently she'd seen too many
horror movies to let those words bring any comfort. Quite the opposite.

"Please, Lane—" Now it was Gabriel who gestured imploringly,
even if she couldn't see it. "Look, I don't know why you're finally
having all these doubts right now, after I've been here for a couple of
hours. I mean, yeah—I was a little surprised you'd let me into your

home like this... somebody you've never even seen before."

He winced, shook his head: *What an idiot.*

"But I swear that's the only reason I'm here. I really *do* need a place to stay." He shrugged, didn't know where he'd go now, but offered anyway. "And if you're uncomfortable having me around, I'll leave. Just call me a cab or something."

Four dollars might at least get him back to the ammo plant where he could pick up another ride. But then he wouldn't be able to pay Lane for the meal.

"I don't have a phone," she finally replied, deadpan.

Several seconds, then: "You... don't have a phone?"

For some reason Lane found this ironic. Or at least humorous. Or merely cathartic. She placed a hand on the stair rail again, released a throaty laugh. More at herself than the incredulity in Gabriel's voice.

"Nope. People around here couldn't believe I did it, but I cut the cord a year and a half ago. Only calls I ever got were from co-workers and friends who wanted to tell me how sorry they were about everything and ask when they could come by to drop off a casserole. *Endlessly.* I know everybody meant well, but it got old, you know?"

She proffered a look simultaneously apologetic and resolute.

"So... it would appear you're stuck out here at the ranch, and the fair maiden who owns it is at your mercy."

She could say this now. Like last night's fog on 97, her fears had melted; how could she have thought otherwise? She waited as Gabriel sighed, brought his right foot down from the next to last stair, shuffled at the bottom as though he still had something to say.

"What is it...?"

He sighed again. "Well... you *still* might want me to leave."

"But I don't. Really, Gabriel. I don't know what got into me. Sometimes I get these flashes of helplessness and I just—"

"There's no need to apologize, Lane. I'm the one who should be apologizing to *you.*"

A heartbeat. "For what?"

Yet another sigh. "I was trying to tell you before dinner. I don't have... I won't have any money to pay you until I get my Bible back.

That's where I keep it."

She recalled how he'd tried to bring up the subject of her Indian basket once or twice, even after she'd explained the rules. And then there was his inexplicable comment about his Bible. She let herself sink down, sit onto the landing at the top of the stairs.

"So. You don't have any—"

"But I *will.* I can pay you Sunday. That's when this trucker I was riding with is scheduled to return—at least, according to one of the guards. If this guy has any sense of decency at all—"

"Trucker?" She suddenly perked up. "He makes deliveries at the plant...?"

"Yeah. Son of a bitch was running late when we hit—"

"This son-of-a-bitch have a name?"

Gabriel paused. If only Lane would let him finish a sentence.

"Vincent. See, after we hit the—"

"Vincent!" Now *this* was ironic. And maybe humorous to boot. "He was just here this morning."

Another pause. Longer.

"He was here?"

Gabriel wasn't so sure he wanted to know what *here* meant. Lane concealed a smile, knew he was wondering about it.

"Sweet guy, Vincent," she replied, nodding fondly. "Not a son-of-a-bitch at all, once you get past the bluster. He was delivering components even before I went to work there."

"At the ammo plant? You?... worked at—"

"Steady client of mine," she went on, "practically right from the start. Came to see me in the hospital, too, even before I was out of the coma. Past year I've gotten to know him well. *Really* well."

She smiled. He frowned. So many questions.

"Not that it's any of my business... you mind if I ask what he was doing here?"

"You're right. It's none of your business."

She was holding back the impish grin now. Gabriel slumped against the anchor post.

"I wasn't asking if... " He stopped, thought of another approach. "Did you happen to see the front of—" Second time: *Idiot.* "Did this guy say anything about hitting a deer?"

He waited while she seemed to be thinking about it, finally shook her head no.

"Did he mention a hitch-hiker he picked up last night, who went back to clean up his mess while he drove off and left the guy in the middle of nowhere?" Still no reply. "Or maybe having a certain Bible in his possession, belongs to someone else...?"

"Actually, he didn't say much of anything. He just came by for a quickie." She raised her chin toward the front entry hall. "That's his thirty bucks down there in the basket. When he stays longer, it's forty or fifty. Time or two it was a brand new C-note."

"Thanks..." Gabriel looked glumly away. "A little more information than I wanted."

She let him visualize it for a few more moments.

"Had ya goin' for a minute, didn't I?"

He looked back.

"Not that it's any of your business either, but Vincent's just a friend." If she couldn't hear Gabriel sigh with relief, she could sense it. "A good one, too. Not exactly simpatico, far as politics goes. But when I needed a father to cradle me like a baby, he was there. Sure as hell couldn't depend on my own.'

She pushed herself up, paused to brush off her caftan where she'd been sitting, started slowly toward him. "Sometimes, after he drops off a load, he'll come by and stretch out on the sofa for a quick nap, like he did this morning. 'Couple times he needed to sack out for the whole day, so I'd give him the second bedroom. He's been so good to me, I tell 'im it's on the house, but he always leaves a few dollars behind."

"Speaking of which..." Gabriel said, leaving the sentence open-ended.

He stepped aside as Lane reached the bottom. She hesitated, as if gauging whether he was still keeping his distance, nodded almost imperceptibly before going into the living room; evidently so.

"Well, I was hoping to buy some groceries tomorrow when I go in for the town meeting. I need to pay Buddy *something* for that mush he's been making for Fabian." She stopped, appeared almost to be scanning the room. "And since I convinced my folks not to sell this place when they moved to Beatty—against their better judgment, my father took care to point out—I'm trying to pay them just like I would a mortgage. They need three hundred dollars, minimum, at the end of every month, to help them make their own payments on the new condo they bought there. More when I can afford it."

Gabriel felt as if he'd just cleaned out the refrigerator at the homeless shelter.

"I'm sorry, Lane. I can't give you anything before Sunday. That's just the way it is. I'm happy to leave money for your next house payment. But if you can't wait that long, you can boot me out, I wouldn't blame you."

"*Oh*, no—" She swirled to face him. "—you're not getting off that easy."

Easy? Gabriel thought he was being more than generous.

"You're right—I can't wait that long. And who knows if Vincent even *has* your Bible. Could be he threw it out. Maybe he didn't know there was anything in it. Or maybe he *is* planning to bring it back, but Halvorsen cancels this week's deliveries because of the sick-out everybody's expecting."

None of which Gabriel had considered, or *wanted* to consider. He was still hoping to get his three thousand dollars back, of course – now if only for Lane's sake. But it was the other treasures in his Bible that really mattered.

"Do you have his number? Maybe we can drive back into town and find a pay phone. You could call him and see if— "

"Who—Halvorsen?"

"No, *Vincent*. You can ask him about my Bible, make sure he's still—"

"Vincent?—not a chance." She waved a hand. "Much as the guy'll talk your ear off when he's around?—he's pretty much a private person. Never gave me his phone number, or even an address where I could send a thank-you note."

Suddenly Lane ran her hands down her hips, pulled the loose folds of her caftan out on either side before letting the fabric fall gently around her again.

"What do you think? Should prob'ly go change, huh?" She waited while Gabriel simply stood there, still unsure what she had in mind. Then: "Wait. Jimmy Two Feathers got the heater in the Mustang working again."

"Lane, what the hell are you talking about?"

She met his eyes almost dead on.

"You can stay here for the next three days if you like. But right now you're driving me back to the ammo plant."

He'd made a U-turn onto the shoulder just west of the entrance road, started to slip the T-bar into *Park* when Lane cracked her window, tilted her head in concentration.

"Funny. Pamela usually has her radio up loud at night."

"Assuming she was here," Gabriel said.

"You mean she's not?" Lane scowled thoughtfully. "She hardly ever misses a shift, and I can't believe she snagged somebody this fast. What time was it when we left?"

"Little before nine."

Gabriel had already asked Lane what time swing shift let out, even before he'd agreed to drive her back. Not that she'd given him a choice. But since he'd met her at the end of the day shift – almost exactly five hours ago – he'd wondered aloud if it made sense to go back to the ammo plant so soon. Assuming the customary eight-hour shifts, the next one wasn't due until midnight.

She indulged him, patiently explaining that swing shift was only six hours long now, which put the next crew change at ten o'clock. During Chiloquin's mini-recession in the mid-nineties, management had cut back swing to only six hours, and eliminated graveyard altogether. After the return to full production, Halvorsen kept the shorter second shift as a favor to the sizeable number of employees who'd grown to prefer it.

Interestingly, Halvorsen also found that shutting down the assembly lines for two full hours of maintenance resulted in an overall increase in the plant's output. It was important to point this out, Lane went on, because Halvorsen liked to use the swing shift "favor" as proof he'd already made concessions to labor, even though that was hardly his original intention.

Gabriel thought it curious how Lane seemed so conversant on plant politics, but the subject bored him as much as building codes must have bored *her*. He finally brought the Mustang to a halt, reached to turn off the ignition.

"It's nine straight up, so maybe Pamela's not here yet."

"Wouldn't bet on it. I can't remember the last time I got here before she did."

"Even if we're a full hour early?"

"Not everybody waits until the whistle blows before they clock out. I'd get here this early every time if my friend Jillian—she's the one who usually drives me over—if she didn't mind hanging out with me that long before her own shift started." Lane turned thoughtfully away, like there might be more to the story, finally shrugged. "Anyway, I haven't exactly been keeping score, but odds are I'll go home with someone who's off early for one reason or another."

"Well, I guess I should consider myself lucky you were still around when I arrived today."

It took only a few seconds of silence for Gabriel to realize Lane might not feel similarly fortunate. And a few more seconds – as if to rub salt in the wound – before she finally replied.

"Start the car again. I want to go across the road and park in Pamela's spot before she does. Maybe that way everybody'll know I mean business tonight."

"Yeah?—and maybe that way everybody will think you're in the *same* business."

Wounded or not, he should've kept his mouth shut. Not so much because of the tirade sure to follow, but because Lane was close to coming out of her seat.

"Don't you *dare* talk to me like that!" she growled. "You have no right to judge me!"

He squirmed backward. "I was only reminding you—"

"You can't begin to know what I've been through, what kind of person I am."

"—how you hate being compared with—"

"You think I have a lot of choices? You think coming here for a handout is easy—?"

Don't argue. "No, you're right. I wasn't being very—"

"*You* try living a life you didn't ask for." She slashed the air with an index finger, jerking his head back. "*You* see what it's like when your whole life changes forever in a single instant... every dream, all the things you still hope to do—*everything*—goes out like a light, goes out like..."

She stopped, her whole body trembling now, eyes shiny in the glare from the floodlights bathing the ammo plant. But she would not give in to tears. She had stopped crying long ago, *refused* to cry, about this one thing at least.

Gabriel found himself gripping the door handle again, waiting until Lane had taken several deep breaths before he loosened his hold. He was thankful she'd given him time to put on his one sweater before they left. It wasn't much protection, but it might be enough if she only grazed him.

"Can I say I'm sorry now?"

She continued to glower – or so he assumed. In the harsh back-light he could no longer see the green of her eyes. Nor could he itemize all the reasons why he understood her anger, only that he *did*.

"It's not just because I need a place to stay, Lane. I really *am* sorry. And like you say—I have no right to judge you. But I want you to listen, carefully..."

Oddly, he found his own eyes beginning to water; when was the last time *he'd* cried? He sat up, facing her now, wished she could see his own truth written across it.

"...I *do* know what it feels like to have your life changed forever.

Not in an instant, maybe, but a whole lot faster than it takes to figure out how to deal with it. And I know exactly what it means to live a life you don't want to live... how not a day goes by without wishing you could change things back to the way they were, how you miss being treated like an ordinary person again... how you begin to think God is some crabby, frustrated old man with a twisted sense of humor, assuming you think of him at all."

Lane didn't need to see his eyes to know they weren't dry. She instinctively reached out for an arm, a shoulder – caught herself when she heard him clunk back into the door, shook her head with quiet sadness at his reaction. And Gabriel, in turn, didn't need to read her mind to imagine what she was thinking: What is it that must have hurt him to the point that he couldn't stand even the comforting caress of a fellow wounded soul? A violent, abusive father, perhaps? Had he been beaten? Molested as a child...?

"I wish I could help," was all she said.

"And me *you*."

It was clearly not the reply she expected. As though he *could* help her, but something prevented him? Really–? She raised the back of her hand to dab an eye, slowly, so he wouldn't feel threatened, was about to speak again when the sound of a car engine drifted in.

Gabriel glanced past her, spotted a van waiting for the entrance gate to be rolled aside.

"What kind of car is it?" Lane asked.

"It isn't. It's a van."

She nodded. "Dark green?"

"Can't tell exactly. Dark anyway."

"Prob'ly brought in the shipment of blasting caps. They come separately, usually arrive an hour or two before swing. Ford Econoline if I'm right, the extended one with no windows on the sides or back."

The van was halfway through the concrete barriers before Gabriel could tell for certain. "Right." He squinted, could now make out another vehicle moving at the far end of the lot. "Something else on its way out, too. Sedan, looks like."

"What color?"

"Yellow maybe... or green, I don't know—can't tell from the fluorescent lights."

He shifted in the seat, suddenly felt foolish acting as Lane's lookout. She didn't have anyone serving as her eyes that afternoon, did she? Then again, he didn't know much about her routine, didn't care to play the pimp for her, either, even if she was only here to earn food money.

"I gotta tell ya, Lane, I'm not real comfortable with all this. Maybe I should just walk back to your house. Anybody sees me—"

"In the dark?—don't be silly. Besides, it's forty degrees out and six miles down the—"

"—with you, they're gonna think you're already taken, or however you put it."

"—highway and it'll prob'ly take you a couple' hours to get there." Had she heard him?

"Okay with me. Two hours should be just about right. Maybe by then..." He paused, thought better of it. "...I can let myself in your front door, lay down on the sofa and nobody'll even know I'm there."

"No," she said adamantly.

The uneven ends of her hair danced in the backlight as she wagged her head, framing her darkened face in spun gold, the whites of her eyes almost glowing. It was enough to make Gabriel catch his breath. He sat in silence for a few more seconds, turned the key in the ignition, dropped the gear into drive.

"Well then. Guess I'd better get over to the other side after this delivery van leaves."

"No—stay here." She shook her head again. "You're right... about the Pamela thing." A few seconds. "For a while my friends were worried that's what I was becoming, even if I didn't ask for money back then. But they understand now. Anybody goes home with me, it's just for the company."

She turned forward, allowing Gabriel to see the color of her irises once more, now fiercely green in the distant security lights.

"You'd be surprised how bad most guys want someone to pay a little attention to them, listen to a gripe or two over a couple' beers, sleep it off and wake up to the smell of coffee and eggs the next morning. Nobody does that anymore, not even girlfriends. A man'll trade half a day's wages for the kind of TLC I give 'im."

Gabriel pushed the gearshift forward again, killed the engine. "My point was... what I *meant* to say is, nobody's going home with you for *any* reason, they see me sitting here."

"Alright. If it'll make you feel better, get in back."

"Get—"

Gabriel couldn't even repeat her words before she suddenly shushed him, tilted her head again to listen. The unidentified sedan was coming out, the roll-away gate having been left open for it.

"Why didn't you tell me someone was leaving?"

"Lane, I told you—I'm not gonna sit here and—"

"What kind of car?"

"What?—like you've memorized everybody's make and mod—"

"Just *tell* me, would you?"

Gabriel huffed, squinted. "Chevy Cavalier... or maybe a Malibu. I'm no expert at—"

"Malibu..." She blinked. "What color?—can you tell yet?"

"Light... *something*. I don't know—why don't I just lay down in the back—"

"Hurry—what color?"

He sighed more loudly. "Kind of a yellowish green. Like I said, the lights make it hard to—"

"It's a Dodge Neon, and it's Scott Murphy, and he's married."

"There's two guys in the car."

"Mmm—prob'ly his best friend Allen. Also married, cheats on his wife with two other women, not including Pamela. Real jerk. I hope they *do* see you."

They did, as it turned out, the Neon slowing to a stop well before it reached the intersection with the highway, both occupants turning to peer into the Mustang. Lane seemed to sense their curious stares, offered a pasted-on smile of apology and a curt nod toward Gabriel as if to confirm she was indeed taken for the evening. Gabriel flushed as the Neon lurched forward and accelerated onto the highway.

"That's it. I'm getting the hell in back now."

"My, my. We're getting just a wee bit sensitive, aren't we?"

"Maybe we are," Gabriel replied, "but there's also another car coming."

He yanked the handle, pushed the door open and stepped out, folded the driver's seat forward.

"What kind?"

Gabriel straightened to glance over the top of the Mustang, then bent down to climb back inside. "Ford F-150. And this time I'm sure 'cause I used to drive one, only mine was white." He hesitated, shook his head. "Jesus, did they really think a full-grown adult could fit back here?"

Lane chuckled, pressed on. "So it's not white. What color, then?"

He rolled his eyes, turned, reached outside to pull the door shut, shifted sideways so his knees wouldn't be jammed against the front seat. "Red... and it's just sitting at the gate."

Despite his backseat perspective, Gabriel was sure Lane was rolling *her* eyes, too.

"Doyle... another real catch. Prob'ly bullshit with the guard for ten or fifteen minutes before he finally leaves." She listened for the sound of his engine idling. It wasn't. "Both divorced. Go hunting together. If they really get into it, Hyatt's gonna hafta close the gate. Can't leave it open for more than thirty seconds unless there's steady traffic. Regulations."

In a few more moments the whine of the drive mechanism could be heard, followed by the clank of chain against metal. Lane smiled, glanced his way before turning forward again.

"Looks like we got some time on our hands. Wha'cha wanna talk about now?"

A good thirty seconds elapsed before he responded. She wasn't sure it came out of a genuine interest, or he didn't know how else to fill the silence.

"So... how did it happen?"

"How did *what* happen?"

Maybe if she gave him a chance to change his mind...

"Look, if you don't want to dredge it all up again, I understand. I mean, if it's too—"

"You mean the accident?" No reply. "You're wondering if I can talk about it without falling apart? God, after two years, you'd think I should be able to."

Although, she admitted to herself, she wasn't so sure. She hadn't had any reason to reel out the details over the past five or six months. Everybody in Chiloquin already knew the story. The last time she'd recounted it, in fact, some state assemblyman with his own political agenda had invited her up to Salem to testify before a grand jury about injustices in Oregon's recently-downsized disabilities program. It was just after her state benefits had run out and weren't expected to be renewed.

At the hearing, she *had* broken down while retelling the story. But the reason was less a matter of lingering emotional trauma than rising anger at having been shuffled back and forth while state and federal agencies each claimed the other was responsible for her welfare. Though the U.S. Army willingly picked up the tab for Lane's initial medical bills and recovery, the costs for her ongoing living expenses and job-training program, they said, fell to the state. It was in the midst of this dispute when she settled for the pittance already allotted her by Klamath County, declared a pox on the other two bureaucratic houses, and gave up any further attempts to breach their defensive walls.

If only to preserve her own sanity and get on with her life.

Perhaps recalling the details of the accident after all this time would confirm that she had indeed moved on. She took a deep breath, blinked as the memories and images began to emerge from their padlocked, padded cells, promised herself she would remain objective.

"A lot of the lines at the plant are fully automated," she began, as though narrating a documentary. "Some are manual labor, some a combination. Take the tail fin assembly on a mortar..."

She paused, could hear Gabriel's measured breathing behind her, confirmed he was paying attention.

"...It screws in by hand, kind of like the tails on the darts down at Corky Girls. But the powder and explosive head on a tank round?— they're assembled by these huge hydraulic presses that line up all the components, then push them together while somebody watches a video monitor on the other side of a six-foot-thick, reinforced concrete wall. So it depends on the type of ordnance you're working with."

Ordnance. The word felt strange on her lips now, so neutral and inoffensive, as if it were just like any other product being assembled at any other factory. She wondered if Gabriel found it equally odd to think she'd once had a hand in this industry, this woman whom he'd now seen bubbling like a proud grandparent over her newborn colt, then sobbing over the sad fate of its mother.

"Anyway," she went on, resuming her documentary, "no matter how it's assembled, everything eventually gets checked by hand to make sure the components are snug and the safety mechanisms are locked in place. And then it all gets hand-packed into double-walled cartons, kind of like big egg crates, only the contents aren't so fragile. You could drop a tank shell nose-first onto the concrete and it wouldn't explode. So they tell us, anyway."

She threw out a hand nonchalantly – a forced gesture, she realized, as if to demonstrate her composure despite the fact that the hardest part was yet to come.

"Course, there's a two-inch-thick rubber mat around all the packing stations, so nobody's taking any chances."

Gabriel emitted a small laugh, hardly more than a gust of air, but enough to indicate he was still with her. Or perhaps he too was growing more nervous as her mental movie reel unwound toward the final scene. She rolled down the passenger-side window another inch, drew in a breath.

"His E'ukskni name—that's one of the three main Maqlaq tribes—means *Stillwater.* Fairly common Indian name, but a good one for him... so even tempered, never a harsh word, not like his older brothers who still work there. Even when he was busy on the lines he had this blissful smile... a knowing little grin, almost. You've seen those paintings of Indian gurus, the Hindu ones, when they're lost in meditation?"

She paused as though he might answer her question despite its being purely rhetorical, nodded to herself. She was only delaying the inevitable.

"So, he was packing canister grenades at a table across the aisle from me. Guess I should be thankful we were twenty feet apart, and they weren't fragmentation grenades. Could'a been a lot worse."

Another pause; another, shakier breath.

"Lane, really. If this is too—"

"No, no," she said quickly, "don't stop me. I can do this." She exhaled, brought her arms down, clasped her hands tightly in her lap. "The investigators claimed he must've dislodged the safety pin when he put the grenade into the carton. They even had the cardboard dividers redesigned afterwards, saying it would prevent anything like that from happening again. But you ask me?—I think it was all for show, to make it look like management figured out the cause of the accident even though they didn't have a clue... get people back on the lines because the accident sort of made everybody realize what they were doing."

Although not completely, she thought, *or else they wouldn't have gone back at all.*

"It was all so simple and safe. I mean, really. You pack the canister, insert the fuse, screw on the charge head—" She went through the motions as she described the process. "—three quick turns, insert the pin and snap on the lever." Then she reached as if to set her imaginary grenade on the car's dashboard. "Nothing to it. I could do it with my eyes closed. I could *still* do it if they gave me my job back."

She coughed an ironic laugh, abruptly sobered as the critical scene began to play.

"It was the last thing I ever saw. One of the doctors told me a concussion usually erases your short-term memory, and I should've forgotten everything that happened in the ten or fifteen minutes leading up to it." She shook her head slowly; if only she *could* forget. "But I can still see it, clear as any memory I have... this silhouette, kind of washed out, edges all blurry... a man with his arms outstretched like Jesus on the cross, and this iridescent yellow light all around him. That was it—hazy silhouette and the yellow light. Except..." Her voice quavered only slightly before she pushed through it. "...for this even brighter blue-white light, more like some kind of heat I could *feel* through my eyes... separating his neck from his shoulders."

She became aware Gabriel had stopped breathing. Then, finally, he drew in a mouthful of air, slowly, as if trying hard not to gasp.

"Did the explosion... I mean, was his head—"

"That's what hit me. It could've been an unexploded grenade—the first doctor tried to convince me it was, prob'ly thought the experience would seem less traumatic that way. And the clean-up crew *did* find canister all over the place, some of it live, some clear down at the other end of our line."

She paused to draw in a few breaths of her own. "Some other people on the line got hit with it, too... in the shoulder, leg... none seriously. But with me so close, if one'a those metal things had hit me, even without exploding, I'd be dead for sure. That's what I think. And anyway—" She paused again, throat sticky, took longer to resume this time. "—they found most of his upper body parts in the same place as me. If Stillwater hadn't been standing directly between me and the blast, I would've been killed instantly, too."

He didn't know exactly when he became aware of the headlights sweeping intermittently through the Mustang's interior, washing over Lane's face as she continued to stare fixedly ahead, adding a few personal notes to her recounting of the actual event. Gabriel wasn't about to interrupt her, even though the shiny red pickup had already wended past all but the final barrier on the entrance drive and was now less than fifty yards away. Besides, she'd basically told him Doyle wasn't on the A-list of potential houseguests.

"What I went through for the next twelve months?—*nobody* should face that kind of torture. And it wasn't just about losing my sight. It was all those insurance forms and idiotic interviews and having to beg for every dime you're supposed to get automatically, like they were doing you a favor. It was having your—" She stopped. Again the sticky throat. "...about losing your family. It was being told your eyesight would come back by itself and it was just a matter of time because, you know, all these specialists with all their expensive degrees and six-figure salaries convinced themselves the reason for my blindness was getting bashed in the skull. But they somehow missed the little detail about part of my optic nerve being fried the instant that grenade went off, and if they'd bothered to run some tests right away instead of telling me to be patient, maybe they could've actually done something about it before the damage became permanent."

It was all Gabriel could do to keep from throwing his arms around her, as much for his own comfort as hers. Life wasn't fair for either of them – but more so in Lane's case. He, at least, had helped to bring on his own suffering. He'd as much as pleaded for his power, prayed like a madman during those terrible minutes when he'd been trapped in the car with his mother, silently offered his very soul to the universe in exchange for some antidote to the fragility of flesh, like Midas bargaining for his Golden Touch. And even though it came too late to use on the one person on whose behalf he'd pleaded, he couldn't undo what had been done. Lane, on the other hand, didn't ask for her fate, didn't deserve what the universe had dealt her.

Out on the entrance road, the red pickup's slow progress came to a complete halt almost directly ahead. Gabriel could see the driver's silhouette, the brim of his baseball cap swinging around as he stared into the Mustang. Even though their windows had become somewhat fogged, Lane was no doubt visible in the front seat. Gabriel wasn't so sure about himself – though he presumed Lane would have *liked* him to be visible, considering her potential client.

"But no," she went on, oddly unaware of the other vehicle, "all they could see was this massive bruise on my forehead, and the hairline fracture in their X-rays. So they just assumed…"

The red pickup suddenly turned from the entrance, tires crunching in the roadside lava rock. Lane reacted, cast a sidelong glance to chide Gabriel for the seeming slip-up.

"Is this Doyle already?"

The pickup's headlamps splashed across both of them as it made a tight semi-circle and swung around to the passenger side. If the baseball-capped driver hadn't seen Gabriel before, he had now.

"Why didn't you tell me?"

"You weren't finished with your story. And based on what you said earlier, I figured he wasn't in the running."

"In the *run*—?" Lane released an exasperated sigh, lowered her voice as though Doyle might hear. "Like I can afford to be choosey right about now?"

She turned back, began to roll her window down as the pickup came to a stop alongside. The truck's window lowered with a faint whirr, its stubble-jawed occupant leaning across the seat with a quizzical frown.

"You running some kinda group special tonight, Laney?" Doyle said, staring directly at Gabriel. "Or did I get here in the middle'a you two ironing out the details?"

She bit her lip, obviously censoring the first response that came to mind, but still managed to beat Gabriel to the punch.

"Uh, no—and you know there aren't any details to discuss, you asshole." She tacked on a coy smile as if to pretend the epithet was more endearing than she'd meant it, then nodded briefly toward her back seat companion. "In case you were wondering, this is my cousin Gabriel, from California. Showed up a little unexpectedly, but I told him he could stay for a few days before he looks for a job further north. 'Bout as broke as I am right now."

Gabriel had to admire not only her on-the-fly fabrication, but the not-so-subtle hint of her own financial need. He shrugged, nodded in agreement as Doyle's eyes returned to give him another once-over.

"Huh. Don't remember your folks ever mentioning family down south..." He nodded back toward the ammo plant. "Guess you told 'im to skip lookin' for work here."

"Yep, he's just passin' through," she said, repeating Gabriel's words. "So, you want a couple'a brewskis, maybe a nice backrub now you're through playing with one-oh-fives?"

"I haven't packed shells for months, Laney. They got me on the forklift now, loading boxcars." A few beats. "Man, it *has* been a while, hasn't it?"

He leaned forward, appeared to remove his billfold from a back pocket to riffle through the contents. Since the window of the pickup was a foot higher than the Mustang's, the door panel obstructed Gabriel's view; but he was certain that's what Doyle was doing. And he was thankful Lane couldn't see him counting his money like some flea market bargain-hunter, figuring out what he could afford. Which, if Gabriel interpreted his expression correctly, he clearly hoped would be more than a massage.

"So is that it...?" he finally said, flipping his billfold shut.

"Is *what* it?"

"You know. Is there..." He hesitated, seemed suddenly uncomfortable with Gabriel's presence. "...I mean, are we talkin' about a beer and a backrub and I'm out the door—?"

Gabriel was close to losing it. He glanced at Lane, could tell she was worried he might say something to ruin her chances, didn't want him to scare off a possible payday.

"Why don't we see how things go, okay, Doyle? But I don't see any reason why you couldn't be around for sausage-and-cheese omelets come sun-up."

Doyle interpreted her reply in the only way possible for him, tried not to let his anticipation show as he glanced past her.

"So, uh, what about your cousin?"

"Listen," Gabriel finally broke in, fed up with all the second-person references, "why don't I take the car for a spin? You two can go back to your place in Doyle's pickup, and I can go check out Chiloquin's nightlife."

"You think that's a good idea?"

Lane turned in her seat with sudden concern. It didn't cross Gabriel's mind he'd be driving without a license, or that Lieutenant Fiske's fondest dream was to catch him doing something just exactly this stupid. All he could think about was *not* being at Lane's house for what was almost certainly on the pre-breakfast menu. He'd sooner go off and park on the side of the road somewhere for the rest of the night.

And once again he cursed Vincent for driving off with his Bible. He'd happily give Lane all the money he had – a good chunk of it, anyway – to keep her from doing what she clearly didn't want to do, assuming she had other options.

Of course the irony was, if the old trucker *hadn't* driven off with his money, Gabriel would never have gone out to the ammo plant to try and find him, and would therefore never have met Lane in the first place.

Ain't life grand?

"An' anyway," Lane was saying, "you can't *afford* to check out the nightlife."

"I got enough on me to buy one drink at the Masonic tavern, whatever the name is."

"Corky and Corky Girls," Doyle chimed in helpfully. "On the main drag 'bout halfway through town on your way south." He leaned forward to dig out his billfold again while Lane sent him an unappreciative glower. "Here's another ten spot. There's some pool tables off to the side where you can play a rack, have another beer or two— on me. So how 'bout it?"

He waved the bill. Gabriel waved a hand.

"That's okay. Save your money—"

He clipped off the last two words of his reply – *for Lane* – could see her start to turn as if she knew it was coming, but restrained herself.

"—I can make one beer last all night."

"Suit yourself."

Doyle grinned, ran a fingertip across the brim of his baseball cap as if giving him a secret salute. Gabriel knew it was meant as an expression of thanks from one man to another, a kind of male-bonding wink-and-a-nod, as though he'd assumed Gabriel's willingness to go off and leave them alone signaled permission to get his money's worth. The very thought made him sick.

"C'mon, Laney. Hop in."

She seemed strangely reluctant, turned so Doyle could neither hear nor read her lips.

"You sure you're okay with this?"

"You're asking *me?* The guy who brought on this whole situation?" He winced, lied. "I'm just happy I've still got a place to stay."

She seemed unconvinced. Or at least not ready to go yet.

"Well, don't stay out too long... midnight—no later."

"Lane, I'm not a—"

"Oh, and—" She turned fully in her seat now. "—it's gonna get a little crazy after the swing shift crowd comes in. Just lay low, try not to draw any attention to yourself, 'specially if one of the badges drops in to check on things. They're a little on edge these days, with what's going on at the plant."

"Fine. I promise not to get into any barroom brawls, or stay out past—"

"Laney, you want somethin' in your basket tonight or not? Let's get a move on here."

Gabriel turned with daggers as Lane, too, spun back to face Doyle, replying before Gabriel could.

"I will, if you'll move your damn truck and give me some room to open the door."

Thirty seconds later Gabriel was alone in the car, still sitting in the back with his knees against the driver's seat, staring through the steam-glazed windshield as the pickup's tail-lights disappeared into the distance. Angry as he was, he found himself marveling at how easily Lane had turned off the story about her accident when Doyle drove up, how she could force herself to smile and swallow her pride along with her sadness, how the image she'd painted in his mind kept forcing itself back into his consciousness... the yellow light and the outstretched arms and the gap of blue-white heat. And how he felt so protective of her all of a sudden.

Maybe he'd head back *before* midnight.

*C*ompared **to what the place would be like** less than an hour later, Corky and Corky Girls was basking in the proverbial calm before the storm. Ten minutes earlier, Gabriel had finally climbed back into the driver's seat and started the engine to wait for a pickup-and-camper shell about to emerge from the gate. Its two occupants – a pair of Maqlaqs, Gabriel guessed – were clocking out early just as Doyle and the others had, but thankfully did not stop to peer into the Mustang when they drove by. When the pickup turned west, he did an immediate one-eighty in hopes of following it back into Chiloquin.

As it happened, the pickup was also headed for the town's primary after-hours attraction. Or its *only* attraction. Few of the other buildings on the main drag even had their lights on. The two vehicles passed the painted brick tavern, turned onto a side street and into a broken asphalt parking lot whose sign offered *Additional Parking in Rear* as though they weren't already in the rear. Gabriel pulled into a space at the far end, switched off the ignition, remained in the car until the two Maqlaqs disappeared around the front of the building. Then, getting out, he pushed the keys down into his right front pocket, felt the four one-dollar bills, now slightly damp and wadded up like a grocery list that had been through the wash.

Gabriel chortled at the prospect of blowing it all on a pint of Rainer Pale Ale – assuming the neon sign in front wasn't just for decoration – recalled a few times he'd enjoyed the same brew when he'd lived near Everett. A decent brand, and not as pricey as Henry Weinhard's, or even Olympia. Maybe he'd have enough left after the tip to put a few quarters in the jukebox.

Through the bluish haze inside, Gabriel could make out only two patrons at the bar – a young Indian in a cowboy hat halfway down the length of the polished walnut, and an equally young, sur-prisingly attractive brunette at the far end. The bartender Gabriel queried for directions earlier that day was no longer pulling drinks. In his place were a matched pair, both gray-haired, one of whom was now feeling twenty years younger with the help of the female patron. Maybe she was a friend, or – who knew in such a small town? – his wife. Maybe she was one of the Corky Girls, or Corky herself. Maybe she owned the place.

The thought took him back to an encounter he'd had not long after a string of narrow escapes finally convinced him to avoid every kind of physical contact – except for the one he would surrender to every three or four months. Before settling exclusively on the com-pany of waitresses, Gabriel picked up a woman in a bar who later turned out to be its owner. Though considerably older than he, she immediately accepted his offer to refresh her drink, and slipped easily into conversation. Even then he was sensible enough to talk about health and fitness before broaching the subject of sex, and after thirty minutes of purposeful banter he found himself in her apart-ment.

Which happened to be directly above the bar. In fact her bed was right over the small stage where a three-piece band was playing that night. It was so loud, he recalled, neither of them could hear the other moan when they climaxed. Or at least when *he* did.

Later, while they were getting dressed and the band was taking a break, she allowed that she owned the bar downstairs, brought out a few snapshots of herself with her bartender and some of the town's movers and shakers as proof, and suggested two hundred dollars was more than a fair price for the privilege of taking a woman of her stature to bed. What's more, she had a strict policy forbidding sex between the bar's staff and their customers. She'd made an exception in his case because he seemed "so innocent and needy" and that was worth some kind of premium, wasn't it?

Green as he was, Gabriel suspected she told the same story to one or more "privileged" customers per night. And it was shortly thereafter he began frequenting coffee shops for potential partners – *and* taking the time to get to know them beforehand.

"Get'cha anything?"

It was the barkeep nearest the front door. He cocked his head, waited several more moments, finally looked down the bar to where Gabriel was still staring.

"Right... Colonel Halvorsen's daughter, Amy. Helluva good looker."

Gabriel shook off the cobwebs, nodded like a local who recognized the name the barkeep had just tossed out, then realized he *did* know it: Halvorsen was the ammo plant manager who refused to see him earlier that day.

"You ask me," the gray-haired barkeep went on, "she's only showin' her face tonight so she won't look so outta place at the town meetin' tomorrow. Prob'ly take notes on what goes on and who says what, then report back to daddy the minute it's over." He shrugged. "Can't exactly keep her out, though. She's got a part-time job in shipping and receiving, draws a paycheck just like everybody else who'll be here."

Gabriel nodded again, pulled up a stool. "The town meeting... it's *here* tomorrow?"

"Seein' as how this is the only place in Chiloquin that'll hold three hundred-plus people at once." The barkeep leveled a critical gaze. "Guess you don't work at the ammo plant, do you?"

"No," Gabriel admitted, "I'm just—"

He caught himself before adding the customary words, *passing through,* thought of a better answer. And why not? – it wasn't any different from the kind of preliminary research he did on other women, was it?

"—staying with my cousin for a few days on my way north... Lane D'Arcy. Know 'er by any chance?"

"Laney? Hell, everybody around here knows the D'Arcy family."

Family?

"Lane'll prob'ly be here tomorrow too, maybe say a few words, even if she doesn't work at the plant anymore." An affectionate smile turned abruptly somber. "Damn shame what happened to your cousin. Sure could'a used a little more support from her other relatives when she needed it."

He shook his head, sent an even more critical gaze as if to ask, *Where the hell were you?*

"Yeah, I didn't even know about the accident until... not long ago. Been on the road pretty much non-stop for the last few years. Would'a come right away if anybody took the time to track me down."

The barkeep was still squinting. "You in a traveling band or somethin'?"

"Band...?"

Gabriel frowned, then smiled. He knew how to play a passable rhythm guitar, could probably sing a few Beatles tunes while accompanying himself if someone asked. He'd even learned a couple of Yiddish folk songs at the guest home run by the Jewish couple. The day before Gabriel had to leave, Morrie got out an old Harmony he'd purchased at Sears back in the 50s, taught him some chords and a few verses and roared with laughter at Gabriel's initial efforts. And then he slapped him on the back – and cured his own arthritis – when Gabriel eventually pronounced *chutzpah* like he'd been raised in a shtetl.

"...You might say. I'm on a construction crew. We move around a lot."

Another man in a cowboy hat – *not* Indian – sidled up to the bar and leaned across it to demand the bartender's attention, lightly brushing against Gabriel's sweater. Gabriel instinctively jerked away, drawing scowls from both men before the cowboy turned back.

"Look, I been sittin' over there by the jukebox with Skip since we came in 'bout fifteen minutes ago...? God *damn*, Artie—you think maybe we could get us a couple'a pitchers sometime b'fore day shift?"

The barkeep took another moment or two before transferring his scowl from Gabriel to the foul-mouthed interloper. "Sure, just as soon as I finish taking this man's order." Then, to Gabriel: "So, what'll it be?"

Gabriel slipped off the stool, looked across the tavern where the two Maqlaqs who'd preceded him had now joined four more friends.

"Just pull me one from the tap when you get a chance." He pointed to a vacant table near the six Maqlaqs. "You can bring it over when you get this guy's pitchers. Will this cover it?"

Taking the wadded bills from his pocket, Gabriel peeled off three of the four, smoothed them out on the counter. The barkeep looked down at the crumpled bills, looked back up.

"Tell you what. As a favor to Lane, the first beer's on me. Here..."

Tilting a pilsner under one of the spigots, the barkeep filled it to overflowing, set it on the counter next to his three damp dollars. Gabriel collected the beer and bills, nodded a sheepish thank you. Then, turning, he stepped past the man in the cowboy hat, ignoring his mocking reenactment of Gabriel's earlier reaction. Nothing new there; he was used to it.

He crossed the tavern's cavernous main room – presumably the hall local Masons used for their meetings and secret initiations – pulled up a bentwood chair at a vacant table near the back. After a sip from his beer, he decided it wasn't Rainer after all, sat back in his chair, listening to the nearby Maqlaqs while they conversed in soft, gentle voices despite the country-and-western blaring from the jukebox. Their sentences, he mused, seemed an elegant mix of English and their native tongue, the words sometimes intertwining in a sing-song fashion for a sentence or two, then separating into long, unbroken strings of one language or the other.

As he reflected and sipped some more, it occurred to Gabriel that there were few places he'd traveled where Native Americans could not be found. They were never far away, even if invisible, alluded to by the local white population in respectful yet patronizing tones. Most references were in the past tense, as if they were some lost civilization whose legacy remained only in the form of the occasional unearthed arrowhead, or the "authentic" dream-catchers for sale in the Earth Treasures boutique at the mall, or the occasional street signs with names like *Cheyenne Avenue* or *South Pontiac Parkway.*

Sad, Gabriel thought, how the only real visibility Indians had achieved in recent years was by way of the casinos they were allowed to build on their tribal lands, like the one just down the highway. *Gambling,* for Chrissake. Another scourge the white man had brought upon them, like chicken pox and firewater.

The first sign things were about to get a bit more lively at Corky and Corky Girls was the trio of Anglo ammo plant workers whose boisterous, Miller-time camaraderie raised the noise level by ten decibels the moment they walked in. No more than fifteen minutes later the tavern was a barely-contained riot, with roughly equal numbers of Maqlaqs and whites who gravitated toward two separate areas of the tavern. One contingent was clustered around the bar and the jukebox, the other in the back half of the room. There was some intermingling along the border between them, as well as in the neighboring pool parlor where stained-glass fixtures hawking Elkhorn and Moosehead hung over the half-dozen tables. And, of course, there was Gabriel's own presence in the midst of the Maqlaqs, though his olive complexion and longer hair made him look completely at home.

What *did* appear out of place was one solitary person sitting at a table designed for four, and would accommodate twice as many people when the room grew more crowded. For a while the unoccupied space around Gabriel was conceded, as if he might be saving it for friends who hadn't arrived yet. Eventually a pair of Maqlaqs pointed questioningly at two of the empty chairs and Gabriel consented for them to sit. Minutes later several of their friends dragged chairs over to join them. Despite very much wanting to stay and enjoy the alcohol-fueled fellowship, Gabriel remembered why he hadn't been to a bar in years – at least one this popular – and he was suddenly, desperately claustrophobic.

He caught the eye of one of the men at his table, inquired whether the building had another exit. The broad-shouldered Maqlaq considered the request as if Gabriel might be asking for a place to throw up – a logical inference, given his sickly pallor and the beads of sweat on his forehead – then gestured to a hallway some distance to their right.

Above the hall was a large, hand-lettered sign with the words *Restrooms & Telephone.* Trouble was, what was once an unobstructed aisle leading toward it was now a standing-room-only throng of tightly-packed bodies.

To his great relief, a heavy-set waitress with four pitchers of beer came by only moments later, the crowd parting ahead of her and simultaneously applauding as she balanced the tray atop her head like a Mohawk maiden bringing water up from the river. Gabriel promptly fell in behind her, felt a mild charge only once or twice as the parted patrons closed ranks after them, then made his break while the waitress continued on toward the pool parlor.

He stopped a few paces down the hallway to suck in fresh air, had to swirl away from two women who breezed out of the restroom without warning, then headed for the exit door where he stopped for a second time. The metal release bar was stamped with bold, red letters: *Emergency Exit Only – Alarm Will Sound!* Gabriel stood there slack-shouldered for only a few seconds before a voice echoed down the hall behind him.

"Don't worry. It won't go off."

He turned back, recognized one of the two Maqlaqs who first sat down at his table, the same one who'd told Gabriel where to find the exit. The hulking Indian waited at the other end, frowning with concern.

"You gon' be okay?"

"Much better now," he said, now reaching for the door.

"I'm Two Bears."

Gabriel turned again, allowed that the man was at least as big as one grizzly, shrugged apologetically. "Gabriel. Didn't mean to be rude."

"You're the one who stays with Magdalena."

It was more a statement than a question. Gabriel frowned.

"If you mean Lane D'Arcy—yeah, that's right. And if you'll forgive me for being rude again, how'd you know?"

"When the wandering son returns from his journeys, even the four-leggeds hear of it."

Gabriel tilted his head, wasn't sure whether the Maqlaq was

quoting his ancestors or putting a new spin on an old parable. For a
moment he thought he might laugh, stifled the urge, finally nodded
a belated thanks before pushing outside.

The cacaphony from within faded as the door slowly closed behind him. He took perhaps ten steps across the uneven asphalt,
still puzzling over Two Bears' cryptic pronouncement when he looked
up, spotted the tailored jacket of a policeman bending over the Mustang at the far end of the lot. On the street nearby was a patrol car,
lights off, engine still idling.

Fiske?

Gabriel spun just in time to watch the tavern door *ker-chunk*
into its metal frame, winced at the fact there was no knob on the
outside. By the time he turned back, the policeman was already
squinting in his direction. Fortunately, in the garish glow of the lone
floodlight, Gabriel could now see that it wasn't Fiske, but Buddy,
the lanky Maqlaq whom the Lieutenant had sent north to have his
blood-stained work shirt tested.

Buddy, who knew Lane.

Buddy, who could have told others in his community – including Two Bears – about the new visitor in town.

But how would Buddy already know he was staying with her?
And what in the world *did* Two Bears mean, anyway?

The deputy made no move toward him merely leaned against
the door of the Mustang and folded his arms, his badge gleaming
softly in the yellow light. Gabriel resumed walking, more slowly now,
stole a glance across the street, then down an alley to his left. There
were plenty of escape routes if he felt the need.

"I could arrest you for operating this vehicle without a permit,"
Buddy said when he'd come within a few car lengths.

Before Gabriel could reply, another pickup barreled around the
corner, bounced into the lot and stopped directly in front of Buddy
so its occupants could exchange greetings. It would have been the
perfect opportunity to bolt if Gabriel had wanted to, but something
in the deputy's manner seemed oddly non-threatening. The pickup
moved on, circled to the next row where it sputtered into a vacant
space.

"Maybe you could," Gabriel finally said, "if you actually caught me operating it."

The lanky cop shrugged, looked away as three men emerged from the pickup. "Laney's keys in your pocket would be proof enough."

"In *this* town, I guess. You hauled me in on circumstantial evidence once already."

Buddy finally broke a smile. "The Lieutenant, not me. But I would, too, all that blood." The upturned corners of his mouth turned south again. "My partner has her own theory."

Gabriel halted two spaces away, leaned against a claptrap Plymouth, waited for more.

"Anyway, I'm not here as a cop," Buddy went on. "I'm here as a friend of Lane. You both need to know Deputy Chino will be coming out to her ranch tomorrow—"

"Chino, yeah—I was trying to remember her name. And you're right, she *does* have some pretty funny ideas."

"She's paying a visit because the Lieutenant told her to. She'll be wearing a wire."

"Wire?" Gabriel again had to stifle another laugh. "Why would anybody—"

"The Lieutenant thinks you're here in Chiloquin to stir up trouble, because of the town meeting tomorrow. When Deputy Chino asks you about it, you don't know anything."

"Well, she's right about that. I don't."

"She will ask you certain questions, because Fiske will be listening to the recording. But you won't talk about the meeting, understand? Neither will Laney."

And with that he started back for his patrol car. Gabriel watched him get in and pull from the curb, stood there silently as the car squealed around the corner before he took another step.

Two Bears, and now Buddy.

Not to mention that jerk in the red pickup.

Lane had been intimate with Doyle more often than she cared to recall; but it had been nearly a year since their last, unsatisfying session. And, now that she thought of it, "intimate" was hardly the proper term. No woman could be *intimate* with Doyle Houser.

True, he was handsome in a lumberjack kind of way; he'd even worked in a lumber mill before getting his job packing mortars and artillery shells at the ammo plant. But life for Doyle was strictly a physical occupation, not an intellectual one. Muscle and testoster-one were tools of the trade.

Which could nevertheless serve a woman's needs on occasion. And it was precisely what Lane needed during the period she later came to call her "blind rage phase."

The words made an apt description in more ways than one. What she hadn't told Gabriel when she first recounted her accident – or hadn't had *time* to tell him – was that after her initial attempts to deal with her new "disability" in an accepting, positive manner, she eventually lost faith in the Pollyanna approach. Whereas at first she'd bought into the standard recovery mantra that "events in our lives are designed to strengthen us," that her doctors were "doing everything they could" and she might even use this new challenge in her life as "an opportunity for increased self-understanding," she had finally and totally lost control.

To say she'd turned self-understanding into self-destruction was an understatement. Though drugs were never a problem – with the possible exception of alcohol – sex *was*. Sex, after all, was some-thing you could still do with your eyes closed. Or with your eyes closed permanently, like hers were. Truth be told, sex was often better that way.

Doyle fit in nicely with this rage to feel and not think. It wasn't that he was particularly irresponsible himself. He wouldn't have mer-ited a job fitting fuses onto high explosives if he weren't responsible, even meticulous, while he was working. But the only thing Lane wanted during this phase was the physical, hormonal side of him, which he, in turn, was tirelessly willing to give, in part because his marriage was simultaneously crumbling. Which made *her* irrespon-sible. Being abandoned by her parents and losing a child in the process only intensified her rage, only confirmed the universe was out to make her life miserable.

It took a good year for the rage to burn itself out. And another month or two for Doyle to figure out that he – like Richard before him, and like the half dozen other men who alternately attempted to fill the hole Richard had left – was no longer needed. And least, not in the same way.

All of this came back to Lane as she sat, legs tucked under her on the sofa, listening to Doyle reel out his own recent tales of woe, and otherwise bring her up-to-date on the six months they hadn't exchanged more than a hurried "hello." Unfortunately, she also sat watching Doyle put away the two Michelob Special Ales she'd brought out to him, then help himself to two more pints of Guinness she kept in the fridge because Richard had liked the brew, and she'd developed a taste for it herself during the lonely nights to which he'd consigned her. And when Doyle went into the kitchen and grabbed the cans without bothering to ask, Lane could only shrug because, well, that's just the way he was.

Which didn't make her any more comfortable, because "the way he was" also included a tendency to lose what little control he kept on his other appetites whenever he exceeded his limit. But she *had* offered him a massage. And at eleven o'clock at night, the combination of beer and backrub just might put him soundly to sleep for the next seven or eight hours. If she wanted to avoid having sex with Doyle and still keep the eighty dollars he'd already put into her basket – with great ceremony, counting out one Jackson at a time – this was probably her last, best chance.

She suggested they use the smaller, twin bed in her guest room so she could get at him "from all sides." He countered, suggested the queen-size Posturepedic in her own bedroom so they could wake up beside each other in the morning.

Before she could stop him, he'd stripped down to his skivvies right there in the living room, and then loped up the stairs three at a time – she could tell by counting his footfalls on the bare oak – and was waiting for her, still breathing hard and way more awake than she was hoping, in the middle of her bed.

"I wanna watch you undress," he said after she reluctantly appeared in the doorway, "just like you used to. Remember, Laney?— how you'd take off one piece at a time, hold it out and let it fall, and make it last, like, ten minutes? And then you'd jump me like a crazy woman, remember—?"

She didn't need to see his silly grin to know it was plastered across his face. She only wished *he* was plastered.

"Not right now, big boy."

She didn't want to tell him *No* outright. She still had hopes of putting him in dreamland with her hands. And if worse came to worst, she suddenly realized, she could take care of other things, too, with her hands.

"Let me do this for you first. I mean, c'mon—a nice massage'll do you good after a hard day's work."

"You take some correspondence course or somethin'? Your hands were never exactly your strong suit, Laney."

She could tell his grin was still plastered on. And there were limits to how much grief she would take from him, eighty bucks or not.

"Is that right? And exactly what *was* my strong suit, Doyle?"

"Let's just say it wasn't your hands." He wasn't completely without tact.

"Well it is now," she replied, trying to keep things playful and yet remain firm. "And you're gonna get a damn massage whether you like it or not."

The problem was, Lane couldn't get *at* him from the sides of her queen bed as long as he lay in the center. Which he purposely did. And her mistake – the second one, anyway – was finally giving in and climbing on top of the bed in order to get more leverage. The *first* mistake, which she'd made even before Gabriel drove her back to the ammo plant, was her decision not to change out of the flimsy caftan she'd donned after her shower.

Because when Doyle laid a hand on her while she leaned over his laterals – and it was inevitable he *would* – he could feel her body as if there were nothing separating his palm from her thigh: Warm and smooth and firm as the high school cheerleader he had the hots for even when he was in sixth grade. As close to comatose as his brain might be, his body was ready for action in an instant, and he wanted inside her in the worst way.

And it *was* the worst way because, as Lane sensed almost immediately, he was going to force himself on her regardless of what she might want. The cotton gown was up over her head before she'd even thought of resisting him. She began to put up a struggle only after he started to yank her panties down, grabbed the elastic band with both hands.

Hanging on to it proved less than futile. The knit cotton that covered her crotch and buttocks ripped away like a tear-off coupon; and through her own protests she could hear him laughing because the elastic band was still in her hands, still encircling her waist though the fabric itself was gone.

Even while she continued to hold it tight, he pushed her back on the bed and came down on her with his full weight, hips thrusting even before his erection was anywhere close, never going more than partway inside as much as she was squirming beneath him, pounding him on the back, then finally twisting a knuckle deep into one of the crevices between his ribs.

Which is when Doyle began to hit back, pummeling only her arms at first, as if meant only to make her stop jabbing him, then punching her stomach and upper body when she continued to resist, and finally lifting himself off her far enough to take a full swing.

The back of his hand came across Lane's jaw with enough force to spin her head sideways into the mattress, drawing a tortured scream from deep inside her lungs, a scream she heard almost as if it had come from someone else.

And then, suddenly, there *was* someone else.

Gabriel had parked the Mustang a good fifty yards from the ranch house, the better to avoid disrupting any activities Lane might have planned – or to awaken them, assuming things had progressed that far.

He'd left Corky Girls not long after eleven, knew it was too soon to go back, but too dangerous to kill time by cruising around town. Besides which a tour of Chiloquin would probably consume no more than five or ten minutes. He eventually decided to go back out the same way he'd come in, find a spot where he could pull off the highway for an hour or two, maybe listen to the radio or gaze up at the stars. He had passed the ammo plant, its rows of parking spaces not yet filled with cars whose owners would be working graveyard, drove as far as the Sprague River before deciding it was too close to the ranch.

He made a tight U-turn, wondered if Lane could hear the faint screeching of the Mustang's tires from so far away, finally pulled into an unpaved turnout a mile or so east of the ammo plant where its lights could be seen glowing over the pines like Oz over the poppies.

For a while Gabriel mulled over Two Bears' comment, regretted not staying to talk with the stocky Maqlaq and his friends, then remembered the feeling of being slowly strangled that sent him running for the exit. And which brought him to Buddy's revelation.

If Fiske was *that* interested in keeping tabs on him, *that* worried about what Gabriel was doing in Chiloquin, maybe he should just save everyone the trouble and move on. He could go back to the ranch, sneak in the house to retrieve his duffle bag, then drive the Mustang back to 97 and leave it on the shoulder just beyond the onramp. Fiske or Buddy or Chino would find it by morning, and return it to Lane before swing shift. And by then he'd be trading stories with his second or third trucker.

He would recover his Bible and his mementos eventually. He could live without them for another week or two – *couldn't he?* – and meanwhile he'd get himself out of Fiske's cross-hairs.

From past experience, he knew Oregon had plenty of places where he could find work. The central part of the state, only two or three hours further up 97, was one of the fastest-growing regions in the entire Northwest. There was a wonderful little town by the name of "Sisters" he'd heard about when he was living for a time in Washington. He could thumb his way there and probably be pounding nails again before Vincent returned to Chiloquin. He'd rent a mailbox at one of those postal centers where you could remain anonymous, call the ammo plant and ask Halvorsen to send his Bible C.O.D. And even if it came back without any cash inside, it would be worth getting out from under the noose hovering over his head.

Gabriel pondered his options a few minutes longer, finally turned the ignition key to *Accessories* so he could tune in some music. The original radio was still in the dash, and therefore without an FM band; but AM was more likely to get reception out here anyway.

He punched its row of black-plastic pre-sets in slow succession, nodded approvingly at Lane's choice of classic rock stations. To his surprise, however, the fifth button pulled in the voice of some smug-sounding preacher who was haranguing his radio audience with "more irrefutable proof" that the end of the world was at hand. *Funny,* Gabriel thought, *a Bible-thumper right there alongside the golden oldies.*

At exactly 11:33 the preacher took a break from his harangue to introduce "The End Times News." Gabriel promptly switched off the radio and turned on the engine. Assuming Lane had left the front door open for him, he could slip in as planned and be asleep on the sofa in two minutes. Or maybe less; it had been another long day, and the glow from the half glass of beer he'd downed before escaping the tavern had begun to make his eyelids heavy. Didn't take much anymore.

His initial clue that something wasn't right came not from inside Lane's house but from the barn out back. Gabriel could hear the colt and its mother rustling in their stalls, baying nervously as if a coyote were skulking nearby. He'd started walking up the drive alongside the house, intending only to look in on the horses, when he heard muffled laughter from a second-story window. It galled him to think Lane and her client were still up this late. He didn't relish the prospect of listening to their bedroom behavior while he drifted off to sleep, then reassured himself he wouldn't be awake for long.

And then he was *wide* awake.

Suddenly, beneath the laughter he could hear Lane's protests, growing from urgent to desperate. He debated whether to intervene for all of two heartbeats, bolted for the front door but hesitated on the porch when the laughter seemed to abate and the protests softened into what might have been the moans of lovemaking.

Which is when a wail ripped outside like a banshee – a horrific, wounded-animal sound, ear-splitting not so much in volume as in its raw, utter helplessness.

Gabriel was through the door and up the stairs in a moment

somehow outside of time, as if Lane's scream had emerged simultaneously with his arrival in the room. He reached down with no thought as to where he might find a hold, latched onto Doyle's shoulder with one hand, his buttocks with the other, and yanked upward with every ounce of his strength.

Doyle was in the air before Gabriel knew what he'd done, sailing in a head-first back flip into the antique mirror above Lane's dresser. The mirror may have absorbed the impact and kept him from going through the lath-and-plaster, but the shattered glass also ripped a gash in the back of Doyle's head that was already spewing blood by the time he'd landed on the oak-plank floor.

For a second or two Gabriel gawked at the sight, astonished at how Doyle could remain bleeding and unconscious when he'd just laid hands on him, realized with a sudden start that the injury had occurred only *after* he'd sent him flying. He shook it off, spun to look at Lane.

She was sitting up now, face darkening with broken blood-vessels and twisted in agony; but her screams had turned into a softer, almost relieved, sobbing. Gabriel quickly gathered up her comforter from the footboard, doubled it over as a precaution before climbing onto the bed. Coming from behind, he wrapped the thick cotton around Lane's shoulders, both to cover her nakedness and protect himself, at the same time taking her fully into his arms. Even through the heavy insulation he could feel her trembling, embraced her all the more tightly.

"I'm sorry, Lane. I should never have left—"

"*Gabriel—?*"

She stopped sobbing, lifted her chin seemed genuinely surprised. He loosened his hold just enough to lean around her, see the side of her face.

"Who'd you think?"

She sniffled, breathed out. He could feel her begin to relax.

"You, at first. But then you hugged me, so I thought it must be Buddy."

Her shoulders lurched with a dry, soundless laugh. Gabriel leaned back, unwrapped his arms completely now, the comforter slipping down around Lane's upper arms like a low-slung bodice.

Her bruises were clearly growing a deeper red, but hadn't yet turned purple. He waited a few more moments before asking.

"So Buddy's another—"

And just as quickly he stopped himself. No, he'd learned that lesson already; it was none of his business. In fact, *none of this* was his business. Still, he found himself wondering what might have happened if he'd stayed away another five minutes, or fifteen minutes, or if he'd decided not to come back at all. Trouble was, his inability to pay Lane is what had made her foolhardy enough to accept Doyle's company. Which meant it *was* his—

"No, he's not," Lane was saying, without any rancor for once, in reply to the question he'd implied without asking. "He's come by a few times over the last couple of weeks, late at night or just before sunrise, to check on Fabian and Tina... so quiet I don't know he's been here 'til I find new hay in the stalls, or a fresh bucket of his apple mash."

Gabriel said nothing, appreciated the fact that she hadn't jumped on him, hoped she'd appreciated the fact that he'd withdrawn his query.

"What did you do to Doyle?"

Gabriel blinked, was mildly surprised he hadn't given a passing thought to the other man since catapulting him into the wall. He turned, winced at the small pool glistening on the floor beneath Doyle's head, was reassured to see his chest slowly rising and falling. He hadn't killed him at least – though even *that* wouldn't matter since so little time had elapsed.

"Looks like the back of his head turned your mirror into a jigsaw puzzle," Gabriel said, leaving out both the blood and Doyle's unconsciousness. "I'll pay for it when I get my Bible back."

"Don't worry about it. Haven't had much use for it lately."

She tried to put on a smile. And once again Gabriel swore at his situation. Events had done nothing but go steadily downhill from the moment the buck had raised its rack into Vincent's headlights.

Or maybe not.

"Guess I'd better send your houseguest on his way," he said, suddenly clambering from the bed.

"You kidding? When Doyle wakes up he's gonna be too drunk to see past his steering wheel."

"Oh I don't know. Some guys can hold their booze better than others." Gabriel knelt beside Doyle, reached under his neck, felt nothing out of alignment, placed a hand on the dry side of his head so he wouldn't bloody himself. "How many beers 'e have, anyway?"

"Four... in less than an hour."

"That's all? Hell, I've seen guys knock back twice as much and it didn't phase 'em. You remember the roofer I told you about?"

She did. She was also curious as to why Gabriel seemed to be moving from one side of Doyle to the other, voice quavering the tiniest amount as if he were straining over him, almost like a paramedic at work.

"Gabe—what *are* you doing?"

Gabe. He loved it. So much better than the *Ralph* or *Rafer* that once substituted for his first name.

"Just trying to wake him up, make sure I didn't hurt him too bad."

"*Did* you—?"

She swung her feet over the edge of the bed on the opposite side, turned as if to glance back over her shoulder, expression filled with more concern than Gabriel expected. He could see her bruises darkening even more. Especially the one on her jaw. *Good.*

Before he could formulate a reply, Doyle's eyes flashed open. He blinked once, twice, pushed himself up on one elbow, then reached back to his right ear with his free hand to feel the warm stickiness. Drawing back his hand, he went wide-eyed at the sight of his own blood, was up on his feet in an instant, immediately slipped in the puddle where his head had lain but managed to catch himself on the dresser just before he went down again.

"What the hell you *do* to me—?"

Gabriel had to force himself to remain serious. Doyle pushed himself off the dresser, stood there buck naked, shrunken with fear in more ways than one, hair spiked from the blood already thickening like styling gel.

"The real question," Gabriel said, "is what the hell *you* were doing when I came in."

Doyle blinked once more, looked away to see Lane sitting on the other side of her bed, face turned just enough for him to see the evidence on her jawline, her comforter lowered on one shoulder to reveal still another patch of deep magenta. His eyes widened again as his short-term memory clicked in, sobering him instantly – if he wasn't already.

"Jesus Christ... *Lane!* I don't know what got—"

He stopped, looked at her almost penitently. She said nothing. Lifting his bloodied hand to his forehead, he poked at his scalp, felt for the source of the flow, finally turned back to Gabriel with an uncomprehending look.

"Hit your head on the mirror when we got into a fight," Gabriel said, stretching the facts; but who could dispute him? "Afraid *that'll* cost you, too."

Doyle continued to scratch his head, unable to recollect their encounter, looked back at Lane. That one he *could.*

"How much money you got?" Gabriel asked.

"Money—?" Another uncomprehending look. "Maybe twenty, thirty bucks. I don't know—my pants are downstairs."

His words suddenly reminded him of his nakedness. He couldn't recall where he'd flung his undershorts, scanned the room in vain, finally spotted Lane's terrycloth robe hanging on the back of the bedroom door and started toward it.

Gabriel stepped in front of him, his left boot coming down just behind where Lane's torn panties had landed on the floor. Doyle halted, looked down with another penitent scowl, no doubt assuming Gabriel had done it on purpose, looked back up.

"I meant," Gabriel said, eyes locking with Doyle's, "in your bank account."

"What?"

"How much in the *bank,* not your billfold."

Doyle hesitated, appeared to be considering whether he could take this party crasher, cousin or not, if he was still in the mood to fight. Then, abruptly, he lifted a hand to his scalp again, vaguely remembering flying through the air before he blacked out.

"About eighteen hundred bucks. Took me a year to save up that much, after I took everything out for the down payment on my truck."

"Well, you can give it all to Lane, or you can spend it on an attorney."

Long pause. "Wait—you're gonna *sue* me?"

"Lane is. For attempted rape."

"Bullshit. She was *asking*—" He stopped as Lane turned partway around, thought better of it. Lane probably wouldn't say anything if it was just her word against his. But her cousin had seen it all, had heard her screaming beneath him. Not to mention the bruises.

Maybe he'd try another angle.

"She'll need a lawyer, too. Thing is, she doesn't have the money to hire one. And from what I heard, neither do you."

Gabriel leveled a confident gaze. "Lane, how much money do I have hidden away in my Bible?"

She recalled their earlier conversation, nodded. "Three thousand dollars. Maybe more."

Her voice seemed thin, tired; but there was an edge to it. Doyle realized she wasn't going to roll over this time.

"You'll be at the town meeting tomorrow, right?" Gabriel asked.

The other man squinted, was at least smart enough to figure out what Gabriel was proposing.

"There's a word for this."

"Extortion?—no way. *Getting off easy*, that's how I'd put it." Gabriel reached down for the ripped panties, straightened, examined it like a piece of evidence. "Unless Lane would rather have you do time for this."

He paused as if awaiting Lane's response. Doyle started to turn, couldn't look at her, turned back, couldn't meet Gabriel's eyes either.

"Bring it tomorrow. *All* of it—in cash. You don't, I take her to the hospital right after the meeting. They'll probably want their own pictures of all the bruises, in addition to the ones I'll be taking tonight on my cell phone." It wouldn't matter that he didn't own one; the threat was enough. "And then there's that test... you know, the one they give rape victims? Or do you wanna risk they won't find anything when they take samples?"

Doyle paused as if trying to remember whether he ever did find her sweet spot, stole a glance at the bruises that would make a rape test only icing on the cake, finally slouched with defeat.

"We done now?"

Then, without waiting for an answer, he started for the door, knocking into Gabriel's shoulder as he passed. It was a collision Gabriel would have judiciously avoided had he not already touched him. Instead, he turned to watch Doyle walk out, knew full well he would go home and wash his hair, would find no sign of any gash, would ponder where all the blood had come from and maybe even regret there were no wounds of his own in case he might want to file counter-charges. Gabriel could only speculate what other physical ailments he may have inadvertently healed, hoped none of it would come back to haunt him.

He decided to follow Doyle down the stairs, stopped to lean against the anchor post, watching in silence while Doyle snatched up the clothes he'd peeled off earlier, then quickly pulled on his jeans. After stuffing his socks in a back pocket, he slipped on his Nike's without bothering to tie them, took more care with his NRA baseball cap, finally slung his plaid shirt over one shoulder and headed for the front door.

As Doyle trudged past the Indian basket, he hesitated, bent long enough to look into it with a begrudging frown. Gabriel thought for a moment he might reach in and snatch the eighty dollars he'd left there, took a step after him.

"You wanna leave the other thirty you still got in your pocket, right?—so Lane can buy herself a new mirror...?"

The other man glanced up sharply. "For eighteen hundred bucks Laney can buy all the new mirrors she wants. Maybe she still thinks she'll have a need for 'em someday."

He started for the door again. Gabriel took several more strides after him, considered throwing him bodily out of the house after so coarse a comment, decided it wasn't worth his energy. Doyle, meanwhile, yanked the door open, turned one last time to glare at Gabriel, found him staring back with a look he couldn't read: Contempt? Satisfaction? *Pity?*

"You got somethin' else to say to me?"

Gabriel shrugged, said the first thing that came to mind. "You gonna be okay, driving yourself home?"

"Am I too drunk?—that what you're sayin'?" And then he gave an ironic laugh, shook his head and looked back at Gabriel as if they were still pals, having just finished with another male-bonding ritual a la *Fight Club*.

"Crazy thing is, I'm sober as a cue ball. Hell, I feel better'n I have in months." He laughed again. "Just hafta pee really bad."

He was in his shiny red pickup ten seconds later – without stopping to relieve himself – and heading into the curve where the Mustang was parked after a few more. Gabriel waited until his lights faded behind a trail of dust, quietly closed the front door, turned back, shocked to find Lane standing on the bottom stair, comforter still wrapped around her.

"Lane!—you shouldn't be—"

"I didn't have a chance to thank you yet," she said sheepishly. "That was really nice, what you did. Or..." She wagged her head. "...I don't know if *nice* is the right word. Heroic, maybe?"

She attempted a smile. Gabriel smiled back, stuck his hands in his pockets.

"I figured if I couldn't pay you right away, least I could do was rope somebody else into it."

"No, I mean coming back when you did, pulling Doyle off me like that. Things could've been... much worse."

"For him, too. I didn't realize I could throw anybody that far."

She brightened. "Yeah—and could you believe how fast he snapped out of it?—drunk as he was, even after hitting his head on the mirror?"

Gabriel took her last comment as a subtle hint, even if she didn't mean it that way.

"Right. I better go back and clean up the mess. There's glass all over your..."

His words quickly trailed off when Lane stepped off the bottom stair and doubled over, face contorting as the pain of what had happened finally, abruptly sank in. The comforter fell open on one side as her body tightened, right hand reflexively clutching the area just above her pubic bone. *Had* Doyle penetrated her?

"You really shouldn't be down here." He hurried over, grabbed the quilted padding to fold around her once more. "But since you *are*, let's go get you looked at. There must be some clinic or emergency room—"

"No, no—I'll be okay." She released a shaky breath, her hunched shoulders straightening, the delayed reaction subsiding. "I prob'ly shouldn't tell you, but this isn't the first time."

"You mean Doyle's done—"

"Not just Doyle." She shivered, pulled the comforter to her chin. "I *do* need to stop this, this... whatever I've been pretending it isn't. Besides, I keep thinking I'm Richard's age, and I'm not." She frowned as if regretting that last thought, quickly moved on. "You know, I really *could* make this old house into a bed-and-breakfast. That's what would make me happy. And I mean it, Gabriel..." She looked up, almost met his eyes. "...I *am* grateful for what you did tonight."

Gabriel backed away, winced at the irony. "You should've kicked me out when you had the chance. All this is my fault."

"Oh, stop it." She casually waved aside his assumed guilt, turned for the hall. "I'll make you a deal. All is forgiven if you'll run me a nice, hot bath. You saw the cast-iron tub in the bathroom down here, right?" She was walking ahead now, gingerly, the incident with Doyle already behind her even if its after-effects weren't. "My dad brought it down from upstairs ten years ago when he decided these creaky old floors might be getting too old to support the weight."

Halfway down the hall she stopped, turned back.

"And when you go back up there to pick up the glass?—take one of the hand towels from my bathroom and make sure you clean up all the blood."

"Blood? What makes you think—?"

She tossed a look to remind him who he was dealing with, then resumed her mini-steps down the hall.

"I heard it dripping when Doyle started to get up. Not to mention he practically fell on his ass when he slipped in it. Some things you don't need eyes to see."

As if he didn't know.

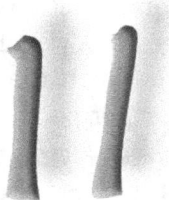

If he'd thought the previous day had been eventful, it was the following morning that turned his world upside down. Gabriel was convinced his life had shifted in some fundamental way, that he'd been in some sense reborn. And at least in respect to Lane, he *had* been.

He'd drawn her bath the night before, just as she'd asked. Leaving him to turn on the hot water valve and clear the pipes of the cold, she'd gone down the hall to search the fridge for another Guinness – "to see if Doyle missed one" was how she put it. Maybe the brew would help numb the inner pain while the bath soothed the outer.

The antique tub was just beginning to fill by the time Lane came back. She told him she would take over from there, that he could go upstairs and clean up the rest of the wreckage, then take a shower in her bathroom if he liked.

She let the comforter fall to her feet even before he was out of the room. As he started to close the door, she called out for him to leave it partway open. Her father had never installed an exhaust fan, she groused, and the room was already thick with steam – though not enough to hide *her*, Gabriel discovered, and not before he'd seen enough to confirm that her body was as lithe and alluring as any of the more youthful ones he'd been privy to.

Fleeing upstairs, he picked up the shards of her mirror first, had to push Lane's dresser away from the wall to collect some of the smaller pieces, then dumped them all into a plastic wastebasket he found in the second bedroom. Removing the broken frame from the wall, he found the hand-carved oak unsalvageable, broke the only intact corner so these pieces, too, would fit into the wastebasket.

Cleaning up the blood was more of a challenge. Reluctant to use one of Lane's towels despite her permission, he poked around for something he could throw out afterwards, searching the cabinet over the toilet and the hallway linen closet for an old dust cloth or even a box of sanitary pads.

He finally sopped up the pool of blood with a dampened washrag – along with a few other drops and smears he hadn't noticed before – making several trips to the bathroom sink in the process. When the terrycloth fabric wouldn't come clean under the faucet, he took it into the shower with him, soaping down both himself and the blood-stained rag. Then, satisfied he'd done the best he could, he hung it over the curtain rod to dry.

Stepping from the tiny shower stall, he grabbed one of two bath towels hanging nearby, remembered as he dried himself that his undershorts were still in his duffle bag. Last time he saw it, the bag was downstairs near the sofa. He quickly wrapped the towel around his waist, went to the top of the stairs to listen for Lane.

She was happily humming another Beatles tune – *Here, There, and Everywhere* – the melody wafting up through the open bathroom door along with an occasional wisp of steam. He listened to the unintended concert for perhaps a minute, awed once more by how quickly she could shift moods, until he heard the plug pop and the water begin to drain.

He hurried down to the living room, spotted his duffle bag on the piano bench and pulled out a pair of fresh boxers. Then, dropping the towel, he stooped over to slip them on, almost immediately noticed Lane out of the corner of his eye. She was rounding the stairs from the hall, peering curiously in his direction. Gabriel stiffened, lifted his shorts in a less than successful attempt to cover himself, suddenly realized how foolish it was.

"Caught you starkers, didn't I?" Lane halted, raised her eyebrows as if she could see him in all his glory, then shook her head with pretended sadness. "One more reason to shake a fist at my fate."

Gabriel dropped his boxers, poked his feet through.

"You feeling any better?"

"Maybe a little, thanks." She squinted with concern. "But I was just thinking how exhausted you must be."

After what she'd been through, she was thinking of *him?*

"Yeah, I'm pretty beat. Prob'ly be asleep in about ten seconds once I'm prone." He pointed up the stairs, realized that too was foolish. "I, uh, think I saw an extra blanket and pillow up in your linen closet. If it's okay, I'll go grab 'em before I flake out on the sofa."

"Sorry. Already taken."

"What?—the blanket or the pillow?"

"The sofa. That's where I'm sleeping tonight."

A scowl. "Why?"

She shrugged, waited for a few more seconds as though hoping he might figure it out himself. Then again, maybe it wasn't something a man would understand.

"I'd rather not be in my own bed tonight, that's all."

Gabriel nodded, absently reached down to pick up his bath towel, straightened with another idea. "What about the second bedroom?"

"Sure, be my guest. Or you can use mine. No reason why it should—"

"No, I mean you. *You* could sleep in the other bedroom. You don't belong down here on the sofa, not in your own house."

"I'd just rather not, Gabriel. Besides, I might get... I don't know— restless, and this way I won't bother you if I get up. Might even decide to take another bath. I'll just be better if I'm down here tonight, okay?"

"Okay," he replied after another moment or two. And that's the way they left it... he thought.

The sun was already bright in Lane's bedroom when he began to awaken. He had the distinct impression he'd slept like a log, that he hadn't moved an inch since he'd pulled up the covers, turned on his side and let his lids go south.

There was just one difference.

It took him several seconds to become aware of it, and several more before he turned his head, slowly, just enough to see. But there, draped over his bare shoulder, was Lane's forearm, her wrist extended perhaps two inches beyond his biceps, hand limp, finger-tips almost touching his chest each time he drew in a breath.

Not that her fingertips concerned him when the full weight of her arm was pressing into his own flesh. And who knew how much more she'd touched him in the middle of the night, while he slept just as soundly as when Vincent blew the tire.

But now Lane would awaken, her eyesight restored. And if past experience was any indication, she would gasp the moment her lids parted, begin screaming like a shill at a Benny Hinn crusade. At first she'd be too engrossed in the reality of her healing to wonder how it might have happened, and unlikely to connect Gabriel with the event – at least until later. After all, the telltale surge which sometimes accompanied the realignment of matter with spirit didn't *always* happen. It was the brief, unintentional touches that gave him away, the ones that snapped like electricity arcing across a bad connection. But if Lane had crawled into bed, pressed a hand or other body part firmly against him, even by accident, she probably hadn't felt a thing.

On the other hand, unless her eyes were shut tight at the time, she should have *seen* something. She no longer drew the window blinds; there was no need to keep out the sunlight, and as isolated as her ranch was, no concern over somebody peeping through her windows.

When he'd turned off the lamp last night, Gabriel could see the moon shining brightly over the barn, casting its silvery glow onto the wall where the shattered mirror had hung. Fact was, Lane's bedroom was brighter at night than the inside of her barn was during the day. He swore at himself now for being too tired to get up and pull down the shade.

Then again, maybe the moon had set by the time she'd finally come upstairs. A moonless night in the back woods of Oregon could be black as the bottom of Crater Lake. Maybe there was nothing to see, even if she *could've* seen it.

He began to plan his escape. Assuming Lane had been unable to sleep – had taken another bath, perhaps – maybe she was as exhausted as *he* was by the time she'd crawled in with him. If he was careful, he might be able to extract himself without rousing her, roll from under her arm and slip out of bed. He could sneak downstairs, put on his clothes there and quietly let himself out the back door.

Fortunately, the Mustang was still parked fifty yards up the drive. He could probably start the engine and drive off before she awoke. But he'd need to find a route to the freeway that didn't pass through Chiloquin. Lane mentioned a back way to Klamath Falls; and even if he had to go that far south, he could get back on 97, then head north as far as the Indian casino. He would leave it parked in the lot and hitch a ride with one of the truckers who stopped for a bathroom break and a few pulls on the quarter slots. Her car might not be as easy to find there, but he could always make an anonymous call to the Chiloquin Hilton from wherever he ended up that night. After all, he still had the four bucks he came to town with yesterday. He could afford one long-distance call.

He experimented with a few modest rolls of his shoulder to see if they disturbed Lane in any way. Then he lay still again, listened to her slow, steady respirations, felt the warmth of her body behind him but no apparent reaction. He took a breath, held it, made the first concerted attempt.

He slowly worked his shoulder forward far enough for her hand to slip down his back and fall gently onto the mattress. It was when he tried to pull his hips away that she seemed to catch her breath, but only for a few moments. He waited for her respiration to normalize, silently counted from one to a hundred just to be safe, started to inch away once more.

"Is it really so—"

Gabriel jerked at the sound of her voice, which in turn stopped Lane mid-sentence. She took another breath, started over, more softly this time.

"Is it really so bad, my touching you?" She lifted the hand that hand fallen, replaced it on his shoulder before going on, almost mockingly. "I was hoping, you know—maybe if I got in bed next to you when you were asleep, you might actually wake up and discover you could live through it."

He tried to scoot further away. She promptly reached around his chest, pulled herself to him again, more tightly now. Gabriel could feel her breasts pressing hard against his shoulder blades, her leg now sliding over his thigh to keep him pinned.

"C'mon, Gabe—it's just skin." A beat. "Okay, maybe not *just* skin. Pretty miraculous stuff, when you think about it. Has some amazing qualities when certain people happen to rub theirs together."

She knew!

Gabriel was out of bed and on his feet in two seconds, swirling to look back at her...

...And utterly shocked to see her casually pushing herself up on one elbow, staring toward him in the slightly off-target way she had the day before.

He froze, blinked, finally moved his head slightly to the right, then left, then did it again. Her eyes remained fixed, unmoving.

"Lane... look at me!"

She corrected the direction of her gaze, drew a shallow gasp from Gabriel as her eyes seemed to meet his, then slipped off the mark once more.

Still refusing to believe, he stepped to the end of the bed and leaned onto it with one hand, waved the other in front of Lane's face like a magician making sure his assistant's blindfold was on tight.

"Tell me what you see."

"Tell you... What—?" She sat up stiffly now, shook her head as if Gabriel must've lost a few neurons during the night, then shrugged her willingness to humor him. "Okay. I see two fingers... uh, make that *three*." Another shrug. "Gabriel, what in God's name are you doing?"

He was visibly shaking now. This was too good to be true, more than he could ask for, all those other clichés combined. He tried to think back: Had he done something to prevent the healing from taking place just this once? Was it only a fluke? – some unknown quirk in the mechanics of this power that possessed him?

It was entirely possible Lane hadn't been healed – for whatever reason – but her sight *would* be restored if he touched her again. On the other hand, maybe he'd lost the power altogether. He would never know unless—

"Gabriel...?"

"Lane, stay there for a moment. Don't move."

"What?—why?"

"*Don't move.*"

He hurried around the bed, sat on the edge, brought up one leg so he and Lane were sitting astride each other, only inches apart, thighs parallel, bodies facing in opposite directions.

"Now... turn toward me."

"You *do* realize you're scaring the shit out of me, don't you?"

"Just your head. Please, Lane—I need you to do this."

She huffed, finally complied. He drew in a breath to steady himself, lifted both hands, left them hovering over her face, one on either side, for several more seconds. Then, exhaling deliberately, he took her face in his hands, held it gently while she continued to stare straight ahead. In a few more moments she blinked – placidly, almost in slow motion – then seemed to look toward him from the corners of her eyes, questioningly, not quite able to lock onto his gaze.

He took another breath, moved his thumbs off her cheekbones, ran them along the inside of her nose, up and over the ridge of her eyebrows, then, ever so delicately, down across her eyelids as she obediently closed them.

Gabriel could feel the supple roundness of her eyes under the moist layers of skin, then, drawing his thumbs back toward her nose, stopped in the hollows above her tear ducts, delighted at how the sides of his thumbs fit almost perfectly. He left them there for a few moments longer, then brought them again to her cheekbones, her face still cupped in his palms, eyes still closed.

"Okay. I need to hear you say this, Lane," Gabriel said, forcing himself to remain calm. "I want you to open your eyes now and tell me what you see."

She kept them closed, brow knitting in thought, then nodded after several more seconds as though she'd finally gotten the point, finally understood what this mysterious exercise had been about. Her lids parted, opened fully, eyes focusing just above his line of sight.

"I see a man... who is no longer afraid to touch... and *be* touched."

Gabriel frowned for only a moment, then nodded, almost laughed out loud. Yes, *yes!* That was it! Lane's explanation for his behavior was far better than any he might've cooked up if he'd spent all morning at it! He gently dropped his forehead against hers, smiling, let his hands slip to her shoulders, then slide back up the nape of her neck.

And then he kissed her.

It was a lilting, lingering kiss, a kiss of thanksgiving, a kiss meant only for Lane yet also transcending her, that conveyed gratitude for what she'd done, but also for the sublime, redemptive power within her that had now, through the serendipity or grace or sheer luck that brought him to her bed, cast off his chains.

It was a kiss that began as a sacrament, then suddenly turned passionate.

For all at once Lane was up on her knees, pressing her mouth and her body against him as if Thanksgiving was long gone and church bells were pealing Easter Sunday's good news. Gabriel's tender feelings were swept aside, replaced with a physical yearning that took only moments to catch up with hers – until he remembered what she apparently had forgotten.

He threaded his fingers through her hair, pulled back hard, their mouths coming apart like suction cups, the resulting *pop* bringing a hearty laugh from Lane even though she was clearly unhappy he'd stopped.

"Wait—wait a second, " he panted. "We need to think about this."

"What's to think about?" She was panting, too. And grinning impishly.

"Well, for one thing…"

He released his grip, started to get up. She clutched him all the more tightly, but he managed to swing both feet onto the floor. She quickly lassoed him from behind, kissed him playfully on the back of his neck.

"For one thing, *what—?*"

"Aren't you forgetting about last night?"

He turned his head halfway around to look at her. She leaned around him, planted another wet one slightly off target on the side of his mouth.

"Yes. Matter of fact, I *am*. Last night never happened. There's only *now*, now."

She was as animated as he'd ever seen her. And utterly, beautifully naked. He finally grabbed her hands, pulled her arms up and over his head, twisted away so he could stand.

"I'm sorry to be the one to remind you, but you were practically raped last night. No, you *were* being raped when I just happened to drop in." He shook his head, waited as she allowed herself to grow serious. "Jesus, Laney. You could hardly move, you were in so much pain. There's no way I can… that I would…"

He stopped, shrugged. Her smile came back, almost coquettishly.

"What makes you think you would've gotten that far?"

Gabriel peered down as she knelt at the edge of the bed, watched her breasts rise and fall as she waited breathlessly, face tilted upward at him, aglow with the morning's radiance.

"Oh, believe me. I definitely would've gotten that far."

"So what are you waiting for?"

He took a step back, his disbelief now bordering on disapproval. She sensed it, nodded.

"It's okay, Gabriel. I'm fine down there… *and* up here…" She raised a hand, drew the backs of her fingers along her jawline. "I don't know—maybe it was the warm baths… but I can't even feel where Doyle hit me. *Really*—like it never happened."

Gabriel reached up to his own jaw, mouth agape. He hadn't even thought to look until now, hadn't noticed because there was nothing *to* notice. Her bruises were gone, as if it truly *hadn't* happened. Lane continued to wait for some response, heard none.

"Look, I know it's hard for you to accept. I couldn't believe it myself. I was feeling a little better after the second bath, and that's when I decided to come upstairs and get in bed with you."

She turned away, recalling what had happened while he was asleep, putting it into words for the first time, no doubt imagining how it must sound to someone else.

"After laying here for a few minutes, just listening to you breathe... this'll prob'ly gross you out, I know... I got up again and went into the bathroom and—" She blushed in spite of herself. "—I *felt* myself, all the way up inside, and out. And then my face. And it didn't hurt at all. Nothing." She glanced up again with an urgent look. "I felt... I feel great, Gabriel. So would you just get back in bed, please? It's a little chilly out here, and if I've got you figured right—" Another grin. "—you prob'ly have some serious catching up to do."

She had the last part right. But not all of it. In fact, Gabriel was having difficulty figuring it out himself. And if *he* was right, maybe this *was* too good to be true.

It would take only a few minutes, he'd said, and then he'd be back. Ignoring the petulant look she sent his way, Gabriel lifted her blanket along with the comforter she'd brought up last night, waited until she reluctantly slipped her legs underneath and lay back down, then drew the bedding around her.

"But why?—where are you going?"

"It's just... there's something I need to do first, okay?"

He left without further explanation, found his shoes, shirt and pants in a heap beside the shower stall, took them downstairs and into the kitchen before stopping to put them on. Then he crossed the room and slipped out the back door, closed the screen as quietly as he could in hopes Lane wouldn't be able to trace his route.

All of which proved futile before he'd even made it to the barn. The horses sensed his presence as soon as he stepped outside, began moving in their stalls, the colt releasing a high-pitched whinny when Gabriel came inside and started toward his mother. Once again it took a good minute for Gabriel's eyes to adjust, but at least he knew the general layout now. By the time he stopped beside the gate to Tina's stall, he could see the mare struggling to get up from where she'd been resting, trying to avoid putting any weight on her bandaged left leg, and succeeding at neither.

"Whoa, girl—stay there," he said as if she could understand.

He entered the stall, remembered the calming sound Lane had made and attempted to duplicate it, but ended up making more of a hissing noise. Despite that – and despite the fearful flashing of her eyes – the horse settled back onto the hay-strewn floor, her energy already spent, watching warily as Gabriel stepped over and knelt beside her.

He began to hum softly, as he had with the buck the previous day, held out his right hand, palm up, to show that he meant no harm. In the neighboring stall, the colt whinnied again, now clearly jealous of the attention his mother was getting and he *wasn't*. Gabriel turned to shush the colt like a fussy child, drew about the same response, felt stupid and turned back to the mare.

Gabriel knew the risk he was taking, but this was the only way he could be certain. For reasons he couldn't fathom, his touch hadn't healed Lane of her blindness, yet the bruises from Doyle's attack had completely disappeared. Maybe it *was* the warm water – he hoped it was – and she had recovered by purely natural means. Whatever the case, either his touch still had power, or it didn't. The greater risk was not knowing.

He hated himself for hoping, *praying*, the horse would remain lame, that her shattered foreleg would remain shattered and she'd inevitably weaken and die. But there it was, ugly and shameful, nevertheless:

Please God, don't let the mare be healed.

He hesitated with second thoughts, just as he had before he took Lane's face in his hands, finally pressed a palm firmly against Tina's upper leg, above the splint. Then, slowly, he moved the hand to her shoulder and across her flank. For several glorious seconds the mare lay absolutely still, only her ribcage moving up and down beneath Gabriel's hand, slowing as he held it there, her eyes seeming to glaze over as if, far from being healed, she might expire from his touch.

And then, without warning, she pushed herself up, front legs thumping forward onto the hay-strewn floor, hindquarters rising in a clattering of hooves that narrowly missed Gabriel before he could scramble out of the way. The colt whinnied once more, the mare snorting with pent-up energy, side-stepping and prancing like a race-horse at the starting gate.

The gate!

Gabriel spun, lunged to shut it, but Tina was already between the posts, her haunch knocking him aside as she pushed out and wheeled for the barn door. And then, just as quickly, she drew up, scuffling to a noisy halt.

Lane appeared in the opening, standing on the cold ground in her bare feet, terrycloth robe slung around her but unbelted at the waist, looking just as surprised to hear Tina's hoof beats as the mare was to see Lane blocking her way.

"What are you—! What's going on... Gabriel?"

She was facing the stall where he was just now pulling himself up on the railing, both of them blissfully unaware she'd nearly been trampled by her own horse.

"Gabriel!"

He had to invent something fast, but found his heart in his throat. He couldn't speak, didn't know what to say. Didn't know what was going on any more than she did.

His powers were still intact, that much was certain. Tina had stopped in her tracks, but she continued to fidget like a high-strung thoroughbred, only the splint and Lane's presence keeping her from breaking outside and into a full, exuberant gallop.

Lane turned her attention to the mare, took a few steps toward the sound of her flaring nostrils, reached past her muzzle. She pressed her hand against the mare's neck, ran it down her shoul-der, chest, upper leg, knee. The splint was still in place, though not as securely; but she also felt Tina's full weight on her foreleg, and her impatience to begin using it.

"Gabriel...?"

By the sound of her voice, he wasn't sure Lane was still de-manding an explanation, or she'd found one. But now he'd had time to compose one himself, even if only for Lane's sake. He sighed, stepped out from the stall.

"I'm as shocked as you are," he began. "I came outside because I had to get some air. You know—*think*. What happened this morning, Lane?—this was big for me. Huge."

It was also true. Whether Lane was actually listening wasn't so clear. She was still busy with Tina's leg, shaking her head in quiet disbelief.

"I heard them making noises, thought something might be wrong, so I came in. After I opened the gate, she just pushed out past me."

True again, Gabriel thought, just highly edited. He could see the doubt clouding Lane's face as he approached. Or maybe it was fear.

"But her leg, it couldn't have mended by itself, not the way it was shattered. No way Tina should be up like this. She must've gone numb to the pain after all this time. Her bones'll break through the skin and she'll bleed to death!"

"Or maybe Buddy was wrong."

Lane turned toward his voice now, glaring almost as though he'd spoken blasphemy, but couldn't hide her elation at the prospect it might be true. In fact it was looking more and more that way. She turned back, slipped her fingers beneath the bindings as far as they would go, could feel nothing amiss; and more importantly, Tina hadn't flinched.

"How could this happen?"

"No clue. But maybe we should stop asking questions and just let it be."

Gabriel stopped a few paces away, could see her eyes darting in thought. Suddenly she rose, hurried back to the barn door and closed it, then stepped over to a pegboard rack mounted to the posts nearby. Hanging from the pegs was an assortment of hand tools and garden implements. Lane felt for the edge of the board, moved her hand toward the center as if she'd memorized the location of each one, came down almost directly over a pair of tin snips. She lifted it off the peg, stepped back to where the mare was obediently, if anxiously, waiting.

"I must be crazy," she whispered. Then, louder: "Buddy said

she wouldn't last another week or two, anyway. So if she goes down again—" She glanced up briefly as Gabriel came around to see what she was doing. "—I'll get the rifle and it'll be your job to put her out of her misery."

Carefully aligning the tin snips alongside one of the slats Buddy had fashioned, Lane began cutting through the buckskin binding, the leather falling off in small loops as she guided the blades downward. Before she could reach Tina's fetlock, the mare was already beginning to prance again, rear hooves dancing in the dirt, her lungs filling and steaming out with increasing urgency. Across the barn, the colt mirrored his mother's excitement, circling his stall and crying to be let out.

The slat on the inside of the mare's leg was the first to fall off. She felt it come loose, instantly pulled back from Lane, side-stepped Gabriel and broke for the other end of the barn, the remaining half of the splint flying off in mid-gallop. It took all of three seconds to get there, just enough time for Lane to stand up again, re-open the barn door and step aside.

The mare saw daylight, swirled, galloped flat-out through the doorway and was gone. Gabriel hurried over to where Lane stood, was about to ask why she would simply let the horse go, then noticed the tears streaming down her face. He stopped beside her, was caught off guard when she flung her arms around him, buried her face in his neck and begin to cry like a baby.

After a few moments Gabriel lifted his own arms, laced his hands at the small of her back and waited for her to settle down, felt a sudden welling in his own eyes. This was all so new, so foreign to him – being able to hold someone who desperately needed healing, deserved it, yet was somehow immune. He felt confused, over-whelmed...

Liberated.

He began to cry, too, the shoulder-wrenching sobs drying up Lane's tears, making her look up in wonder, then reach to feel the moisture on his cheeks. She couldn't remember the last time a man had cried in her presence, couldn't understand what Gabriel had to cry *about.*

"Why are you...?"

He put a hand behind her head, pulled her face back against him, didn't want Lane to see him crying, then remembered she *couldn't*. He stopped as quickly as he'd begun, fought the urge to laugh at the bitter irony of it. Turning to look down at her, he ran his fingers through her tousled, sunlit tresses for several more moments before looking up to survey their surroundings.

There was the split-rail corral to his left, the packed earth between the barn and the front of the house where a trail of dust pointed in the direction the mare had taken. There, too, was the emerald meadow to the south rimmed with lodgepole pines and, beyond them, a view of the Cascades that seemed to extend all the way back to California.

Could heaven be any more beautiful than this?

"Tell me what you're thinking," Lane said.

She turned her face up again, her gaze reassuringly off-line with his. He shook his head, honestly couldn't tell her, was tempted to begin with the phrase *To tell you the truth* because he didn't want her to rely on anything he might say after that, wasn't sure he could believe his own words.

"I'm thinking I might want to stay here for the rest of my life." He brushed a palm across her cheeks to dry what remained of her tears, raised a shirtsleeve to wipe his own. 'I'm also wondering how far Tina will get before someone finds her running loose out there."

"Don't worry, she'll be back in a few minutes," Lane said, "if her leg really is healed. There's a trail out through the trees and down south of the meadow. The deer made it going between North Butte and the river. Tina likes to follow it out to the highway, come around and cut across the meadow on her way back. We've ridden the loop a few million times. She's prob'ly done twice that many all by herself."

"The meadow... that's not where the ground squirrels were?"

"No, the burrows are on the north end. She'd never go there—except when I made her."

Lane grew quiet at the memory. pulled her robe tighter against the morning chill, then rotated in Gabriel's arms to lean back against him, content in his embrace, facing southward as if scanning the treeline for the mare. Neither of them spoke for several minutes, not so much anxious as expectant. Then, just as Lane predicted, Tina appeared at the far end of the meadow, still kicking up dirt as she slowed to a trot and began heading their way, the distant thumps of her hooves resonating with Lane's heartbeat. Inside the barn, the colt raised an impatient whine. Moments later the mare's reply drifted back across the dew-covered grasses.

"I better go let Fabian into the corral," she said excitedly, "put Tina in there with him when she gets back." Lane shook her head again, as amazed as she was thankful, turned partway around, face and hair even more aglow than before. "Am I just dreaming all this, Gabe?—or did some kind of miracle just happen?"

Gabriel smiled, pulled her close enough to feel the heat from her body through the terrycloth, breathed in with a sense of unfettered lightness he hadn't known in years.

More than one, he thought to himself. More than either of them could count.

12

hey stood at the railing along the south side of the corral for perhaps ten minutes, enjoying the sounds, if not the sight, of mother and son frolicking together. It took that long for Lane to finally acknowledge the cold, despite the warmth of Gabriel's embrace, and suggest they go back inside.

The day promised to be a busy one, she said – as if yesterday hadn't been – and they would need a hearty breakfast to hold them until dinner. She made a quick trip back to the stalls to make sure the horses had fresh hay and water, then took Gabriel by the hand and started for the house.

It was then Tina called out in the same tone with which she'd answered Fabian from across the meadow, trotted over to the fence and stood stock still. Gabriel looked back as the colt sidled up to his mother and poked his head between the rails. Lane frowned, realized the horses had suddenly gone quiet, turned her face up with concern.

"What is it? What are they doing?"

"Saying thank you," he replied without thinking, then chided himself as he reached for the back door. Hopefully Lane would assume the "you" meant *her.*

And evidently she did. They immediately went about making preparations for breakfast, Lane digging out a pair of skillets from her Hoosier while Gabriel was assigned to search for eggs and bacon in the fridge. But even before he'd counted out the half-dozen eggs Lane had asked for, she ordered him to stop and put everything back. The house was still too cold, she complained. She hadn't thought to turn on the furnace when she'd dashed outside earlier. Gabriel agreed it wasn't much warmer in the house than the barn, which provided Lane with the perfect excuse to insist they march back upstairs and crawl into bed while they gave the propane time to do its job.

Gabriel suspected she had ulterior motives, agreed anyway, wasn't a bit surprised when she threw off her robe without changing into her nightgown and got into bed as he undressed. She pressed herself into his side the moment he joined her, frowned when she realized his boxers were still on, but made no comment. Then, after sliding her hand across his chest, up his neck and along the line of his jaw, she began tracing his facial topography with the tips of her fingers.

"I've never felt anyone's face I hadn't already seen," she said. "Mind if I try to get a mental picture?"

"Be my guest. I'll give you all the money in my front pocket if you can tell me what color hair I have."

She giggled like a teenager, used the remark to justify reaching down to search his imaginary pants, in the process brushing her palm across his boxers in a less-than-subtle ruse for determining if her bare body had drawn a response yet.

"Not to be a stickler, Gabe, but you don't *have* any pockets... although there's this slit here—"

He grabbed her hand before she could slip it through, eliciting another raft of giggles.

"I think it was my *face* you were trying to picture, wasn't it?"

Still more giggles. She strained against his grip, finally extracted her hand and lifted it back to his stubbled jawline to resume mapping his face. Gabriel craned his neck to study hers at the same time, was amused to see her lips puckering in concentration, brows knit while she moved her fingers slowly upward across his cheekbones and around his eyes, much as he'd done to her an hour earlier. From there she slid her palm further upward to his scalp, fingers furrowing into his hair, following it back to where it splayed atop the pillow.

"How 'bout that? Before this morning I didn't think of you as having long hair." She chuckled at herself. "Guess it was all that business about not being touched. I figured you for short hair, crew cut even, maybe light brown."

"And now?"

"Now I'm thinkin' tall, dark and handsome." A pause. "God *damn* this being blind."

Gabriel wasn't sure she was being sardonic or serious, looked down once more, found her eyes squeezed tight, beads of moisture now seeping into her lashes.

"I'm sorry, Lane," he said. "I wish there was something I could do."

Again, it was clearly not a response Lane might have expected, and apparently still found puzzling. Gabriel, meanwhile, pondered once more his failure to heal her, considered whether he'd risk doing so now even if he *could*, admitted that his staying here would depend on keeping his otherwise potent power under wraps. And he *wanted* to stay here – more than any place he could remember.

He shifted to his side, turned toward her. She took it as an invitation, and he did not stop her. In moments they were in each others' arms, lips pressing together, mouths opening into one another's sultry warmth, Lane's right leg rising up over Gabriel's thigh. He was surprised that he roused so quickly despite his earlier concern for her. He was even more surprised when she pulled his boxers to his ankles and guided him between her legs, more so at how easily he slipped inside her, as if her body had been ready for as long as they'd lain there in bed. Or longer.

Gabriel paced himself, waited for her to come – and she did, with a series of shallow gasps and a final deep-throated moan that made him want to hear it all over again before he would take the opportunity to satisfy himself. When he asked her how long it might be until she was ready to repeat the process, Lane only grinned, pushed him onto his back and began riding him like the first time was only a warm-up.

Unfortunately, Gabriel couldn't hold out for another twenty minutes, not as unrestrained as she was, and not as glorious the vision of her swaying rhythmically above him. After only a few more minutes he let himself go with such abandon that, once he'd finally slowed, he felt an apology was in order.

"Don't be silly," she said, bending forward to stretch out atop him "We've got all weekend, and nobody's counting."

She kissed his lips, then lowered her head to press the side of her face against his. Gabriel was surprised yet again when, moments later, he felt moisture trickling into his ear, pulled back to find both of Lane's cheeks shiny with tears.

"Just happy, that's all," she said, answering his unspoken question. She reached behind her to pull up the blanket, lifted a hand to wipe her face with the top sheet. "My horse can run like the wind again, and I just made love to a man who's more concerned about *my* pleasure than his own." She let loose a laugh, rolled off Gabriel, nestled beneath his ear. "What more can a country girl ask for?"

It wasn't long before Gabriel was inside her once more, and a scant few minutes until Lane climaxed again – a "personal best," she chortled. He hurried to finish out of concern she might still be overly sensitive, remembered that his touch had restored everything but her sight, then realized all this thinking was beginning to soften him. He hurried all the more, which only made matters worse, had to unlock memories of friends' *Playboy* magazines and past lovers – a vision of Natalie finally did the trick, even as it made him feel guilty – all the while hoping Lane wouldn't suspect.

He was bathed in sweat by the time he'd finished, partly from the exertion, partly because the house had heated up nicely over the last hour. *More* than nicely. Her bedroom was practically a sauna. Lane ran a palm along his spine where perspiration had pooled on either side, brought her hand up, flicked it as if to wring it out.

"I didn't mean for it to be so much work," she said with another grin.

"Sorry. Feels like summer back in Visalia." He lifted himself off Lane, flopped almost breathlessly on his side. "This rate, you won't have any propane left for winter."

"Not to worry. If Doyle comes through, it'll be toastier in this house than it has been in years."

Except that now Gabriel *was* worried. Because, it suddenly occurred to him, if Doyle decided not to turn over his bank account to Lane later today, Gabriel's threat of taking her to the hospital to prove his attempted rape no longer had any foundation. Not only were there no bruises to prove she'd been beaten, the E.R.'s rape kit would turn up no vaginal tearing or other signs of distress – and would probably find only Gabriel's semen inside her.

Lane sensed his change of mood, though not the reason for it.

"That was really dumb of me to bring up right now, wasn't it?" She threw an arm across his back despite the slippery sheen. "I try to make each man I'm with feel like they're the only one, at least while they're in my bed." She flashed a fake smile, felt nothing to indicate he shared her humor, poked him in the side. "That was a joke, you know."

"I was smiling, couldn't you tell?" He grabbed her hand out of self-protection, pressed it down onto the mattress, held it there. "Actually, I was thinking—" And suddenly it was no longer Doyle he was thinking of. "—about a conversation I had with your friend last night... Buddy."

She propped herself on an elbow. "You saw him again last night?"

"Again—?"

"Yeah, you know—after you met him yesterday morning?"

Gabriel was glad she couldn't see him roll his eyes. The incident with the pair of deer was still hanging over his head, along with the two versions of his arrival in Chiloquin. With any luck, maybe he wouldn't need to explain the discrepancies. He hoped Deputy Chino wouldn't bring it up, either.

"Right. Well, when I saw him at the tavern—"

"Why didn't you tell me?"

Gabriel blinked; it wasn't as if they'd had many opportunities for small-talk after the incident with Doyle. And as far as Lane was concerned, last night was ancient history.

"Oh, yeah," she finally allowed, nodding. "Guess it wasn't exactly the first thing on your mind."

"Well it is now. Because he said Deputy Chino was coming out to pay us a visit."

"Chino—when? ...Why?"

"Sometime before the town meeting, I'm assuming." He paused again, not sure how to answer her second question without raising even more. "Buddy told me Fiske thought... and I have no idea how he got this impression... that I might be some kind of union activist. Like I'm here because of what's going on at the ammo plant."

"That's crazy. You've been with me the whole time," She suddenly stopped, put on a suspicious expression Gabriel assumed was only in jest. "Well, except for those two hours you went off in my car."

"Yeah, and in those two hours I talked to a grand total of three people: The bartender who gave me a beer, an Indian who told me where the back door was, and Buddy."

"Why'd you go out the back door?"

Maybe her suspicious look *wasn't* in jest.

"The place was getting too hot and crowded for me, okay?" What with all the sweating he'd just done, it wasn't so far-fetched. "Besides, from what I gather, Fiske is worried precisely because I *am* staying with you."

Lane sat up fully now, frowning in thought.

"Why would that bother him? I'm not the one who cooked up the idea for the sick-out. I don't even work there any more. If it was up to me..."

And then she stopped again. And it began to make sense.

They were halfway through breakfast when Deputy Chino showed up. Lane had spent the entire forty-five minutes prior to that – during which time they'd gotten dressed, then gone downstairs to make coffee and omelets – telling Gabriel about her dream. Not the one about the bed-and-breakfast, but the one about the ammo plant.

While the vast majority of locals were focused on labor conditions there, it had become Lane's fondest desire to see the U.S. Army simply vacate the facility and return it to peacetime use. She admitted, of course, it wasn't all that "simple." She had no ready-made answers for those who asked how it might be accomplished or what would happen to the local economy as a result, or who would oversee the plant conversion. She only knew that Chiloquin had changed for the worse since it had been turned into a community of munitions makers – even if others saw it as their salvation, and even though Lane herself had taken an active role in its mission for over a decade.

The past need not determine the future, she said, quoting from some book she'd read in school. And if it were up to her, the production of ordnance would be phased out as quickly as possible. The town could never be whole again, and she would never be fully recovered, as long as the ammo plant remained in operation.

"So you'd rather have the ammo plant gone than your sight restored?" Gabriel asked, sitting down to the Denver omelet Lane had just plunked on the table.

"You kidding?—I'd trade both my eyes any day, and maybe a kidney, to have things back the way they were before Halvorsen came to town."

And what impressed Gabriel most was not *what* Lane said, but how she said it, how her eyes lit up while she related her dream. They were even more luminous than before, could see what most sighted eyes couldn't, something beyond the range of ordinary vision, something more important than the way things were.

"Have you told anyone else about this?"

"A few people. Even the tribal council, once."

"You'd think if anybody could understand, *they* would."

"Some of them did." She paused with a cynical look, and in only that much time the fire in her eyes dimmed. "Problem was, the Kla-Mo-Yah casino wasn't doing well at the time. That was supposed to save the local economy, too. And since it wasn't exactly a resounding success, no way they'd consider giving up those ammo plant jobs."

"Sounds like white man's logic to me."

"You got *that* right. Some of the Maqlaqs, they still understand the old ways. But you'd be surprised how quickly most of 'em took to white corporate culture."

Lane brought her own plate to the table, sat down, seemed to gaze thoughtfully out the kitchen window. "Outsiders like to think of Native Americans as more spiritual, less materialistic. And many are. But they're also, I don't know—so innocent, in a way, which makes them even more vulnerable to the temptations of Anglo ways. Some of the most materialistic, most unspiritual people I know are Maqlaq. And a lot of those sit on the Council."

"But the others... they were open to this idea of yours?"

"Oh, yeah. Believe me, most Maqlaqs know what they're giving up in exchange for telephones and central heating and a Sunday drive down to K Falls for a Big Mac. Talk to 'em and they'll tell you their problem is about working conditions. But on a deeper level?— they know what they're doing goes against who they are."

Gabriel nodded to himself, likewise turned to gaze outside. He could see Fabian and his mother standing at the corral railing, breath still visible in the chill morning air, presumably taking a break from their play. As he continued to watch, the colt bent down for a quick snack, the mare turning contentedly to nuzzle her son's flank.

"I assume that's what you're going to say at the town meeting?"

"I don't know what I'm gonna say. Maybe nothing. The few Bustins who know what I think figure it's because I've got a chip on my shoulder. Like my new goal in life is to shut down the ammo plant, out of revenge or something."

"Then tell them exactly what you just told me."

"What would that accomplish?"

"Just share your dream." Gabriel shrugged, shoveled a mouthful of omelet. "You plant a seed and let it grow. The soil seems fertile enough around here."

"You think?"

"Yeah, I think."

And then she was quiet for a long time, quiet enough for Gabriel to hear a car slowing out on the highway, to hear it braking, the steady shooshing of rubber on asphalt replaced by the muffled thumping of its tires on the powder-covered washboard drive.

"That would be Deputy Chino, I presume."

Lane looked up, waking from her thoughts, raised an admiring brow. "Huh. You might just make a good blind person yet."

"You think?"

"Yeah, I think."

A minute later Chino's boots were on the concrete steps and then the broad wooden porch that wrapped the front and west side of the house. Lane was already opening the door as the deputy raised her knuckles to knock.

"We heard you drive up," she said almost apologetically. "We're having kind of a late breakfast. Can I fix you something?—it's no trouble."

"Oh, no thanks," the deputy said, a bit uneasily. She stepped in, glanced past Lane to where Gabriel stood beside the stairs. "Had a bite earlier. Could go for some coffee, though."

Lane closed the door, gestured toward the kitchen. Chino hesitated, seemed to search Lane's face for a moment, as if she looked different but wasn't sure just how.

"Been a while, hasn't it, Connie?" Lane said brightly. "I think the last time you came out here was to give me that ride up to Salem."

Connie, Gabriel repeated to himself. He realized he hadn't heard anyone speak Chino's first name yesterday; but if he'd thought about it, he might've expected something slightly more... how to put it? – *indigenous.*

Chino glanced his way again as if sensing his thoughts, continued to stare at him as Lane started across the living room. Gabriel walked ahead to the kitchen, found a mug in a cabinet next to the sink, reached for the pot on the stove. The deputy halted beside the table, waited as he poured her coffee and turned back.

"Short for Constance," she said, holding his eyes, making sure he knew *she* knew. "My mother always assumed I'd want to move away when I grew up, live among the Bustin, gave me a name that would help me fit in. Most of us have Bustin names, too."

She paused as Gabriel nodded back, acknowledging her "medi-cine," watched as he set her coffee mug on the counter without hand-ing it to her, in much the same stand-offish way he'd behaved in the jail cell.

"Anyhow, I'm here this time for similar reasons," the deputy said, finally turning back to Lane. "I was just wondering if you needed a ride to the meeting later today. Somebody mentioned you were on the agenda."

She peered at Lane, spotted the quick, knowing glance she sent in Gabriel's direction. It was clear they'd both been clued in.

"Nice of you to offer," Gabriel said before Lane could respond, "but she already made arrangements for a friend to pick her up... knowing I don't have a drivers' license."

Lane spun at the belated confession, frowned with still more surprise at the index finger Gabriel pushed preemptively to her lips, but remained silent. Maybe she understood that, once again, he simply hadn't found an opportunity to tell her. Nor, Gabriel sud-denly realized, had he told Lane about the wire Chino might be wear-ing. He leaned down to whisper *Later,* hoped she would let it go, quickly changed the subject.

"That term you used a minute ago..." He turned to the deputy, could see her concern that perhaps Lane hadn't been clued in. "...*Bustin,* is it? Heard it maybe half a dozen times since coming to this area. I take it that's what Maqlaqs call white people...?"

"One of the names," Chino said, finally picking up her mug from the counter. "The first whites in the upper Klamath were trappers, down from settlements along the Columbia. Most of those people came from Boston, or else they worked for the companies in Boston where all the pelts were shipped so they could be made into coats and hats and mufflers."

"Boston... Bustin..."

Gabriel nodded as he repeated the words, smiled at the expla-nation even as he suspected the name alluded to more than a city northeast of New York. Intruders was more like it – descendants of Europeans who came to strip the land of resources that weren't theirs, who would eventually strip the natives of the land itself, if not their whole way of life.

Chino could tell Gabriel had grasped the deeper significance, glanced at Lane who continued to frown as if she'd missed something. She waved at their half-finished omelets, slid a chair back from the butcher-block table so Lane would hear.

"Please—your eggs are getting cold," she said, waiting until both of them returned to the table. "So, Lane... did you invite Gabriel to go with you to the meeting?"

"Why would *I* go?—it doesn't concern me," Gabriel broke in again, perhaps a bit too eagerly. "Although, I don't know, I might tag along, see if anybody can tell me where that trucker is who drove off with my money." He was mildly surprised when both women sent scowls his way. "Or, maybe I'll just hang around here this afternoon, see if there's anything needs fixing. I'm in construction, you know."

He winced, aware how stilted his retraction sounded, especially if Chino *was* wearing the wire. He couldn't help squinting at her jacket, doubted she would have some sort of radio transmitter, couldn't imagine he'd merit a full-blown surveillance operation complete with a pair of sound technicians sitting in some van out on the highway, wearing headphones and sipping lukewarm coffee from a thermos. A small tape recorder, he guessed.

"Construction," the deputy repeated. "You belong to a union by any chance?"

Her tone was casual, but she stared across the table at Gabriel in a way that warned him this was one of Fiske's required queries. He nodded back.

"Never really been in one place long enough for my membership to kick in. Or else the jobsite wasn't union to begin with. Anyway, I wouldn't exactly call myself a joiner." He hesitated, wasn't sure he should follow up with the next question, but decided it might make the conversation sound more natural. "Why do you ask?"

"Just curious. You know, there are some union organizers who travel from place to place same as you do, never staying anywhere for very long..."

Gabriel cocked his head, noticed that Lane seemed equally dumbfounded. If anything sounded *stilted*...

"You should hear Gabriel's stories about the places he's worked," Lane said helpfully. "Some are pretty funny, like the roofer in Visalia who could drink a case—"

"You know, Deputy—" Gabriel quickly cut Lane off. Having her back him up wasn't such a bad idea, but not at the expense of leaving clues that might enable someone to retrace his past. "—I happen to like Lane's idea the best."

"Lane's idea—?"

He could see both women grow tense.

"Well, look at it this way. If there was no more ammo plant, there wouldn't be any labor problems, would there? And no reason to worry about union operatives skulking around."

Chino stared back incredulously. Out of the corner of his eye Gabriel could see Lane gawking in similar disbelief, couldn't under-stand either reaction until he imagined Fiske listening to what he'd just said. Because if the Lieutenant might no longer think of him as a labor organizer, he now had reason to believe Gabriel was some kind of peace activist, some outside agitator whose ultimate aim was to bring down the whole military-industrial complex. Assuming Gabriel wanted to reassure the local powers his presence in town this particular weekend really was a coincidence, he'd pretty much ruined his chances.

So what was there to lose?

"Look, Deputy, let's be honest with each other. I know this isn't exactly a social visit, even if Lane still thinks it is." No reason to take down everybody with him. "And I don't know what I can say to as-sure you and your Lieutenant I'm here only because of some freak accident, and all I want to do is get my Bible back so I can move on." He paused, had to ask himself: *Was that really the case anymore?* "But to tell you the truth, that's the only thing I care about."

Lane abruptly swung her head back, eyes drilling him with the question of whether he'd used that phrase as purposefully as she suspected. Deputy Chino, on the other hand, was suddenly looking away toward the window over the sink with a puzzled expression, almost as if she hadn't heard him. In a few more moments the rea-son became clear.

Out in the corral, Tina and Fabian were romping again, the dull thumping of their hoof-beats audible through the clapboard walls, an occasional whinny punctuating their play. Chino cast another incredulous look at Gabriel, then quickly reached up under her jacket, presumably switching off the device she'd hidden there.

"Is that your... Appaloosa...?" Her words trailed off as she pushed her chair back from the table, stepped to the window and leaned over the sink to peer outside. "I could swear Buddy told me your mare's leg was broken badly, but you couldn't bare to put her down yet."

"Good thing I waited, then, isn't it?" Lane said matter-of-factly, carrying her plate over. "She's spunkier than ever. Gabriel went out to check on her this morning and she practically broke through her stall, she wanted out so bad."

Chino turned from the window, stared once more at Gabriel. He immediately looked down, busied himself with a last morsel of egg before getting up to clear the rest of their dishes. As the deputy continued to watch in silence, he joined them at the counter, placing a hand on Lane's shoulder as if to prove her assumption wrong.

See? – blind as ever.

"You know, even if Buddy did make a mistake," he said, "I'm sure the splint helped. Keeping the weight off her leg probably made the sprain heal that much faster."

Lane leaned aside far enough to slip an arm behind him, gave him a playful shake.

"What's this?—an hour ago you were willing to call it a miracle."

"Yeah, well, even miracles have an explanation."

Chino nodded dubiously, finally turned for the back door. "Listen, I need to get back to town so I can help with traffic control. But I meant to ask earlier, about Lane's car...?"

"What *about* my car?"

"Well, it's almost blocking your drive where it's parked, down by the curve. I was just wondering if you were having engine trouble or—"

"No, no—" Gabriel broke in, noted Lane's questioning look. "—I took the Mustang for a little spin last night and didn't get back 'til late." He promptly made a face, scratched the back of his head; there was no use hiding the fact that he'd been driving, license or not. If Chino had spoken to Buddy lately, she knew anyway; and as far as he could tell, she hadn't turned her recorder back on. "I parked away from the house 'cause I didn't want to disturb Lane in case she was already asleep."

"I see. But you might want to move it. I could barely squeeze by. Keys are still in the ignition, too, and I know you wouldn't want any of the local kids to be tempted."

She gave an urgent nod toward the back porch as she finished her statement, making it clear she wanted him to follow her out. Gabriel squinted back for several moments, wasn't in any hurry to face more of her questions, but finally relented.

"Right. Maybe I should bring it around to the front door." Then, to Lane: "Save the dishes for me, okay? You'll prob'ly want to check on the horses one more time before the meeting. Bet they've worked up even more of an appetite by now."

He gave her a squeeze, reminded himself that his powers were still intact – in regard to everyone else, at least – waited until the deputy pushed open the back screen before starting after her. Stepping down from the porch, he watched her throw a final, wondering glance back at the corral, continued to remain a few steps behind as they circled to the front of the house. They halted beside the police car before Chino spoke again.

"You might as well know. You've created quite a stir among our people, Gabriel Woods."

He didn't respond for several moments, peering at the small bulge now visible beneath her tan jacket, just back of her right hip. She acknowledged the implied query by lifting the bottom edge, casually unbuckling the strap that secured a mini-cassette to her waist. Then, unclipping a tiny microphone from inside her collar, she began drawing down the wire that had been laced between the buttons of her shirt.

He looked up again, met Chino's gaze. "That's what I don't understand. I mean, your Lieutenant—he's got reason to be concerned, even if he is totally wrong about me. But the Maqlaqs—?"

She wrapped the wire around the recorder, opened the door of her patrol car, tossed it casually onto the front seat.

"No reason you'd know this. I'd forgotten the teaching myself until Two Bears reminded me."

"Two Bears... he's the one I met—" Gabriel stopped, squinted.

"Teaching...?"

"An old legend, actually."

Chino lowered her forearms atop the window of the open door, watched Gabriel position himself a safe distance away on the opposite side. For a moment she seemed to be reconsidering whether she should go on, finally nodded, stared evenly at Gabriel.

"It speaks of a time when the Maqlaq lose their ways. Another tribe comes to settle where the two rivers meet. They grow in wealth and numbers, so the people hold a pow-wow and decide to take on the other tribe's customs. They think their lives are better for a while, but inside they grow sad. *More* sad when one of the Mo'dokni leaders, a medicine man who has just taken a new wife, dies in a hunting accident, and his widow leaves for a far land to start a new life."

She paused again as Gabriel shifted his stance. If her steady gaze wasn't already making him uncomfortable, the story was.

"Not long after the widow goes away, she bears a son who grows up without knowing who he is or where he comes from. I won't bore you with all the details, but the son eventually finds his way back and helps the people remember who *they* are and where they came from."

Gabriel recalled Two Bears' cryptic comment, suddenly understood why Chino was telling him the story, folded his arms almost defensively.

"So, bore me with an answer to this: If the son doesn't know who he is, how can he possibly help *them* remember? And how do they figure out who he is to begin with—?"

"Because they recognize him."

"And how do they—"

Gabriel clipped the end of his question, wasn't sure he wanted to know the answer. He turned, looked at the lodgepoles and sun-gilded aspen across the parkway in front of the house, noticed the hoof-worn deer path where Tina galloped off earlier that morning.

"Recognize him?" Chino completed Gabriel's sentence, lifted her arms off the edge of the window glass. "Let's just say the meaning of his Maqlaq name is, *He who heals.*"

Gabriel turned back, stared at the deputy as she glanced conspicuously toward the corral, his memories rewinding to a conver-

sation he'd had with Morrie, the old man at the boarding house.
Morrie was slumped before the TV one winter evening when, out of
nowhere, he turned to ask Gabriel if he was aware that his name
came from the Bible – which of course Gabriel had known since he
was a child. What he *hadn't* known, what his mother had never told
him despite her conviction he was destined to "do the Lord's work,"
was that Gabriel meant *Warrior of God.*

"A strong name," Morrie said. "A name you should be proud of,
not like Morrie." And then he laughed his self-deprecating laugh
and, still staring at the tube from his easy chair, asked, "What about
your other one?"

"You mean Woods, my family name?"

"No, your middle name."

"Actually, Gabriel is my middle name."

Morrie finally pulled his eyes off the starlet who'd just been introduced by a fawning Jay Leno, waved impatiently. "So, my-middle-
name-is-Gabriel, what's your *first* name?"

Gabriel paused, never liked having to say it out loud.

"Ralph."

"Ralph..." the old man echoed, turning back to the TV. "From
the Hebrew word *refuah.* Another name you should be proud of. But
I can see why you like Gabriel better."

He waited for the old man to go on, but the TV starlet had taken
a seat and was now bending forward, laughing overmuch at some
quip from her host, breasts practically spilling from a low-slung
cashmere sweater. Gabriel had to press him to finish.

"So, what's it mean?"

Morrie turned with renewed impatience. "What's *what* mean?"

"Ra-*fu*-uh... whatever the word was."

"Oh, your name... Raphael..." He spoke the name with its Hebrew pronunciation, stressing the last syllable. "It means healer...
healer of God."

"*Gabriel?*"

Deputy Chino stood behind the open door of her cruiser, moving her head into his line of sight, not unlike Gabriel's earlier efforts
to determine whether Lane could see him. The difference was, when
Gabriel blinked, his vision suddenly returned.

"Sorry. I was just thinking how wrong you are."

He could be fairly certain the deputy didn't know Hebrew, even if she remembered his first name from his driver's license. What she *did* know, and had now seen for herself, was that Lane hadn't been healed. At least not in any way that was obvious.

"How *wrong...?*" she repeated.

"That this legend of yours has anything to do with me." Gabriel stepped past the patrol car, started for the Mustang parked down the drive, glanced back with a shrug. "I mean, if it did, how do you explain the blind woman who lives here?"

13

Rather than leave the clean-up chores until he returned, Lane had not only washed and dried the dishes, but put everything neatly away. By the time the Mustang was parked beside the front steps and Gabriel was back in the kitchen, she'd also tended to the horses and was just now swinging the barn door shut.

Gabriel caught sight of her through the window above the sink, immediately stopped to watch her turn and start across the open ground for the house. Again he found himself struck by the confidence with which she moved. True, she'd had nearly two years to become accustomed to her darkness, to chart the spatial relationships between the objects that filled her world. But even with two good eyes, Gabriel could hardly find his way from bed to bathroom at night without stubbing a toe.

Of course, he rarely had more than a few months to learn his way around the boarding houses where he stayed – as little as six days in one Alabama backwater where a sidewalk collision with a wheelchair-bound Iraqi war vet betrayed him. Which is why Gabriel generally paid scant attention to most of the physical objects in his environment, focusing instead on his proximity to other living beings. Watching Lane now, he couldn't imagine having to gauge the lay of the land through the soles of her shoes, or detecting nearby objects through subtle changes in reflected sounds, or simply walking from the barn door to the back porch by counting paces of a precisely measured length.

The thought crossed his mind – and he was genuinely stunned by this – that Lane didn't need a miracle in her life. *She'd already had one.* Or at least she was in the process of undergoing one. She was adjusting to her new circumstances in a far more miraculous way than if she'd had a merely physical healing. Not to mention that it was more inspiring, at least for anyone blessed with the opportunity to witness it.

Gabriel suddenly felt guilty, even angry, for healings that should never have happened, for all the bodies and the lives returned to their previous status quo. For all he knew, there was purpose in the injuries or diseases he'd had a hand in curing. After all, the true miracle was found down the path of greatest difficulty, wasn't it? – where the challenges and obstacles seemed most daunting, most insurmountable? Physical healings and so-called signs and wonders might get all the headlines, but they rarely *changed* the people involved.

No. Miracles were properties of heart and soul. They had more to do with attitudes changed, with lives rebuilt and relationships mended. And that took concerted, consistent effort, not a mere touch or the wave of—

The back door thumped. Gabriel turned from the window to see Lane pause just inside the glass-enclosed porch, cocking her head to listen.

"You were supposed to leave the dishes for me," he said, at least in part to reveal his whereabouts.

"And *you* were supposed to move my car sometime before next Monday," she said without missing a beat. "When I heard you and Connie shooting the breeze out front, I figured I had some time to kill."

Gabriel smiled – he hadn't heard that expression in years – then just as quickly frowned. "So you could hear us talking?"

"Your voices, not what you were saying."

Lane halted beside the Hoosier, reached up to feel the hands of an electric clock perched on one of its shelves. Gabriel noticed the small alarm clock last night during dinner, had assumed its clear plastic cover had broken off in some previous mishap. She faced him as he nodded with realization, propping a fist playfully on her hip.

"Why?—should I be jealous?"

"No, we were just..." Gabriel turned, shrugged. "You know Chino. She has some pretty interesting ideas."

"She's psychic, if that's what you mean. Doesn't much like being around me because I make her nervous."

"Nervous?"

"Too much going on in my head. Like I have this radio playing up there, and I keep changing stations—that's how she describes it. Could be why I don't sleep very well." She tilted her head again, allowed her own quick smile. "Though I gotta say, I had three, four really good hours last night for the first time in months."

She paused; Gabriel waited. The question he expected – about what he and Chino had been discussing beside her patrol car – never came.

"The town meeting doesn't start until one," she said. "That gives us over an hour before we need to leave."

And then she broke into her impish grin.

By the time they arrived, the street in front of Corky Girls looked less like the traffic jam it was than a pull-out-the-stops tailgate party before the final Series game between the Braves and Yankees. Not that there were any fistfights or mob control problems. Or, thankfully, any sign of the police.

Nor had Gabriel seen any patrol cars on the highway into town. Maybe his for-the-record comment about Lane hitching a ride with a friend had kept Fiske from lying in wait. But the two-lane road through the center of Chiloquin was now a virtual parking lot, people opening the doors of their cars to get out and chat while they waited, milling between them as if they were pieces of furniture rather than automobiles.

The curbside parking spaces up and down the full length of Main Street had long since been filled. Presumably, too, the lot behind the tavern. A well-muscled Maqlaq wearing a hunter's vest over his otherwise bare torso was positioned in the center of the side street, waving off any vehicles threatening to turn, sending them away to the north or south where, hopefully, they could find a place within walking distance.

"I told you we should'a left a half-hour earlier," Gabriel said, glowering into the rearview mirror at the jacked-up Blazer looming inches from the Mustang's rear end. Ahead of them, the crush of crowd and cars precluded any alternate route for at least two more blocks. "It'll take fifteen minutes before I can even get off the main drag."

"Relax, Gabe. They're not gonna start until everybody's inside. And anyway—" Lane reached across the seat to touch his arm. For once he didn't flinch. "—I'd say the extra time was well spent."

She raised an eyebrow, waiting for him to agree. He responded with a hand on hers.

"You're right. It's just... I feel like a sitting duck here."

"Trust me. Fiske won't come within two miles of this place. And if Buddy or Chino shows up, they'll look the other way." Suddenly she squinted, brightened, began to roll down her window. "Good—the drummers are here. You're gonna love this."

With their car still fifty yards from the tavern, Gabriel could just make out two clusters of Maqlaqs arrayed on either side of the entrance, hunched over tub-sized ceremonial drums. They appeared to be sitting on split-log stools, positioned around each drum like points on a compass. They were also completely blocking the sidewalk in both directions.

Which didn't exactly help the flow of foot traffic, because anyone who wanted to enter the tavern had to first step into the street, circle one of the two pickups parked directly in front, then pass between the drummers as they crossed the sidewalk to the door.

Worse, the long line of attendees was hardly moving, what with handbills being distributed and name tags dutifully inscribed in felt pen on the backs of others waiting ahead of them. If Halvorson or Fiske needed proof that labor activists *weren't* involved, the front door fiasco should have been enough. Union people would've had the crowd zipping along like one of the plant's assembly lines, the Maqlaqs' metronome drumbeats serving to set the pace.

Nevertheless, Gabriel found the drums comforting. He'd heard the pow-wow pounding in movies and reruns of TV westerns, of course. He'd also heard of the 90s "wild man" movement, remembered an article in *Atlantic Monthly* or *GQ* about weekend retreats where men took off their dress shirts and Dockers, sat around a campfire and beat on hollowed-out logs or tom-toms until they'd connected with their primitive selves and thrown off the shackles of civilization. Maybe there was something to it.

But this was a bona fide Native American call-to-community, all the more authentic for being felt as much as heard. Even if the drone of the surrounding Jeeps and Dodge pickups sometimes muffled their sounds, there was a steady concussion, like a communal heartbeat thumping in his chest. As Gabriel continued to listen, he could hear voices adding themselves to the beat, which he mistook for women's wailing until he noticed the mouths of the drummers moving in unison. *Wey ha wey hi ya ho wey,* they sang. *Oh wey ya hey oh...*

"Kinda makes you wanna go over there and bang right along with 'em, doesn't it?" Lane said, acknowledging Gabriel's reverent silence.

He didn't reply for several more seconds, mesmerized by the drumsticks' rhythmic rise and fall over the taut buckskins, their multi-colored shafts and ochre knobs leaving perfect rainbows as they arced repeatedly.

"Yeah, if only to give somebody a breather. You think they can keep this up until the meeting starts?"

"Well, it's not like they play the same thing over and over. They're on their third song since we came into town, 'case you haven't noticed."

Gabriel was forced to admit he hadn't. Rap music had the same effect, he mused, each song blending into the next unless you listened closely. Then again, he felt more of an affinity for Maqlaq drums than Wu Tang. There was something... *familiar* about it, like a place he'd been to but long since forgotten.

They were almost directly across from the drummers now. Nearby, at the tavern door, one of the men passing out handbills glanced toward the Mustang, then turned and spoke to someone inside. Within moments two more men emerged, pushed through the line of people and the northbound traffic and circled their car. The young Bustin on Lane's side bent down and looked through the open window, practically shouted to be heard over the drums.

"Glad you could join us, Laney."

"Hey, C.J. Packed house today, huh?"

"Yeah. Halvorsen agreed at the last minute to run day shift with just the maintenance crew, so more people could come. Trying to look magnanimous and all that."

"Or maybe he *is*. I never thought Halvorsen was a bad guy."

"Yeah, well..." The young man shot a glance at Gabriel before settling on Lane again. "...we saved you both a seat at the table in front. I'll show you inside while Danny parks your car."

"That's sweet of you."

She turned appreciatively as both men popped their respective doors open. Gabriel grabbed the half-lowered window frame as soon as the driver's door began to swing out, promptly pulled it shut again.

"I think I'll sit this one out, if it's all the same to you."

The long-haired Maqlaq on Gabriel's side was taken by surprise, couldn't help throwing Lane a questioning frown before looking back at Gabriel.

"You're not gon' be talkin'—?"

Now it was Gabriel who frowned. He turned, saw Lane's own surprise morph into puzzlement, guessed she was wondering if he must be some kind of labor activist after all. Problem was, the only other explanation for the Maqlaq's query was Deputy Chino's update of the Prodigal Son parable. Considering the alternative, leaving Lane to wonder about his identity seemed the least troublesome.

"I'm sure Lane will deliver the message a lot better than I could." He turned back, nodded ahead where a gap of almost two car-lengths had now opened in front of them. "We're holding things up. You go on, Lane. I'll poke my head in a little later."

C.J. reached over the door to touch Lane's hand. She obediently took it, even as she glanced back over her shoulder with the same puzzled frown.

"I won't let anybody take your place," she said, climbing out. "Just get back here soon as you can."

"Lane, I may be okay around *you...*" Gabriel left his sentence half finished, waited until she leaned back through the window so he could lower his voice. "...but there's no way I can walk into a crowd like that. Maybe I'll just stand in the back or something."

She finally returned a nod to say she understood, started to leave.

"Oh, and Lane... like we talked about?—just plant the seed and you'll do fine."

He smiled. She grinned back the way she had two hours earlier.

"Could be you already planted one."

They'd saved her a seat at the table nearest the podium, which had been set up not far from the hallway where the telephone and restrooms were. A century ago, what now passed for the rear of the building had actually been the focal point – or rather the main stage – of the old Masonic hall. What most people assumed was a crude wainscot attached to the brick wall was actually the support rail for a low platform. When the hall eventually lapsed into a succession of businesses – and for the preceding two dozen years, an Adventist church – the wooden railing was left intact for its historical value.

Today the tavern appeared more like its original incarnation. All of the small round tables had been moved into the neighboring pool parlor, their matching bentwood chairs left behind and rearranged into neat rows which now faced the podium. A narrow center aisle provided a straight path from the tavern door to a pair of rectangular, cloth-covered tables where the council members, speakers and other special guests were seated.

Not that the pathway was visible at the moment. There were probably more people standing in the aisle than seated in chairs, the Maqlaqs and Bustins equally intermixed, unlike the segregated groupings which characterized last night's bar crowd. Lane's progress toward the front was therefore sluggish at best, even with C.J. guiding her – though less from congestion than the succession of former workmates who came over to say hello or ask how she was getting along.

There was Alex Round Tree, for example, elder brother of the Maqlaq who'd died in the explosion that took Lane's eyesight, and with whom she'd gone through all twelve grades of public school. He too was quiet, though in a fashion more brooding than serene; and it was a bittersweet moment when he stopped Lane to offer the traditional welcome – *All my relations* – on behalf of his fellow Modocs.

Jillian and Waneta, the tag-team on whom Lane depended for her end-of-month rides to the ammo plant, were there. And Martha O'Connell, who'd worked on the grenade line alongside both Lane and Stillwater – between her every-other-year bouts with childbirth – was especially happy to see her, and embraced her so tightly that Lane could almost guarantee the gender of her next child.

When she was not quite halfway through the crush of people, Lane suddenly felt an object being pressed into her right palm by someone who'd come up from behind. She closed her fingers around it, shook off C.J.'s hand long enough to feel the item with both of her own, realized it was a small, sealed envelope perhaps a quarter of an inch thick. *Dollar bills?*

She spun. "Doyle—?"

The voice that responded was already retreating behind her, fading quickly amidst the surrounding hubbub.

"It's all there. You don't believe me, your cousin can count it."

And just as quickly he was gone.

Lane had barely managed to slip the envelope into her jeans pocket when C.J. latched onto her once again, pulling her forward, though she would stop several more times before reaching her seat. Two of her subsequent well-wishers, both Maqlaqs, asked where Gabriel was, calling him by name and reacting with great disappointment when she expressed doubt he'd be joining them up front.

For the second time she found herself wondering if Gabriel might be more than he seemed. She made a mental note to resolve her doubts once and for all after the meeting was over.

Assuming she would have the chance.

Because it suddenly dawned on her that if Gabriel *was* a union organizer, if any of the locals had invited him to Chiloquin for some kind of last-minute consultation, maybe he'd already accomplished what he came to do and he would now vanish from her life as quickly as he had appeared.

And it was this thought that nagged Lane as she finally took her seat at the makeshift dais, and continued to worry her when the moderator – an assembly-line worker known for having turned down an offer to join management – called the meeting to order. It was the same thought, too, that caused her mind to wander even as the first two speakers took turns behind the microphone.

She *did* regain her focus when her former suitor, who hadn't bothered to greet her despite sitting only a few chairs away, got up to make his own statement. After thanking members of both the city and tribal councils, Richard argued that conditions at the plant were considerably better than the Maqlaqs had recently made them out to be, citing several "generous" twenty-five-cent pay raises and all the special provisions giving Maqlaqs time off for pow-wows and other seasonal events. And though Lane hadn't been paying as much attention as she might have, she was fairly certain it was the first time the issues had been articulated along ethnic lines.

Even if sentiments tended to fall into those camps, Lane thought, the distinction added nothing useful to the discussion. It also set her mind to wandering again, mostly about why she'd had little choice but to turn down Richard's marriage proposal.

True, he'd always made her feel fifteen years younger when they were together, as if she still had all the time in the world to decide what she wanted to do with her life and whom to do it *with*. And their frequent trysts deep within the recesses of the ammo plant? – they were like interludes from reality, a place where decisions about the future could be put off indefinitely, where the universe was reduced to only the moment, only their immediate pleasure.

But when it came to politics and social issues, they began to diverge even as their physical relationship grew more intense. Richard saw no reason to change the status quo, either as it related to the Bustin/Maqlaq balance of power, or to what the Great Father in Washington happened to be doing around the globe at the time, which could only benefit the local economy.

Yet even this growing divergence couldn't tear them apart. If anything, their disagreements gave them something to be passionate about when they weren't being passionate with each other. No, it was the simple fact that Richard wanted – *desperately* wanted – to be "married with children" while she, just as desperately, wasn't ready. And might never be.

Lane realized she wasn't paying attention again, re-focused, was reassured to hear the speaker who followed Richard stressing the point that the issues they'd gathered to discuss transcended any group or individual who might have raised them. They were now the whole community's problem. And the problem was simply this:

Orders for munitions were still way up, and were expected to continue at the same pace for several more years at least. Not only did the stockpiles of ordnance expended in Iraq Two and Afghanistan need to be replaced, but supplies for the ongoing campaigns against ISIS and its ilk – in the Middle East, of course, but now also in Africa, Asia and Europe – had to be massively increased. What had once seemed only a temporary spike requiring extensive overtime, weekend rotations and cancellation of most summer vacations, had now become routine.

What's more, management had been unable to hire additional workers, simply because the local labor pool was pretty much fully employed. Outsiders were unwilling to move to Chiloquin despite the availability of jobs because there was nothing else *but* those jobs to attract them. Local government had done little to create additional housing, or the community amenities that might also lure new residents and businesses.

It had long been a joke throughout southern Oregon, the speaker reminded them, that Chiloquin had only one local eatery where existing business owners could enjoy a hot lunch, which wasn't so "local" since it was across the Williamson River closer to Highway 97. Corky Girls offered snacks, of course, and cellophane-wrapped sandwiches delivered every other day by truck from Klamath Falls. But the nearest "family restaurant" was either thirty miles south or thirty miles north, not counting the No Smoking section at the Kla-Mo-Yah casino coffee shop.

At this point one of the town's white council members came to the lectern to defend the town's "steady progress" on a number of other projects. The fact was, most of the tax revenues from the ammo plant had been used to catch up on a forty year backlog of capital improvements – from deteriorating roads to long-delayed sewer extensions into areas of town where many of "our Native Americans" had never known indoor plumbing until recently.

One of the tribal elders followed, thanked the councilman for helping to raise their standard of living to the level enjoyed by most of the town's other residents – avoiding "Bustin" or "white" or "Anglo" to describe them. But he also wondered why almost two-thirds of the new tax revenues went straight back into projects designed primarily to benefit the ammo plant.

Yes, a new waste treatment facility and electrical substation had been built just east of town. But as much as eighty percent of their capacity was immediately absorbed by the ammo plant's needs. The highway spur from 97 through the north end of Chiloquin and out past the D'Arcy ranch was now widened and repaved, and the roadsides regularly freshened with lava rock; but most of the streets within the city limits were cracked and repaired only as potholes grew large enough to swallow a tire.

All of which finally brought up the call for the question that had necessitated the town meeting in the first place: What action could plant employees take to pressure management – technically, the United States Army – to shift some of their production to other sites and thus reduce their workload, while at the same time encouraging Chiloquin's leadership to shift tax revenues to projects of greater benefit to the townspeople?

To everyone's surprise, concerns about the legalities of any potential labor action were quickly overcome by the next tribal leader to speak. There would be no "strike," Roy Soars-Like-Eagles assured them. However, he added with a nearly straight face, he'd heard a particularly virulent strain of Asian flu was already headed this way, even though the first day of winter was two months off.

"A lab technician I know at County Med tells me some kind of genetic mutation makes the Maqlaq people more, ah ...*susceptible* to this strain. But she also tells me the rest of the population isn't immune, either. And if management wants to send medics to the homes of anyone who calls in sick—" To make sure they actually *were* sick, the elder was implying. "—well, we've all been asking for in-home doctor visits, haven't we?"

The room erupted in laughter and applause. And without any further discussion it became clear not only how the labor action would play out, but how confident everyone was that nothing could be done to stop it.

When Colonel Halvorsen's daughter, Amy, bravely stood up to confide she'd "heard a rumor" about management considering free flu shots for everyone in town, no less than a dozen of her fellow workers shouted her down, saying the shots couldn't be made mandatory and might even conflict with native spiritual practices. Besides which, Matthew White Elk asked, didn't it take at least a week or two for the flu shots to confer immunity?

A warehouse worker whose sister was a nurse in Medford confirmed that, yes, it *did*. But what was more, someone else quickly added, even if the flu shots took effect right away, he was beginning to feel sick already; and now, with everybody breathing the same stale air in the meeting hall, he wouldn't be surprised if much of the plant's labor force became afflicted by Monday, if not sooner.

There were more laughs. The moderator promptly thanked "the floor" for all their comments, and a voice from the front row called for a show of hands.

"Alright, then," he responded officiously, "let me put it to you in the negative, so there won't be so many to count. How many of you are pretty sure you're *not* going to catch the flu starting next week?"

Someone further back in the hall called out for clarification. "You mean, who *doesn't* plan to call in sick on Monday?"

The moderator glanced toward the dais, covered the microphone while he whispered to the council elder who'd just spoken, then faced the crowd once more. "What I'm asking is, how many of you still feel immune to the flu, based on what you've heard so far?"

Unfortunately, some of the eyes that had shifted from the moderator to the dais during their brief conference happened to fall upon Lane. And remained there.

"Wait a minute—what about Laney?" a voice rose from the floor.

"Yeah," another voice chimed in, "some of us would like to hear what she has to say before we vote."

The moderator hesitated as a wave of murmuring roiled through the hall, finally raised his hands for quiet.

"My mistake. We, ah, *did* invite Lane to say a few words... if she wants to."

He turned questioningly in her direction, tried to appear pleased when she straightened in her seat and smiled as if welcoming his invitation."Well, then. Most of you know Lane D'Arcy as one of the very first residents hired at the Chiloquin Army Ammunition Plant, and the only employee in a full decade of operation whose job-related injuries forced her to quit work as—"

"Correction—" Lane abruptly stood, waved as if to dismiss the need for any further introduction. "—I never *did* quit. And I bet I can still pack a grenade as good as anybody here if they'd let me."

There were few more laughs, a smattering of applause. That was the Lane most of them hoped would show up today – the fearless, feisty, get-down-to-business woman they'd come to know and respect, at least before the accident.

The moderator shrugged, gestured as if to concede the microphone. Which is when Richard pushed his chair back from the table, stepped over to escort Lane to the podium, then leaned down to whisper that he'd never stopped loving her.

It took thirty minutes before Gabriel could find a space in the elementary school parking lot on the south end of town, then walk the half mile back to the tavern. It was another forty-five before the two men assigned to register late-comers finally moved away from either side of the tavern entrance, presumably to get a better view of the proceedings.

Gabriel promptly ducked inside but remained near the door,

suddenly became aware his heart was racing, not so much from his proximity to the crowd but the fact that Lane was just now stepping to the podium. A younger, lightly-bearded man – perhaps the one he'd seen with his wife and two kids at the ammo plant – was helping Lane center herself behind the microphone, leaning over her in a way Gabriel couldn't help thinking was a shade too familiar. The man waited until Lane took a breath and suddenly glanced back at him – in a way no less familiar – before returning to his seat.

She stood at the podium for several more seconds, seemed to be shaking off a few distracting thoughts rather than collecting them, finally laughed as if remembering a joke. "Then again," she said, "even if they *did* let me come back—and I'm kinda surprised they haven't called, what with the labor shortage—I'm not sure I'd really *wanna* pack any more grenades."

She paused for a few cautious chuckles, a few uncertain coughs, and then a mounting silence. Was she still joking around or not?

"Because what I've come here to say this afternoon, what I really need to ask you..." She paused again, raked her hair as she took in another breath. "...what I think we all need to ask ourselves is, should *any* of us be packing grenades for a living?"

Obviously she *wasn't* joking.

"Or mortars, or tank shells for that matter. I mean, is what we've been hearing for the last hour really all there is to talk about? How to force management to lighten up on the overtime? Or at least dole out more money for all those extra hours you've been working, maybe beg the town council to throw a few scraps at us for all those new tax revenues they've been piling up lately?"

The pin-drop silence disappeared as a murmur of surprise, if not uneasiness, swept the room. For many of the workers, it was the first hint there might be more at stake here than working conditions. Gabriel could see some of the dais big-wigs exchange annoyed glances. He hadn't heard much of the discussion leading up to Lane's remarks; in fact he'd spent most of the previous hour leaning against one of the pickups at the curb, despite repeated invitations from the two doorkeepers to come inside. Still, he had the distinct impression the meeting had been proceeding smoothly, and Lane was now the proverbial monkey-wrench.

Not that the murmuring surprised Lane as much as her opening remarks surprised them. She hesitated once more, scanned the
hall from left to right as if she could see the faces before her, waited
for the buzz to die down.

"Look, everybody... we've known each other a long time, okay? I
grew up with most of you. I know your families and you knew mine.
Some of you even went to the same church I did."

She stopped like a comic who knew where the laughs would
come. Several floated across the room. Gabriel could only assume
the response was out of irony. No doubt Lane's past indiscretions
and current bed-and-breakfast activities were common knowledge
in this small community. What more there was to it – if there *was*
more to it – Gabriel couldn't imagine.

"Most of us went through the same run-down schools, too. And
we were poor—God, were we poor." Lane turned her face up with a
reflective look that seemed to take the crowd along with her; and
once again the room fell silent. "But only in a material sense, and
only because we like to compare what we didn't have then with all
the toys and conveniences we have now. So, we figure we must be
doing better now, right?"

She turned back at her audience only briefly, nodded with a
sigh.

"I can remember the field to the west of town where Alex Round
Tree and Clifford Trait used to grow alfalfa. And Buddy Spear's family... how they raised horses on the grasslands between the Sprague
and the Williamson, and sold them at the round-up in Pendleton.
Best stock in Oregon, ranchers up there said. And the hatchery...
you remember when it was the town's pride and joy, after the lum-
bering days were over?"

Again Lane paused, a smile coming naturally to her lips. "I can
still see Edison Red Buck straddling one of the wooden flues when
he was thirteen years old. The water's rushing between his legs and
there are salmon and steelhead jumping all around him, trying to
climb the stairs. And meanwhile he's trying to grab them in mid-air
for the sheer fun of it, and he finally snags one and holds it up like
this..."

She raised her arms out over the lectern as if grasping one of the wriggling silver trophies, looked up like she could see it there. The eyes of her audience seemed to follow her gaze, as if they, too, could see it.

"And then... and then I have another mental snapshot of Edison. He's holding up a mortar, all bright and shiny before they've sprayed on the olive drab, tail fins catching the light while he inspects the seams..."

She continued to hold her hands dramatically aloft for several more seconds, then slowly lowered them. The heads dropped, the collective vision fading.

"And now there he is, thirty-four, and this is what he does to put bread on the table for Shelly and the twins. Instead of working at the hatchery as his father did, raising trout and steelhead and salmon to fill our streams and give us life, Eddie's packing boxes with flying fish that rain destruction and take life away."

The squirming in the bentwood chairs was palpable. If the crowd had been uneasy before, they were now clearly distressed. Which didn't mean Lane had changed any minds. Not yet. If anything, her audience resented what she'd said, resented that she'd breached their unspoken agreement to repress any consciousness of what they were really doing at the ammo plant.

Colonel Halvorsen and the U.S. Army had done their job well when they'd first come before the town council to propose their plan. They'd all been sold a new future, with a renewed economy that put money in their pockets. And just as importantly, the Colonel told them, they'd be helping their country protect itself. A grenade was a guarantee of security, a mortar their method for keeping the peace. *That* was what Halvorsen had really sold them – the illusion everyone agreed not to question, not to think about.

As Lane was forcing them to do now.

"Most of you know it hasn't been easy for me since the accident. But it turned out to be the best thing that ever happened because... because..."

She seemed to falter. Gabriel felt his heart racing again. Lane looked down at the lectern with an almost hopeless expression, then suddenly up again, eyes seeming to scan the room once more, stopping for the briefest moment, Gabriel thought, on *him*. It was as if she knew he was there, knew he was rooting for her.

Just plant the seed.

"...we seem to get, I don't know—caught up in the flow of things, and we no longer notice how we're changing, how we've already changed. But the thing is, we still do know. Even if we pretend not to see, we know when we're doing something that goes against our nature. We know, deep down, when we've let our souls be bought by somebody else's plan for our lives. But it's not our plan, *our* dream. And it's like we're just waiting for some event, or some*one*, to come and wake us up."

And just like that the tension in the room abated. Gabriel could feel it. Lane seemed to sense it, too. If the crowd still resented her for what she'd made them remember, at least they understood her. And maybe their understanding was enough for now. She remained at the podium a few moments longer, listening to their silence, then gave the slightest nod and turned to the dais.

"Can someone help me back to my seat?"

There was another moment, and then almost a collective gasp, as if the assembly had assumed she would go on, as if she'd brought them to the point where she would finally tell them exactly how to recover what they'd lost – but stopped just short. At last Richard got up, took her by the elbow again while the moderator hastily returned to the lectern. Before he'd managed to speak, someone in the third row stood up.

"So, Lane, you're saying, what?—we should try to force the ammo plant to just shut down? Go back to the way things were before?"

Lane halted behind her chair, thanked Richard once more, turned calmly to face her questioner.

"That's for you to decide, Stuart. Along with everyone else here."

Another Bustin near the back: "And what about our jobs? How are we supposed to make a living once they're gone?"

And a third, rising in Lane's defense: "I don't remember anybody starving. Maybe we didn't have a regular paycheck, but we were all making ends—"

"*Alright, people!*" the moderator's voice finally boomed through the microphone. "Let's get back on track, here. Before Lane spoke, we were about to have a show of hands on whether the flu—"

"Before Lane spoke…" The only other woman at the dais, a wispy-haired grandmother who worked in payroll, stood up and somehow managed to raise her voice over the P.A. system "…this meeting was being run by a few hand-picked people at this table. I say we act like a democracy, and we don't vote until we discuss *all* our options."

Now a dozen people were standing, some asking for permission to speak, some not bothering to wait, most of the others turning to those around them to launch their own private discussions. Amidst all the confusion Lane felt another tug at her elbow.

"Thanks, Richard, but I'll take my seat when I'm good and—"

"Actually, I was hoping you'd split this sock-hop with *me*."

"Gabriel—?"

During the commotion he'd circled the crowd, wended between the tables in the adjacent pool parlor and approached the dais from the side. If anybody had been watching, no one seemed especially concerned.

"Maybe this'd be a good time to go check on your horses," he said.

She turned around to face him, gaze reassuringly off target, still uncertain whether she was in the presence of some undercover activist, or the no-less-mysterious wanderer who had stumbled into her life quite by accident.

"So then, you think I've planted the seed?"

"I think," Gabriel replied, "that thumb a'yours couldn't get any greener."

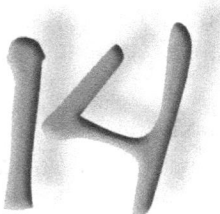

*S*omewhat *to her own surprise,* Lane's premature exit from the meeting had gone largely unopposed, if not exactly unnoticed. Amidst the chaos she'd left in her wake, her name was called out only twice – once to plead with her not to leave, a second time to say they'd all be better off if she *did.*

Of those who sat at the dais, only Richard turned his head when the pair made a bee-line for the same exit where Gabriel made his escape last night. Fortunately, no one was waiting outside this time. Nor did they meet anyone during their walk back to the school parking lot or, to Gabriel's relief, on the drive back to Lane's ranch.

At least no one who stopped them.

Because on the north end of Chiloquin, where the new pavement pointed the way to the ammo plant, a patrol car was hiding behind a clump of jackpines. They were fifty yards past it before Gabriel caught the glint of its windshield in his rearview mirror. He immediately lightened up on the accelerator – as if speeding were the issue – watching the brown-and-white car as it continued to sit there, expelling a grateful sigh when the ammo plant came into view and there was still no sign of pursuit.

Maybe Fiske had decided – assuming it *was* Fiske in the patrol car – any damage Gabriel might've caused had already been done, and now it would serve no purpose to haul him off to jail again. Or maybe one of his spies had already reported in by cell phone. Gabriel had no doubt that Halvorsen and Fiske would have at least one informer at the town meeting, in addition to the Colonel's daughter; and since Gabriel was basically a no-show, and Lane's remarks only left the crowd *more* confused, the various powers were suitably reassured he was no longer a threat.

Which is why the unofficial delegation that showed up at Lane's front door just before dinner came as yet another surprise. The group, consisting of two Bustins and three Maqlaqs – Two Bears and C.J. among them – purportedly dropped by to fill them in on the discussion that followed Lane's departure. As usual, Lane greeted them before they'd had a chance to knock, promptly invited the five to join them around the table since she and Gabriel were just sitting down to eat. After throwing their two mugs of navy bean soup back in the kettle, along with what remained of last night's chicken gumbo and two more cans of diced potatoes, Lane was able to serve each of her guests a small bowl – along with one slice from the last loaf of homemade bread in the house.

"Don't worry," she whispered as Gabriel bent down to help her find the tub of butter he'd misplaced that morning. "I've got money to buy groceries now. *Lots* of groceries. We can pick up some things on our way back from my folks' tomorrow."

He found the butter, straightened with a secret sigh of relief. Despite having spent the last two hours brushing the horses, then letting them out for a romp while she and Gabriel strolled the south meadow, Lane hadn't so much as mentioned her brief encounter with Doyle. Gabriel hadn't forgotten his demand – and now empty threat – that Doyle empty the contents of his savings account on Lane's behalf. He was simply afraid to bring up the subject, fearing Doyle might have called his bluff after all.

What Gabriel *had* forgotten, however, was tomorrow's drive to Beatty to visit Lane's parents – and the reason he was staying with

Lane to begin with. Truth was, he couldn't care less about what had originally brought him to Chiloquin, only that he'd found someone else in the universe with whom he could act like an ordinary human being with ordinary human feelings. And, best of all, no special powers.

Unfortunately, there were now five other people in the cramped kitchen with whom he *couldn't* act like an ordinary human being. And at least one of those people knew it.

Gabriel caught Two Bears stealing a glance as he and his four compatriots pulled their chairs up to the table, then quickly look away.

"You're gonna join us, right?" C.J. asked.

Lane slid her own chair around to the corner nearest the sink, gestured toward the living room. "Go get the piano stool for me, would you, Gabe? You can sit here."

Gabriel remained at the stove, turned to hide his reluctance while he replaced the lid on the soup kettle. He was hoping the six occupied chairs would give him a ready excuse to opt out of the conversation, if not the kitchen itself.

"I was thinking..." He turned back, looked down at the bowl he'd just filled. "...I might take this out to the living room instead. I found an old issue of *End Times* on the coffee table when I got up from the sofa this morning..." *There.* He would even help Lane preserve her reputation, should any of their guests be wondering. "Maybe I'll finish the article I started, something about Jerusalem and the new temple."

Lane laughed, assumed he was making a joke, quickly sobered when no one else saw the humor.

"Come on, Gabriel—don't be silly. There's plenty of room around the table."

He winced, allowed his reluctance to show. "This is really none of my business, Lane."

Dead silence. Two Bears turned partway around, then back to his bowl, mumbled a few syllables which were repeated by the two other Maqlaqs – a blessing, perhaps? – then picked up his spoon and began noisily slurping his soup.

"I don't know how you can say that," Lane said, allowing her own emotions to show as well. "It's you who gave me the courage to stand up and say what I've been thinking. Without all your plant-the-seed stuff, I probably wouldn't have gone to the meeting today."

"Yeah—stay," C.J. chimed in. "We feel bad enough we barged in on you like this."

Cornered. How quickly all the old feelings came back to him – the wariness, the claustrophobia, the calculating of escape routes and the length of a man's reach so he could evade contact. The same thing happened every time he returned from one of his pre-arranged getaways. If he'd had any illusions of a life where he would no longer be bothered by such concerns, he could stop dreaming now. Even Lane's ranch was part of the real world.

Gabriel blinked, realized it wasn't only C.J. who was waiting for an answer.

"Aw'right," he finally said, stepping behind Lane to set down his bowl, "but you keep the chair." He started for the adjoining hallway, took the long way around the table since there was more room to pass there. "And don't expect me to say anything."

Lieutenant Fiske remained unconvinced, even if Halvorsen was now satisfied Woods played no role in today's events. After all, the Colonel reminded him, it was Lane D'Arcy who'd always harbored the most potential to stir up trouble, and she didn't need Woods' or anyone else's help to do it. Still, there was something about Lane's current houseguest that rankled Fiske.

Halvorsen himself was getting on his nerves, too, come to think of it, by essentially ordering him to back off – not once, but twice – the most recent instance being his radioed-in report that he'd spotted Woods behind the wheel of Lane's Mustang. "Listen, Albert," Halvorsen called back to say, "if we leave him alone, and if he really was sent here on behalf of some activist group, he'll tip his hand soon enough. When he does, that's when we'll find out which of our locals are involved. In the long run, that's more important."

Fiske couldn't argue with the strategy. Nevertheless, he took it upon himself to keep an eye on the D'Arcy ranch for the rest of the evening. Relocating himself from the outskirts of town to the north side of the Sprague overpass where eastbound cars couldn't see him, he parked and waited.

Byron Red Hawk's weather-beaten Jeep Cherokee passed by half an hour later, two more Maqlaqs in the car with him, one of whom may have been Two Bears judging by the sheer bulk in the back seat. No surprise there. But if Fisk wasn't mistaken, Ken Chisholm was riding along, too; and the possibility that any members of the white population might actually conspire with the native hot-heads *would* be surprising.

It was less of a shock when, only minutes after Fiske had positioned himself, Richard McCaffery sped past him in his Chevy pickup, then came to a dead stop on the pavement opposite Lane's drive. He must've sat there a good thirty seconds debating whether to turn in, until a camper with California plates practically rear-ended him coming around the curve, forcing Richard to decide. He floored it just in time, smoking a one-eighty back toward town, flying by Fiske moments later, their eyes locking for a split second. Richard's eyes almost popped out at the prospect his antics had been seen.

Fiske found it mildly amusing, actually. Richard's long-time crush on Lane had provided an endless supply of grist for the local gossip mills, as did Lane's mistreatment of him – leading on her younger paramour for years until he finally proposed and she promptly rejected him, then going on to bear another man's baby seemingly out of spite. Not to mention going through another half-dozen-plus lovers after her accident.

The fact that Richard continue to not-so-secretly pursue her was almost laughable were it not so pathetic. Then again, Fiske might have pursued Lane himself if he hadn't recognized her for what she really was. Once a whore, always a whore.

So maybe Woods was just another temporary, younger plaything, stuck here by circumstance, and only too happy to pay room and board by servicing her needs. But with four other men in her house at that very moment, and a looming sick-out their likely topic of conversation, the coincidences were just too improbable.

The discussion was already well underway when Gabriel returned with the piano stool. Though he'd been gone for nearly ten minutes – paying a visit to the upstairs john and even taking time to slip on a heavier shirt – it didn't take Gabriel long to catch up with the conversation.

And the gist of it was that Lane's brief talk had indeed left today's town meeting in disarray. Following the five solid minutes of chaotic debate that ensued, the grandmother from payroll had retaken the lectern, presiding over a slightly more controlled discussion about whether the ammo plant really *was* a boon to the local economy – an assumption virtually everyone accepted as gospel until just that afternoon.

It was true, one of the subsequent speakers admitted, most of the townspeople had been poorer before the ammo plant arrived. But the local economy had finally begun to diversify over the decade since the lumber industry imploded. If the ammo plant hadn't come to town, he argued, Chiloquin might very well have pulled itself up by its own bootstraps before long, with a mix of industries from agriculture and animal husbandry to small manufacturing and recreation.

And, of course, the project begun in the late 1980s, whereby the Maqlaqs would eventually regain full control of their former tribal lands, might have gone ahead at a much faster clip. If anything, the appearance of the ammo plant had brought those efforts to a screeching halt. A few Maqlaq voices – including Alex Round Tree, Stillwater's brother – were even raised in support of the theory that the ammo plant was a ploy to keep the area under federal control indefinitely. The Bureau of Indian Affairs, along with its universally-disliked local representative, had conspired to make what was known as "The Restoration" nothing more than a sham.

The ousted moderator – to his credit for once – wrestled back control of the discussion at this point, convincing the assembly that the topic just raised would open yet another can of worms and further distract them from the purpose for which they'd gathered. It helped when the tribal elders backed him up, agreeing The Restoration was still too hot a topic for debate, and maybe tempers would someday be calm enough to allow a separate town meeting on that subject.

"But why?" Gabriel broke in. "What makes this restoration thing too hot to handle?"

"Excuse me—I thought you weren't going to say anything," Lane chided.

"Because it's about where people live," Byron Red Hawk replied, squinting gravely through his metal-rimmed glasses. "It's about the land. *Our* land."

"Not to mention money," C.J. added. "All a result of what they call The Termination."

"Termination...?" *Another four-syllable word.* Gabriel looked from C.J. to the Maqlaq beside him, rocked back on the piano stool. "Fraid I don't get it."

Oddly, despite his implied request for more information, Gabriel found himself mulling over how the bookish-looking Indian between Two Bears and C.J. could easily pass for Caucasian if he were living back in Visalia or Bakersfield. In the company of other Maqlaqs one might notice the family resemblance... the tighter check bones, the cut of jaw, the heavier brow and creaseless drop of his eyelids. But walking down the street, the young man looked no more Maqlaq than, well, he did.

"Actually, The Termination came first," the Maqlaq rejoined. He pushed back his eyeglasses, waited until Gabriel appeared to refocus. "And it wasn't only the Klamath tribes, either. Just after the Korean War, the U.S. Congress voted to abolish services to every tribe in the country. Basically, they said we no longer existed as independent peoples, and they would no longer deal with us as one sovereign nation to another. The Klamath Reservation was terminated in '54, and the federal government sold off all of our lands."

"Yeah. A million-and-a-half acres for as little as five bucks per." It was C.J. again. "And then they divided the money among only those Maqlaqs who agreed to deny affiliation with their tribe."

"Unbelievable," was all Gabriel could say. *Although on second thought, not really.*

One of the Bustins took over. "A few of the local Maqlaqs were able to purchase the land their own homes sat on, but not much more. And a lot of outsiders who knew about the land grab were able to snatch up huge tracts for the cost of a beat-up Volkswagen bus. Most of the big ranches in this area... prime riverfront property, good farmland, grazing land... were practically stolen."

"Including the D'Arcy Ranch." Lane stared blankly at her soup bowl, nodding as if to say *Guilty as charged.* "So here I am, trying to buy the property from my parents, when I really should be paying the tribal council. Assuming they'd sell it to me."

"We will *give* it to you," Two Bears said, "when the lands come back to us."

Lane smiled, reached across the table to clasp Two Bears' left hand as if she knew right where it was. "That means a lot to me. Thank you."

"So, when *does* the land come back to you?" Gabriel asked.

"It's all very complicated," Byron answered. He pressed the metal rims into his brow once more. "The remnants of the original tribes, the ones who refused to go along with The Termination?—the burden is now on them to prove to the government they can become self-sufficient. They call it the E-S-S-P... covers things like health services, democratic elections, education, jobs of course—"

"And that's where the conspiracy theory comes in."

It was the other Bustin in the group, the only one who hadn't spoken until now. In fact, he seemed to be taking a dim view of the entire conversation, Gabriel thought, raising a dubious brow as each of the others would comment, shaking his head in apparent disagreement whenever someone would try to make a point. Gabriel couldn't help wondering why he was part of the delegation.

"Conspiracy theory?"

"Ken Chisholm," the Bustin said by way of introduction, "and as long as ninety percent of the local job market is dependent on the ammo plant, the Indians here don't stand a chance of proving they're self-sufficient, do they? Only way to demonstrate they can run their own dog-and-pony show is if the U.S. Army isn't around to give everybody a damn job."

"And there's at least two reasons the feds won't let that happen," C.J. said, relieved at the opportunity to jump back in. "First, the plant's doing well. The locals are good workers, and the subcontractors are making a profit. But the second thing is, if the tribes ever *did* prove they were self-sufficient, their ancestral lands would have to revert back to them. That's the deal the feds worked out back in the eighties. But it can't revert until the present owners—"

"Occupiers," Byron corrected.

"—Until the people who bought all that dirt-cheap land are compensated at today's market value. I mean—hey, it's not *their* fault the U.S. government sold them the land for peanuts, and now they're sitting on a ton of equity. Or will be soon, now that real estate is coming back."

Gabriel could see where the argument was heading. "And it's the U.S. government who's gotta make up the difference. Which they don't want to do if they can help it."

"Exactly."

He turned, squinted at the more dubious Bustin. "So, you think this conspiracy's for real?"

"I wouldn't put it past 'em, would you?"

Gabriel declined to say. But he admitted to himself that, if nothing else, the connection between the ammo plant and the Maqlaq self-sufficiency requirement was a happy coincidence for the feds. But why would anyone other than the Maqlaqs want to press the issue?

"You mind if I ask—" He looked from one member of the Bustin contingent to the other. "—what's in it for you? I mean, let's say you're a white rancher. Wouldn't you be happier if things stayed just as they are?"

"I *am* a white rancher," Ken said. "At least I *was* a rancher. I didn't go to work at the ammo plant until two years ago. And that was only because I gave up trying to compete with it."

"Compete—? With a weapons factory?"

"That's right. A goddamn ammo factory put my ranch into Chapter Eleven." The man paused, could tell how strange it sounded, seemed to be considering how best to explain it. "See—I used to grow hay for some a'the locals who raised horses. I still do, only I sell maybe one-fifth what I did ten years ago, because demand is way down."

He scowled at his own words this time. Perhaps, Gabriel thought, his dubious looks weren't so much a rejection of others' comments but a reflection of his own pain.

"Also got a blacksmith shop in one a'my outbuildings," he went on. "Used to make custom tackle, bridles, shoes—that business fell off, too. See, when an industry this big comes into a town this small, it's kinda like one a'those black holes you read about? Sucks everything else into it."

"But not all at once." It was Byron Red Hawk again. "Some farmer who's had a couple'a bad years, he figures he can make a few dollars back by letting his land go fallow for a year or two, and he signs on to assemble mortars. And his neighbor, who sells him gas for his tractor, or maybe insecticide or fertilizer, his business dries up a little." He pushed his soup away, folded his arms. "So then a few more farmers bail out, and the gas station owner goes belly up. But it's not so bad, because the station owner can always find work at the ammo plant, right?—and then maybe he can still afford to send his boy to college."

At this point the former rancher turned conspicuously to his fellow Bustin. "Thing is, when he closes down his business, it affects some other guy who depends on *him*, and then that guy figures, what the hell, why beat 'em when you can join 'em, and pretty soon everybody's workin' for the ammo plant and you basically end up with a goddamn one-crop economy."

He gave a frustrated shrug, as did his Anglo compatriot. Gabriel simply nodded back, turned to look at Lane, sitting uncharacteristically silent ever since Two Bears' offer to tear up her mortgage. It was C.J. who finally packaged the reason for their visit into a nutshell.

"We all have our reasons to see the ammo plant shut down, hard as that'll make things for a while. And it's Lane who, well, sort of put that into words for us this afternoon. So now we want her..." He turned from Gabriel, leaned forward onto the table. "...we want *you*, Lane, to be our spokesman. You know, lead the charge for us."

Lane blinked, shook off whatever daydream she'd been entertaining, turned with a questioning frown.

"Who exactly *is* us, anyway? Surely not everybody at the meeting wants to send the Army packing."

"Hell, no," the rancher replied, "which is a damn shame."

"My best guess is, about a third of the people who attended would be happier if the plant was gone," C.J. said, "and only half of those were Maqlaq." He paused with a scowl. "That part threw me, I gotta admit."

"Our people will come around," the bookish Maqlaq assured him. "They're just waiting to see some leadership. We've been burned too many times by broken promises—on both sides. Once the tribal council is officially on board, most of the Maqlaqs, and many of the Bustins, they will join us."

"Meantime, it looks like fifty or sixty percent of the folks there today are gonna call in sick next week. Even if they're doing it for different reasons."

"More time off. Better pay."

"New asphalt on Main Street."

"A work slowdown will help our cause, too." C.J. leaned forward again, patted the table to jolt Lane out of yet another daydream. "So, Laney. What about it?"

She blinked once more, shook her head. "I don't know—I just... I can't imagine what else I could do at this point."

Just then Gabriel glanced away at Two Bears, saw him staring back so fixedly, so unabashedly, he finally raised his eyebrows as if to demand why.

"Talk to Magdalena," Two Bears said, still riveting him with his gaze. "Tell her what to do, what to say. She is Chiloquin, from a child. Most of our people do not know you yet." He stood; the other two Maqlaqs did likewise. "She will be your mouthpiece for now."

Gabriel didn't bother to explain Two Bears' statement, didn't even give Lane the chance to ask, until the five men had gone.

Not that the two Bustin members of the delegation had any idea what Two Bears was talking about either. They seemed as stupefied as Lane, like they'd joined the conversation late and missed something important.

The Maqlaqs, on the other hand, took the comment in stride, as if privy to inside information. It was time, Lane thought, to finally get a straight answer to the question that had bothered her since the town meeting, if not before.

"I have no right to know everything about you, Gabriel. I get that. I mean, we all have our secrets." She turned from the front door as the soft thrumming of their visitors' Cherokee disappeared down the dirt drive. "But if I'm being used for some ulterior purpose everybody seems to know about except me, that's not really fair, is it?"

It also, she thought as the last word left her lips, *changes our relationship.* For one thing, Gabriel's obsession about not being touched – was it only some kind of ruse? And all that drama when he woke up in her embrace and discovered he hadn't caught some dreaded disease – or whatever it was he was afraid of – was it all just for show?

But *why?* To distract her from the real reason he was there? To give her the impression she'd helped him overcome some great personal challenge and thereby create an emotional connection between them?

Talk about conspiracy theories!

And how was she supposed to think about what they'd shared physically? The fact that other men would have filled her basket for such favors didn't matter. She actually enjoyed the sex for its own sake. Really, truly *enjoyed* it. What's more, it meant something. And that hadn't happened since, well, Richard. *Richard,* who apparently still loved her, or thought he did. But what could it mean to Gabriel if he was only there because—

"*Lane.*"

"What?"

"Are you gonna let me say something, or do you want to stand there and make up your own answer?"

Lane realized she'd drifted off again. She caught Gabriel in a similar daze more than once, thought it odd how easily he could go off in his own world, figured it was a by-product of living alone. Or being a loner. Maybe she wasn't so different.

"Sorry," she said at last. "I *did* ask you a question, didn't I?"

"I wouldn't call it a question, exactly. More a statement of concern, like I'm not being honest with you."

"*Are* you?"

"Lane, look..." Gabriel finally put down the piano stool he'd carried back from the kitchen and held protectively in front of him
during the entire time their guests were leaving. "...I'm trying to be
as honest as I can here. But what you said, about all of us having
secrets? There are some things I can't tell you about myself. Not
now. Not yet."

That alone was mildly reassuring. At least, she thought, his
statement referred to the future. And if she wasn't mistaken, it
seemed to include her.

"But I *can* tell you those secrets have nothing to do with what's
going on at the ammo plant. I'm not some kind of labor activist or
union organizer, or anti-war crusader, not that I have anything
against anybody who *is*."

Lane folded her arms, sent a glance across the space between
them so dead-on accurate that Gabriel was momentarily frozen.

"So, what did Two Bears mean about my being your mouthpiece?"

He stepped slightly out of her line of sight, exhaled with exas-
peration. "You wouldn't believe me if I told you."

"Try me."

He opened his mouth to reply, realized he hadn't thought it
through, wondered how much he could tell her without digging an
even bigger hole for himself. Maybe the labor activist persona might
have been better after all. The Prodigal Son story could only be understood in light of the incident with the deer, and divulging those
details risked coming closer to the real truth of his identity. Giving
himself away, even to those whom he trusted – or thought he could
trust – had always been a mistake. *Always.*

Then again, if he was serious about putting down roots here,
she would find out sooner or later. He nodded to himself; it might
work.

"You remember what I said about Chino having some strange

ideas about me?"

"I thought we were gonna talk about Two Bears."

"Well, they're kind of related."

"Both Maqlaq—I'll give you that."

"Yeah, and that's what's behind what I'm trying to tell you." Gabriel sat onto the squeaky stool, watched her eyes try to stay with him. "See, there's this legend, okay? I don't know how far back it goes, but it's about this outsider—well, he's not really an outsider because his mother comes from around here, or wherever the story takes place, only she's gone off to live some—"

"Is this the one where he comes back and reminds the locals how they've gone astray, then leads them back on the right path?"

Gabriel's jaw dropped. "You know the story?"

"Gabriel? *Hello...?*" Lane unfolded her arms, held out her palms as if to ask whether he could see what was in front of his face. "I grew up with these people, remember? Some of my best friends and all that?" She shifted on her feet, drew a breath through pursed lips. "Although, really?—most of my Bustin friends never made the effort to learn about Maqlaq traditions. Lot of Maqlaqs themselves, sad to say."

She stopped, lowered her chin, squinted dubiously. "You're not serious—they think *you're* the prodigal son?"

Jesus. Not only had she jumped ahead to the conclusion, she'd used the same analogy for the story he did.

"Crazy, isn't it? I knew you wouldn't believe it."

"Well *yeah*—'cause this guy doesn't just come back. He does all these miraculous things when he first appears. That's how they recognize him."

And then there was silence. Loud-as-it-gets silence. Lane was off in her inner world again. Gabriel practically cowered at the thought of what she would ask next. The only question was whether she'd start with the deer or her horse. He cleared his throat to break her reverie.

"I mean it's, well, it's almost funny. If only because I'm not even from around here. And my mother?—she never lived here either."

It didn't matter that Gabriel wasn't all that certain. His mother had revealed very few details about her life before Salem. He was born out of wedlock – that much he knew. But as for the rest, she had just as much a right to keep her own secrets, didn't she?

"So it looks like they got the wrong man."

Lane, however, was already two steps ahead of him. "You said the truck you were riding in... Vincent's rig. You hit a deer yesterday, right?"

He swallowed hard, hoped her ears weren't sensitive enough to pick it up. "Hit one, rolled over another that somebody else must've bagged first. I *think* so, anyway, judging by the pool of blood I found."

He decided right there to be as truthful as he could without lying outright – and to try jumping two steps ahead of *her*, assuming anyone could. "Thing is, after I went back to where I thought they'd be, which is when Vincent drove off, they weren't there."

"You mean the deer were already gone, even before you went back to look?"

And just that quick she'd pulled out front again.

"It was foggy. *Thick* fog, laying right on top of the ground, chest high. Really weird. They could've dragged themselves down in the gully nearby, or gone off into the forest and you'd never know. That's when Fiske comes along."

"Fiske—? I thought you said *Buddy*."

"No, I met Buddy at the police station."

"Bureau," she corrected.

"Whatever. Look, Lane—we've been over this, haven't we?" Then again, maybe a little extra guidance would help her make sense of it. "We ran over a couple' deer on the road, okay? Chino and Buddy hear about it after Fiske hauls me in, but Fiske tells them there are no deer to be found – or at least *he* can't find them." Gabriel stood, pushed the stool back under the piano. "And then Two Bears gets wind of it, which is how the vanishing deer and this legend somehow come together. Suddenly I'm the long-lost son, come to bring the wayward tribes back into the light."

And if only Lane would leave her horse out of the sequence of events, Gabriel might leap another two steps ahead and *stay* there. The fact that Lane let the whole thing drop, that she stopped grilling him like one of Fiske's henchmen, was all the more amazing in light of what she said next.

"Fine. So I'm gonna go out to the barn one more time, give Fabian the last of Buddy's mash, maybe have another look at Tina's leg just to be safe. And then I have a little favor to ask."

Gabriel winced, waited.

"Would you mind doing the dishes for me? I'd like to take a shower soon as I'm done out there, try to get to bed early tonight. We can't afford to sleep in tomorrow if we want to be at church on time."

hey didn't sleep in. In fact it was just after six when Gabriel first opened his eyes to find Lane straddling him. She was leaning forward on her hands, her warm, moist breath coming in shallow gusts over his left shoulder, hips moving so slowly and so gently that the whole experience had merged seamlessly into his dream long before it dissolved, slowly, into wakefulness.

"How long?" Lane said when she realized he was conscious.

"Long...?" Groggy as he was, he was already beginning to move in tandem with her.

"Yeah. How long have you been awake?"

"Oh." He lifted his arms from the mattress, laced his fingers across the hollow of her back. "I don't know... maybe fifteen seconds...?"

"Damn. So close."

As he turned questioningly to look at her face, she arched her head back and began to shudder, opening her mouth but making no sound, as though he might still be asleep and she was still trying

not to disturb him. Then at last she lay down against his chest –
breasts, tummy, clavicle, in that order – released a long, luxuriant
sigh and tucked her head into the crook of his neck.

"I've always wanted to see if I could do that and not wake the
guy up."

Gabriel stopped moving. "So, you've... done this before?"

"Nope. First time. And I was *that*—" Suddenly she pushed back
up on her hands, scowling down at him. "What?—you think this is
some experiment I try out with all my house guests?"

She added a grin to show she was only playing. He was relieved;
he hadn't meant any offense.

"Just wondering." He pulled her down against him again before
resuming his own steady rhythm. "I mean, the real trick would be to
see if you could get the *guy* off without waking him up."

"You are *so* nasty." Another grin. "You wanna go back to sleep
and let me try?"

He didn't, but even so they were twenty minutes later getting on
the road than Lane had originally planned.

"I know, I know," she said as the Mustang bounced onto the
pavement. "It's my own fault. Course, you could try saying *No* after
the second or third time."

Lane paused, listening as the Mustang's acceleration slowed
and then leveled off, frowned when the pitch of the RPMs didn't
sound high enough.

"You'll need to pick it up if we want to get there before the service starts."

"Can't. Visibility's less than a hundred yards."

"It's foggy? It didn't feel that way back at the house."

"It *wasn't* back at the house."

Lane fastened the seatbelt she hadn't bothered to put on when
she first got in, withdrew a hair brush from her buckskin handbag
and began running it through her still-damp tresses. The punk style
she'd sported when Gabriel first met her was now a respectable-
looking shag. He nodded approvingly, wondered how women could
get their hair to look so different with only a few brushstrokes and a
little mousse.

"Prob'ly just moisture from the river," she said. "The highway follows it for a while before turning south, then doesn't meet up again until just before Sprague River—the town, that is. Should clear up long before that."

She was right. The fog disappeared less than fifteen minutes later, but by then it was doubtful they'd be able to make up for lost time. The poor visibility had kept their speed down between thirty-five and forty when they should have been going the limit. And after the mist melted, Gabriel was reluctant to push the pedal too much harder what with all the curves on the road – *and* after glimpsing an OHP cruiser on the bridge just this side of Sprague. Fiske might no longer be a concern, but driving without a license *was*. So despite the empty, two-lane road running straight east from Sprague, Gabriel stuck the needle at fifty-five and left it there for the duration.

Not that the longer drive time was wasted. They spent most of the eighty-plus minutes talking about their respective childhoods, growing up in southern Oregon as compared to northern Virginia. And it slowly became evident, despite the topic, how little was being said about either set of parents. Gabriel had divulged only that his mother was no longer alive and he never knew his father, and then changed the subject to Lane's folks. She, in turn, tried to change the subject back.

"No—you first," Gabriel insisted. "We're going off to see *yours*, not mine. C'mon Lane—I need a little help here. What should I know about them before we meet?"

"What should you know...?" She mulled the question, seemed to grow more uneasy as she thought about it. Finally: "You know, Gabe, why don't I just let you be surprised?"

"You make it sound like they're a birthday present or something."

"I just want you to form your own impression. Which will prob'ly be way different from mine because, well, I'm the one who had to live with 'em for twenty years."

"In other words, I'll think they're sweet and endearing, and far as you're concerned they scarred you for life."

She forced a laugh. "Well, I'm not sure about sweet and endearing. And yes, there were a few scars. But that doesn't mean you won't like them."

"So you *don't...?*"

"You're starting to put words in my mouth, Gabriel Woods."

Lane could sense he was watching her as much as the road, turned away like she was merely gazing at the scenery – now more a mixture of juniper-covered hills and intermittent grasslands than the pine-forested buttes around Chiloquin.

"Okay, so maybe there were *lots* of scars. And maybe I don't exactly like them for what they did. But I can still love them. There's a difference, you know. And to tell you the truth, I never—"

She stopped herself, turned partway back as if to admit the slip, then faced away again. Her voice sounded strong enough, Gabriel thought, but he couldn't see whether her eyes were dry. He decided to let it go. What her parents did or didn't do was none of his business. Besides, he had more pressing concerns.

"Are they... in good health?"

"My parents?"

"Isn't that who we're talking about?"

She turned with an unappreciative glower. Her eyes were moist, but no more than usual.

"They're fine. My mom just has a little bursitis now and then. One of the reasons they chose Beatty. Besides all the new building going on out there lately, the climate's a lot drier. When it would get damp back home, she'd complain about her joints. Actually, *before* it would get damp."

She turned forward again, though her eyes remained downcast. Up ahead, what Gabriel assumed was another high mountain meadow now appeared to be a vast field of alfalfa, with the kind of automated sprinklers that looked like long pipes mounted on wagon wheels. Beyond the next bend in the highway was a shed stacked high with hay bales, still green.

"They also liked the new church," Lane went on. "Some friends of theirs started coming out here when it was first built, eventually moved into one of the retirement villages nearby. My folks were thinking about joining them even before... before I moved back in with them."

"Because of the accident," Gabriel offered helpfully.

"Well, sort of. I was renting a little two-bedroom house in

Chiloquin after Richard and I split up. But then I couldn't take care of everything, so my—"

"Wait—you can keep up a forty-acre ranch, but not some two-room rental?"

"I had other responsibilities at the time." She lifted her gaze to the scenery again. "And it took a while to get used to things. Good thing is, I have people who'll help me now, if I ever need it."

He'd meant to ask about her "other responsibilities" when the Mustang crested a rise. Below, in the scrub-covered plain between two gently rising escarpments, a grid of earth-tone structures were interspersed with wispy, gray-green trees.

"That should be Beatty across the valley," Lane said, sensing their descent. "And it's about frigging time."

Gabriel turned left at the BP gas station just past the Lost River Trading Post in the old section of town, found the modest stucco church – beige, freshly-painted – a block-and-a-half north. The box sign on the front lawn, the kind with plastic grooves and interchangeable letters, featured the sermon title, "Hungry for a Miracle? Inquire Within." Above that, in permanent cursive letter-ing, was the name, *Beatty Bible Church.*

"I thought your family was Seventh Day Adventist."

"Dyed in the wool. My father's trying to be flexible, though. I mean, you can't be too exclusive in a place that's even smaller than Chiloquin. But his five-year plan is to convert everybody in the con-gregation. He's already talked the board into meeting on Saturdays, which is pretty amazing considering how hard it is for people to break old habits."

Once again the next logical question had to be deferred. Be-cause no sooner had Gabriel pulled into one of the two remaining spaces in the parking lot than an earnest-looking teenager in a baggy, pin-striped suit ran out to greet them. Before Gabriel thought to warn her, he'd circled the car to Lane's side and yanked open the door.

"Morning, Miss D'Arcy. Your mother wanted me to save a place up front, but your father said it would disrupt the service if you came in late. Best I can do is the balcony."

Lane didn't seem the least bit startled as her door popped open, raised a hand to take his.

"Anywhere's fine, Jared. You know I can't stomach special treatment."

The escort service notwithstanding, Gabriel thought with a smile.

"How far along are we?"

"The second hymn's coming right up."

"We're that late?"

She turned almost accusingly in Gabriel's direction as he slammed the driver's door, waited while he stepped around the car to take her other arm.

"Oh, so now it's *my* fault?"

Lane let go of Jared's hand, landed a punch on Gabriel's shoulder as thanks for the reminder. "Hurry or we'll miss the sermon."

As if that was an incentive.

The fifty or so congregants were well into the third verse of *Coming in the Clouds* by the time they'd climbed the stairs to the tiny, two-tiered balcony. It turned out to be fortuitous. Their footsteps on the hardwood floor were conveniently drowned out by the chorus – and by the slightly dissonant strains of a Hammond organ that must've gotten considerable punishment in some previous life.

Gabriel thanked the young usher, helped Lane into the rearmost pew and took the seat next to the aisle. He quickly scanned the loft to gauge the relevant distances, was reassured to spy a small niche where he could safely stand aside while the assembly filed out after the service.

He was mildly surprised when, at last, he glanced down at the chancel area only to find the eyes of the black-robed clergyman peering up at him. The sixtyish pastor seemed to be staring not out of simple curiosity, nor even to chastise them for being late. There was more to it, Gabriel thought, to the point of making him feel even more claustrophobic and out-of-place than he already was. If this was how the soon-to-be-Seventh-Day-Adventist Beatty Bible Church welcomed visitors, there had to be some other, unknown reason the pews were packed.

"Why in the world," Gabriel said, turning to Lane as the hymn came to a close, "would your parents pick *this* church?"

The final chord of the organ abruptly subsided as he completed his query, the words *pick this church* hanging out over the pews below so that several heads twisted around to stare up at the balcony. Lane winced, tried to shush him without drawing even more attention, stiffened in her seat like a Sunday School third-grader promising to be good.

Gabriel allowed another smile, thought, *Funny how religion does that to people, even when they're grown.*

Down on the chancel, the pastor cleared his throat as if to acknowledge the distraction, stepped past the altar to a speaker's platform more like a dictionary stand than a pulpit.

"Just before our last hymn," he began, sending another stern glance toward the balcony, "we listened as one of our young people read for us the story from Matthew, chapter fourteen—and retold in almost identical fashion in each of the other three gospels—about the feeding of the multitudes."

The pastor lowered his gaze to the congregants in the first few rows, missing the sight of Gabriel rolling his eyes. It wasn't that Gabriel disliked the familiar New Testament tale; the bare bones, eight-verse passage was among his favorites. But he had yet to come across anyone with a genuine understanding of it – from the chaplains of his childhood to the Mack truck missionaries who unknowingly abetted his periodic escapes to the next safe haven. He took Lane's hand, felt her squeeze back, then lean close.

"You okay?" she whispered.

"Just feeling a little closed in all of a sudden." That was part of the problem, anyway. He shifted in the pew. "If I need to bail out before the service is over, you'll understand, right?"

She pressed a finger to his lips, nodded. Gabriel caught another glance from the man in the robe, was surprised that his reply, as careful as he'd been to keep his voice down, had evidently carried that far. Maybe it was the acoustics.

"Everybody knows this story about one of countless miracles Jesus performed during his ministry on earth," the pastor continued. "But we often forget it was also meant to be a sign. A sign, first of all, to show that the end of an era was at hand. Just as miracles preceded the giving of the Hebrew Law to Moses – the ten plagues, the dividing of the Red Sea, manna from heaven – Jesus' feeding of the five thousand was one more demonstration that a new age, the reign of Christ Jesus, was about to commence."

Not exactly how his fellow Jews saw it, Gabriel mused, but certainly consistent with Christian theology. Especially the Seventh Day Adventist kind, if the magazine article on Lane's coffee table was any indication. It appeared Lane's father had already converted the pastor, if not the congregation.

"Second, it's a sign God is in absolute control, and that what we think of as the immutable laws of nature are only playthings in God's hands." The pastor paused dramatically, picked up the Bible from the platform. "Let's take a moment to reflect on what happened two thousand years ago, there beside the Sea of Galilee."

Here it comes. Gabriel rolled his eyes again, realized he hadn't fully considered how hard this was going to be when he accepted Lane's offer to come along; it had been years since he'd sat in church. He also realized how tightly he was now clenching Lane's hand, tried to loosen his grip, slowly, without being conspicuous.

"Jesus had come into that area to find solitude after the death of John the Baptist," the pastor was saying, "but people from the surrounding villages heard he'd be there, so they came out to see him. And kept on coming... and *kept on coming...*" He flashed a grin from the pulpit as if he'd made a joke, gave the congregants a few moments to show they'd gotten it. Apparently the Energizer Bunny was still a fond memory for at least a few souls in Beatty.

"Now, what happened was that the crowd was sitting around, hoping Jesus might preach to them. But it was already growing late and people were still arriving. We can assume everybody was getting hungry by then, and probably complaining about it—you know how people can be sometimes." Another flash of enamel. "So the disciples, they wanted Jesus to just send them all away, to go back home and feed themselves. But the Savior had other plans..."

Another pause, yet another theatrical smile. Gabriel looked down at his hand in Lane's, hoped she couldn't sense his growing agitation. It was even worse than he expected.

"...because he wanted the people to know who it was that was speaking to them. Not just another itinerant Jewish preacher roaming the countryside, but God's only-begotten Son. So Jesus blessed the five loaves and two fishes, and what was barely enough to feed his own disciples ended up feeding five *thousand*... with more left over than they started with!"

"Except that's not what happened," Gabriel said.

It was barely a whisper, spoken more to himself than for anyone else's benefit. Still, several of the balcony-bound congregants turned. The pastor hesitated, cleared his throat once more before going on.

"Wouldn't you *love* to have been there? And me?—well, I'd give just about anything to have been one of the ushers at that particular event, passing the Lord's basket from one row to the next... watching as someone would take out a morsel of fish or a piece of bread, only to have two more fishes or another loaf replace it—"

"That's not what *happened*," Gabriel whispered again, only this time it was more like a secret he'd decided to share with everyone else in the balcony, and the dozen or so nearby weren't the only ones to hear.

Lane was squeezing *his* hand now. She turned with pursed lips to quiet him, the muscles on her neck taut like ropes. *Too late.*

"Excuse me..." The black-robed pastor stepped from behind his dictionary-stand pulpit, propped an elbow on the edge, drew a breath for composure's sake. "We're a small congregation here in Beatty, and we *do* like to keep things informal. But frankly, I've never been accustomed to other people talking while I'm delivering my Sabbath message."

Gabriel knew without looking that Lane was glaring, could practically feel the heat from the deepening red of her face. Still, he found himself peering over the railing, down at the clusters of upturned faces in the pews below; and he sensed not so much their consternation as their curiosity.

Perhaps the pastor did, too. "You're telling us that's not what happened that day?"

"It's *not.*"

Lane dug an elbow into his ribs, as if the only proper response was to remain penitently silent, or at least beg forgiveness for the interruption.

"Well, friends," the pastor said, scanning the pews, "I just told you how I wished I'd been there that day. It appears we have someone in our midst who actually *was*."

He donned an insincere smile. A few congregants chortled with discomfort.

"No need to be there to know that's not the real story."

Beside him Lane slumped, brought a hand to her brow like a mother giving up on an incorrigible child. Gabriel wondered which of the upturned faces belonged to her parents, suddenly felt bad he'd embarrassed not only their daughter but them.

"Maybe now would be a good time to excuse myself," he said softly to Lane. But evidently even this was heard.

"No—please. Why don't you stay and tell us exactly *how* you know. I'm sure we're all dying to find out. And I'm sure—" His voice went flat. "—our dear Miss D'Arcy wouldn't have brought along a new friend this morning unless she wanted all of us to meet you."

Lane looked as if she might crawl under the pew. Gabriel, in contrast, was oddly invigorated, felt all the more inclined to confront this condescending man-of-the-cloth. He stood, took a step out into the aisle.

"I know because the story, the way you're telling it, isn't all that miraculous."

The graying pastor frowned, cocked his head much as Lane did when a thought or a sound would capture her attention.

"I'm sorry—did I hear right? You don't think feeding five thousand people with a few fishes and crumbs of bread qualifies as a miracle?"

Gabriel took two more steps onto the next lowest tier, halted at the balcony railing.

"Why should we think it's a miracle when God does something everybody already knows he can do?"

"Maybe the point is, we don't know it's God *doing* it, until we see the miracle."

The pastor drew a smug look, gazed out over his congregants to see them nodding back. Round one to the man in the black velveteen.

"Sleight-of-hand. Pulling rabbits out of a hat. That's not God, that's David Copperfield doing his show for people who pay to be wowed. And all those other so-called miracles? All the healings?—the cripples throwing down their crutches and the blind seeing again...?" Gabriel leaned forward, braced himself on the wooden rail. "Just like you said, playthings in God's hands. I'm afraid that's just not good enough to get me down on *my* knees, Reverend."

There were a few gasps now, a few congregants stiffening their spines and turning away as though Gabriel had just crossed the line between respectful debate and atheist insolence. And he was just warming up.

"You want to know the *real* miracle? You want me to explain why Jesus was God incarnate at that moment?"

Some of the faces turned back.

"Because he listened to all those hungry people, the ones who brought nothing with them, who didn't own much to begin with. He knew there were people out there who were well-off, who came with their picnic baskets full—or at least with more than they needed. He knew there was enough food for everyone if people would share. And he believed they *would* share, if someone would just, you know?—set an example."

Even Lane turned back now. He stole a glance over his shoulder, could see her earlier dismay replaced by something more like surprise – at this new, bolder side of him, perhaps. And he had to admit: this passion, this sudden energy, was no less surprising to *him.* Just as it was two nights ago when he'd lifted Doyle like a ten-year-old schoolboy and hurled him across her bedroom.

Gabriel caught the wondering looks of several others sitting nearby, turned forward to find the faces in the pews below still fixed on him.

"So what does Jesus do? Something so crazy, so totally unexpected, the people can't even conceive of it. He starts passing his own basket around. Maybe he tells them all what to do, asks them to take out what they need and put *in* what they don't. But my hunch is, he doesn't say a word. He just..." Gabriel lifted a hand from the rail, swung it gently, as if sending his own imaginary basket down the row nearest him. "...sets the example. And then others, who *get* it, who see just how amazing, how divine, this crazy act is—they start passing their own baskets around, too."

Gabriel straightened, lifted his gaze above the modern, crimson-draped altar and gleaming brass cross to the more traditional stained-glass image of the fair-haired wunderkind.

"With all due respect, Pastor, the miracle wasn't about magically turning take-out for twelve into a free lunch for the whole crowd." He lowered his eyes again, nodded. "It was about a loose-knit assortment of self-centered individuals accepting responsibility for one another and becoming a living, breathing community."

He stopped, heard his final words echoing from the simulated ash paneling like they weren't entirely his own, saw the stern expression of the pastor as he peered steadily back. He could also feel the eyes of the congregation, wondered if their utter silence was out of appreciation for what he'd said or just a matter of suffering patiently through his rant until such time as they could get on with the service. Either way he'd said enough.

He pushed off the railing, turned up the aisle. "I'm sorry, Lane," he said, now moving quickly for the staircase. "I'll wait outside."

She didn't reply, nor did anyone else break the silence until Gabriel was halfway down the stairs. Since the doors to the sanctuary were closed when he reached the narthex, the pastor's ensuing words were muffled; but it was clear he'd reasserted control. Whether to berate Gabriel or simply pick up from where he'd left off wasn't clear. Gabriel assumed Lane would let him know. That is, if she ever spoke to him again.

He decided not to sit in the Mustang while he waited, nor even remain on the church grounds. There was a new Dairy Queen on the corner opposite the BP station where he'd turned earlier. He retraced the block-and-a-half on foot, went up to the window to buy a cup of coffee before he remembered that his four dollar bankroll was still in the pocket of the Levi's he'd traded for his one pair of wrinkle-free Dockers. Apologizing to the banana-clipped cashier, Gabriel stepped away empty handed, sat down at one of the nearby patio tables where he could keep an eye on the front steps of the church.

Another twenty minutes passed before the arched doors swung open. Roughly half the congregants proceeded straight to the parking lot and departed. The others, including Lane and the young man who'd first greeted them, could be seen walking around the sanctuary to a smaller building in back.

Probably the post-service coffee-klatch, Gabriel mused. Or did Adventists foreswear caffeine as Mormons did? They didn't eat pork – that much he knew. But did they also keep meat products separate from milk, like orthodox Jews? So many rules and regulations for the religious. Why couldn't they all just concentrate on the important things – learning to live together, for one, or beating swords into plowshares?

He let his mind wander, didn't notice at first when Lane's pinstriped escort came out – sans jacket – and peered into the Mustang to see if Gabriel might be sacked out in the rear seat. At last it occurred to Gabriel the young man was searching for *him* and decided to go back – though he vowed to decline any invitations to join them inside.

As he started across the street, the young man spotted him and waved excitedly, then inexplicably bolted toward the adjacent church building. Gabriel could only hope he was running off to fetch Lane. Maybe she was ready to leave now and sent Jared out to tell him so. Maybe he could avoid having to face her parents, or anyone else for that matter.

Unfortunately, by the time Gabriel opened the driver's door of the Mustang and glanced up to see Lane coming, his hopes evaporated. Not only was Lane walking past the front steps of the sanctuary on her way out to the car, she was bringing the pastor along with her. The gray-cropped clergyman was no longer regaled in his black robe, but he *was* wearing the same stern expression.

Oddly, Lane appeared neither stern nor particularly upset as they approached. If anything, she had what Gabriel could only describe as a self-satisfied smirk. He waited in the relative safety behind the opened door, watched the two halt on the sidewalk directly ahead, leaned against the door so that it creaked loudly enough to give Lane his coordinates. Her head promptly rotated in his direction.

"Gabriel Woods," she began, "I thought you might want to meet the senior pastor here at Beatty Bible Church—the Reverend Paul..." The space between his first and last name seemed to lengthen, as did the upturned corners of Lane's lips. "...D'Arcy."

The fact that Gabriel had just figured out what was coming made it no less of a shock. His jaw fell, and Lane knew it.

"You remember when I said I'd just let you be surprised...?"

The Reverend D'Arcy took a step forward, extended his right hand. "They call me *senior* pastor not so much because of my age," he said congenially enough, despite his unabated scowl, "but because I'm looking for a younger associate to take over some of my duties. If you're willing to preach the sermon every third Saturday, you let me know."

He left his hand out. The hint of a smile came to his eyes, though not his lips. Gabriel finally brought his own lips together, stepped around the car door even as he pondered how to avoid taking the pastor's hand, then recalled that it was Lane's mother who had the bursitis.

"I was out of line in there," he stammered, reaching out at last.

"Yes, you were," Lane's father said. "However, I must say I enjoyed your exegesis, even if that's not exactly what the scripture says."

He withdrew his hand from Gabriel's – not in an unkind manner – then stepped back alongside Lane to place an arm across her shoulders. The gesture seemed a bit forced, Gabriel thought, and perhaps untypical given Lane's reaction.

"My daughter told me over juice and cookies just now, you considered the ministry while a younger man...?"

"My mother considered it *for* me, would be more accurate." Gabriel frowned, looked at Lane. "Speaking of which, where's *your* mother? I figure I'd better apologize to her, too."

"Went to the nursery to collect our little Jenna," Reverend D'Arcy said, giving Lane another squeeze. This time she appeared more distressed than surprised. "In the meantime, we thought the two of you might want to go on ahead, assuming my eldest remembered to bring her key." He glanced down; Lane nodded back with barely concealed ire. "We'll catch up in a few minutes."

And with that he unwrapped his arm and turned back toward the church.

Gabriel had driven from the lot before he considered broaching the subject again. And even then he was careful to work up to it.

"I want you to know I wasn't planning to make a scene back there, Lane. And the funny thing is—" He broke off, wheeled the Mustang around the next corner where Lane was pointing. "—I gave up trying to debate these things long ago. I have no idea what got into me."

"Don't worry about it."

Her reply was oddly distracted – perhaps, Gabriel thought, because she knew he was only biding his time before popping the question. She blinked, seemed to refocus.

"And you know, maybe he didn't sound like it—he hardly ever *does*—but my father was impressed. Told me so after the service, said it wasn't like me to bring anybody along who had a brain in his head." She expelled a breath, then squinted, sensing the car's gentle rise and fall as they crossed an intersection. "Should be a little yellow house up on the left, new owners turned it into a pottery studio. Entrance to the retirement complex is just on the other side."

Gabriel spotted the sign – Council Bluffs Condominiums – slowed.

"Listen, Lane, you may love your parents, but if you don't like them that much—or at least your father—why do you bother coming out here?"

She remained purposefully silent, eyes downcast, still waiting for his question. He obliged her.

"Okay, tell me about... Gina, is it?"

"*Jenna.* Genevieve, actually." Lane looked up again, eyes resolutely forward as the car turned up a long drive leading to a row of two-story, Cape-Cod-style units set well back from the street. In a few more moments she rolled her neck, sighed loudly as though trying with great effort to relax. "We're looking for Eight-B."

Gabriel slowed, finally pulled into an empty space alongside a shiny new Jeep with dealer plates still on. Nearby, a wooden stairway rose to a barn red door on the second level marked 8-B.

"Should've bought a place on the ground floor," Lane said, "what with my Mom's knees. My father said it would be brighter upstairs, and they'd have a better view of the bluffs northeast of here."

She gave a sullen shake of her head, as if this was yet another strike against her father – *and* as if admitting she'd been avoiding Gabriel's question but was now ready to answer it. He switched off the ignition, turned to face her.

Another sigh. "Jenna's my parents' adopted grand—" She bit her lip, corrected herself. "Adopted daughter. Most people in the church think she's one of those orphaned kids from Croatia or Venezuela or wherever, the ones you sponsor through Childreach or some other missionary program...? And they look at my folks like they're doing this great, admirable thing so late in their lives, bringing home some poor waif from overseas so they can raise her in a loving, Christian home. The two couples who knew my family in Chiloquin promised to keep their secret."

Gabriel waited until he could speak without his voice cracking. "Meaning she's really... yours."

He could see her eyes were moist; but this was evidently one more thing she was determined not to cry about. In fact she was doing far better than *he* was.

"She was less than a year old when the grenade went off. I couldn't take care of her anymore—obviously. Klamath Day Care already had her eight hours a day, but they couldn't take her twenty-four-seven. Besides, I needed round-the-clock care myself for the first six weeks." Lane paused at the memory, went on more deliberately. "When I was finally released from Medford General—after they airlifted me there from Klamath—my folks already had Jenna for two-plus months. They'd moved most of my stuff back into my old bedroom at the ranch, and it was pretty much a done deal."

Gabriel had a dozen questions but held them back, found it ironic that Lane had wrapped her right hand around the Mustang's door handle the way he had when he was still afraid she might lunge across the seat.

"You said they, what...?" He watched her hand tighten still more. "...*adopted* her?"

She turned away, didn't answer for several more seconds. "I wasn't so easy to live with, okay? I admit it. Maybe for a week or two when I was still pretending, but then I sort of... I didn't..." She stopped again, composed herself, swallowed. "Let's just say I went through a lot of changes before I decided to accept my fate. And during the time things could've gone either way, I wasn't any kind of mother to Jenna, even when I tried to be."

Still another pause; Lane was clearly aware she was beating around the bush, finally gave in.

"My dad sued for legal custody, the idea being to physically take her away someplace where I wouldn't be a bad influence, which I definitely *was* right about then. He offered to work out a deal with the ranch—you know, like that would be my consolation prize? And now the only way I get Jenna back is if I prove to the state of Oregon I can maintain a stable home life, and you can guess the odds a' that happening."

"You could get married," Gabriel said. It was the only response he could think of.

Another huff. "Like I'm the marrying type? I could've been Mrs. Richard McCaffery right now if that's what I wanted. And if not him, then at least..." She shrugged, let the sentence hang there.

"Jenna's father."

He let his own words hang. She turned partway around, frowned. "You're not gonna ask—?"

"What is it you were saying about secrets?" He reached over to caress her shoulder; she loosened her grip on the door handle. "What I *am* a little curious about is what she thinks of you. I mean, you had Jenna for a year before it happened, right?"

"She doesn't seem to remember. I'm just her sister now. Her *big* sister." She forced a laugh. "*Really* big sister." And just as quickly she turned somber. "She called me Mama once, on her second birthday. Broke my heart. My mother's, too. I don't know—I guess she must understand at some level that our family is different from other people's. But she seems happy enough, and my mother loves her dearly, and I suppose I should be grateful for that."

Gabriel simply stared, his own heart breaking at the thought of one more tragedy for Lane to cope with, one more injustice – even if she was partly at fault in this case – paying scant attention when a Ford Taurus pulled into the parking space on the other side of the Jeep. It was after the passenger, a woman in her late fifties, reached into the back seat and straightened with an armload of wriggling energy that Gabriel suddenly leaned forward, squinted past Lane.

The Reverend D'Arcy was already busy removing something from the trunk. Lane's mother, meanwhile, was quickly coming to the conclusion Jenna wanted down. And when the dark-haired cherub was finally let loose, Lane was opening the door to greet her, all smiles and outstretched arms and not a trace of the sorrow Gabriel could only begin to imagine.

*S*he *was plainly half Maqlaq,* a handsome combination of coarse, ebony hair and light brown skin, her childhood chubbiness already lengthening into the lithe, slenderness of her mother. Gabriel could see how the elder D'Arcys could pass her off as a South American import, a Bolivian orphan, perhaps, with a not-untypical trace of European blood.

Lane told him later, as they started back for Chiloquin, how her parents had "leaked" a story about their flying off to La Paz the year before to adopt her. As it happened, the Reverend D'Arcy had actually taken Jonelle – Lane's mother – on an AARP-sponsored cruise to Mazatlan the week Jenna was due to arrive. Such was his elation over a granddaughter born out of wedlock, whose father Lane adamantly refused to identify.

Their drive back began uneventfully enough, just as their visit with Lane's parents had begun. Surprisingly, Gabriel found them both quite cordial, even if Lane's father was clearly Lord of the Manor and Jonelle the dutiful serf. It wasn't hard to imagine the young

Maggie rebelling against this brand of paternalistic rule – in addition to her name – not only refusing to take on her mother's subservience, but to try and be everything she had never tried and had never been.

While Lane and her mother went into the living room to play with Jenna, the Reverend D'Arcy – *Paul*, he now insisted – pointed to a chair at their dinette and asked to hear more about Gabriel's "religious convictions." Despite his seeming interest, however, virtually every avenue of discussion eventually became an excuse to demonstrate how the world was slipping ever faster toward the New Testament's prophetic climax. Having politely nodded in response to three or four such demonstrations, Gabriel finally raised the possibility that all of these end-time predictions might be "coming true" only because a few zealous Christians were determined to *make* them come true.

"And how about this?" he said, in hopes of ending on an upbeat note. "The Second Coming isn't about Jesus returning in the clouds to set up some kind of worldly kingdom. It's when we all accept responsibility to take care of each another, just like he asked us to, and work for peace with just as much dedication as we once waged war."

"I like that," the Reverend said generously, "but who says it can't it be both?"

It was then that Lane invited Gabriel over to play with Jenna while her mother went into the kitchen – refusing any offer of help – to prepare lunch. Gabriel hadn't found an opportunity to slip the query into their conversation where it wouldn't seem as obvious, so Lane thought it a bit odd when Gabriel asked if Jenna was "as healthy as she looked."

"Her usual case of the sniffles is all," Lane replied. "But at least it's not from the flu that's probably hitting Chiloquin right about now."

She laughed and shook her head, surprised at herself for having brought up the subject. As it turned out, they would discuss the situation at the U.S. Army Ammunition Plant in much greater detail over lunch, despite Jenna's constant efforts to hijack the conversation and focus on more important matters like her toy collection, her third birthday party last month, and the bedtime prayers she repeated every night asking Jesus to make Sister's eyes work again. Amidst all the jumping between topics, no one noticed that Jenna's nose had stopped running.

Only partway through the meal, the Reverend expressed his amazement that things had deteriorated at the ammo plant to the point where a sick-out was being considered. "Must be outside agitators," he stated with certainty, though he made no connection with Gabriel, and Lane didn't so much as glance his way.

On the other hand, Lane *did* admit to her own role in yesterday's town meeting, and to publicly posing the question as to whether Chiloquin might be better off without the ammo plant. Her father, turning to her as if she *was* Jenna's older sister – and as rebellious as ever – told her Chiloquin would surely be committing economic suicide if the workers pushed the army out, especially after all the good they'd done.

"How do you feel about all those bombs they produce?" Gabriel inquired, thinking a man-of-the-cloth might be sympathetic.

"A holy commission," the Reverend said with no apologies to the Prince of Peace. "Do you think Armageddon will be fought with spears and slingshots?"

Her parents' hospitality notwithstanding, the comment put Gabriel in the mood to leave whenever Lane might be ready. Which she soon *was* – but not before she'd posed one other question. After she and her mother began clearing the table, Lane suddenly halted behind Gabriel, salad plate in each hand, casually cocked her head as if she'd just thought of it.

"Hey—what if we took Jenna home with us for the weekend?"

"What?"

"Well, why not? Gabriel's staying at the house for the next couple of days."

Both of the elder D'Arcys abruptly turned toward Gabriel as if on cue – and as if the possibility that he was sleeping under the same roof had just occurred to them.

"He can help me watch her."

In equally scripted fashion both parents' gazes promptly shifted to Jenna, sitting regally in her second-hand, molded-plastic Thomas the Tank Engine booster seat. The center of attention again, she furrowed her brow and clunked a spoon against the tabletop.

"I wanna go home with Sister."

"We've talked about this before." her father said softly to Lane, clearly hoping a simple reminder would end the discussion, even if he knew better.

"Daddy—"

"Lane, this is exactly the kind of message we don't want to send."

"Message?—*here's* the message..." Lane spun, stormed toward the kitchen. "First, you tell me I can't care for Jenna because I'm not able to watch her, even though you've seen us play hide-and-seek a hundred times and she wins only if I let her. But then, if I offer to bring someone over to help me keep an eye on her—male, female, younger, older, it doesn't matter—it's like you think we're gonna have sex in front of her."

"Lane!"

The name erupted from both mother and father in unison. Gabriel had to bite his tongue to keep from joining the chorus himself.

"And God forbid Jenna should stay overnight when a man might be there with me."

"Lane..." It was only the Reverend this time.

"Daddy, Gabriel may not be one of your hand-picked bachelors from the church, but you know him by now—"

"I wouldn't say I *know* him—"

"—and you can tell he's a deeply spiritual person—"

Gabriel almost blushed at this point, grateful everyone's attention was on Lane – except for Jenna, who had suddenly blossomed with a silly grin she'd now fixed on Gabriel. Back in the living room, she and Gabriel had invented a game of funny face, which she continued to play throughout lunch, usually when "Papa" and "Sister" were engrossed in grown-up talk, as they were now. At least there was someone with whom she could have fun.

And Gabriel was clearly having as much fun with Jenna as she was with him. He couldn't remember the last time he'd been around a three-year-old child – or *any* child – for more than a few moments. Working on a construction crew all day, then going home to the

sterile, spare bedrooms of the senior citizens with whom he boarded
– he rarely had an opportunity to enjoy their innocent, focused-on-
the-moment companionship.

If anything, Gabriel had learned to avoid children altogether.
Their unpredictability made him fearful, and that fear became an
aversion. He almost broke into tears when, in the middle of showing
him the collection of *My Little Ponies* Sister had given her, she ran
over to throw her arms around him for no apparent reason, and
then, two seconds later, ran back to grab Sundance Pony and gallop
away down the hall. And now here he was, staring across the dinette table in Lane's parents' second-floor condo, mugging and making faces like a three-year-old himself.

He suddenly became aware the room had gone quiet, his face
frozen into a monkey-like simper Jenna was trying her best to mimic,
and that Lane's parents were staring.

"Yes, it's quite obvious Mr. Woods is deeply spiritual." The Reverend paused to clear his throat. "Still, I think it's best if we—"

"Lane, dear," her mother broke in, "why don't you let your father and me talk about it before we decide one way or the other."

Gabriel, still red with embarrassment, glanced at the Reverend
to see his color likewise deepening, then back at Lane, who managed a tiny nod at her mother as if this was progress. For *both* the
D'Arcy women.

The conversation grew increasingly sparse after that, the
lunch dishes rinsed and stacked in the dishwasher, excuses eventually made and goodbyes exchanged. As they stopped in the doorway on their way out, Gabriel distracted Jenna's attention from the
tears welling in Lane's eyes by making a few more silly faces – and
by promising, without having any basis for it, that she would be
able to visit Sister "very soon" to see her new colt.

And as the Mustang swung back onto the highway, it was this
remark that continued to weigh on Lane's mind.

"I wish you hadn't said anything to Jenna about seeing Fabian."

"Why not? I thought she loved horses."

"She's crazy about 'em. I just don't want to get her hopes up."

"I don't know—it looked to me like your mother's on your side now. By my count, that's two against one."

"Not a majority when it comes to my father."

Gabriel glanced at his watch: *Two-thirty.*

"We should've stayed longer. I can turn around if you want."

"No, that's okay. My friend Jillian, from the plant?—she's dropping me off next weekend before going on to Lakeview. I might even spend the night with my folks." Lane shrugged, finally fastened her seatbelt as the RPMs leveled off. "Anyway, I've imposed on you enough. I know how hard it is to make small talk with people you don't know."

"Not really. It was, uh, an interesting discussion. And Jenna's so incredible. I just hope you can...'

He let the sentence trail off. Lane faced him, finished it with no hint of sadness or regret.

"Get her back...? Let's just say I'm not getting *my* hopes up, either." She nodded wistfully. "I really hurt my folks, Gabriel. And scared them. I can't blame my father one bit for taking Jenna away when he did. And this is too funny—" She tried to laugh. "—the only time they ever drove up to Chiloquin to visit me, six months ago...? They never told me they might be coming. It was an hour before day shift, Richard dropped by and we were in the shower together."

"Richard? But isn't he—"

"Yeah, yeah—married, children, devoted family man—all of it. And really, it was only the second time we'd been intimate in the last two years. For old times' sake, didn't mean anything." She paused, blinked as if suddenly reconsidering, then managed an ironic smile. "Anyhow, that's when they show up. I mean, what are the odds?"

"I take it your father knew Richard was married."

"Knew—? He performed the ceremony!"

The car left Beatty behind, headed up the gentle rise and into the open road toward Sprague. Gabriel wound up the Mustang's 289 a few clicks before he remembered there was no hurry now – and that at least one OHC cruiser was somewhere this side of Chiloquin.

"You wanna take a drive anyplace, long as we're footloose and fancy free?"

Lane smiled again, raised an eyebrow, appeared tempted. And she *did* have money in her buckskin bag for a change.

"I guess we could see what K Falls is like on a Saturday night. Haven't been down there since I was in the hospital. Problem is, our top priority right now is buying some groceries. You saw yourself— there's nothing left in the house. If you're planning on staying a few more days, we'd better stock up."

Her voice was hopeful, Gabriel thought, as if she wished he might stay even longer. Which gave *him* hope. It also made him feel slightly foolish. How long had they known each other – all of two days?

"There's a little market in Sprague River next to the PetSmart, where they put in the town's only traffic signal last year. You ran the yellow on the way out this morning, remember?" Lane paused to flash another smile, knew he'd gunned the car to beat the red light and assumed she hadn't noticed. "Frozen stuff should be okay. Won't take that much longer to get home."

They found the newly-enlarged Squaw Flats Country Store on the south side of the highway, waited almost a minute until the signal just up the road could stop oncoming traffic long enough for them to turn. The market, offering an unlikely combination of groceries, guns and hardware, was only moderately crowded. They filled a shopping cart to overflowing in less than twenty minutes, but with only one register open, the check-out line was beginning to back up into the canned goods aisle. Gabriel had just told Lane he was going off to complain to the manager – less so because of the long wait than the crowd thickening around him – when the crash occurred.

By the time Gabriel ducked at what sounded more like a bomb going off than two vehicles colliding, a bright red big-rig could be seen through the store's plate-glass, jack-knifing southward out on the highway. A pastel green Caravan was cartwheeling across the center turn-lane, one side virtually ripped off. As a dozen other heads jerked around to gape in horror, a Ford pickup coming northbound smashed into the other side of the van after the briefest of skids, ejecting its rear seat occupants like so many sacks of cement.

Gabriel had already taken two steps toward the exit before he remembered Lane – *and* his injunction against getting involved. He halted, turned back to find her wide-eyed and rigid with shock, was sure she'd guessed what happened but told her anyway.

"Eighteen-wheeler and a mini-van. A few people on the street. A pickup was involved, too, but it didn't look—"

"So why aren't you going out there!?"

He was surprised Lane would ask such a question, blinked uncertainly, then glanced past her to see the checker already turning back to her register, expression more angry than sympathetic.

"Swear to God," the young woman said, reaching for a head of lettuce on her conveyor, "it happens at least once a month. Even the new signal doesn't help."

"Gabriel—?"

He shook off the checker's comment, looked back at Lane. She continued to stand there with an urgent, reproving frown, as if waiting for him to rush outside. As if he could do something.

As if she *knew* he could do something.

Maybe it was only her small-town sense of responsibility. After all, no one should stand around with their hands in their pockets if they could be of some help. Lane obviously couldn't pitch in, but Gabriel could. That's all she was saying to him – *wasn't it?*

"Right. Lemme see if I can make myself useful."

He glanced at the old woman in line ahead of them, a deeply-creased Maqlaq in a bright red poncho who nodded back as if she understood both his predicament and Lane's need for assistance. And with that Gabriel started for the exit once more.

He crossed the parking lot in a strangely-swirling haze, as if he'd entered a time warp, halted on the sidewalk to gawk like the other lookie-loos, none of whom could possibly know – as Lane could not have known – how the scene tore at his memories. He finally stepped off the curb, fought off the urge to throw up, half-walked, half-stumbled across the eastbound lane to where the first body lay.

She was a young girl, stark white and unmoving, with a teen-aged boy standing over her, eyes transfixed as he sobbed violently, a bicycle helmet still strapped on like he'd been pedaling by and stopped to see if he could help. Oddly, Gabriel's first thought was that the bicycle rider was about the same age *he'd* been when he experienced his first accident, when, far from standing by as an observer, he was pinned inside the wreckage of his mother's Chevy Nova. And equally transfixed by his helplessness.

He could almost hear her voice now, rising softly, cooing to him in the way she once sang lullabies, using words in a language he couldn't understand but didn't need to, assuring him everything would be okay, that he could go on without her now, asking him to reach across the space between them so she could feel the touch of his hand one last time, so they could pray together in silence before she left him. The memory of her somehow galvanized him, and he was suddenly as calm and focused as he always became when he gave up control.

He knelt down beside the little girl – nine or ten years old, Gabriel judged – looked with an almost scientific fascination at the foot-long shard of pastel green sheet metal that had bisected her jugular and lodged in her collarbone. As he reached down to grasp the shard, he heard another voice, this one definitely not his mother's, looked up to see a man in a white smock bending over a second child perhaps ten yards away.

"Didn't you hear me?—the girl's gone already, 'case you're too blind to see. But this boy here just might make it—if I can get a little help."

Gabriel looked back down, ignoring the other man, gripped the edge of the torn metal, felt how solidly it had imbedded itself in the bone. Slowly, he began to work it loose.

"Hey! I'm talkin' to you!" It was the white smock again. "I'm only a vet from the pet store over there, but I know how to take a goddam pulse, okay? If you really want—"

The veterinarian broke off as another pair of sidewalk gawkers finally ran to his aid. He cast one more disgusted look in Gabriel's direction, started barking instructions to his new-found assistants.

Gabriel, meanwhile, had extracted the metal shard, caught himself wondering which part of the car it might have come from, immediately put the thoughts aside along with the bloodied metal. He ran a finger along the length of the gash it had made, the viscous blood on the little girl's neck smearing, covering all but a telltale depression where the opening had been.

In only a few more seconds the girl coughed once, twice, three times, her hacking barely audible over the surrounding street noise and distant siren, but wet enough to indicate that her throat was filled with more blood. Gabriel quickly turned her onto one side, rotated her head toward the pavement to let the fluids drain, at the same time feeling her ribs, abdomen and legs. Aside from a scrape on her right arm, there were no other signs of injury, no blood soaking through her pink Osh-Kosh overalls or yellow t-shirt. Whatever internal damage there may have been would now go undetected.

He looked back over his shoulder at the teenaged bike-rider, now standing slack-jawed and no longer sobbing, waved him down alongside the little girl.

"Hold her head and shoulder like this," he said matter-of-factly. "Let her cough until she's cleared everything out, then I want you to sit her up straight. Got it?"

The teenager nodded and did as directed, thankfully without drawing any further attention to what had just transpired. Gabriel pushed himself up, turned to look for the van's other back-seat occupant. Nearby, the vet was busy wrapping a tourniquet around the second child's thigh – this one appeared to be two or three years older, a boy, conscious enough to be moaning in pain. The vet looked up as Gabriel started over, did a full-blown double-take when he noticed the little girl spitting up blood but clearly alive.

"Where's the other one?" Gabriel asked.

"What kind'a medic *are* you?" the vet replied, blinking with customary disbelief.

"The other kid," Gabriel repeated.

"Past the van. Don't think you'll be able to do anything with that one. Skull's caved in." He finished cinching up the leather belt one of his aides had donated, eyes following Gabriel as he walked past. "I'm telling you, that girl you just treated—? No pulse when I checked 'er. Abdomen felt like a goddam waterbed."

"Easy to make a mistake, all this confusion."

Gabriel found the third child behind the mangled van, head and upper body concealed beneath someone's blue windbreaker. Two shopkeepers with name-tags were standing guard, though their attentions were fixed on the efforts of four other men struggling to get at the van's female driver through the gaping hole in its side. The crushed front doors were evidently welded tight, the woman trapped by a steering wheel thrust hard against her chest despite an airbag having been deployed.

He winced as memories of his own accident flooded back once more. For some moments he considered joining the men – his mother had been pinned behind the wheel, too – but knew it would be too risky, stepped over to the windbreaker-cloaked body instead. He knelt, reached for the jacket when the two name-tagged bystanders spotted him.

"You don't wanna look under there, pal," one of them said. It was obvious he was speaking from recent experience.

Gabriel pulled the windbreaker aside despite both men's protests, fought not only a renewed urge to vomit but his own doubts he could do anything to bring this teen-aged girl back to life. Assuming she *was* a girl. Aside from long brown hair, there was little evidence to suggest a gender, and certainly no clue in what was left of her face.

He let his doubts dissolve, let the men continue their protests, began pushing the glistening overflow from the girl's split skull back inside where it belonged, trusting the torn flesh and bone fragments to reassemble themselves beneath his fingers, knowing all the while his fingers had nothing to do with it. As he kept working, the coagulated blood became liquid again, smearing, dripping from his wrists as he moved one hand along the base of her neck and down her spine, the other across her chest and down over her abdomen.

It was then that Gabriel heard another voice, this one filled with anger despite its being muffled and far away. Or maybe not so far away. Because someone's hand was now at the base of *his* neck, shirt collar suddenly tightening like a noose before his body lurched backward. The girl promptly slipped from his field of vision, replaced by a swirl of blue and white that faded to black when he heard his own skull crack against the pavement.

The next thing Gabriel knew, he was staring straight up at a highway patrolman whose accusing glower could be seen through his Ray-Bans. Then, abruptly, the expression turned quizzical, the face disappearing entirely. Moments later one of the two men who'd been standing guard over the teenaged victim bent into view, frowning with concern.

"You okay...? Hey, doc—whoever you are... you *okay?*"

"I think so. What about the girl?"

Gabriel attempted to sit up, reached for the man's hand when he offered it.

"The badge here didn't realize what you were doin' when he drove up. 'Course, *I* didn't know what the hell you were doin' either..."

He stopped mid-sentence. Less than ten feet away, two paramedics were now crouching over the blood-smeared teenager, one wrapping gauze around her head while the other waited to slip on an oxygen mask. Stooped over all three was the highway patrolman, quizzical look still intact.

"...an' for the life a'me, I still can't believe my eyes."

Another paramedic appeared from behind, pushing a gurney.

"Anyways, looks like she's breathin' again. Could'a sworn she opened her one good eye just before you got decked."

The baffled bodyguard – *Hank,* according to his drug store name-tag – glanced ungraciously away before helping Gabriel to his feet. The sudden movement to his flank caught the patrolman's eye; he swirled, stepped back to grab Gabriel's arm.

"Hold on! This guy's not going anywhere."

"This *guy,*" Hank spat back, emphasizing his words between clenched teeth, "just *happens* to be some kind of *doctor.* He was trying to save that girl's life—he *did* save that girl's life—before you came along and knocked 'im on his keester."

The officer squinted back dubiously before reluctantly letting go. Gabriel couldn't feel any transfer of energy to either of the two men; but he was too distracted by all the confusion to be certain. Either way, things were getting more dangerous by the moment.

He glanced toward the grocery store parking lot, could see the Mustang but not Lane, turned to survey the highway. To the south, the big-rig was frozen at an acute angle, radiator and fender bashed in, though not as badly as Gabriel might have expected.

In the northbound lane, the driver of the Ford pickup was standing beside its opened door, talking animatedly to a policeman busy taking notes. A few yards to Gabriel's left, the woman in the Caravan was finally being extracted by the four men who'd been at it from the beginning, now supervised by another medic. Her head and neck were bound in a brace, two splints strapped to either side of her torso. She was also groaning – loudly – a fact for which Gabriel was thankful, in part because it meant she was alive, more importantly because his presence would no longer be needed.

He started to step away, suddenly felt a hand on his shoulder. He instinctively twisted from beneath it, the reaction eliciting scowls from both Hank and the patrolman.

"Sorry," Hank said, staring wonderingly even as he apologized. "Just thought you might want to get some medical attention, too. I mean—" He nodded, indicating the back of Gabriel's head. "—looks like you might need a few stitches yourself."

Gabriel reached up, felt the wet hair and split skin where his head hit the pavement.

"Not now."

He turned away again, headed for the grocery store, halted after only a few strides when the white-smocked veterinarian came around the back of the van. Some distance behind him were Lane and her elderly Maqlaq escort.

"Your name Gabriel?" the vet queried.

"Lane!" He stepped past the vet. "You shouldn't be out here."

"You were gone so long, I came out to ask if anybody knew—"

"My God!—that can't be the—"

The vet cut her off, sucked air before he could finish his own sentence, did yet another double-take as the teenaged girl was wheeled past him toward a waiting ambulance. Her skull was bandaged and bloody but round as a cantaloupe, clear plastic oxygen mask now strapped over a mouth and nose no longer skewed like the label on a crumpled soda can.

Lane looked up questioningly as Gabriel took her arm.

"C'mon. We're only getting in the way here."

He nodded his thanks to the Maqlaq woman, started for the parking lot. The vet continued to gape while the paramedics prepared to load the gurney, shook his head incredulously for several more seconds before he noticed the two of them walking quickly away.

"Hey!—you're no doctor, *are* you?"

Lane glanced up once more, perhaps trying to fathom how the question – if it *was* a question – could be meant for Gabriel. He saw her uncertainty but kept on moving, guiding her back through the metal debris and shattered glass, past the newly-arrived truck with the words *Klamath County Rescue* on the side, slowing only briefly when he met the eyes of the little girl he'd helped not more than fifteen minutes ago.

She was sitting on the pavement where Gabriel first found her, the bike-rider still dutifully at her side, looking across the twenty yards that separated them with the most serene expression, an expression that seemed to say she'd been to another place, a beautiful place, and now she was back and there was at least one familiar face in the crowd.

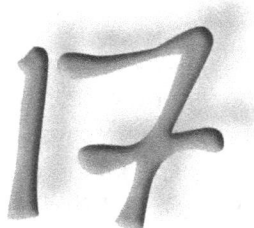

hey drove from the parking lot onto the side street, paused at the intersection where the town's only signal teased the long line of cars in both directions with a meaningless green light, then turned left to get back on the highway. The Mustang was still gaining speed when Lane finally spoke again.

"After what you saw back there, you're doing what?—seventy-five, eighty?"

Gabriel eased up on the pedal, checked the speedometer – *seventy-eight*. Straightening himself in the seat, he shifted his perspective in the rear-view mirror, lowered his gaze from the highway behind them to the paper grocery bags in the back seat. At least one appeared to be growing a dark splotch along the bottom.

"Didn't want to give the frozen stuff time to thaw out, is all."

He winced, thought, *She knows better.* And she did.

"Likely story. I haven't seen you this nervous—" She paused to allow a laugh; maybe it was her use of the word *seen.* "—since you thought I was going to reach over and touch you that first day."

Gabriel turned to see Lane staring purposefully at him, stifled a gasp, quickly moved his head forward and back to see if her eyes followed. They didn't, thankfully; but he was suddenly reminded how careless he'd been when he took Lane by the arm and walked away from the accident scene, the power still coursing through him, his hands still hot from the rush. And the fact he'd been so vital, so fresh from bringing two bodies back to life, that he might've healed her right then and she would've begun screaming how she could see again – the reality both shocked and frightened him.

And now, for the first time, deeply saddened him.

Because it made no sense: Why *couldn't* he heal her? Her alone? Why should this power work through him so indiscriminately, so *uncontrollably,* no matter who he might touch and despite all his prayers to the contrary, and then fail to work in this one, isolated case?

Not that he wanted to heal Lane. He didn't want to heal *any*body... except for the children back there, perhaps, and the mother who ended up not needing his help. At least he hoped she didn't need his help. *God,* he thought, *what if her injuries proved fatal after all?*

His own mother had died before they could pull her from the wreckage, before *he* could be extricated for that matter. True, he'd been able to exchange a few last words with her. He'd prayed with her, too, since she seemed to want it, though his silent petition wasn't the usual request for her soul to rise peacefully and for the heavenly angels to welcome her with loving arms.

Still, he was thankful for those final moments, thankful she hadn't died without the opportunity to say goodbye. And maybe it was just as well he couldn't see her when she took her last breath, couldn't reach across the seat to take her hand, couldn't turn his head or even open his eyes because the dashboard was pressed into his forehead and his eyes were filled with blood. One of the paramedics who finally cut him out of the Nova told him his mother's injuries had been massive, and the twisted metal which trapped her had also done things a son should not be allowed to see, should not be forced to store in his mental memory banks. And for that, too, he was—

"Gabriel—?"

He blinked, checked his speed, assumed Lane was simply re-minding him to slow down. *Fifty-seven.* If anything he needed to pick up the pace.

"What?"

"The accident. I was just wondering if it had some special sig-nificance for you?"

"Oh, *that...*"

He winced again, not so much at his most recent relapse into daydreaming but at how stupid his response sounded, as if the ac-cident had simply slipped his mind, as if what had just taken place was nothing out of the ordinary. Which was hardly the case. If he'd done nothing but stand on the sidewalk and watch, the accident scene would have still sent his mind reeling.

"I mean, yeah—it did, actually. The woman who was trapped in the van..." He tried to say it as objectively as possible. "...that's how my mother died. And I was just, you know—hoping she makes it. All those people around her, there was no way I could—"

He stopped himself, couldn't believe he'd almost said it, couldn't believe it when she said it *for* him.

"Heal her?"

Lane had been staring in his direction the whole time, but turned away now without another word, fixing her gaze in typical passing-scenery mode. Gabriel could no longer see her face, couldn't tell by her expression whether she was already convinced, or she was merely trying to draw out the truth. Assuming the latter, the ruse was work-ing.

He looked ahead, spotted a viewpoint coming up fast where the Sprague veered north from the highway in a tumble of whitewater and boulders. Not that he cared about the view any more than she did.

"What were you saying about the frozen food?" Lane wondered aloud when she sensed the car slowing. In a few more moments she could feel her weight shift to the left as the car swerved right, heard the sweaty clenching of Gabriel's hands on the steering wheel, the scrabble of crushed lava rock underneath their tires.

"Uh, Gabriel...?"

The Mustang skidded briefly on the loose surface before coming to a halt. She could hear the T-bar chunk into *Park*, the ratchet of metal teeth as Gabriel removed the key from the ignition, the plunger in the driver-side door lock pop up just before it opened. She turned questioningly in his direction, could picture him getting out and slamming the door, then crunching around the front of the car to her side.

She looked up as her own door opened, felt a sudden flush of vulnerability, the way she had that first night after inviting Gabriel into her house despite knowing so little about him. And now here she was, twenty minutes from home, parked in some remote turn-out on a two-lane road that might as well be deserted because of the bottleneck back in Sprague.

And she knew something about him he didn't want anyone else to know.

"Gabriel, before I get out..." She took a shallow breath, didn't want to let on she was afraid, or had reason to be. "...I just want you to know I can keep a secret."

"Yeah, well, that's pretty obvious." He paused as if to underline his disapproval, then: "What?—you think I'm gonna do you in right here and dump your body in the river or something?"

If he'd meant it as a joke, she wasn't laughing.

"Wait a minute."

She could hear Gabriel place both hands onto the door sill, bracing himself while he looked down at her through the open window.

"My God, Lane—I just met your parents and fell madly in love with your daughter. What do you think I am?"

"I don't *know* who you are! That's the point."

She was trembling now, no longer hiding her fear. And maybe, she thought, it wasn't so much because he might hurt her. Of *course* he wouldn't hurt her; she had to know that by now, didn't she? It was because, if what she suspected was true, she wouldn't know what to think of him anymore, or how to think of him. Or worse, how to *be* with him.

"Lane, please—this isn't something I could just blurt out while we're breezing merrily along on our way back home, like it's some minor detail in my life story. This is..."

He broke off, pushed away from the door. She could hear his hesitation as he opened his mouth, closed it again, the friction of fabric on skin as he lifted an arm, nails against scalp as he ran fingers through his hair.

"I haven't told this to anyone, Lane," he said at last. "Ever."

She got out without further comment, offered her arm, allowed Gabriel to guide her to a knee-high stone wall that he took care to brush off before gently lowering her atop it. The warmth of his body was tangible as he stepped past her, then threw a leg over the wall so he could straddle it while facing her. She could sense him gathering his thoughts, wet his lips several times like he was about to speak but didn't. At last she could wait no longer, broke the silence herself.

"When Seska and I—the old En'skni woman at the store?—when we put the bags in my car and went out to find you, there was this young girl standing on the curb wearing a bike helmet. She told us how she and her boyfriend were riding on the side of the highway when the accident happened, and they barely got out of the truck's way as it jack-knifed. Her boyfriend went back to see if he could do anything because he recognized the van."

Gabriel drew a breath, released it, the tenor of his exhalation signaling that he'd let his head fall back. He obviously realized where her story was heading, probably understood she was trying to make things easier for him. And just as obviously, he was letting her.

"I guess this little girl he found in the street was a neighbor of his. And she was already dead. But then some man in tan Dockers and long hair—" She forced a laugh now, heard Gabriel take another breath as he brought his head level again. "—that's how she described him. Anyhow, she told me he went over and two minutes later the little girl was sitting up."

She turned toward Gabriel, tried to fix her gaze on where his eyes should be.

"Gabriel, *you* healed my mare. It wasn't some spontaneous recovery. Buddy wasn't wrong about her shattered leg. And the story about the deer?"

"Lane—"

She pushed ahead, if only to finish verbalizing what had been percolating in her mind as early as yesterday, and certainly by last night, though it was no less difficult to accept now.

"Maybe Chino doesn't have such crazy ideas about you. And this *thing* you have about being touched..."

She suddenly reached out, wagged her hand in front of Gabriel, asking him to take it. He seemed unwilling at first – maybe he thought she was only emphasizing some point – but finally obliged. She stood, steadied herself in his grip so she could throw her right leg over the wall and likewise straddle it.

"That night, after Doyle left, I hurt so bad. Everywhere. I didn't want you to know how bad. And come to think of it, I can't believe I *didn't* ask you to drive me to the E.R. like you wanted to." Lane shook her head at the recollection, became aware she was still squeezing Gabriel's hand. Bringing up her other hand to clasp his palm in both of her own, she pulled it toward her. "But then I got into bed with you—I can't believe I did that, either, after what he'd tried to do to me. And then the pain went away."

She sensed his head turning, his energy draining as if to admit she'd uncovered his secret but still didn't understand, *couldn't* understand. She tried to hold his gaze, leaned to one side to look back at him.

"It's true what I told you, Gabriel. It was like it never happened. And when you woke up three hours later, now I know why you were acting so crazy that morning, trying not to show you were upset with me. And then you began touching me, touching my eyes—"

"*Why* was I touching you, Lane?"

His abrupt re-entry into the conversation startled her. She frowned, tried to imagine the purpose of his query. Perhaps she could answer the question he couldn't.

"Because I was still blind. And you were having trouble believing it." She finally withdrew her hands, tried to smile. "And I guess, for you, that was more of a miracle than if I'd been healed."

"It *was*, Lane. I know that's hard for you to understand, but—"

"No, I do. I *do* understand. And it would've been an even bigger miracle if you weren't able to heal Tina, either."

"It would've—yes."

She could hear him shift his weight atop the stone wall, sense the electricity as he learned closer; perhaps she *did* understand.

"And you probably went out to the barn that morning to see if you still had this..." How could she characterize it? How did *he*? "...this ability, this power. And you found you could still do it—"

"No. It's not something I *do*—"

"—which must be why you still won't let anybody else touch you."

"That's right. Because it just happens, Lane. I really don't have any—"

"And you don't want it to happen."

"I *don't*. I wish it would never happen. It's been nothing but—"

"But you went out to those children back there. After the accident. You healed them."

"I *let* them be healed. Through me. Nobody should die like that. My mother—"

"So you pick and choose when to let it happen?"

Lane could sense the electricity being sucked from the air, the fleeting vacuum in the space between them as Gabriel pulled back.

"You were the one who told me to go out there."

It was a weak reply. She bit her lip, hadn't meant to turn on him this way, but she'd come too far now. She had to know.

"So you want to help... *sometimes*."

Two heartbeats. "When it's safe."

"Safe?"

"When I won't be noticed, won't draw attention to myself. Or at least when I'm sure I can get away without being followed."

She could sense his growing defensiveness, couldn't blame him, paused while he spun his head at the sound of an approaching car and exhaled in relief when it passed.

"Lane, can you imagine what would happen if people knew this about me? What *does* happen?"

"So people have found out?"

"In the beginning they did. Before I knew enough to keep it hidden. Now my life is a constant battle to keep people from finding out. Either that, or I'm on the road to somewhere else before they *do*."

"And that's why you were traveling with Vincent? Somebody was about to find out?"

"Yes."

"And Chiloquin was the next *somewhere else*."

"Yes... well, no. It wasn't really my choice. But that's nothing new. I end up staying in a lot of places by accident."

"And you end up meeting a lot of people by accident."

The rustle of shirtsleeves betrayed that he'd folded his arms against his chest. If he'd been defensive before, his tone was now almost icy.

"Lane, I don't know why it doesn't work with you. Is that why you're so angry?"

"Am I angry?"

"Why shouldn't you be? I mean, I touch someone, or someone touches me, and they're healed just like that. But not you. At least not your eyes."

"I'm not sure that's it. Maybe it's because you have this amazing gift and you won't use it. Or you're afraid to."

She paused, listening to the sudden tension in Gabriel's throat, heard the constricted air escaping from his lungs as distinctly as she could once see steam venting from the ammo plant's signal horn. She could tell his mouth was open, head turned just slightly away as if he was looking askance at her, waiting for her to go on.

"I don't know if I'd *want* to see again," she said, hoping that might help. "I could survive without having to look at another howitzer shell, or a scene like you witnessed back there." She felt a sudden shiver, turned her own head back toward the southeast, toward the low, cottonwood-covered hills beyond which Beatty lay. "But I will miss seeing Jenna. I'd trade all the other snapshots I still carry around up here—" She rolled her eyes upward to indicate the inside of her skull, attempted a smile. "—for one clear, mental likeness of my little girl on her third birthday."

"Lane..."

She heard him sigh with the heaviness of regret, of not knowing, of unanswered questions, could tell what the next sentence would be before he spoke the words.

"If I knew what to do, how I could fix it, I swear I would. Right now, right here, on this spot. But I've never really known how it works. I've never been able to get rid of it, and wouldn't have a clue how to get it back if I *did.* I'm telling you, this has never happened to me."

Gabriel reached for her hand now. "...*You've* never happened to me, Lane. It's not just that you're the first person who's given me back some sense of who I used to be, or could've been. It's who you are. It's your..."

He paused, groped for words. Strangely, this unsolicited – and unexpected – confession was making Lane uncomfortable. Richard used to talk this way, this boyishly romantic, impractical way. Being responsible for other people's feelings had always scared her, but it was more than that this time. Because Gabriel was more than that.

"...your confidence, your completeness—even without your eyes. Or maybe *because* of that. Lane, you're someone I could—" He stopped again, as if suddenly thinking of a better way to make her understand. "You're the first somewhere else I've ever wanted to stay, for the rest of my life."

She didn't reply for several seconds, wanted to pull her hand away but knew Gabriel would take it wrong. And how ironic: She'd imagined hearing him say such words as these, *hoped* he might; but that was when he was... what—? Ordinary? Simply mysterious? Merely mortal?

"Don't lie, Gabe. I know it's just the fabulous sex. Gets 'em every time."

He'd waited a few more moments before letting go of her hand, sat there silently debating how to take her reply: Maybe it was just an innocent attempt to lighten the mood. Or another of Lane's bad jokes that was too close to the truth to be funny. But the fact was, he'd just admitted two things he never thought he would – one of which he'd promised to keep to himself whatever the circumstances, the other of which he never imagined himself capable.

He finally lifted himself from the stone wall and simply said, "Those green beans aren't gonna stay frozen much longer," then started for the car without her.

By the time she caught up, Gabriel had opened the car door to discover it wasn't just the two packages of green beans that had begun to thaw. Six of the eight grocery sacks had soaked through on the bottom from all the melting frozen goods. The tuck-n-roll ridges in the back seat upholstery were filled like miniature water troughs.

"Gabriel—"

"Am I wrong, or did we buy out the store's entire freezer section?"

He cut her off, didn't want to hear another contrived explanation, another belated apology. He began to busy himself by brushing the puddled liquid from the leatherette vinyl onto the floor mats, suddenly stopped when he found it wasn't merely water.

"Gabe—"

"*Damn*. Look at this—there's... hamburger juice, chicken juice..."

He'd been an idiot to tell her. He could've kept his mouth shut. Or simply denied it. She might have continued to suspect him, but she would never have known for sure. Or if she did find out eventually, he would be gone by then.

He looked around for something to wipe his hands on, saw that the backseat snowmelt had also begun to dissolve the dried blood he hadn't wiped off after the recent accident, some of which was his own. He immediately backed himself through the open door, tried to shake off the moisture.

"Great. Everything that's not in a can is now sopping wet, maybe even ruined."

"Gabriel, listen to me—"

"You got anything in the trunk to wipe the seat with?"

She threw up her hands in frustration, brought them back to her hips, struck a pose.

"I don't know *what's* in the trunk, actually. I don't have a key."

Gabriel turned, squinted.

"You're kidding."

"I'm not. When I bought this pony five years ago, they never gave me a trunk key. Jimmy Hoffa could be in there for all I know."

Gabriel continued to stare for several seconds, was finally unable to hold back a smile. Lane sensed the break in his mood, allowed her own grin, then a hearty laugh – as much for the release of tension as the silliness of the situation.

"It's true. I really have no idea what's back there."

"You can get into the trunk through the back seat, you know."

"Yeah, somebody *did* tell me that once. Guess I never thought it was all that important. Besides, I'm already driving around with enough baggage as it is."

Gabriel allowed a brief smile for her effort, glanced back at the grocery bags. Wiping his hands on his Dockers, he suddenly found himself hoping he could get in at least one load of laundry before he left. That is, assuming he ever got his Bible back from Vincent. And assuming he must mean so little to Lane.

They were ten miles and ten minutes of small-talk closer to Chiloquin before she made one last attempt.

"I was the idiot," she said, without making any effort to ease back into the subject.

"What?"

It wasn't just that her comment came out of left field. It was the fact she'd used the same term he had applied to himself.

"I mean, I shouldn't joke around with other people's feelings. Bad habit of mine. I'm really sorry if I—"

"We all have our reasons for not letting others get close."

Lane spun to face him but held her tongue. Perhaps, Gabriel thought, she'd realized her cavalier response to his last confession had cut him deeply. She could afford to let him throw back a minor barb.

"So, what do you want to do about the groceries?" he asked.

"Groceries?"

"They say you shouldn't re-freeze stuff, once it thaws out."

Lane released one more sigh, seemed to accept the futility of pressing him at least for the time being. She settled back in her bucket, turned toward the scenery again.

"Well, I guess we could try to eat everything over the next few days."

"Us, and half the Maqlaqs in Chiloquin."

She nodded, thought for several more moments, brightened.

"That's it! The tribal administration runs a soup kitchen at their headquarters. Kinda like their version of the Salvation Army. They serve over a hundred people a day, mostly with profits from the casino. I'm sure they'll take whatever we can't use by this weekend."

Gabriel looked past Lane in the direction she appeared to be gazing. A hundred yards north, the Sprague River was visible once more, paralleling the highway after meandering among the same buttes and escarpments he remembered seeing that morning when the fog lifted. It was obvious he hadn't missed much by way of scenery. The sparsely-wooded hills with occasional clumps of bitterbrush and thistle seemed utterly unremarkable.

"We need go back through town, do we?—to get to this tribal headquarters?" The thought of Lieutenant Fiske briefly crossed his mind.

"It's on the south road between Chiloquin and Ninety-Seven. Like we're going to Corky Girls, then on out the west side." Lane turned back to raise an eyebrow. "Not the same road the B.I.A. station's on, in case you're wondering."

She turned away without waiting for his reaction. He shook his head – she'd done it again – squinted into the distance where the river and highway converged, knew the ranch wouldn't be much farther.

"Want me to drop you off while I go on into town? Maybe you ought'a see how Tina and Fabian are doing."

"That's okay. Buddy's prob'ly stopped by once or twice already. I'm sure they're fine."

Gabriel recalled how she'd mentioned Buddy's regular visits more than once, supposedly for the purpose of checking on the horses. He also recalled how Lane assumed at first it was Buddy who'd pulled Doyle off her, as if the barn and the corrals weren't the only places he might be expected to appear. Gabriel wondered whether Lane was reading his mind right about now.

In less than five minutes the powder-covered drive to the D'Arcy ranch flashed by on the right, and seconds later the bridge over the

Sprague. Lane felt the thump of the tires crossing from asphalt to concrete, abruptly awoke from her own secret thoughts.

"Whoa—did that sneak up on me or what? You must be speeding again."

Maybe she *had* been trying to read his mind.

She sat quietly for the next few minutes, concentrating on the curves in the highway, her body anticipating a few of the tighter turns before the road would straighten and descend gently into the broad plain where the U.S. Army Ammunition Plant was located. Soon she placed her hand on the dash, nodded through the windshield.

"Just a little further. Look for the ammo plant on your left."

"I've been this way a few times, remember?" Gabriel huffed. "It's not like I don't know where—"

He suddenly broke off, squinted. As they passed the turn-out where he'd stopped to burn some time the first night, several dozen cars came into view perhaps a mile ahead. Some were backed up on the highway – Gabriel couldn't tell yet if they were moving – while others could be seen on both shoulders, parked at odd angles.

"Jesus. Not again."

"What?—another accident?"

"Can't tell if it's a car wreck, or..."

The Mustang slowed, rounded a final curve overlooking a more expansive vista toward the west. The traffic jam and roadside parking lot seemed to extend a good half mile from the ammo plant on this side, and at least as far on the other. And though it was hard to make out from this distance, there appeared to be no vehicles inside the gates.

"Gabriel...?"

"Not an accident, thank God. Something's going on at the plant."

hey didn't make it to the Tribal Administration soup kitchen, but neither did their once-frozen food go to waste.

A Maqlaq plant worker whose brother owned a catering business in Chemult was sent to retrieve his brother's "barbeque-on-wheels." The tribes often used the portable grill for pow-wows since its upper and lower racks could easily accommodate an adult stag, in addition to assorted waterfowl and fish. The two month's supply of hamburger, chicken and rainbow trout Lane had purchased in Sprague River was gratefully received, and mostly consumed by the end of swing shift.

Not that there *was* a swing shift.

As C.J. explained once the Mustang was parked in the space they'd saved, the employees on day shift turned out to be the last workers allowed inside the plant. The entire crew, from assembly lines to office staff, were subsequently asked to go home an hour early – "for maintenance reasons," as management put it. Then, after their vehicles were cleared from the lot, the gates were closed and padlocked. When cars began arriving around 3:45 for swing shift, employees were told the lines had been shut down until further notice.

Many of the workers simply turned around and drove off, expecting a phone call within an hour or two informing them the plant had reopened. Others parked alongside the highway to wait. Temporary shutdowns, after all, were not unheard of. Whenever safety supervisors detected a danger of any kind, some or all of the site would be evacuated – and *had* been, occasionally in mid-shift. A full-scale evacuation had happened perhaps a dozen times over the last decade, and the problem never caused more than a half-day's delay. Usually less.

But such shutdowns had occurred only twice since the ten-to-midnight maintenance period had been inaugurated. And the fact that *this* one was happening only one day after the town meeting – and two days before the predicted "invasion" of the flu – began to seem more than coincidental. After a few phone calls to workers who'd finished day shift, as well as consultation with various leaders in the community, it became apparent that plant employees were being locked out.

"But if it's illegal for federal workers to go on strike," Gabriel asked, still sitting behind the wheel, "isn't it just as illegal for management to stage a lockout?"

"They're not calling it a lockout," C.J. replied, "just like we're not calling our action a strike. Plus, there really *are* safety issues, so it's not a lockout anyway."

"Safety issues?" Lane echoed, leaning a hip against the fender.

The clique gathered around her suddenly grew quiet, exchanged glances.

"One way to put it." It was Ken who finally answered, the Anglo rancher who'd been part of last night's dinner discussion. "Two Bears got wind of it this morning. Seems there was at least one other group who got together after the meeting yesterday. Word is, they decided there's only one way to make sure the U.S. Army gets the point that some of us locals want 'em gone."

"They can't be that stupid."

Apparently Lane had already figured out the other group's plan, leaving Gabriel to shake his head in confusion.

"Well, if the feds can drag their feet like they're doin' on the Restoration," one of the Maqlaqs shrugged, "can you really blame them?"

"You can," C.J. said, "'cause this kind of thing isn't good for *any*body."

"I know this really isn't my concern," Gabriel broke in, "but what exactly are we talking about here?"

"We're talking about sabotage. And it *is* your concern."

Sabotage, in fact, had always been a possibility at the Chiloquin ammo plant, even if it wasn't high on the list of potential threats. Terrorist attacks from outside sources were far more worrisome in management's view, given the increasing incidents since 9/11 and the country's latest misadventures in Africa and the Mideast. Combined with the lack of anti-war sentiments or political activism within the local community – at least before now – sabotage was considered unlikely.

Still, an inside job couldn't be ignored completely. Numerous countermeasures were always in effect – from entrance drive scanners to German Shepherds sweeping the lot for hidden explosives, from keeping employees' cars at a safe distance to ongoing video surveillance both inside and out. And of course there were the half-dozen SWAT-trained soldiers always on site, in addition to the counter-terrorist unit stationed at Kingsley Field south of Klamath, only ten minutes away by Blackhawk helicopter.

"Report is, there are at least three people from day shift, maybe more, who are still inside the plant."

"They don't know the exact number?"

Another Bustin posed the question as he walked over to join the group beside the Mustang. Gabriel, meanwhile, was still digesting C.J.'s earlier remark.

"What do you mean, it's my concern...?"

C.J. ignored the Bustin's query for the moment, took a step to where he could see both Lane and Gabriel simultaneously.

"It's everybody's concern, you want my opinion. But most a'the people I've talked to in the last hour pin responsibility on you." He nodded at Lane.

"That's bullshit!" Gabriel shot back. "Just because she raised the question about the ammo plant doesn't make her—"

"...And on *you*."

C.J. turned, fixed his gaze on Gabriel now. There might've been the hint of a smirk.

"You can't be serious."

"Plenty of people in this town think it's a little suspicious you're staying with Lane this weekend."

Jesus. It was Fiske's conspiracy theory all over again.

"This is crazy. I had absolutely no part in what Lane said."

"True," Lane conceded. "Except you convinced me to *say* it."

Gabriel peered through the windshield at her, aggravated she'd so easily accept responsibility for what was happening, much less palm some of it off on him.

"Anyway," he said, looking back at C.J., "Lane never said a word about what action they should take. And sabotage?—totally off the wall. She only asked people to stop and think about things, for Chrissake!"

"Just plant the seed, is how Gabriel put it."

He frowned again, now leaning out the window to send Lane a baffled look she obviously could not have seen, though his elbow banging on the door panel made it clear enough.

"Well, you *did*."

"Maybe. But *this*—" He waved at the hubbub surrounding them, pulled his head back into the car. "—is not the seed you planted."

"Look, there's always a few people in any group who are more radical than everybody else," C.J. said. "Whenever the majority decides to do something, you run the risk these people will want to take things a step or two further."

If anything, Gabriel thought, *it's C.J. who sounds like the union activist.*

"Then it's possible they would've done this, even if Lane *hadn't* said anything yesterday."

"Possible."

"So why pin it all on Lane and me?"

"I'm not. I'm just telling you what some people are saying."

There was that smirk again.

"You think this is funny, getting the rap for this?"

"Not hardly. If it turns out a few of our people *are* in there, and they're intent on doing some damage?—there's a SWAT team hunting them down right now with orders to shoot first and ask questions later. Nothing funny about that."

"So, what could they do?—the Maqlaqs who are inside?"

"What makes you think they're all Maqlaq?" It was the rancher again. "One a'the day shift workers who's unaccounted for is Richard McCaffery."

"Richard? No way!" Lane's sudden surprise just as quickly turned fearful. "No. You heard him at the meeting. Richard was against the whole idea of a sick-out, not to mention anything like this."

Gabriel was no less shocked Lane's ex-suitor might be involved, but he still wanted an answer. "What could they do?" he repeated.

"I don't think they'd go anywhere near the ordnance," Ken ventured. "For one thing, half the SWAT guys'll be guarding the finished product. But there's plenty a'places in there to hide. The original building wasn't constructed with security in mind, and the Army's retrofit was basically a Rube Goldberg job, y'ask me. Richard knows that, good as anybody—he was on the construction crew at the time. Prob'ly some nooks and crannies he knows about the SWAT team doesn't."

Gabriel noticed Lane's eyes widen just slightly at the rancher's remark, saw her start to glance his way before catching herself.

"Anyhow," the rancher went on, "unless they posted guards at every machine, somebody who knows his way around could probably avoid detection long enough to raise some serious havoc, maybe shut down some a'the lines for weeks. Be easy enough to take a crowbar, a little motor oil, gum things up big time. Easy to pull a few circuit boards or bash in a few computers, too, so much of the stuff's gone high-tech now."

"They'd actually *do* that?"

"They might," C.J. said, "if they thought the ammo plant could be used as leverage for settling our Restoration issues. *And* if they thought they could get off without much jail time. Feds have been known to be lenient, long as things don't get too far out of hand."

"What if they think it's *already* out of hand?"

Gabriel gestured out the driver-side window in the direction of Chiloquin. Two olive drab military vehicles were now making their way through the outer fringes of the crowd some distance up the highway.

"Son of a bitch," C.J. spat. "Here come enough guards to post at every machine."

Lane reacted nervously, reached back through the window to lay a hand on Gabriel's shoulder. "Who is it?—who's coming?"

"Looks like Army trucks, maybe National Guard."

"Least it's not the AT unit from Kingsley," somebody added.

The low rumble of diesel engines droned over the increasing crowd noise. Gabriel shifted from side to side, trying to peer through the group clustered about the car. He could see several more men on the road beyond turning back with questioning faces, as if asking C.J. and the others what they should do. By the looks of it, the people now gathered around them – Lane included – were considered the *ad hoc* command center for the employees.

It was possible, Gabriel suddenly thought, the workers might be instructed to block the two trucks, perhaps lay down in the roadway *en masse* or set up a line of pickups to prevent them from coming through. Maybe they were asking the leaders for permission to act. Unfortunately, it was also possible the leadership hadn't had time to develop any such contingency plans. C.J. admitted as much, simply shrugged and nodded, essentially telling the others not to interfere. Not that his decision – or lack of one – was a mistake. Even if they'd had a plan, a roadblock was a pretty extreme measure to use this early in the game.

It *wasn't* too early, however, to expect a more complete explanation of what plant officials were doing. A small delegation had come back from the gates thirty minutes ago with nothing more than a restatement of the previous announcement that the plant would remain closed until further notice. They were also told in no uncertain terms to remain outside the restricted zone surrounding the plant, as if they were members of the general public and not its employees. With the approach of the two troop transports – at least that's what they appeared to be, with their camouflaged canopies pulled taut to hide their human cargo – the stakes were obviously going up. And so, therefore, was the need for information.

Behind the two trucks, Gabriel could see even more cars driving in from Chiloquin, along with at least one highway patrol cruiser. With sympathies likely to fall equally on either side of the sick-out, and the probability of ill feelings because of the lockout, the potential for some kind of flare-up was escalating by the moment.

The two trucks were now less than thirty yards away, beginning their turns into the plant's winding entrance drive. Beyond them, the chain-link gate was already rolling, a pair of security guards positioning themselves on either side. Gabriel noticed for the first time that Deputy Chino was among the crowd on the edge of the highway nearest the gate. She was waving aside a small group of employees who were blocking the entrance, whether inadvertently or on purpose. Gabriel also noticed, as the trucks swung end-wise to him, the movement of soldiers beneath the canvas canopies, as well as the telltale glinting of gunmetal gray. Colonel Halvorsen obviously meant business.

And, obviously, the tension was beginning to wear on Lane.

"We need to do something. We need to stop all this. Why can't a few of us go into the plant and talk to them?"

"To management?—we tried that," C.J. said. "They won't even let us inside the yellow line. And nobody's answering the phone in the front office, either." Suddenly he turned to a nearby Bustin. "Anybody seen Amy Halvorsen? Think she'd give us her father's cell phone number?"

There was a brief discussion over the hood of the Mustang while several people were assigned to search the crowd for Halvorsen's daughter, assuming she'd been locked out, too. The point was made, however, that Amy would likely have known about the administration's move in advance, and warned not to come in. Either way, it might be possible to call her, perhaps even use her as an intermediary. More than one objection was raised to this proposal.

And it was during the ensuing debate when Gabriel poked his head out again and reminded Lane about the groceries. Lane nodded, called over a pair of Maqlaqs whose voices she recognized in the crowd nearby and asked them whether they could use their now un-frozen goods for the Klamath Emergency Meals program. Gabriel strained to hear the reply, something to the effect that the program would happily accept their donation, but plans were now being made to set up some kind of meal wagon for the locked-out employees. Would she consider letting them use her food for that purpose instead, they wondered? *Of course,* Lane replied.

To Gabriel's relief, the *ad hoc* leaders had migrated some distance away from the Mustang during their conversation. Gabriel took the opportunity to slip out the passenger-side door and find relative safety behind the neighboring pickup. Not a moment too soon, either, because a troupe of four Maqlaqs immediately descended on the Mustang to strip the back seat of all its groceries. And just as suddenly Lane rushed over to stop them.

"No, wait—*wait* a minute!" she called out as both car doors popped open. "You need to give Gabriel some room to get out."

Gabriel watched her from perhaps fifteen feet away, smiled at her unexpected – and oddly gratifying – protectiveness. She groped for the opened driver's door, reached inside to feel for him, drew back anxiously. A heartbeat or two, then:

"Lane... over here."

She straightened, squinted with realization, swirled. "You are *so* cruel. I don't know why I ever let you into my life."

Even so she shook her head and grinned like a good sport, found her way across the open ground to the pickup with the same effortless aplomb that continued to leave Gabriel awestruck, stopped directly in front of him.

"My fault for not paying attention," she said.

"My fault for thinking you didn't care," he replied softly.

Lane turned in the direction of the Maqlaqs as they set about collecting the groceries – canned goods and staples right along with freezer items – then back, the whites of her eyes luminous as ever. "Maybe if you'd given me ten more seconds to explain myself back there at the turnout, you'd know how I feel." She lowered her gaze, shrugged. "Not that I'm quite so sure anymore, because—"

"It's okay, Lane. I'm not asking—"

"—there's this other side of you that'll take—"

"—you to explain yourself."

"—some getting used to, and I don't know if—"

"Lane!"

She stopped with a wince – he *still* couldn't get ten seconds without interruption – was about to speak again when the crunching of multiple shoes nearby turned her head. Gabriel likewise glanced away, spotted C.J. rounding the pickup, followed by Two Bears and, to his surprise, Deputy Chino.

"You need to come with us," Chino said. "Both of you."

It was only natural they'd want Lane for the job. For one thing, last night's group of five had already asked her to be their spokesperson based on what she'd said at the meeting. For another, virtually everyone in Chiloquin had a soft spot for Lane D'Arcy, partly because of what she'd been through, partly because so many of them had grown up with her or watched her grow up.

They also admired her spunk as a preacher's kid, even more so now that she seemed to be pulling her shattered life back together. That kind of grit trumped personal or political differences. And besides, as the rancher so tactfully put it, what were the guards going to do? – shoot down a blind woman as she came to make peace?

Gabriel, however, was reluctant to go along. To accompany Lane was tantamount to admitting he *was* the activist Fiske and Halvorsen had suspected almost from day one; and now, as they would surely see it, he was merely taking off his sheep's clothing. Worse, Gabriel was playing into the misguided Maqlaq legend making him out to be some kind of Messianic figure. He wanted no part of it.

Chino was fully prepared to escort Lane to the gates herself if Gabriel refused, even if the act would almost certainly cost her deputy's badge once Fiske found out. It was one thing for the Lieutenant's underlings to wear their sympathies on their sleeves, quite another for any of them to openly take sides. Gabriel's suggestion that Chino could claim she was only protecting Lane from plant workers who didn't want her to go, or holding back others who wanted to march to the gates *with* her, wasn't convincing; Fiske would see through it. If the deputy could prevent other people from going along with Lane, she could damn well keep Lane from going in the first place.

It was only when Chino took Lane by the elbow and started across the highway that Gabriel swore under his breath and finally loped after them.

"I don't have a job to lose," he explained to the deputy, grabbing Lane's opposite arm. "And if I don't keep on Lane's good side, I won't have a place to *stay*, either."

"About time you realized that," Lane said, starting for the gate once more.

Chino nodded and let go – as if she'd expected him to come around, Gabriel thought – then hurried ahead to clear the crowd at the top of the entrance drive. Inside the chain-link fence, the two military vehicles could be seen parked next to the employee entrance. A company of soldiers in camouflage fatigues were off-loading both themselves and their gear, M-16s strapped across their shoulders. Some had already disappeared into the plant as their C.O. waved them on, but when the officer spotted two members of the crowd approaching the gate, a squad peeled off to join the four guards already posted there.

The original quartet had been watching Gabriel and Lane through binoculars even before they'd started down the drive. While their own rifles hung at an unthreatening angle toward the ground, one of them raised a bullhorn, pointed it at the pair.

"The two of you headed this way... be advised you're approaching the restricted zone. Do not—repeat, do *not*—cross the yellow line."

Until that moment, most of those in the crowd extending a half-mile up and down the highway were still unaware Lane and Gabriel had been dispatched. The sound of the amplified voice drew a momentary hush, followed by a buzz that roiled along the pavement in either direction like waves in a pond. Lane was briefly distracted by the sudden clamor, but quickly turned back toward the guard hut.

"Stop it, Whitley," she scoffed. "Don't talk to me like you don't know who I am."

The additional soldiers were now taking positions behind the chain-link, one of them quietly asking for orders. Lane picked out the whisper despite the crowd noise behind her.

Gabriel felt Lane's pace slow, then resume, didn't know why. "You're not having second thoughts, are you?"

She squinted, still straining to hear, didn't reply for several more moments.

"Who is that, came to the gate just now?"

"A few Guardsmen from the trucks," Gabriel replied.

"Trigger-happy bastards. Warning shots, for Chrissake." It must've been something she'd heard. "They're the ones we need to watch out for."

"C'mon, Lane," Sergeant Whitley went on, now more informally, "don't make us do anything we don't want to." He lowered the bullhorn halfway through his plea, belatedly realizing there was no reason to broadcast their conversation. Besides which Lane was finally within earshot. "You know we gotta keep this area clear when there's a security breach."

Lane kept walking. Gabriel tried not to look down as they stepped past the bright yellow line in the asphalt.

"That's what we've come to talk about."

"We may know who *you* are, Lane—" It was the other guard Gabriel remembered from his initial visit to the plant, the less friendly, more strident of the pair on duty that day. "—but we sure as hell don't know your friend. Now stop right there before we—"

"But, see, that's all you need to know, Hyatt—he *is* my friend, and he came with me only because I..."

She broke off when Gabriel tugged on her upper arm. An instant later the whine of the motorized gate could be heard as it began to roll aside, then almost immediately stopped. They both halted, now perhaps ten feet away.

"Are they letting us in, or is someone coming out?" Lane whispered.

"I'd say the latter, but nobody's moving yet."

"Listen, Laney," the first guard resumed, "the Colonel gave us explicit orders to arrest any civilian or employee who approaches the gate without authorization, and get out the tear gas if things heat up. Now look, I know you two don't want—"

"We're not here to cause trouble, Sergeant," Gabriel broke in. "We just want to know what's going on inside—is that too much to

ask? I'm sure the Colonel understands he's not helping the situation by keeping us all in the dark out here."

Gabriel regretted his last remark as soon as it left his lips. If
he'd wanted to admit his involvement in the labor action – if he *had*
been involved – he could hardly have made it more clear.

The guard moved his eyes from Lane to Gabriel, seemed to be
sizing him up. "Well, Mister Woods... it does appear you got yourself
in pretty deep since you came to town, doesn't it? For a guy who's
just biding his time until his ride shows up, seems like you've become quite the celebrity."

And just like that the benefit of the doubt he'd extended Gabriel
in their first encounter was gone. Then again, it was worth a try.

"Have you heard anything? Is Vincent still on schedule for tomorrow morning?"

"Assuming you really *were* waiting for him?—I'd say the chances are pretty damn slim at this juncture. And if I know Colonel
Halvorsen, he's already cancelled all pick-ups and deliveries 'til this
thing blows over. Not to mention it's a bad idea to bring in new
hardware while our guys are combing the rafters for bogies."

"So that *is* what's going on?" Lane queried. "You're conducting
a search?"

Lane took a few steps closer to the fence, stopped when she
heard boots in the gravel on the other side. Gabriel followed, grabbed
her arm to indicate she'd gone far enough, ended up standing just
behind her.

The second guard was clearly chafing to send out the fresh
troops, all of whom had now formed a single line behind the three-
foot-wide opening. Gabriel suddenly heard movement in the crowd
some eighty yards behind him, turned with mild surprise to see a
contingent of Maqlaqs fanning out on the shoulder of the road like a
football team preparing for kickoff. In spite of himself he held up a
hand for them to hold their position, had no reason to think they
would. But if plant officials and half the townspeople thought he
was part of the conspiracy, he might as well play the role.

The guards were evidently impressed with this display of control, exchanged relieved glances. Even Lane took note. She'd no doubt
heard the scuffling of the opposing forces, the rustle of Gabriel's

shirt as he raised an arm, the sudden quieting of the crowd. She cast a mystified look his way before turning back once more.

"Look, Whitley," she said, "I know you're not supposed to give out any unauthorized information—"

"*Any* information, period," the second guard corrected.

"—but if Richard is one of the employees that security's looking for?—it's really important I know."

"Yeah?—*why?*"

If the sergeant hadn't asked, Gabriel would have.

"Because..." She lowered her eyes slightly, lifted them again in earnest. "...because I can talk to him, talk him out of whatever he thinks he's doing. And then maybe whoever else is in there with him will come out, too."

"First off, Laney girl—" Again the second guard. "—this is an internal matter. Last time I checked you don't work here. And even when you did, I don't remember *talk* bein' one a'your strong points."

"Hey!—don't you ever—"

The guard tightened his grip on his M-16 as Gabriel took an angry step forward, but continued without stopping, eyes fixed on Lane.

"Besides which, when our guys find out where Richard is?—I'm sure they can talk him outta whatever he's up to real easy."

He offered a grim smile Lane thankfully could not see, raised the barrel of his rifle from ground to sky to bring home the point. She swallowed the insult – the guard was friends with Doyle; what else could she expect? – pressed ahead for the answer.

"So you're saying Richard *is* one of the people who's in there?"

Now the guard swallowed, blinked with chagrin for as much as admitting it, after making a point not to divulge anything.

"Look Lane," Sergeant Whitley cut in, "I know you're concerned about any friends of yours who might be inside. I get that. I also know the Colonel's always been fond of you. How 'bout I convey your offer to him, and if we get into a position where you might be able to help, we'll get a message to you."

He paused, stepped closer to his partner, stood just behind him as if what he was about to say was meant equally for his ears.

"Meantime, let's all try not to do or say anything 'might raise the level of tension higher than it already is. What we don't need is an incident, if you know what I mean. 'Fact, the best thing you can do right now is go back across the highway and tell everybody we're doing everything we can to handle this without using deadly force."

Gabriel could feel Lane stiffen beneath his palm. He glanced away as the last few soldiers from the two military transports disappeared into the ammo plant with their carbines and clear plastic bags containing gas masks, pondered for a moment how people could still think the best deterrent to violence was the threat of still *greater* violence.

"And whatever we do, it's gonna be by the book. You know same as me, we're bound by procedure when certain things happen. Just like we followed it two years ago, when that grenade..."

The sergeant let his words trail off. Gabriel assumed he was simply biting his tongue, suddenly aware how inappropriate his reference was – especially when he rolled his eyes as if regretting his words. But then Lane abruptly swirled, turning toward what sounded like a backhoe scooping lava rock. Gabriel turned, too, saw a brown-and-white Blazer laboring diagonally across the rock bed between the highway and the fence line. Even if the route *did* circumvent the crowd at the top of the entrance drive, the police car was paying for it in spades, nearly bogging down in the protective perimeter designed to thwart terrorist attacks.

"That could only be Fiske," Sergeant Whitley sighed.

It took another ten seconds for the police car to plow through the lava rock, engine roaring, chunks spewing from behind like the rooster tail from a speedboat. At last the car bounced onto the drive between Lane and the gate, front tires suddenly biting pavement and nearly sending it off the other side. Gabriel yanked Lane back as the car skewed sideways to a halt, dirt and crushed rock still skittering about their ankles. Lieutenant Fiske threw open his door, rose into the cloud of dust.

"I *told* the Colonel you had a hand in this!" He practically beamed, reached behind him to extract a pair of cuffs from his belt. "We find out the people inside are following your instructions?—it'll be conspiracy to infiltrate a government installation, not just driving with an expired license."

Lane heard the jingle of the stainless steel cuffs, stepped in front of Gabriel, sent an urgent look toward Sergeant Whitley.

"Is this the kind of incident you were talking about?"

"Hold on, Lieutenant," the sergeant said, slipping through the gate past the Guardsmen. "Everything's under control here... so far." He halted beside Fiske's Blazer, glanced conspicuously toward the highway where Deputy Chino – and now four other officers including Buddy – had positioned themselves in front of an increasingly noisy crowd. "I don't know exactly what you've got in mind, or what charges you're bringing against Mister Woods here. But you are *not* going to arrest him in front of all these people."

Fiske scowled at the guard's request – his *demand* – looked away at the hundred-plus townspeople now lining the highway, evidently cognizant his intended action might be less than wise. Even so, it wasn't easy for him to be overruled like this. He turned back, squinted.

"You're aware I outrank you, Sergeant?"

"Not on this side of the yellow line... sir."

The Lieutenant blinked, bested once again, glanced from the guard to Gabriel.

"And you're planning to *stay* on this side of the line, are you?"

"Actually, they were just about to leave when you drove up," Whitley answered. "Good thing I made 'em wait, 'cause I hate to think what might'a happened if you'd intercepted them up the drive there, closer to all their friends."

He stepped around the rear of the Blazer, halted beside Lane and Gabriel in a defensive posture that caught them all by surprise. "So, unless you've got some serious paper to serve, Lieutenant... murder, rape, drug trafficking, maybe... my advice would be to let these two walk on back without further delay. And I believe Colonel Halvorsen would concur."

Fiske continued to squint. After making such a high-visibility entrance – and hardly an elegant one at that – he couldn't let Gabriel go without something to show for it.

"I want your word, in front of all these witnesses—" He scanned both the security guards and soldiers, returned his gaze to Gabriel. "—you won't skip town, and once this is over you'll turn yourself in."

"On what charge?" Lane asked.

"Like I said, driving without a... valid license." Fiske blinked several times, barely able to mumble the last two words.

"Driving without—" Lane held back a laugh. "And did you actually *see* the accused committing this horrible crime?"

"Me personally?"

"Or Deputy Chino? Buddy maybe?"

"You know they wouldn't tell me even if they did."

"So how do you—"

"Friend a'mine, OHP captain down in Sprague River."

Gabriel tensed, as did Lane.

"He saw you driving away from the scene of an accident down there earlier this afternoon. Got a make on both the car and the driver." Fiske stared evenly at Gabriel, knew he'd regained the upper hand. "He also saw... some other things."

"You're saying Woods had something to do with the accident?" the sergeant asked.

Gabriel could see Fiske hesitate at the guard's query, as though he might actually be thinking of some way to implicate him. At last he blew out a breath.

"Not that we know of. But there were some pretty wild reports filed by a few of the eyewitnesses, all concerning someone who fit Woods' description. They're still trying to sort 'em all out."

"And what exactly do these reports say?"

"Whitley," Lane jumped in, "what does any of this have to do with what's going on here?... now?"

The guard nodded. "You're right." Then, to Gabriel: "So what about it, Woods? I heard the Lieutenant ask you a question."

Now it was Gabriel who hesitated. Lane caught her breath, turned partway around as if to show she was just as interested in his answer as Fiske was. Depending on what the OHP reports contained – depending on whether Gabriel was beginning to feel things closing in – there was a very real chance he *would* try to leave Chiloquin. The possibility suddenly terrified her.

"Look, I haven't done anything wrong. Besides, I'm still waiting for my things to be returned."

"That story again?" Fiske sneered. "Even if you *weren't* lying, you prob'ly won't see Vincent again for at least another week, with what's goin' on here."

Gabriel traded glances with the guard; it was basically the same thing *he'd* said. But there was more than a mere *I-told-you-so* look in his eyes. A residue of suspicion, perhaps? Curiosity about the reports from Sprague River?

"So what are you waiting for?" Whitley finally spouted. "Go on, both'a you. Go tell everyone the situation's being handled. Tell 'em nobody's gonna get hurt, long as everybody stays calm and we can all do our jobs the way we know how. Agreed?"

There was a brief pause before Lane, then Gabriel, nodded their assent and Fiske reluctantly did likewise. As they went their respective ways, Lane wondered if she was the only one who noticed that Gabriel hadn't answered Fiske's question.

W_hy Richard would not only switch sides_ in the dispute but engage in such potentially violent action became the hot topic out on the highway. Almost to a man, the entire assembly seemed shocked by his apparent conversion. With the possible exception of Lane.

And Richard's wife, Elizabeth.

She'd come out to the plant to pick him up as she always did, figured her husband must have gotten a ride home when his shift let out early, then dropped her two young boys off at the day care center she relied on whenever she had errands to run. Hoping she and Richard might have some time alone together, she hurried home only to find he wasn't there, waited expectantly for most of an hour before receiving the phone call to come back to the plant because her husband was still inside.

And it was all Lane's fault.

Only Lane could have turned him around so suddenly, she railed, storming over to the group still clustered around the Mustang. Only

Lane had that kind of influence over her husband. *Still*. And it became obvious to Gabriel, as he sat in the safety of the car once more, there was far more history between Richard and Lane than he knew, or cared to know. Which is when he leaned out to call Lane over, suggesting they go back to her ranch and wait out the stand-off there.

C.J. was quick to agree. Lane, after all, had become a source of increasing division at the highway vigil – not merely because of the confrontation with Richard's wife, but because her views were still shared by only a minority. Most of the people along the highway supported a sick-out, but fewer wanted the ammo plant gone; and only a handful were sympathetic – at least openly – to some kind of physical takeover designed to force the issue. The possibility that Lane had something to do with what was now transpiring, even if indirectly, was making her continued presence less than welcome. Any lingering suspicion about what role Gabriel might've played wasn't helping either.

With a still-empty pantry at home, they stayed only long enough to have some of their own chicken and vegetables from the portable barbeque. Deputy Chino offered to drive them back to the ranch and notify them should anything significant develop – even to return for Lane should she be needed for any reason. When it was determined that Fiske had gone back into Chiloquin, however, Gabriel politely declined Chino's offer and revved up the Mustang. They took C.J.'s cell phone with them, as well as a few epithets from a pair of Bustin stockroom workers who were only too happy to see them go.

The eastern sky was an almost iridescent azure as Gabriel drove through what remained of the crowd and finally broke out onto the open highway. Behind them the sun was already below the buttes defining the western boundary of the Klamath tribal lands, and with the sun's descent went Lane's mood.

"I'm sorry things haven't turned out the way you expected," Gabriel said after a minute of brooding silence.

"I don't know *what* I expected. But you're right... anything but this."

He hesitated before pressing her, wasn't the least bit curious for his own sake, but knew she needed to talk about it.

"I know you're worried about Richard..."

"Terrified. He's still such a child in some ways." She paused with a look bordering on pity, then expelled a breath. "You want my opinion?—he married Elizabeth just to spite me. And even *then* he's never been able to... I mean, he just can't—"

"You mean he still loves you."

She blinked, dropped her chin. Gabriel could see, even in the fading light, it wasn't merely her own emotions she wasn't "good at." Maybe the idea that others could love her, could care deeply about her, was difficult for her to accept, or even recognize. He'd had a taste of her emotional blindness himself, though in his case it was more understandable.

Gabriel let his foot off the gas, didn't want to hurry Lane back to her horses and her household chores before she'd had a chance to finish what she'd started.

"It's complicated," she said at last. "It's not like Richard is doing this because he's trying to get my attention, or he thinks this is what I'd want. He can't possibly think this is what I'd want." Another pause. "Although..."

She grimaced at the apparent difficulty of recalling the memory. Or the emotions which accompanied it.

"Although...?"

"He once threatened to blow up the ammo plant. Right after the accident. Funny, isn't it? One of his friends told me a few months later. It was just an idle threat—you know, something you say without really meaning it. Like the plant was somehow responsible and it deserved to be punished." She shook her head. "Heard he went a little crazy those first couple' days when nobody was sure I'd even survive, much less—"

The tires thumped as they met the concrete span over the Sprague. As expected, Lane jerked her head up, was about to speak when Gabriel beat her to it.

"I know, I know—just ahead on the left."

The Mustang slowed, turned into the drive, slid in the soft dirt until the treads regained traction, headlamps brightening the three-legged mailbox where Gabriel first realized Lane was blind.

"Want me to stop and grab your mail?" he asked. But even before she could answer, he fired off another. "Wait—you think they'd send the U.S. Army out here to keep tabs on us?"

In the narrow swath through the lodgepoles, the headlights now reflected from the beveled edges of countless tread marks, presumably left by the movements of one or more heavy vehicles. They were consistent, Gabriel mused, with the troop transports he'd seen back at the ammo plant. He came to a full stop.

"What—? What is it?"

"Tire tracks, big ones. More than one set, looks like. Can't tell whether they're only going in, or coming out. Maybe both."

Lane pondered a moment, finally nodded. "Going in is my guess."

Gabriel turned with mild surprise. "You know who it is?"

"Yeah. And so do you."

Fiske couldn't put his finger on it, and it continued to erode whatever peace of mind he still clung to. Maybe, like his chronic ulcer, the current problems had been simmering beneath the surface since the 70s, long before he'd done his five years with the Bend P.D. and applied for the top spot at the B.I.A. field office in Chiloquin. He'd simply assumed the underlying tension between Indian and white man was the natural state of affairs; and only during the mid-90s did he sense things beginning to boil over.

He was sure the ammo plant wasn't the cause – although its presence *did* aggravate the differences between their cultures, even as it improved both groups' economic conditions. No, the real motivation came from elsewhere, from outside agitators, special interests with their own not-so-hidden political agendas, or economic ones.

The casino hadn't been the Maqlaqs' idea either. Even the Restoration was an imported notion. The Platte River Indians had been infected with it by the Lakotas, and the Lakotas from secessionists up in Canada who were prodded by French separatists for their own self-serving reasons. The locals were somehow related to the Plattes, and it didn't matter that the B.I.A. could make concessions of large tracts of barren, undeveloped plains without undue cost or consequence. The Chiloquin natives were now convinced they deserved their land back as well, even if white landowners had already invested millions of their own dollars in it.

All of which failed to explain what Gabriel Woods was doing in Chiloquin. Fiske had researched every available database and couldn't confirm his involvement in any political cause or peace movement. Chino let slip that Woods had relatives in the area. After the town meeting yesterday, Doyle Pollard had told him Gabriel was somehow related to Lane, but wouldn't say precisely how he'd come to know this. Some of the locals were even passing a rumor he was Maqlaq. Woods *was* olive enough to possess some Indian blood, but he could just as easily be of Latin or Mediterranean descent, or even Middle Eastern.

It was the latter possibility that worried him the most – or had earlier, at least. The reports from Sprague basically put everything up for grabs. The doctor's account – or was he a veterinarian? – about someone fitting Woods' description, someone who had helped him revive two of the victims using techniques the likes of which he'd never seen, was unsettling enough. The teenage biker's claim that Woods had essentially brought one of the victims back from the dead, and without any help from the vet, could be dismissed, of course.

But then there were the two shop owners whose testimony was so similarly bizarre that the OHP officer refused to file it. Another three or four accounts *were* filed, simply confirming that two of the victims had been pronounced dead at the scene; but the same victims were later ID'd after arriving at Klamath General – one in good condition, the other serious but stable.

The bottom line was, Fiske didn't know *what* to think now. But he also had enough on Woods to take him back into custody and hold him for as long as it took to discover his real identity. And he would do exactly that, just as soon as he'd escorted Vincent through the roadblock and into the safety of the ammo plant's concrete barriers.

It hadn't occurred to him Vincent would be parked anyplace but where he said he'd be. Actually, Fiske approved of the location chosen by the old trucker as soon as he'd been informed. The firebreak was well east of town, beyond the territorial claims of the local tribes. There were no ranches or other dwellings within a mile, and the break formed a loop behind a stand of jackpines thick enough to keep the truck well hidden from the highway.

Which is why Lieutenant Fiske was mildly surprised to find no trace of the big-rig's tires in the thirty-foot-wide firebreak where it intersected the roadbed. It was possible Vincent had taken a pine bough and swept the soft dirt to conceal his presence. But by the time Fiske had driven two hundred yards back into the trees and seen nothing more than the impressions of someone's ATV, he began to feel downright foolish.

Almost as foolish as when he was told to leave the ammo plant gates two hours ago, without having taken Woods into custody. Right there in front of half the population of Chiloquin.

His first impulse was to call in and report the truck missing, or at least tell plant officials Vincent's rig wasn't parked where he'd claimed. But Halvorsen had told him to direct all calls through the front gate for the time being, and Fiske wasn't about to talk to Sergeant Whitley again. Besides, he had an idea where Vincent might've parked instead.

He kicked himself for not checking out the possibility when he passed Lane's driveway on his way out to the butte twenty minutes ago. Because as soon as his headlights skimmed across the powder beside her mailbox, the semi's tire treads stood out like those footprints in the photos of Armstrong's first steps on the moon. And if the same thought now crossing his mind had occurred to him only a week earlier, he would've considered that, too, sheer lunacy.

Vincent arrived a half-day ahead of schedule, it turned out, specifically to look for Gabriel, though he hadn't told anyone the real reason. Nor had he any idea he would find Gabriel at Lane's ranch.

Soon after returning to Long Beach from his last run, he'd made arrangements with his next two pick-up points to come by twelve hours early, with the intention of making his delivery in Chiloquin at 6:30 p.m. Saturday rather than 6:30 on Sunday morning. Management at all three stops assumed he was only being judicious, moving up his delivery time in view of the expected sick-out due to begin on Monday. At that point there'd been no hint a pre-emptive lockout was in the offing.

He'd planned to overnight at Lane's all along, but only *after* dropping off his load. He was crossing the Oregon state line, perhaps ten minutes north of the little burg where Gabriel had slept through the tire change, when his cell phone rang. The dispatcher told him his delivery was now "on hold."

Having to reschedule *en route* was a rare enough event that Vincent had to get out his three-ring binder and look up the nearest location where the trailer could be safely parked for the duration. There was the airbase near Midland, of course, and a National Guard headquarters in Klamath. There was also a forestry station south of the border whose maintenance yard fence was topped off with razor-wire. As the crow flies, that was actually his closest option; but it was also twenty minutes in the opposite direction, and Vincent hated retracing his steps almost as much as he hated missing his scheduled arrival time.

Last Thursday had been his first delayed delivery in decades. And even if the blown tire and the damage to the front end of his truck weren't exactly Gabriel's fault, it was beginning to seem as if he wasn't the luckiest person to be around.

All of this would be explained later, after Lane and Gabriel had come inside. But even before that, before they'd slammed their car doors and started back for the house, Gabriel had gone to great lengths to assure Lane the truck driver was unlikely to greet him with open arms. When they found Vincent sacked out on the living room sofa – and apparently still asleep despite their noisy entrance – Gabriel took the opportunity to retreat into the safety of the kitchen while Lane went over to awaken him.

She shook her head as Gabriel's footsteps faded down the hallway, crossed the living room and stopped beside the sofa to tap on

Vincent's shoulder... once... twice..

"What the hell's goin' on at the plant, anyway?" were the first words out of his mouth. Then, throwing his stocky legs over the edge of the sofa, he sat up as straight and clear-eyed as a soldier waking from a foxhole catnap.

"You're not gonna like it when I tell you," Lane replied.

She did, and he *didn't.* And it was after he'd recounted the travails of his most recent trip north that Vincent finally asked her who was responsible for putting this crazy idea in her head about getting rid of the ammo plant – as if she hadn't been thinking about it for most of the last two years. Before Lane could respond, Gabriel re-emerged from the kitchen, the sound of his shoes on the oak floor turning Vincent's head.

The truck driver went slack-jawed as Gabriel halted beside the staircase, hadn't known anyone else was in the house, much less the very person he'd come twelve hours early intending to locate.

"Hey!—you're—!"

"Nice to see you again, Vincent... or is it *Mister* Vincent?—nobody around here will—"

"Jesus Christ," the trucker said with sudden realization. "Good thing I didn't tell dispatch where I finally parked or they'd think I was part a'your damn conspiracy."

"Where *did* you tell them you parked?" Lane asked.

"In the trees, mile-and-a-half east, where the Yainax Butte firebreak crosses the highway. Came in the back way from Klamath, after I heard the plant was locked down. An' I pulled off the road near the butte like I said, long enough for them to verify my coordinates. Guess if they took another fix on my GPS, they'd know I moved since then." He paused, eyeing Gabriel as he finally came into the room. "By the way, I brought back somethin' belongs to you, case you were wondering."

"I was hoping you would." Gabriel sat onto the piano stool nearby, tried not to show how much it meant to him. "Where'd you find it?— under the dashboard?"

"Back under the seat. Never would'a seen it either, 'cept for the mechanic at the body shop where I went in for an estimate. Spotted it when he opened the passenger door—" Vincent allowed a chuckle.

"—knows me well enough, a Holy Bible isn't the kind of reading material I normally bring along."

Gabriel forced a smile, shrugged as if the answer to his next question hardly mattered.

"This mechanic... he take a look inside by any chance?"

"He didn't, but *I* did. That's when I figured you might be in a world a'hurt without it."

Gabriel squinted back, mildly surprised by Vincent's empathy.

"Yeah, well, it *is* all the money I've been able to save up over the last three years."

"You know that's not what I meant."

Vincent looked Gabriel up and down just like he had in the cab of his truck, found him just as mysterious as before.

"When I was in Vietnam I carried around a little stash I brought from home. Picture a'me and my mother in front of her house on Bay Shore Avenue... tickets from a boat ride to Catalina Island with my first wife, a high school ring my dad wore the whole time he was in Korea—stuff like that. Carried 'em all in a blue flannel Cutty Sark pouch, drawstring looped around the choke knob on my dashboard. Took everything out whenever I needed to remind myself who I was before the war."

He squinted at Gabriel again; it was obvious he'd finally struck a chord. "Dumb little ritual is what kept me sane. An' anybody try to mess with my pouch?—they'd never do it a second time. Anyhow, I figured the least I could do is get your own stash back soon as I could. Lucky break I didn't hafta chase you all over Oregon to do it."

"You'd'a done that for me?"

Vincent rose from the sofa with a look advising Gabriel not to press his luck, walked over to a duffle bag beside the credenza and carried it ceremoniously back to the coffee table. The bag was not unlike the one he'd noticed next to Lane's four-poster, after he'd let himself in and cased the house when no one came to the door. He reached into the bag, found Gabriel's zippered Bible resting against his Army-issue .45, pulled it out.

"Count the money if you want," he said as Gabriel started over to retrieve it. "It's all there... all three hundred and fifty bucks."

Gabriel halted in his tracks, relaxed when the gray-haired wiseacre grinned up at him.

"Got'cha, didn' I?"

Vincent handed him the Bible, smile fading slightly when Gabriel accepted it in the same careful-to-avoid-contact manner he'd displayed three nights ago.

"I see you keep somebody's ring in yours, too. Wedding band?"

Lane suddenly swung her head in Gabriel's direction. It was enough he hadn't told her there were other valuables in the Bible besides money. With Vincent's mention of a wedding ring, she could barely contain herself.

"My mother's," Gabriel said, answering her unspoken question. "She died wearing it. Or... let's just say it was on her hand when they found it."

Vincent winced, looked over to see a similar reaction on Lane's face, though neither made any comment. Gabriel, meanwhile, continued to gaze down at his Bible, hefted it for several moments as if remembering its weight, its leatherette texture, finally drew the zipper pull with the brass cross around the top, side, bottom. Then, tenderly, he reached into the hidden compartment, pushed aside the folded greenbacks, fingered the gold band with the nick along one edge, the safe deposit key, lifted out the tarnished pillbox to uncover his boyhood picture.

He took another moment to recall how, just before the snapshot was taken, he'd been riding a tilt-a-whirl at some county fair with his best friend, how the rush of adrenaline made him feel like he could do anything, anything at all, just like his mother had always taught him, if he could only focus all that energy, if he would decide what one thing he would use it for, if he would just *let it be used.*

He suddenly became aware of the other two staring, glanced up sheepishly. Vincent returned a knowing look. But Lane, clearly, was hoping for something more – confirmation that all of his things were there, perhaps? Maybe an explanation for the last two minutes of reverent silence? Or could it be that she wanted reassurance he wouldn't simply leave now that he had all his treasures safely returned?

"Thanks," was all Gabriel said; and for Vincent, it was enough.

Not for Lane. "Well, then," she huffed, "I guess you've both ac-

complished what you came here to do, and you can leave now with
a clear conscience."

The two men traded glances at the flare-up, less astonished
than amused. This was, after all, the Lane D'Arcy they had both
come to know.

"Well, not quite," Vincent responded at last. "I still have a delivery to make." He glanced away at his bag. "Maybe I'll just give the
Colonel a call, get an update."

Lane's eyes went wide. "You can do that? You've got Halvorsen's
cell number?"

The truck driver seemed surprised. "Wha'd you expect? I *do*
work for the guy."

And suddenly the irony of Vincent's being there hit them all.
The fact that a big-rig full of shell casings and fuses and tail-fin
assemblies was parked alongside the house of the *de facto* ring-
leader of – or at least the inspiration for – the current situation at
the ammo plant, seemed all at once absurd and laughable.

Not to mention unwise.

Vincent joined the other two in a nervous outburst of laughter,
then quickly turned more serious. "I should prob'ly go, shouldn't I?"

"Well, for your own sake, I wouldn't want anyone else to find
your truck here."

"Trouble is," Vincent shrugged, "Jack already knows I've spent
a few afternoons on your couch. I just hope he thinks I stopped at
one of the secure sites down Klamath way." He frowned, reconsid-
ered. "Naw. Dispatch prob'ly gave 'im my position back near Yainax.
Lord help me if they send Fiske or somebody else out there, thinkin'
I could use help guarding the truck."

It was then the cell phone chirped, its electronic notes muffled.
The two men assumed at first it was coming from inside Vincent's
duffle bag until Lane looked up past it, toward the hallway.

"You brought in C.J.'s cell phone, right?"

"Yeah. I left it on the—"

Lane was already up, crossing the living room with her customary confidence, only a hand out to brush the stairway anchor post
as she headed for the kitchen. Gabriel and Vincent traded another
glance, this one admitting their mutual admiration, then turned

back to listen as Lane answered the phone. They could hear the ringer tones break off, the low, anxious tenor of Lane's voice as she answered and exchanged a few words, followed by the higher-pitched *No—oh, no!* which sent shivers up both their spines.

Lane was coming down the hall as Gabriel started for the kitchen, her face pale, walking slowly as she continued speaking into the mouthpiece.

"Well, do you know if anyone was hurt? I mean, did you send anyone back to the gate to see what—"

She frowned as the reply came, eyes darting.

"They what—? *When?*"

By now Vincent was standing just behind Gabriel. "If there's an operation of any kind goin' on," he whispered, "they'll prob'ly move everybody back at least—"

Lane waved him silent, pressed her hand against her other ear. "So you're saying, *don't* come? You actually expect me to just stay here and do nothing?"

In the sudden quiet, Gabriel could hear the reply almost as clearly as Lane.

"There's nothing you can do," the voice said – presumably C.J.'s, "Coming back here right now would only make things worse."

"Will you at least—"

She stopped as C.J. anticipated her question, told her he would stay in touch, then disconnected without bothering to say goodbye. She blinked, seemed to stare at the phone a moment longer before letting her arm go limp.

"How d'you like that?—they don't want us to come anywhere near the plant," she said, avoiding what was more likely her real concern. "And guess what?—they brought in two more Guard trucks to enforce the mile perimeter. Even closed the highway at Sprague and Chiloquin to anybody but locals."

"Told ya that's what they'd do," Vincent chimed.

Gabriel continued to peer at Lane. "What happened to bring this on?"

She hesitated, seemed to be waiting until she could reply without losing her composure.

"C.J. said they heard shots fired. Weren't sure it was gunfire at first, it was so faint. But then there were three or four explosions, right in a row."

"Explosions?"

"And bright flashes through the skylights." She was bordering on tears now.

"Could've been stun grenades," Gabriel offered, looking to Vincent for help, "like SWAT teams use sometimes?—so they can avoid shooting anybody."

"Yeah—could'a been," Vincent nodded, though his tone was unconvincing.

"And then there was more gunfire," Lane added.

Which eliminated *that* theory.

Several silent seconds piled up before Vincent walked back to his duffle bag, withdrew his own cell phone.

"Lemme see if I can find out what the hell's goin' on."

"You're calling the Colonel?" Lane asked hopefully.

"Front gate. They'll have some idea. Besides, I wanna tell 'em I'm bringin' in my load, like it or not. Damned if I'm gonna sit around *here* any longer."

It wasn't as if he'd intended it. He hadn't gone to work that morning knowing ahead of time he wouldn't be clocking out. And it wasn't out of sympathy for the mostly-Maqlaq contingent who'd turned against the presence of the ammo plant either. If anything, he found their tactics completely counter-productive.

If they'd mustered a few dozen men – maybe even a handful of women to show it wasn't a violent protest – and then simply "occupied" the plant until the administration agreed to labor talks – such a demonstration might've won his sympathy. True, participants in a sit-in would've been carted off to jail. But the news media would be waiting outside the gates while the paddy wagons left one by one – not kept a mile away in case of "accidental detonations" – and the Army might've caved to public pressure. Chances are all the charges against the protestors would've been dropped as well.

In fact, that's exactly what Richard was determined to tell the would-be saboteurs after he stayed behind to talk them out of mucking up the machinery – which he'd overheard the more radical Maqlaqs whispering about weeks ago. He never imagined they'd actually be stupid enough to carry out their plan.

Assuming there ever *was* one. According to some of the Maqlaqs he still counted as friends, their so-called plan was hardly more than a "vision" one of the Yahooskin elders had after spending an afternoon in their sweat lodge. And the basic idea simply called for two or three "braves" to begin committing acts of minor sabotage every few days, slowly but surely poisoning relations between management and the local community to a point where the Army would end up trusting no one and eventually close down the plant for security reasons.

Among the vision's leading advocates was Alex Round Tree, whose brother was killed in the same explosion that had blinded Lane. Richard strongly suspected Alex harbored his own, more personal reasons – a vendetta perhaps, even though he seemed stoic enough about Stillwater's death and was one of the first to go back to work following the investigation. But whatever the individual motives might be, the collective hope was to see the ammo plant revert to civilian use, or otherwise disappear. Let some other place and some other people become cogs in the wheels of war; it was no longer the will of the natives to beat those drums.

And Lane, while no peacenik herself, only fed their vision with her sentimental journey back to the good old days of Chiloquin, back to its roots in fishing and agriculture and the raising of livestock – conveniently leaving out the poverty, the failed economy, the lack of public services and private conveniences. She could be so unrealistic. Then again, Lane's rose-colored view of the world was one of the things he found so seductive about her – along with her vibrant, younger-than-her-years, spur-of-the-moment spirit. And her hunger for new experiences. And her laughter in the face of any challenge. And her...

Damn her, Richard thought. Damn her for being who she was, for making him love her, and then for not taking on that ultimate challenge, the one he'd finally put to her three years ago in the form of a long-overdue ultimatum, and despite the differences in their age and their temperaments: *Committing to one man and forsaking all others.* After all, she could commit to raising a child, to taking on that particular challenge, couldn't she? If the baby had been his, he was certain they would have eventually tied the knot.

He would feel bad for being the second husband to walk out on Elizabeth, of course. She was a good wife, had a quick temper and a passion for things like gardening and cooking and horses much like Lane did. She also aroused enough passion in him to forget Lane for days and even weeks at a time, though he couldn't help but notice Lane parked outside the plant toward the end of every month and thoughts of her would inevitably return.

Sometimes he fought back by pretending to be all the more in love with Elizabeth. But just as often he would fantasize about the possibility that Elizabeth might take the boys over to see their grandmother in Grants Pass, and he'd hop in Lane's Mustang and go home with her like all the other "overnight guests" and friends who had successively taken his place. Including, if recent rumors were accurate, Doyle Pollard.

And he *did* love Elizabeth's kids. As if they were his own. In fact, unlike her first ex, he would gladly continue to take care of them financially, even after he would leave Elizabeth for Lane.

But Lane's child *wasn't* his. He didn't need a blood test to know that. Besides which, the accident changed everything. As independent as she was before it happened, her year-long recovery had ultimately made Lane so fiercely self-reliant she didn't seem to want or need anybody else – except as occasional playthings, or sources of funding for her otherwise hermit-like life and her dubious dream of running a bed-and-breakfast. And if her recent "coming out" against the ammo plant had struck a chord in him, it was only because the plant had played such a pivotal role in finally destroying whatever remaining hope he had for their getting back together.

Maybe, as he looked back on it all, that was why he didn't clock out today. Maybe in some subconscious, long-suppressed way he wanted the radicals to succeed. And if he couldn't talk them out of their plans, maybe *he* could be talked into *theirs*.

Although it really didn't matter now. He might as well be one of the saboteurs as far as the SWAT team was concerned. Because by the time Richard found Edison Crow and Alex Round Tree pouring battery acid into the motor control boxes for the tank shell line, the SWAT team had caught up to them too. It didn't help things when Edison lobbed a mortar fuse against the catwalk behind the half-dozen soldiers, designed only to distract them long enough to allow an escape. Three of the SWAT riflemen let loose before the team leader ordered them to cease fire, and a ricochet off the nearby fork-lift caught Richard in the side.

The wound didn't seem serious, and not all that painful. In fact he was fairly certain the blood had begun to soak through his jersey only after he'd squeezed through the A/C register behind the casing press. Which meant there would be no trail of blood to give him away, and hopefully no telltale droplets inside the walls – once they'd figured out his only possible avenue of escape – to show where he was headed.

As far as he knew, he and Lane were the only ones to use the secret room he'd first stumbled onto when he was on the retrofit crew. Hidden within the maze of false walls and crawl-spaces throughout the plant was an eight-by-ten-foot cubicle originally built to house a bank of electrical transformers. The units were eventu-ally relocated to the southeast end of the property when one of the subcontractors insisted at the last minute that the transformers should be placed outside where they would better dissipate heat. Meanwhile the room had gone completely unused – except for his once- or twice-weekly rendezvous with Lane over a span of almost three years.

Richard had taken refuge there once already, before he'd tracked down any of the three men reported to be loose inside the plant, when the first volley of blasting caps and gunfire sent him running for cover. To his surprise, he'd opened the metal panel to the cubicle and found it pretty much as he and Lane had last seen it. Though a bit more dusty, the multiple layers of foam packing they'd dragged in to use as a makeshift mattress were still in the corner beneath the air vent, a few crumpled lunch sacks still scattered on the floor. Not that lunch was the primary reason for meeting there.

But now, ten minutes after the second round of gunfire, while pausing beside the metal panel to listen for his pursuers, he noticed a small pool of blood beside his right foot. The blood had apparently trickled over his belt and worked its way down his Wranglers during his retreat. It was just then he realized how weak he'd become, how desperately he needed to lie down.

Maybe if he stopped moving for a few minutes the bleeding would stop. Then he could regain his strength and go turn himself in. He was fairly certain Edison Crow had been wounded, too; and assuming Edison or Alex had now been captured, they'd surely vouch for him, for the fact he had no part in their conspiracy. He'd be exonerated, maybe even commended for his efforts to stop them, however ill-conceived, however futile.

But right now he needed to rest. He only wanted to rest.

he phone call - actually three calls by the time Vincent managed to work things out - gave Lane and Gabriel time to go upstairs and change clothes. Lane was "feeling grungy," as she put it. And Gabriel admitted he hadn't spent this long in a pair of Stay-Press Dockers since he'd returned from one of his quarterly "three-day getaways" - which he didn't bother to explain - only to find his duffle bag and all of his work clothes stolen by a fellow boarder who'd moved out during his absence. Fortunately he'd left his Bible on the nightstand as he always did, in full view of everyone, its secrets unsuspected by all who saw it, and it had remained un-touched.

He placed the same Bible on Lane's bedside table now, even though he wasn't sure he'd ever lie in her bed again, much less sleep in it. Taking off his clothes now, he watched Lane as she too undressed, not the least bit self-conscious and utterly unaware of his presence. In a few more moments she faced the wall over her dresser where her mirror had been, eyes straight ahead, unhooked her bra and let it casually slide off. After opening the top drawer to pull out fresh underwear, she nodded back over her shoulder.

"I want to make love to you again..."

Gabriel finished pulling up his jeans but didn't fasten them.

"Right now?—with Vincent down—"

"...before you leave," she said. "I don't know when, what with everything that's going on. But I *do* know there's nothing keeping you here now—"

"*You're* keeping me here, Lane..."

"—and every reason for you to leave—"

"...and not because of the sex."

"—especially with Fiske waiting to haul you in." She turned away, giving no indication she'd heard him, shook her head with determination. "You can't let that happen, Gabriel. I won't *let* you let that happen."

She slipped the fresh bra over her head like she was putting on a T-shirt, breasts rising gloriously as her arms went up. Gabriel realized he *could* make love to her right then, Vincent notwithstanding, and was mildly disappointed when she finished fastening her bra and stepped past him, heading for the bathroom.

"When the time is right, I want you to take your things and go. Don't even tell me. You can use my car to get a head start. Just leave it parked where somebody will find it." She disappeared through the door, words echoing off the tile. "I'm sure you can hitch a ride east, out through Beatty to Lakeview. Have you ever stayed in Idaho during your travels?"

"Lane—"

"I know a couple who moved to Cour d'Alene. Got tired of working on the lines. They tell me the hills around there are just gorgeous. Some new developments nearby where you could prob'ly find work."

"—I can't leave now."

"Well you sure as hell can't stay here—don't you see?"

"I can only see—"

"And after what happened down in Sprague today? You think Fiske isn't gonna get his own copies of those reports and figure out—"

"*Lane!*"

It was Vincent, calling up from the living room. Gabriel walked to the bedroom door, looked down the stairs to see him folding his outdated cell phone shut.

"Did you find out anything?" Gabriel said, lowering his voice as if Lane wouldn't hear.

"Yeah. They caught one of 'em during the second—"

"They did? Who was it—did they say?"

Lane had not only heard, but was stepping into the doorway behind Gabriel, belatedly pulling her terrycloth robe around her. Vincent flushed, looked quickly away.

"One of the Maqlaqs—all they could tell me."

Gabriel could sense Lane's relief even without turning.

"Another one got away somehow," Vincent went on, "and they think there's a third who split up from the first two. They're pretty sure both of 'em are somewhere over by the grenade lines, on the east end of the plant."

Vincent looked up the stairs again, noticed Gabriel's unzipped Levi's but pretended not to.

"So, anyhow, they agree it's just as safe for me to come in now as hunker down in the forest—which is where they still think I am, thank God. Might be an hour or two before they're ready for me, so if you wanna go back... I mean, if there's any unfinished..." He gave up, shrugged. "I'm just gonna go over to the couch here and catch some winks while I wait for the call."

It took that long for Lane to realize what Vincent assumed they were doing, and a moment longer for Vincent's shoes to squeak on the hardwood as he turned back for the living room.

"Uh, Vincent—"

Another squeak. Lane stepped over to the railing.

"The one they caught? Did he give up without a fight or—"

"Don't think so. Whitley said they opened the gate long enough to let out the plant ambulance. And they just let *in* two more, up from K Falls, to stand by just in case."

Though Lane was now in front of him, Gabriel could picture the apprehension spreading across her face. He could also see any chance for a more intimate goodbye slip away with the name that emerged

from her lips, even if she only breathed it, even if she was sure
Gabriel could not have known.

"Have you lost your mind, too, Laney?"

Vincent had returned to the sofa, had genuinely intended on
grabbing some extra zzz's before the call came. And whatever Lane
and Gabriel wanted to do during the interim was their business.

Which is why he was surprised when Lane padded downstairs
only minutes later, poked at his shoulder again after he'd just managed to get comfortable, couldn't believe she would even *think* of the
idea on her own much less come right out and ask him. He immediately turned to Woods when he joined them, assumed he'd put her
up to it – except that her houseguest appeared just as dumbfounded
by Lane's proposal as he was.

"You just said they're not gonna unload your truck, even after
you've driven inside the fence, right?"

"They can't," Vincent replied. "Whitley told me I could park by
the dock, but there's no crew left to off-load the stuff. Said it's up to
me if I wanna stay at the fish camp across from the airstrip, or take
a Greyhound back to Long Beach 'til all this blows over."

"So, that would work."

"*What* would work?"

"If I hid in back. Nobody'd know I was there. You could leave the
tailgate unlocked, and I could let myself out after you went inside."

He wasn't sure he should give her scheme the dignity of a response, but did.

"You could. And they'd nail you about five seconds after you hit
the pavement."

"*Who* would? They won't bother posting any guards outside on
the loading dock. Not when the place is in lock-down."

Vincent huffed as if Lane had missed the obvious. "No, but they
will have guards posted along the fences. And if *they* don't spot
you, there's always the surveillance monitors in the security office
on the other side of the wall there." Another huff. "And Lane, for
Chrissakes!—do you think they're just gonna leave the back door

open for you?"

Her blank expression gave Vincent his answer. But to both Lane's and Gabriel's surprise, the old trucker wasn't finished.

"Nope. You'd hafta slip in through the roll-ups, and they wouldn't leave those open either unless they were off-loading. Or unless..."

He paused to consider the alternatives, which was still *more* surprising. Even Lane seemed taken aback by his thoughtful silence. She brightened but held her breath, as if the slightest sound might bring Vincent back to his senses.

"...unless I offered to bring in some of the hardware myself. I mean, I can still operate a damn forklift good as anybody." He squinted, nodded. "They wouldn't let me transfer the whole shipment. Hell, prob'ly take me three or four hours to do it all by myself. But there's a couple' racks it'd be wise to get under roof rather than let sit outside in the trailer. I could prob'ly talk the guards into that much, create some kind of distraction."

Another pause. Vincent looked from Lane to Gabriel, then back. Lane couldn't see the corners of Vincent's lips turn up slightly, but Gabriel could.

"He's just jerking you around, Lane. You don't actually think he'd—"

Vincent interrupted with a snicker. "What?—and jeopardize my job? Forty-odd years a' service, not to mention my commendation from ol' Tricky Dick...?"

He continued to grin, shaking his head at the absurdity of it, then abruptly sobered at the sight of Lane as she slumped and turned away.

"C'mon, Laney." He frowned almost tenderly. "How can this crazy idea be worth getting yourself all worked—"

"You *know* why!" She swirled back. "This is Richard we're talking about here! Have you forgotten the day you made that extra trip just to visit me in the hospital, after I'd come out of my coma? How you spent the whole afternoon holding my hand, and all I could do was blather on about Richard?—how we'd been lovers since he was in high school and he would do anything—'

She stopped as if suddenly remembering Gabriel's presence, suddenly aware how much more Vincent knew about her feelings and her personal history than she'd shared with *him*. It wasn't fair to cast Richard's shadow over Gabriel that way, wasn't fair that the past still had a hold she couldn't fully explain.

She turned to Gabriel like she might try nevertheless, had no way of knowing he was staring down at the carpet, now lost in his own thoughts. At last she shook her head, sent Vincent a pleading, almost forlorn, look.

"You know Richard has never been a violent man. He's not some terrorist. But that's not the way they'll treat it inside the plant. They won't think twice about doing whatever's necessary. And if shots have already been fired, they're *way* beyond talk at this point. Richard won't last the night unless someone goes in there and stops him..."

She tried to lock eyes with Vincent, filled her gaze with every ounce of determination she could muster.

"...and I'm the only one who knows where he is."

He'd heard all he needed to. Thank God these old clapboard farmhouses were so poorly insulated. Pressing his head against the wood siding, he could catch enough of their words to know Vincent hadn't stopped at Lane's just to pass the time while the situation at the plant was resolved. Besides, why would he lie about his truck's position unless he had something to hide?

Fiske felt like congratulating himself. No one else would – at least not until later, when the right people would understand what he'd done, what he was about to do.

The moment he'd laid eyes on the tire impressions, he cut both his headlights and the Blazer's engine. The lights probably hadn't penetrated the trees between the highway and the house, but Lane's hearing was legendary; he would take no chances. Leaving his car beside her mailbox, he approached the ranch on foot, the sound of his boots swallowed in the soft dirt. He circled Vincent's truck where it was parked alongside the house, made sure it was still secure, then silently climbed the front steps. A Maqlaq couldn't have done any better.

For a heart-stopping moment, he was afraid he'd been seen when he crossed in front of one of the parlor windows – Lane always left her drapes wide open – and noticed Woods standing near the piano. He quickly spun out of view, held his breath for several seconds until the conversation inside continued.

And it was about as shocking a conversation as he could imagine. When Vincent suggested he could create some kind of distraction at the loading docks so Lane could sneak inside, he knew it was time to act. But he also knew Vincent was in possession of the same Army-issue .45 he'd carried during his Vietnam days. He would need to take them all by surprise.

The front door was out of the question. Not only was it in full view of everyone in the parlor, the squeaky screen door would give him away before he ever got inside. Fortunately, besides leaving her windows uncovered, Lane left all her doors unlocked. Which meant he should be able to let himself in through the back where he wouldn't be heard. As long as the oak floorboards didn't give him away, he could sneak through the kitchen and down the hallway and have his service revolver trained on them before anyone could react.

He hadn't counted on the horses. The mare whinnied twice as he came around the house, and again he held his breath to listen for any sign those inside suspected someone else's presence. At one point he could hear Lane raise her voice, but as distant and muffled as it was, her outburst seemed to be in anger, not in alarm. Once more he exhaled with relief, started up the back porch as the horses continued to rustle in their stalls.

To his own amazement, his deputies' gossip about Lane's Appaloosa came to mind, how her mare's broken foreleg was found to be fully functional the day after Woods arrived. On top of which were the various accounts from Sprague River. And though he still couldn't make a water-tight connection to Woods, was it only coincidence he hadn't felt any pain from his ulcer since the morning he'd found him on the highway?

Damn, Fiske thought, *who in God's name was he dealing with?*

He refocused, was reassured when the rear screen door pulled open with barely a sound, as did the half-glass door. Fiske was through the kitchen and peering down the hall thirty seconds later, could hear Lane's words plainly again even though the three of them were still outside his line of sight, somewhere toward the west end of her parlor.

"I don't care if they *do* catch me before I get to him," she was saying. "Once I'm inside, I don't see how they can turn me down."

"That's not the point, Lane," Vincent replied. "Point is, they're gonna know it was me who smuggled you in."

It was time to make his move. Fiske lifted his revolver, padded sideways down the hallway as Lane continued to plead with Vincent, careful not to brush up against the family photographs. He knew he'd caught them unawares when he took a final stride past the stair post and into the parlor, sighted down the barrel of his gun at Woods' ribcage before anyone had even begun to turn.

It was Lane who first sensed the intrusion. She couldn't see who it was, of course, or the gun leveled at Gabriel. Vincent had returned to the sofa to ponder the challenge of getting Lane past the loading dock. And it was when he followed her sudden, questioning gaze that he spotted Fiske, badge gleaming against his dark brown uniform, both arms outstretched in target practice fashion.

"What the *hell* are you doing, Albert?"

Gabriel turned as well, shocked not so much to find Fiske pointing his gun at him for the second time in three days, but at the fact he and Vincent were on a first-name basis. He was still more shocked by the Lieutenant's self-righteous anger.

"I gotta admit, Vincent, you sure had me fooled."

"Fooled?"

"*Yeah* you did. But I know your plan. I heard everything."

The truck driver frowned, then gave a quick, eye-rolling nod when he inferred what Fiske was thinking.

"You have no idea what you heard."

He started to lift himself from the sofa. Fiske jerked his revolver around.

"Stay right there. And no sudden moves—I'm warning you."

The command clearly startled Lane, who was still unaware Fiske was pointing his gun. She took a step toward him.

"Look, Lieutenant, I don't know why you're—"

"You either, Lane!"

The barrel came around again. Lane halted, tilted her head in disbelief, somehow knew.

"You are *not* standing here in my living room with your revolver unholstered!"

"I'm sorry, Lane," Fiske said, suddenly feeling like the uninvited guest despite his certainty, "but I'm putting you under arrest. All of you."

"Don't be a jackass, Fiske," Vincent spat. And just that fast the first-name basis was history. "You're completely off-base here. If you seriously think I was—"

"Oh, I'm *dead* serious. And I don't want to warn you again."

The Lieutenant wagged his gun as if to invite the trucker to sit back down. Gabriel frowned, was mildly surprised Vincent had taken a couple of sideways steps closer to his duffle bag where it sat on the far side of the coffee table. He stole a glance, noticed a worn leather pouch through the unzipped opening, lying between a neatly folded shirt and the bag's lining. The cross-hatched handle of a handgun protruded from beneath the snap-button flap.

Gabriel blinked, turned back to see a strangely familiar expression on Vincent's face. And then it hit him; it was the same hardened look he'd worn just before their truck collided with the deer.

"You know what, everybody?" Gabriel broke in. "Seems to me there's been another misunderstanding here, and if we can all just sit down—and calm down?—I'm sure I can explain how—"

"*You* can explain—?" Fiske spat back. "Like that little misunderstanding out on the highway? You think I'm about to believe anything you say, mister so-called itinerant construction worker?" Another swing of the barrel. "How 'bout I explain three things I know about you?"

Gabriel took a step backward and to his left, began to slowly lower himself onto the piano stool, palms out to show he posed no threat.

"Okay. And how 'bout you lower your gun while—"

"First, I know you're not who you claim to be," Fiske said, plow-

ing ahead. "Or at least there's something about you... some big secret you'll do anything to keep other people from finding out. Second—"

"Look, would you mind just putting down—"

"—I know that from the time I picked you up the other day,
everything in this town has gone to hell."

"Oh—and you don't think it would've anyway? Even if I never
set foot—"

"Shut up!" Fiske snapped. "And three—"

Only he never got to *three*. While Fiske and Gabriel were facing
off, Vincent had somehow managed to come around the coffee table
and already had his right hand in his duffle bag. Fiske swirled and
fired before he could possibly have taken aim. The first slug shattered one leg of the coffee table, the second tore through Vincent's
right wrist, blood from his radial artery splattering upward across
his chin.

An instant later, before Gabriel could suck in a breath and Lane's
scream had just begun to split the air, another brown-cloaked figure emerged from the hallway, streaking toward Fiske and grabbing
him from behind. The Lieutenant's right arm went vertical, the gun
firing a third time, bullet dislodging a dish-sized chunk of plaster
from the living room ceiling.

Fiske, too, went down, or rather backward. Buddy was behind
him, simultaneously twisting his head against his chest with one
big hand, other arm reaching forward to strip the revolver from Fiske
like a parent taking a toy from a child.

He crumpled at Buddy's feet before Lane had stopped screaming. She heard the thud above her own shriek, broke off with a gasp,
turned wide-eyed toward Gabriel as if to confirm he was still on the
piano stool. And if he was, who had silenced Fiske?

"Buddy," Gabriel said before she could ask.

"Buddy!?"

No sooner had she spoken his name than the dull patter of
dripping blood could be heard. Gabriel spun to see Vincent kneeling
beside his duffle bag with a look of fearful agony, bravely clutching
his right forearm with his left hand, but the self-applied tourniquet
was clearly insufficient. His artery was still spurting despite his grip,

the bright crimson now streaming down his arm.

Gabriel rushed to his side, reached to encircle Vincent's wrist as though he were simply taking over the job, closed his eyes.

"Another hand won't do it," the old trucker said hoarsely. "We'll need a belt or something to tie me off below the elbow. And Lane—" He stopped, squeezed his eyes at the searing jolt he assumed was from pain. "—you better use my cell phone to call an ambulance."

"Make that *two*." It was Buddy, now bent over Fiske's unmoving form, the latter's head wrenched unnaturally to one side. "I think I might'a broke his neck."

Lane started obediently toward Vincent's duffle bag, then abruptly halted; an ambulance wouldn't be necessary.

"Alright," Gabriel said, opening his eyes again. "Be there in a minute."

Vincent turned with a disbelieving gape, as if to ask Gabriel how he could even consider stepping away, then scowled, all the more astonished to find him no longer gripping his wrist so much as massaging it. And when Gabriel let go entirely, not only had the bleeding stopped, the torn flesh atop his wrist had smoothed over and the shard of bone splintered from the base of his palm – at least he *thought* he'd seen bone – was no longer there.

"Have your doctor order some x-rays if you want," Gabriel said softly. And with that he rose and crossed the room to Fiske.

Buddy's mouth was agape, too, but not so much that he couldn't speak.

"I... I didn't mean..." he stammered as Gabriel knelt down. "I was only trying to stop him. Should'a come in sooner."

But Gabriel was already shutting out his words, disconnecting once more from the sounds and the room and his own body while the Unknowable took over, flowed through his hands, turned the clock back, restored the original blueprint – however it worked; it made no difference. Witnessing rather than performing, he grasped Fiske's head on either side, gently rotated it forward, then cupped the back of his neck and let the vertebrae fall back into place. Nor was Gabriel aware, at first, when Lane stepped alongside him, quietly leaned over and pressed her cheek against his left shoulder blade.

Fiske's groan began to bring Gabriel back, along with the vague consciousness of pressure against him.

Lane?

He straightened without warning, throwing her backward, off-balance and flailing, directly into Vincent's arms.

The trucker had started over moments before, his strength nearly restored, flabbergasted by what had just happened to him and even more so by what Gabriel was doing to Fiske. He caught Lane just before she hit the floor, dropped to his knees to support her while she lay back without moving for several seconds. After blinking a few times, she began to glance from side to side as if she were looking around the room.

Gabriel turned slowly, only now coming back into himself, saw her eyes moving.

"Lane...?"

It was barely a whisper. More like a prayer, actually, because it no longer mattered. *Let her be healed.* He was as exposed as he'd ever been, anywhere, at any time. He would be leaving at the first opportunity, anyway. The fact that Lane's heart belonged to another man only confirmed the necessity.

"I could feel it, for just a moment," Lane said, eyes still darting but not seeing. "Like a pipe when water's running through it. It was the most... *amazing* sensation."

Gabriel could only turn away as Vincent helped Lane to her feet. What had just happened – or failed to happen – was all too obvious. As stunned as they were by what they'd witnessed, as seemingly contrary to the laws of nature as the healings were in the first place, Buddy and Vincent had both jumped to the very same question now haunting Gabriel.

Why not Lane?

Lieutenant Fiske, however, was the one person in the room who hadn't been privy to the events, nor did he seem remotely aware of his own escape from death. Despite his senses' rapid return, it was clear he couldn't remember how he'd come to be on the floor with Woods standing over him, or why his left arm and belt were firmly in the clutches of the deputy who now crouched behind him. He tried to break free, felt Buddy's hold tighten, looked up to see Lane and

Vincent also standing nearby and, in the ceiling just beyond them, the ragged hole his third slug had ripped open.

Fiske dropped his gaze, spotted his revolver lying on the floor, tried once more to pull away, winced as though his head still hurt and finally stopped struggling. Despite the discomfort, he craned his neck to look back at Buddy, then around at the gun, desperately trying to reconstruct what had happened before he blacked out.

The other three men could see the wheels turning. It was Vincent who spoke first.

"You're wrong about all this, Albert, about what's going on here. Wrong about Buddy, too. I don't know if he was out with the horses or what, but he must'a seen you sneaking around back and followed you inside. He was only trying to keep you from killing somebody. Which you'd'a done if it weren't for Woods here."

Vincent paused as Buddy allowed Fiske to sit upright, even as he kept a restraining hand on his shoulder. It was then the Lieutenant glimpsed the fresh bloodstains on the carpet near the coffee table, immediately shifted his gaze to Vincent, more blood spattered across his neck and jawline, crimson stains on his wrist. His eyes went wide at the sight, then straight up to see Gabriel staring back with quiet resignation.

The other two men saw Gabriel's look, too. Lane seemed to sense it from the silence that suddenly filled the room, and she also knew the decision they had to make. This time it was Buddy who put it into words.

"I think it would be wise for our brother to leave Chiloquin now. And you..." He leaned forward to meet the Lieutenant's eyes. "...are not going to stop him."

Fiske seethed at what seemed to be a direct command from an inferior.

"*Are* you, sir?" Buddy quickly added, but too late.

"No way you're getting away with this," Fiske snarled, still unable to pull himself from beneath Buddy's grip, and still no less convinced of his mission. Then, glaring at Gabriel: "And you're not leaving this town until I find out who the hell you really are."

Vincent had bound Fiske to a pair of dining chairs using a good fifteen yards of the flat polyester strapping tape he carried in his tool chest in case his load shifted. It wasn't the first time he'd employed the tape for something other than securing a rack of shell casings or a carton of fuses. He'd tied up the hands and feet of several POWs during his tours of Vietnam and, after landing stateside, the driver of a Honda GTX who tried to run from the scene of an accident he'd caused. The polyester tape was not only stronger than the rope Buddy retrieved from the barn, it was less likely to cut into Fiske's hands and ankles.

For what it was worth, Buddy promised his commanding officer he'd be back in a couple of hours to remove the bindings. That would allow Gabriel plenty of time to make his way across the state line either to the south or east in Lane's Mustang. Vincent advised Fiske to spend those same two hours seriously reconsidering his threat to arrest everyone in sight.

And if push came to shove, it would be his testimony – along with Lane's and Buddy's – that the Lieutenant had acted recklessly and irrationally during the incident in Lane's living room, and he'd been hog-tied to the chairs as much for his own protection as for theirs. The bullet holes in Lane's coffee table and ceiling, plus the bloodstains on her carpet – from a flesh wound Gabriel had suffered, they'd say – would corroborate their story.

And so, with their testimony thus agreed upon, it came as an unwelcome surprise when the four of them walked outside, stopped beside Vincent's big-rig, and Lane began pleading once more for his help in smuggling her into the plant.

"But Lane," Vincent replied patiently, climbing up to unlock the driver-side door, "that would only prove Fiske was right. Deadly force isn't so reckless and irrational if it turns out we really *were* conspiring to smuggle you in."

"Oh, not just me..."

Buddy and Gabriel traded frowns. Vincent stepped down from the running board.

"...Gabriel, too."

"This is getting ridiculous," Gabriel said.

Lane spun imploringly, as if he were the only one she had to convince.

"I know I have no right to ask you. But if anyone gets hurt in there, or somebody's already hurt, you might be the only way to—"

"The only way to keep somebody from getting hurt now," Vincent broke in, "is to keep anybody else from getting involved."

"Except Gabriel isn't just anybody. He prob'ly saved your life a few minutes ago, in case you didn't notice. Not to mention Dudley Do-Right back there."

Vincent went silent as Lane gestured back at the house. Granted, if Gabriel hadn't been in Lane's living room that night, he probably *would've* bled to death. But if Gabriel hadn't been there, hadn't had any reason to stay in Chiloquin to start with, the shooting and everything leading up to it would never have happened.

But it *did* happen, and Vincent had to admit how stupid he was to reach into his duffle bag when Fiske was aware that he packed heat. What Fiske *didn't* know about was the Medal of Valor he also carried, which he'd been awarded during his second tour of Vietnam along with a Letter of Commendation from President Nixon he'd paid three bucks to have laminated. Like the Cutty Sark pouch he'd hauled all across Vietnam, both the medal and the certificate were among the small collection of personal items he took with him on the road now. And if only he could've brought them out for Fiske to see, maybe the paranoid peace officer might have understood he wasn't there to play Trojan Horse for some hastily-conceived ammo plant insurrection.

Not that he wasn't sympathetic with their ultimate goal. Maybe more than he wanted to admit. After all, the countless hours he spent behind the wheel gave him time to think about things, and he couldn't exactly say he was happy with the direction the country had taken since 2001 had changed Life as We Know It. If he was too naive at the time to recognize all the mistakes leading to the quagmire of Vietnam, he could've predicted the even deeper cesspool his leaders had dug since the first deployments to Iraq and Afghanistan. Collecting a paycheck dependent on such unceasing stupidity had never made him particularly proud.

"Vincent—?"

It was Buddy who finally brought him back. Vincent nodded at the lanky Maqlaq, glanced past his front fender where Lane and Gabriel had stepped away to talk. He knew it was up to him now. And maybe the risks wouldn't be all that great. What could his superiors do? – slap him on the wrist for abetting a former plant employee who enjoyed the sympathy of even those who disagreed with her, and whose only aim was to prevent more bloodshed? Force him to retire a couple of years early?

No way would they touch Lane. It was Woods he was most concerned about. Not merely because he was a street-smart young male whose motives were unclear, or even perceived as a threat to local officials. No, it was because Woods was special; Vincent could see that now.

He could also imagine the kind of life he led, having to hide his mysterious talents, never staying long in one place. Which must have been the reason he'd been thumbing for a ride last Wednesday, why he lived out of a duffle bag not much bigger than the one he himself packed for his two- and three-day delivery runs.

He nodded once more, this time for Buddy to join him in front of the truck where Lane was now in Gabriel's arms but apparently no closer to convincing him.

"It's *my* fault for making false assumptions, not yours," Gabriel was saying. "I didn't realize you and Richard still had..."

He stopped as the other two men approached. It was suddenly – and uncomfortably – clear to Vincent and Buddy that their discussion wasn't so much about the dangers of being smuggled into a certain ammo plant, but risks of another, more personal kind. Gabriel shrugged as if to acknowledge as much, to admit his healing powers weren't all he'd exposed tonight, turned back to finish his sentence.

"...things to work out. But that's okay, Lane—really. The last two days have been like a revelation for me. And even if I couldn't..."

He trailed off again, bit his lip. Vincent took another step closer, now more impatient to tell them what he had to say, could see in the light of the moon rising over the lodgepoles there were tears in their eyes, backed off.

"I mean, I wish I could leave here with everything changed back to the way—"

Lane abruptly reached up, pressed her fingers to Gabriel's lips. She said nothing, nor did anyone else, for several more moments. At last Vincent cleared his throat.

"The best thing you could do right now," he said to Gabriel, "would be to get out of here while you still can. Nobody'd blame you. But if you *did* go in there with Lane...?" He paused to wait for her reaction; it didn't take long. "I'll do whatever I can to get you back out again."

Gabriel sent an incredulous look, not only for Vincent's sudden change of heart, but for further complicating the situation.

"Wait. You actually think you can get us... Lane, anyhow—inside to begin with?"

"Hell, that's the easy part."

Then, to Lane: "And you think you can just waltz around the place until you stumble into Richard, when a SWAT team still hasn't managed to hunt him down?"

"If you'll be my eyes."

Gabriel frowned in disbelief, finally laughed out loud at the irony – it was usually *him* who drew the disbelieving stares – then glanced past Vincent to where Buddy was standing.

"And you... you're going to just let this happen?—gonna just stand there with your badge and your thirty-eight special and your promise to uphold the law?"

The Maqlaq stared back steadily, waited several more seconds as if Gabriel should have come to the same conclusion himself.

"I *am* upholding the law."

"You're all three crazy," Gabriel had replied. And there was a moment before he nodded *Yes*, a moment of perfect clarity he would reflect upon only much later, when he imagined himself walking away from them, getting into Lane's beat-up, sky blue Mustang without so much as a glance in the rearview mirror and taking the car out on the highway toward the next chapter of his life. He pictured himself heading east to Sprague, through Beatty where they'd been the very same morning, though it already seemed days ago; and then he would leave the car in Lakeview around the corner from the Trailways bus depot.

Maybe he would try Utah this time. There were lots of small towns south of Salt Lake, he'd heard, where people kept to themselves – even jealously guarded their secrecy – as long as they figured you were Mormon. Gabriel could play that role.

Once, on a four-month long sojourn near Twin Falls, he stayed at a roadside motel-turned-boarding-house owned by an LDS couple. When they saw him carrying his Bible but no Book of Mormon, they insisted he join their Wednesday night study group. Gabriel eventually agreed, sat safely outside their circle but ended up learning much from the two pale-as-milk missionaries.

He also remembered thinking, back then, how easy it must be to invent a new religion – or at least a new sect – not unlike his hosts' religion was born and bred in the badlands of the west. And it wasn't so much a new idea or new theology that always seemed to inspire the upstart religion; it was one solitary, charismatic leader.

He himself might've been such a figure if he'd wanted. He could feel the temptation to build his own following in those early days. In addition to the skeptics and naysayers who believed he wielded some sort of Satanic power, there was also a core of willing converts who could hardly wait for boy wonder to declare himself and his ministry. But the power had come upon him so suddenly, and in such a fog of grief for his mother, he hadn't thought of anything to say. He had no... *message.*

Of course there were others who would gladly volunteer to speak on his behalf. Before he'd finally made the decision to disappear permanently, a traveling evangelist found him out, had even witnessed one of his lesser healings, and that was enough for him. The evangelist promised Gabriel a six-figure income if he would only join his troupe. Gabriel wouldn't need to do any talking, he'd said. In fact his written contract would specifically prohibit any potential sermonizing.

Gabriel made him a counter-offer. If the evangelist could give him one good reason why God would allow a speeding speed-freak to cut short his mother's life, he would sign on the bottom line and go on the holy road for no more than the cost of his room and board.

The excited evangelist reached into his box of ready-made answers and began spewing forth. *Had his mother been saved?* the evangelist probed. Or had she done something terribly wrong in her life for which she'd never sought forgiveness, and therefore deserved God's righteous punishment? Did Gabriel know of any dark secrets in her past? Did she practice magic or witchcraft or read tarot cards? Was she... an *adulteress...?*

When the evangelist belatedly detected the rage Gabriel was struggling to suppress, he quickly changed tactics, explaining how those who are perfectly reconciled with God – whatever their past wrongdoings – are often taken up to heaven so they can avoid any further temptations or tribulations. After all, that's what the Rapture was about: The true believers would be lifted up while the bad and the borderline would be left behind to suffer under the Antichrist.

Surely Gabriel's mother had earned the honor of being swept up early, even if it took a grisly car accident to transport her. The crucifixion of God's only-begotten Son was just as grisly an event, wasn't it? And all those who believed in Him – Gabriel included – would be Raptured soon, perhaps any day now. Wasn't the war against terror and the rediscovery of the Lost Ark a clear sign of The End?

"Save me from your kind of salvation," Gabriel said before walking out of their meeting. And that was as close to a message as he could think of then, and perhaps even now.

Still, Gabriel spent more than a few sleepless nights wondering what life might've been like had he accepted the evangelist's offer. Maybe in time he might've come up with a message worthy of his miracles. At the very least, religion would have provided a context for who he was.

How he longed to stop hiding, longed to stop running, longed for his own End Times. Until then the D'Arcy Ranch was his glimpse of heaven. Lane had swept him up, enraptured him, if only temporarily, if only in the flesh.

And now, ironically, she hunkered with him, uncharacteristically silent, in the rear of Vincent's big-rig, between cartons of 108mm shell casings and the boxes of mortar fuse caps that would provide their excuse to slip through the roll-up doors and into the U.S. Army Ammunition Plant in Chiloquin, Oregon.

*A*lex **Round Tree had always hoped** his younger brother would remain unpolluted by the Bustin business of war. Unlike him, Stillwater seemed destined for a different role in life. Even before he'd come of age, after their father died unexpectedly and his mother left them both with an aunt, Two Bears told the elders the sacred pipe would someday be passed to Stillwater. Chino had the gift, too, but she was a woman. And so, right up until he took the job at the ammo plant, Stillwater spent most of his afternoons learning the Old Ways.

The cost of their aunt's ongoing medical care may have forced his hand, though he claimed it wasn't the only reason. Once, over a brew at Corky Girls, Stillwater explained his decision to work the lines by saying his main task in life was to help "bring his lost brothers home." Actually he'd said *brother*, as if he was referring to only one person, perhaps even to Alex himself, since he'd lived most of his life without a spiritual compass.

Stillwater adamantly refused to explain further, but Alex was certain – at least looking back on it – that he must have been talking about *all* of the Maqlaqs, and to their goal of reclaiming what rightfully belonged to them. And when he died before that purpose could be accomplished, Alex felt the burden fall on his own shoulders, though he hardly knew where to begin and could only assume the task was related in some way to the ammo plant.

Until Edison's cousin had his vision, when everything became clear. Two Bears himself could not deny it. Hadn't he told everyone at last year's pow-wow how the Restoration would never happen without pain and struggle? That lives might be lost? Perhaps his brother's death marked the beginning.

Alex quickly volunteered to become one of the three who would continue the struggle, along with Edison and Truman Crow. But then the sick-out confused things. Or else it was a sign, Edison said. And instead of taking months to persuade the U.S. Army to leave, perhaps they could deliver their message in one single stand.

Edison was certain Richard McCaffery's unexpected appearance was also a sign. If the Bustin leaders joined their protest – especially one who previously opposed them – how could they lose? So when Richard finally got close enough to begin pleading for them to stop what they were doing, it nearly broke the Maqlaqs' spirits. Worse, the SWAT team stumbled onto them minutes later and at least three of the four were wounded – Edison bad enough that he was unable to crawl back to the supply room, much less pull himself up through the ceiling panel again.

Which left Alex… *where – ?* He'd already spoken the sacred words for those who face death. If it came to that, he was ready now. All the more so if the hole below Edison's collarbone proved fatal. He would have no blood brothers left, and no blood relatives ever since his aunt had joined their ancestors just like Stillwater. Unless, of course, his mother remained alive somewhere; but no one had heard from her since she'd headed east.

Maybe there would be another sign. Yes, Alex thought, he would hold out until he could be certain. And in the meantime, he would hold on to the mortar round.

Buddy preceded Vincent's semi in Fiske's Blazer, then pulled forward onto the shoulder to wait as the big-rig began negotiating its way down the entrance drive. Wisely, he'd donned the flat-brimmed ranger's hat Fiske left on the front seat, figuring he'd look more like the Lieutenant if anyone happened to be peering through binoculars.

Getting past the roadblock a mile east had been easy enough. The Guard troopers had probably been given orders to wave through the next truck escorted by a B.I.A. police car. They had no way of knowing the escort wasn't Lieutenant Fiske; and when the few plant employees still keeping vigil on the east perimeter saw Buddy behind the wheel, they broke off their protests and name-calling so fast the soldiers could only wonder why.

The plant gate, however, did not roll aside as it usually did when Vincent entered the final S-turn. Instead the chain-link opened only wide enough for a lone trooper to emerge and step past the beams of his headlights.

Vincent scanned the guard hut as the black-uniformed soldier marched around to the driver's side, saw none of the ammo plant's own security crew posted. The three figures still standing beneath the hut's greenish glare were National Guard, and the man now gazing up through his window, Vincent reckoned, was a member of the unit from Midland. In short, nobody at the entrance knew him from Adam.

It dawned on Vincent that, for the first time in years, he would need to show his I.D. and bill of lading before he'd be waved through. He nodded, lowered his window with one hand, at the same time reaching into the compartment above his seat with the other.

"That's okay—I know who you are," the soldier said perfunctorily, glancing down at his clipboard.

Which turned out to be fortunate. The canvas strap on Vincent's duffle bag was still so sticky with his own blood he had to grab a shop towel to wipe off his hands. Nor had the soldier noticed the sticky sheen as Vincent transferred his bag from the cubbyhole to the seat. Tossing the towel back on the floor, Vincent quickly composed himself, turned to look down at the soldier.

"Guess you didn't get our last message," the Guardsman said, looking up again, none the wiser.

"Message?"

"Tried to reach Fiske, too." He squinted at Vincent before glancing toward the Blazer idling beside the highway. "Nobody told you guys to maintain radio silence, far as I know."

Vincent scowled as if to agree it was odd, twisted around to poke through his duffle bag. The top of his cell phone could be seen, message screen face up, blank. He reached into the opening, careful to avoid the damp crimson on the knit shirt against which it lay, was thankful for the soldier's upward angle. He was even more thankful when he withdrew the cell phone to find the bottom sheared clean off, presumably from the same slug that had torn through his wrist.

"Dammit," Vincent said with a purposeful wince. "Looks like the battery's shot. Must'a gone dead while I was parked out there so long." He looked in the rearview mirror on his left, then the newly-installed mirror on his right, spotted the tail lights of the police car glowing in the darkness. "Don't know what the Lieutenant's excuse is."

"Doesn't surprise me," the soldier said, likewise looking away. "After watching the guy in action this afternoon, you gotta wonder how he keeps his job." He returned his gaze to Vincent. "Anyhow, Cap'm Romano rescinded the order to bring you in. Nobody in receiving right now. They're all busy guarding the assembly lines, or else the product awaiting shipment. Word is, a couple mortars went missing from one of the cartons when they first got there."

"No kiddin'?" Vincent cocked his head, frowned. "So what exactly are you telling me?—Halvorsen pulled the dock crew to help you guys guard the equipment?"

"Halvorsen—?" Now it was the soldier who frowned. "He's got nothin' to do with it. Romano's in charge now. The plant supes and remaining employees were relieved of duty."

"When did this happen?"

"Bout forty-five minutes ago. Prob'ly when they tried to call—"

"No—I mean the new rules. Since when does outside brass get to boot the local C.O. from his own command?"

The soldier reached around to scratch the back of his neck. "Guess it's part of the latest Homeland Security regs. Ever since the New York subway thing, they figure if local authorities can't get the job done within a certain period of time, Special Ops steps up."

It didn't sound good. Lane was probably correct in thinking the two remaining protestors would be treated as terrorists. And with no home-grown staffers to mitigate the SWAT team's actions, it seemed all the more likely that lethal force would be option number one.

Which meant it was even *more* idiotic to put Lane into the thick of it, even with Gabriel around. The miracle man might be able to heal other people – assuming they weren't already blown into bone meal – but that didn't mean *he* was indestructible, did it?

He would off-load the fuses; those definitely deserved the extra precaution. Then he would make some excuse to get back in the truck and—

"What's it matter, anyhow?"

"Huh?"

The Guardsman stared up at him, now almost suspiciously. "What difference does it make *who's* got jurisdiction, long as we get the place fully secured?"

"I couldn't care less," Vincent lied. "I just need somebody who'll open a roll-up so I can get these mortar caps outta my trailer and into the warehouse."

"No can do. The new C.O. might let you park your rig in back, but like I say, there's nobody who can take delivery. You're not even supposed to be here."

"Well, I *am* here, okay? And I was scheduled to bring in this load five hours ago." Vincent peered down, blew out a breath, tried to relax. "Look, sergeant, if you guys are smart as I think you are, the warehouse is cordoned off, besides being surrounded by eighteen inches of concrete. It's the most secure place in this facility—more than your south forty back there, which happens to be within hunting-rifle range of the ridgeline across the river. Any a'your guys scout that area since you arrived?"

The sergeant appeared slightly less confident. Vincent went in for the kill.

"All I need is one guy to open one door. I'll handle the forklift myself. Take me ten, fifteen minutes tops to get all the explosives inside. Your guy doesn't even need to hang around. And the open door'll be concealed behind my truck the whole time." He nodded toward the guard hut. "Go call your captain. I can wait."

As it turned out, Vincent waited long enough to cut his engine rather than waste any more fuel, and *then* long enough to wonder if Captain Romano suspected something. The thought also crossed his mind that his two ride-alongs couldn't be terribly comfortable crammed into the spaces between the stacked cartons where he'd made room for them. If nothing else, the air was probably growing a little stale. There was some circulation of outside air, yes, and both a humidifier and temperature control system designed to kick on every so often. But the trailer's heavy insulation wasn't designed for human cargo.

In fact, the insulation also made the interior of the trailer black as a bat cave and virtually soundproof. Like he'd told them before they left Lane's ranch, there was no need for them to remain quiet the whole time. The two of them could talk at anything short of a scream and no one outside would hear. He'd found that out for himself years ago when he accidentally locked a dockworker inside the trailer. The trapped teamster swore he'd been yelling for ten minutes at the top of his lungs, and only when Vincent opened the door to re-check his load did he finally hear his cries for help.

Neither did Vincent hear the ammo plant's chain-link gate when it finally began to roll aside. With his window shut tight because of the cold night air, and his eyes closed while he pondered the fate of his passengers, Vincent didn't realize the gate had been opened until its metal frame banged against its stops.

Gabriel felt rather than heard the renewed rumble of the truck's diesel engine, elbowed Lane as if she hadn't already noticed.

"Yeah—guess it means conditions are right," Lane said, and then retreated into silence once more.

Much to Gabriel's consternation, Lane had been mostly silent from the moment Vincent had padlocked the rear doors – and despite his assurances no one would be able to hear them if they talked. Repeated attempts to initiate a conversation were met with one- or two-word responses. Only after the truck came to a stop outside the gates did Lane open her mouth to report that she could hear someone who'd come out to speak with Vincent. Gabriel couldn't hear anything beyond his own breathing, but Lane positively identified the voice as belonging to a man in his mid-thirties who did not work at the plant, even while admitting her inability to make out a single word he said.

"How can you possibly know that?" Gabriel challenged, more for the purpose of making small talk than questioning Lane's hearing.

"Same way you heal people," she said simply. "I just *do*."

And other than Gabriel's subsequent expressions of impatience at the delay, followed by Lane's unfounded assurances about Vincent waiting until conditions were right, they hardly spoke.

He estimated that twenty minutes elapsed before the truck began to move again. The trailer shuddered as the diesel strained against its weight – just as it had three days earlier, Gabriel mused, when it left him stranded on the fog-bound highway – then rolled forward for several seconds before turning laboriously to the right. In another half-minute the truck began a barely-perceptible arc to the left that seemed to go on forever.

"Is he taking us back out?" Gabriel ventured.

"No. He's gotta bring the right side flush with the loading dock, is all."

Gabriel nodded to himself. He and Lane had climbed into the trailer through the rear doors because Vincent had parked too close to the house to get inside any other way. But he remembered seeing what appeared to be hinged doors along the right side, similar to those on a large moving van. Sure enough, soon after they'd come to a halt Gabriel heard a faint clattering on the right, saw a wedge of light slice into the interior a few yards forward of where he and Lane were crouched.

"Change a'plans. Nobody's com—!"

Vincent broke off before he could poke his head in – or get another word out. A second voice wafted inside the trailer, seemingly in mid-sentence.

"...in the office, before you get started."

Gabriel immediately pressed himself back against the trailer wall, saw Lane do the same.

"Be right there," Vincent replied, raising his voice. "I just wanna check on my—"

"And I told you to *leave* it, okay? Romano wants this done by the book."

The second voice was close to the opening now. Gabriel turned, could make out Lane's profile in the dim glow, her expression concerned but unafraid.

"Alright—no need to get all worked up, Corporal. Your C.O. wants it done by the book, we'll just..."

Vincent's words faded, disappeared entirely.

"They went into the security office," Lane whispered after a few more heartbeats. "The guy's gonna make Vincent sign in, then go over the entire delivery list."

She emerged from behind the cartons, reached for Gabriel's hand. He hesitated, less from trepidation than surprise, couldn't remember Lane ever asking him to guide her.

"It'll take a while to check off the items they're gonna let him bring in. Now's our chance."

Far from letting him guide her, she began pushing him ahead, up the narrow aisle between the boxes toward the opening Vincent left for them.

"Wait a minute. Don't you think it might be kind of important, what Vincent was trying to tell us before the other guy came over?"

"*Nobody's coming*—didn't you hear? All they can spare is this one guard. And they prob'ly had to pull 'im off duty from somewhere else in the plant. Maybe that's why it took so long before they could let us in."

Maybe. In any case, they were beside the opening now. Gabriel squinted through, could see perhaps thirty yards of concrete loading dock and three metal roll-up doors – all shut tight – as well as an orange door with the letter "S."

"See the fluorescent orange door?"

"I thought Vincent said we were going through the roll-ups."

"Not now. The hallway past the security office leads straight to the lunchroom, exactly where we need to go. This is *way* better." Two beats. "So what about the door?"

"I see it. Closed, just like the others."

"Course it is. But the spring bolt can be set so it won't lock. Usually how they leave it when there's a lot of traffic in and out, like when there's a delivery."

Gabriel glanced upward through the crack in the trailer door, noticed a video surveillance camera, peered back at the orange door.

"So how are you supposed to tell?"

"You can't."

Vincent was wondering about the door, too. He routinely retracted the bolt whenever he went through it the first time, usually without even thinking. And now, standing there in the security office with this painfully deliberate young Guardsman, he couldn't remember whether he'd done it or not.

He already regretted not securing the trailer door. But the soldier was coming over so fast, the only thing he could do that wouldn't appear suspicious was turn and head for the office in an effort to draw him away. Replaying it in his mind now, he remembered the orange door had already closed behind the Guardsman – which meant the bolt must have been retracted or they'd never have gotten back inside.

Vincent waited as the soldier searched for his schedule of delivery, considered pointing to the print-out where it hung on a clipboard next to the inventory computer. Instead, he took the opportunity to scan the banks of video consoles that provided 360-degree coverage of the ammo plant's exterior, from fence line to the front entrance, including four separate screens trained on the loading dock. One was pointed at the side of Vincent's trailer, the six-inch opening starkly visible – as was an unidentified figure moving just behind it.

As Vincent watched with increasing alarm, the opening began

to widen until, all at once, Woods was out on the dock in open view, reaching back through the door for Lane.

Damn.

"What?"

The corporal turned from the counter where he was still shuffling papers, the offending video monitor to his right, just above eye level. Worse, to the Guardsman's left was a five-foot window overlooking not only the adjacent hallway, but the orange door that would be bursting open at any moment.

Vincent hadn't realized he'd spoken the word aloud, suddenly stepped past the soldier to grab the clipboard off its hook. Hoping it wasn't too obvious, he made a tight half-circle, jabbed a finger at the print-out to distract the Guardsman, pulling him around like a tango partner so he'd be facing away from both the hallway and the monitors.

And not an instant too soon.

Gabriel swung the door just wide enough to push Lane through ahead of him, stepped in after her, instantly froze at the sight of the security office, arrayed in all its technological glory through a plate-glass window. It took another instant to realize the Guardsman's back was turned.

He met Vincent's eyes only long enough to glimpse anger – wasn't sure to whom it was directed – before the truck driver's voice rose to berate the corporal for taking so long. Either way, his sudden bellowing would hide any noise he and Lane might make rushing down the hall, not to mention the soft hissing of the automatic door closer.

Lane, too, assumed Vincent was covering for them, signaled that the room they sought was down the hall and to the left. Grabbing her by the wrist, Gabriel began pulling her behind him, glad he'd changed into his gum-soled work boots, and even more relieved when they'd passed the security office without the Guardsman hearing their footsteps.

Perhaps twenty feet beyond the first doorway, the hallway intersected another corridor. They turned left, came to a second doorway before which Gabriel paused despite Lane's urgings to keep moving. This room also appeared to be some kind of security office, with three banks of monitors showing various sites inside the plant, including tooling stations, assembly lines, ordnance storage rooms – as well as the enamel-painted corridor in which they themselves were now standing.

Gabriel marveled to find no one at the console, though soldiers were posted at most of the sites now being displayed on the monitors, with the exception of those at their end of the building. Probably the beat assigned to the Guardsman still being harangued by Vincent.

He felt Lane nudge him forward again, now more insistently, continued another twenty yards toward a double doorway through which a much larger room came into view. Inside were a dozen or so circular tables surrounded by plastic chairs, and a bank of vending machines covering most of two walls. Gabriel paused again, remembered seeing such a room on one of the security monitors, leaned through the doorway to scan for occupants until Lane shoved him inside, having already decided it was vacant.

"Storage room on the far wall," she whispered.

He spotted an alcove across the room, above which hung a sign with the words *Wash Rooms*, began moving through the haphazard arrangement of tables toward it. Gabriel sensed that Lane was actually allowing him to lead now, which he attempted to do by pulling one way or another on her wrist, like the reins on her horse. Halfway through the maze, however, Lane went right when he pulled left, stumbling over the leg of a chair someone neglected to push back under a table. His grip kept her from falling, but the chair bounced noisily across the uneven tiles, skidding to a final *ker-thunk* as it came to rest against another table.

They stopped, held their breath to listen for any reaction, heard silence long enough to presume Vincent and the Guardsman had gone back out on the dock. Then, suddenly, the muffled echoes of boots filled the hallway.

"The one in the middle!"

In two more seconds they were inside the alcove, doors to the men's and women's lavatories on either side of a third one, unmarked.

Judging by the thudding in the hallway, they had no time to lose.

Gabriel reached for the knob of the unmarked door, stifled a gasp at the sight of the key slot and the possibility it might be locked, blinked in amazement when the knob turned freely in his hand. He swung the door open, stepped through ahead of Lane, turned as she followed him in and pulled it shut.

The storage room wasn't as dark as he might have expected, the dusky light coming in beneath the door giving amorphous shape to a few objects lining the walls – a water heater, cartons of paper towels, a galvanized bucket with rubber wheels and a mop. To the left of the bucket, Lane was already on her knees, busy with something on the floor or just above it. As Gabriel continued to watch, a fuzzy rectangle appeared against the darker gray background, then, a blur of movement.

"Crawl through," Lane said, waving him over.

"What?"

And then another voice, faintly.

"What makes you think it was *this* room?"

It was Vincent, still trying to cover for them – and the Guardsman, hissing for the old trucker to keep quiet.

"Hurry!" Lane whispered. "You first!"

Gabriel stooped, squared himself in front of the dim rectangle and squeezed through, then forward far enough to make room for Lane. He was scrambling to his feet when the storage room doorknob turned again.

Or at least someone *tried* to turn it.

There were several metallic clicks, followed by another muffled hiss that Gabriel took to be an expletive. He waited until Lane replaced the metal grating, rose into the darkness in front of him, then pressed his mouth against her ear.

"So how did *we* get in if the door's locked?"

"Richard left it open, same way he did when we'd meet for lunch. I just re-bolted it."

"And you knew it'd be open?"

"Had a hunch."

Gabriel swallowed his first reaction, knew it was futile anyway, turned to scan his new surroundings. It was slightly less dark here than the storage room, a wan, ethereal glow drifting down from somewhere above them. As his eyes began to adjust he could see the two walls they were standing between, one made of concrete blocks, one of peeling, corrugated tin that must have been a room divider within the original framework. The separation between them was only slightly wider than his shoulders. Perhaps twenty yards ahead, several more walls appeared to intersect, the clearance even less.

From his own experience in construction, Gabriel quickly deduced that the ammo plant had probably been retrofitted with new interior walls – for fire protection perhaps, or else explosives containment. He remembered Lane's description of her own accident, how shrapnel from the grenades had gone through the metal roof and been found at the other end of the assembly line; but nothing had penetrated the walls into neighboring work areas.

Apparently the original metal skeleton had been left intact to support the roof and exterior shell. The more recent – and more solid – additions had been erected like separate buildings within the larger structure, at the same time allowing crawlspace for air ducts, electrical cables and insulation.

Gabriel turned back, noticed Lane peering diagonally upward in the dim light, apparently listening for any sounds of activity in the lunch room. In a few more seconds he stepped close enough for her to feel his breath on her face. She immediately redirected her eyes toward his.

"I'm pretty sure they're gone," she whispered. "I just hope the other guy doesn't put two and two together and decide Vincent's involved. Either way, they're not gonna let him off-load his fuses if they think someone's loose at this end. Prob'ly bring some more flak-jackets over with a key to the storeroom."

"Do they know about these spaces between the walls?"

She shrugged. "Only reason *I* know about 'em is because Richard was on the retrofit crew." She nodded away as if to start him moving again. "The maintenance crew—they'd know, but they were prob'ly sent home."

"Yeah, well, I'll bet the contents of my Bible whoever's left will be unrolling a set of blueprints within the next two minutes," Gabriel whispered back, "and kicking themselves they didn't think of it sooner. Assuming they *didn't* think of it sooner."

He paused at the junction between the intersecting walls, felt Lane nudge him to the left, hesitated again at a long stretch of tilt-up concrete whose far end disappeared into the darkness.

"Don't worry," Lane said, "it gets lighter around the next corner."

"I might've brought a flashlight if you'd told me where we'd be going."

"I was more concerned you'd be claustrophobic—"

"Yeah—thanks for the heads-up about *that,* too."

"—and besides, Richard and I used to do it without a flashlight."

"In the middle of the night like this?"

"Oh, stop whining. There's plenty of leakage from the shop lights. And yes, we were on graveyard together when we first started sneaking in here. Lunch was three in the morning." She clucked softly. "Sometimes we actually brought along something to eat."

Gabriel winced, began moving again. He didn't think she'd said it to taunt him; maybe it was just the reckless way she dealt with people's feelings. Or her own. Still, it was enough to make him question once more why he was doing this, why he would risk helping Lane rescue her former – and, it now seemed, *ongoing* – lover from the spot he was in.

"You mind telling me what your ultimate destination is?"

"Sure, if you'll tell me yours."

Gabriel lowered his head, simultaneously pushing Lane's down so they could pass under a rectangular air duct crossing diagonally between the walls.

"Huh. Don't remember that being there," Lane said.

"Three years since you've been in here, chances are lots of things have changed. Maybe even wherever it is you think we're going."

"Not after everything that's happened. Not after the way things have worked out so far."

"Like this is all pre-destined or something?"

"Are you so sure it *isn't?*"

Gabriel slowed, tried to peer into the darkness ahead, found the only thing he could see with any real acuity was a narrow portion of the metal roof thirty or forty feet above them. He couldn't believe the SWAT personnel weren't already up in the rafters, or at least hadn't done an initial overhead sweep. They might even be able to hear them now, but for the consistent drone of air conditioning pumps that pervaded the space.

"You think physical healing is the only way God—or whatever it is—works through you? C'mon, Gabe—maybe there are other things going on in your life just as miraculous, and you're not even aware of it."

The crawlspace ahead made a sharp right turn, then, as Gabriel drew close enough to see beyond it, appeared to make a series of right-angle switchbacks as if the corners of four concrete bunkers had come together, but didn't quite match. Fortunately, the space between the parallel slabs was just wide enough to squeeze through by turning sideways. It was also fortunate, Gabriel thought, that Lane kept on talking. Without the distraction, he almost certainly *would* be claustrophobic.

"I mean, haven't you ever wondered if all this moving around, all this running from one place to the next, might not be so accidental?" Lane was whispering now, her voice within the narrow space more like the sound of his own thoughts. "—and every town you end up in was *meant* to be your next destination? You know, like there was someone there who needed your help, or maybe something that needed doing and only you could do it? Maybe everything that happens, everything from hitting a deer on the highway to stopping somewhere for groceries... all these chance events are really unfolding according to some plan."

Actually, Gabriel *had* let those thoughts keep him awake on more than one lonely night. Which is why, in contrast to his mother's wish to see him pursue the ministry, he began to consider himself an atheist. After all, any God who could endow him with his so-called gift, then send him off on an endless string of missions designed to exploit it – not only against his will but without the slightest concern for what *he* wanted in life – was a cruel and hateful despot.

Not that these sentiments defined him as an atheist. A Catholic priest once explained through the screened window of a confessional box that Gabriel was actually closer to God than many so-called "believers." God would much rather have someone shake his fist at Him in heartfelt anger, the priest said, than to be ignored – or worse, to listen to the vacuous praises of congregants who were only going through motions they'd memorized in childhood, and paid attention to Him only because they thought it might earn them a pass to Paradise.

"Do you see it?... there, to your left?"

Gabriel blinked, looked back at Lane instead, then beyond her, suddenly aware he'd passed through the narrow switchbacks and was now in the clear. The ambient glow was indeed brighter, as Lane had predicted, light enough to see two ways of proceeding from where they now stood. In one direction was a crawlspace that disappeared into more darkness straight ahead; the other, to his left, dead-ended into a cinderblock wall no more than fifteen feet away.

"I can see we'll be trapped if we go the direction you said."

"No we won't. Look for a steel door, like a gym locker only bigger."

He turned fully now, squinted, spotted the louvered panel near the end, slightly ajar. It was then Gabriel noticed a dark splotch on the dusty concrete directly in front of the panel, not unlike the smaller droplets he could now see trailing back toward them, beneath their feet and into the blackness of the other passageway.

There was another louvered panel in the ceiling inside the secret room, admitting a diffuse light that seemed not so much to illumine Richard's body as to make it appear to glow from within. As Gabriel expected, more blood trailed across the floor, and a dark, foot-wide oval had spread into the layers of foam where he lay.

Lane's eyes drilled him with the question. He nodded, finally spoke.

"He's here alright."

"He is? Richard...? Oh my God, *Gabriel*—I can't hear him breathing!"

Gabriel wasn't sure how Lane *could* hear him breathing, what with the incessant drone of A/C pumps filling their ears. Then again, she'd surprised him when they first entered the dead-end corridor and she told him flatly that he must not be there after all. She could hear no movement, no telltale scuffling over to the metal door to see who might be coming. Only then did Gabriel tell her about the blood puddled there. And it was all he could do to keep her from shrieking in horror and giving themselves away.

"Hurry, Gabriel—please!"

"Give me a minute." He reached around Lane to close the metal door, still concerned she was being too loud, then clasped one shoulder as if to tell her to stay put. "I need to see if—"

"Are we too late? I mean, do you think you can still—"

"*Lane.* Do you mind?"

Gabriel waved for her to keep still, a gesture she seemed to sense, then walked over to kneel beside Richard. He focused on his own breath for several moments, found the effort to remove himself more difficult than usual, finally realized he would need to check the artery on Richard's neck to determine if he was alive. If there was any pulse at all, Gabriel knew, Richard might be saved; it was when no pulse was present that he could never be sure.

Earlier that day, at the accident scene – or maybe it was yesterday by now – he had the distinct feeling the first girl he'd brought back had already glimpsed the other side. Gabriel had been a little surprised by the possibility, frankly. Not that he'd done any research. How long could a person – or some doe out on the highway – be clinically dead before his power no longer worked? He didn't know, and could only wish for the day he would have no more occasions to find out.

A split second before his fingers contacted Richard's neck, Gabriel abruptly stopped himself, left his hand hovering there a few more seconds before pulling back slightly. All at once it was clear he had more control over his own life in that moment than he'd had since his mother's death. Because if Richard *wasn't* breathing, if his pulse *had* stopped – or was about to – there might yet be hope for a relationship with Lane. If Richard were out of the picture, perhaps Lane would finally let go of the past and let Gabriel back in her present. He might be doing both of them a favor. Maybe all three of—

"Gabriel...?"

It was barely a whisper. He blinked, stole a glance at Lane, slowly withdrew his hand.

"I can't feel anything," he said, not quite lying outright. "There's so much blood. It looks like he's already—"

"Oh please—no... *no!*" Lane moaned, crumpling to her knees

with such a look of anguish Gabriel found it almost repellent. "What have I done? What—"

"What've *you* done? Lane, this isn't any of your doing. People are responsible for their own actions, their own—"

"But I could've said yes when he asked, and none of this would've happened. Maybe everything would be different. This whole—"

"Stop it, Lane!" It occurred to Gabriel that *he* was being too loud now. "You did what you thought was right at the time. That's all you can ever do. You can't be anybody but who you are."

He straightened, saw in Lane's eyes the same question now assaulting his own mind: *And who am I?*

He turned away, winced at the terrible truth. Richard might indeed be beyond help now, but maybe not. If it was within Gabriel's ability to bring him back, and he refused for purely selfish motives, what did that make him? – a murderer? How many other people had he essentially condemned to death because he would not use the power the universe had entrusted to him? How long would he continue to avoid being who he was?

Raphael.

Gabriel swirled back, peered at Lane where she now hunched beside the louvered door, face in her hands, quietly sobbing.

"Did you say something?"

She lowered her hands, looked quizzically in his direction, her eyes glistening and off-line by several inches, her reply as obvious as it was unspoken.

He shook his head sadly, let go a sigh of submission, tried to refocus. Richard's wound was evidently on the side he'd turned toward the layer of foam. Maybe he'd hoped, futilely, that the pressure might stop his bleeding. Gabriel reached down with both hands, paused once more while he took in another series of breaths, slowly, deliberately. Then, placing one hand on Richard's shoulder and the other on his hip, he pushed him gently onto his back.

Grabbing a fold in his blood-soaked jersey, Gabriel pulled the material up to expose a small gash where a single bullet had evidently entered just below his ribcage. He inserted his right index finger up to the second knuckle, moved it within the soft tissues, could feel nothing metallic.

Probing was unnecessary, of course; even if the slug showed up on an x-ray, there would be no visible damage to any interior organs or arteries. Nor could Gabriel tell whether Richard's flesh was cold, whether there was any life remaining before he touched him. All he could feel was the liquid light flowing again, and a sudden constriction around his finger. He immediately withdrew it, found the hole almost fully sealed by the time he lifted his hand.

Some moments later he became aware of Lane kneeling beside him, speaking Richard's name, growing louder with each repetition. By the time his vision began to return he could see Lane bending over to embrace Richard, burying her face into his neck, Richard's eyes opening, then blinking in bewilderment. Gabriel, too, blinked as all of his senses flooded back, could also hear something else, something over and above Lane's exuberant sobbing, and now her name on Richard's lips, like the answer to a prayer: *Laney... Laney.*

"Quiet—both of you!"

A clattering of boots could be heard on a metal catwalk somewhere overhead, then more thudding, as if several of the soldiers were clambering atop the walls nearby. And then the *crack, crack* of gunfire.

Gabriel rushed to the metal door, opened it partway as another shot echoed amidst the droning of the A/C, peered through as bits of crumbled concrete showered the corridor.

Who are they shooting at?

He pushed the door all the way open, leaned out.

"Not a good idea," he could hear Richard say hoarsely. "They're in take-no-prisoners mode now."

"Exactly why I'm gonna draw 'em away from here," Gabriel replied, though he realized that wasn't his real motive.

"Gabriel—*no!*"

He looked back at Lane, her eyes now even more luminous in the light from overhead, then turned and disappeared through the louvered door.

It didn't take long to discover why the soldiers had opened fire. No sooner had Gabriel retraced his steps down the dead-end corridor than a dark shape vaulted the span directly overhead. He glanced up just in time to see a blur of denim and plaid flannel, shiny black hair streaming behind. The Maqlaq was carrying some kind of blunt object, clutching it the way he might hold a hammer or pipe wrench.

Gabriel swirled, listened, could hear the muffled thumps of his pursuers not far away. He could also hear the voices of Lane and Richard, if only barely, suspected that if *he* could, so could the advancing soldiers.

He quickly scanned the concrete floor, spotted the drops of blood that might have led the SWAT team to the secret room had they looked more closely. But unlike the debris-filled crawlspaces at construction sites where Gabriel had worked, there were no scraps of wood left behind, no tailings of sheet metal to pick up and bang against the walls or girders and thereby draw the soldiers' attention.

He swore at the ill-timed tidiness, turned right, squeezed between the concrete wall slabs through which he and Lane had passed earlier. There was some ductwork along that route, he recalled, where he could probably generate enough noise to create a distraction.

The long stretch that had once seemed so dark was considerably brighter now. He'd been in these catacombs for close to an hour, more than enough time for his eyes to adjust. Even so, Gabriel did not see the figure who had climbed onto one of the girders above him. He was caught completely off-guard when the hulking shape dropped virtually without a sound into the narrow passageway ahead, completely filling the space. It took a few moments for Gabriel to realize it wasn't some SWAT soldier blocking his path, but the Maqlaq he'd seen fleeing minutes ago – and only moments more for the Maqlaq to recognize *him*.

"You're the one Chino calls Healer," the other man said, frowning dubiously. "How did you... what are you doing here?"

"We came for Richard."

"We?"

"Lane and—"

"Lane D'Arcy? You brought *Laney* in here?"

"More like she brought me."

Gabriel peered back in the dim light, could now discern the object clutched by the Maqlaq, saw it wasn't a pipe wrench but a mortar round, complete with tail fins and fuse cap. He could also make out a dark splotch in the fabric on his opposite arm, another on an inside pant leg.

"Are you hurt?"

"Not that bad. It's my friend might not make it. He told me to go on, not give up. I wasn't sure it was right to leave him there. But now I—"

The big man suddenly jerked his head, stared upward, listening. Gabriel stiffened, could hear only the pumps, watched the Maqlaq for a good ten seconds before he lowered his gaze, presumably satisfied they hadn't been detected.

"So what's your plan?" Gabriel whispered.

"Plan?"

"Well, it's only a matter of time before you're cornered. I don't see what you'll gain by—"

"You sound like the Bustin—McCaffery. He was trying to—"

The Maqlaq broke off again, this time with a grimace, tried to reach up as if to massage his bloodied arm with the hand gripping the mortar, but couldn't.

"Here, let me."

Gabriel took two steps to close the gap between them, reached with his own hands to cradle the big man's arm. The pained expression relaxed almost immediately, the Maqlaq's eyes darting with surprise, then widening as expected. Gabriel took a slow, deep breath, retreated slightly.

"So it's true, what Two Bears says." The other man stared now in almost child-like wonder, obviously taking Gabriel's silence as assent, then turned abruptly somber. "My brother... you must be the one he spoke of."

Gabriel looked away – a *again the legend* – looked back, squinted.

"Two Bears is your brother?"

"Two Bears is the one who was teaching my brother."

"So who's—"

But the Maqlaq was already moving on, thrusting up an impatient palm.

"I overheard the soldiers talking about a truck, came in a while ago?"

"That's right." Gabriel cocked his head, had a sudden, uneasy feeling he'd met this man before, but couldn't imagine how or where. "Prob'ly the same one brought us here, Lane and me."

The Maqlaq brightened. "Maybe it can take us out."

"That was the idea. Only Lane never let me in on her escape plan."

"Lane doesn't make plans. Not her way."

Gabriel shrugged, felt foolish he needed to be reminded.

"Besides," the other man went on, "she's in the hands of the U.S. Army now."

"She's— How do you—"

"That's why they stopped chasing me. That, and the tank rounds stored on the other side a'this wall. You heard the commotion a minute ago?" He paused long enough for Gabriel to shake his head *no*, nodded back with a wry smile. "I'm Alex Round Tree, brother of Stillwater. And you, Healer, you will be my hostage."

The storage room by which he and Lane gained access to the crawlspace had no doubt been put under watch almost immediately. Which meant that, in order to reach Vincent's truck, he and Alex would be forced to climb back up into the metal superstructure and return to the loading dock by way of the attic.

Gabriel found himself staring nervously at the mortar tucked into the waistband of the Maqlaq's jeans as he shimmied up the I-beam directly above him. The round was fully armed, Alex had explained, and would almost surely detonate if it fell nose-first onto the concrete below. Of course, this fact was key to pulling off their ruse. The soldiers needed to believe the hot-headed Maqlaq might let it drop if he were "cornered," as Gabriel had predicted; and Gabriel needed to appear certain Alex would drop it.

"But would you, really?" Gabriel had asked.

"In a drumbeat," the Maqlaq replied, "if my only other choice is prison."

Convincing the soldiers would be no problem.

What passed for the ammo plant's attic was a maze of steel beams, girders and tilt-up concrete. Some of the interior walls rose the thirty-plus feet to the metal roof, others only partway, with sheetrock ceilings supported by the same two-by-fours Gabriel had cut and nailed down in hundreds of houses over the years. The administrative offices where they were headed, however, had fiber-board ceiling panels set into an aluminum grid. It would be simple enough to yank out a panel and lower themselves through the open-ing into one of the rooms, then commence with their hostage act. That's when things might "get dicey," as Alex put it, adding that he'd heard someone say it on a cop show.

Not that their passage through the attic wasn't *already* dicey. Alex had warned him about the two snipers with night-vision scopes posted on a catwalk near the east end of the plant. The taller of the interior walls mostly obstructed their sightlines toward the west end, but there were several places where the two of them might be visible while they negotiated their way along the lower walls and the six-inch-wide beams atop them. It was here Alex would grab Gabriel around the neck, hostage style, then hold the mortar out conspicu-ously so it would fall and explode if the snipers tried to pick one of them off.

"What makes you think they'd give a damn if both of us died?"

"They wouldn't. But I drop this, it might set off a chain-reaction, or at least start a fire. That's what they give a damn about."

Thankfully, the two arrived at the west end without another shot fired, and were safely hidden from the snipers' view by the time they stopped over what Alex guessed was Colonel Halvorsen's office. And as far as he could tell, they still weren't being pursued.

Even so, Alex seemed mildly surprised when he lifted a ceiling panel and could see no soldiers posted either inside the room or out in the hallway. Perhaps the security squad had decided to wait for them elsewhere. Or maybe they were afraid of the mortar.

After removing a panel next to the east wall, Alex motioned for Gabriel to lower himself onto one of the built-in cabinets that lined Halvorsen's office, then quickly followed, mortar held out threateningly just in case. It wasn't until they'd walked out of the office and down the corridor past the cafeteria that anyone confronted them.

The sight of four M-16s aimed his way brought Gabriel to an immediate halt. Alex, however, remained unfazed. He simply tightened his forearm around Gabriel's neck, turning them both sideways so he could see down the hallway in either direction.

"Who's the officer in charge?" he demanded, raising the mortar over the linoleum.

"That would be me."

Another soldier sporting a brown beret stepped through the security office doorway, positioned himself behind the four guards now blocking their way out. Gabriel recognized him as the C.O. who'd supervised the off-loading of the troop transports that afternoon.

"Can't let you take me," Alex said as if he were merely reporting a fact. "I'd rather die where I stand. Anybody else wants to come with me, that's—"

He broke off as a second figure stepped from the security office.

"*Lane!*—what're you—"

Gabriel had almost twisted from beneath the Maqlaq's forearm before he was yanked backward by an even tighter choke hold. He felt certain he could've broken away if he'd really tried, but he didn't, and, without intending to, the brief scuffle convinced the soldiers that Gabriel must be a genuine hostage after all.

"So," Alex said with a sneer, "the U.S. Army uses human shields, too?"

"No, Alex," Lane answered calmly, "I asked Captain Romano to let me talk with you."

"He put you in danger like this—he's no different than me. You being here won't stop me from dropping this mortar. You know that, Laney."

"I *do* know it, Alex. But there's no reason to take Gabriel with you. The Captain knows he's here only because I made him come with me, and only because I knew where Richard was hiding."

"So I give him up, and I get a free pass?" Two beats. "Tell me another white man's lie, like this land is ours forever."

"You toss me the keys to that Dodge pickup of yours—" It was the Captain again, voice as calm and measured as Lane's. "—and I'll have one of my men bring it around to the dock. Listen to me, Alex. I will *guarantee* you safe passage through the gate and out past the east end of the property where you can drop off your hostage. After that you're on your own." He shrugged, tried to appear hopeful. "But you'll be under B.I.A. jurisdiction out there, and maybe Lieutenant Fiske will be lenient. If that's not good enough, I figure there's plenty of places to ditch your truck between here and the roadblocks if you want to make a run for it."

By the slight loosening of Alex's grip around his neck, Gabriel could tell the big Maqlaq was considering it. Then: a tense breath.

"Lane, what do you know about Edison Crow?"

The query obviously caught the Captain by surprise – and worked like a charm. Alex clearly knew Lane well enough to assume she would ask about his friends after she fell into the soldiers' hands. He *also* knew her well enough to decipher what she'd learned by the look on her face, and the news wasn't good.

"Last report was," Captain Romano quickly jumped in, "he's in surgery down at Klamath General. I'm sure the doctors are doing everything they can."

The Maqlaq's arm grew tighter against Gabriel's collarbone. "Reach into my left pocket for my keys," he said softly, and Gabriel knew things wouldn't go as smoothly as the Captain had promised.

During the five minutes it took to retrieve Alex's pickup from the front lot, the soldiers had cleared the corridor, escorted Lane back to the cafeteria – all but kicking and screaming – and propped open the orange door. Captain Romano was the only soldier to follow them out onto the loading dock, but Alex whispered to Gabriel he was "dead sure" snipers were already positioned on the rooftop and behind the concrete barriers along the fence line.

In a not-so-subtle breach of protocol, the lights normally flooding the expanse of lava rock outside the perimeter had been extinguished. Gabriel could only imagine the night-vision scopes pointing at them through the chain-link by marksmen who were now concealed in the darkness. Which is no doubt why Alex was holding the mortar high above their heads again and in such a fashion it could be thrown as easily as dropped.

The moment the Dodge came around the corner of the building, Alex turned to the C.O., nodded pointedly at Vincent's big-rig still parked at the north end of the dock.

"I want the semi moved away about fifteen feet, enough space to drive my truck in on this side."

"What—? *Why?*"

The Captain pretended ignorance, knew the Maqlaq wanted to be screened from his snipers by the trailer, also knew he'd been caught off guard again.

"I don't know if..." He shook his head, flustered. "...I mean, it might take some time to locate the driver so we can get his keys. For all I know, he's not even—"

"Horseshit," Alex spat back. "Security keeps a set of duplicates for every vehicle docks here, 'case of emergency. Like *this* one."

The Captain hesitated, drew a breath, looked away at the security office door now shut behind them, then up at one of the video cameras beneath the overhang.

"Corporal MacEvoy," he said, raising his voice only slightly, "get me the keys to Vincent's truck." He glanced back at the Maqlaq. "I'll move the damn thing myself."

Gabriel couldn't be sure Alex picked up on the Captain's tone, but his last remark seemed insincere, if not duplicitous. Whatever his intentions, the Maqlaq wasn't about to wait and find out. Because when the corporal opened the door and waved the extra set of keys for the Captain to catch, Gabriel could feel the muscles in Alex's arm galvanizing for action. And when the unsuspecting soldier lobbed them through the air in what suddenly appeared to be slow motion, the big Maqlaq pushed Gabriel away as easily as a carton of empty shell casings.

In two bounds he snatched the keys in mid-air, immediately swung the mortar with his other hand, catching the C.O. on the side of his head, not so much with the mortar as the fist holding it. The Captain's beret flew off like a wayward Frisbee, arms flailing as he went backward, eyes open but lights out.

And then, before Gabriel had time to figure out why, small bits of concrete began spattering the dock around him, jumping from newly-made chinks in the concrete walls. He swirled, saw Alex break for the cab of Vincent's truck, finally became aware of the *pop-popping* of rifles from the fence line, realized he couldn't simply stand there amidst the whizzing bullets and bolted after him.

The firing ceased once they'd disappeared behind the trailer, then resumed the moment the Maqlaq was spotted inside the cab. Gabriel grabbed the passenger side door just before Alex could close it, shouted "I'm coming with you!" and jumped in after him. "Your funeral!" the big man bellowed back, but allowed him to stay.

They traded anxious looks as the big-rig's diesel engine turned over several times before it revved, and again when the driver's-side window shattered from the impacts of successive slugs. Amazingly, Alex didn't appear to be hit, but simply hunkered down as he shoved the gearshift forward and let out the clutch.

The firing stopped again as soon as the truck began to roll. Probably the danger of a stray bullet hitting the fuse-caps in back, Gabriel thought, or the mortar Alex tossed onto the dashboard as if it were a pair of sunglasses he'd just removed. Or maybe it was the fear of hitting the soldier just now circling in Alex's pickup, or else the Captain.

Gabriel raised his head slightly, glimpsed the passenger-side rearview mirror, could see Romano already being attended by a Guardsman who'd rushed out the orange door. Beyond him two more soldiers were also bursting outside, apparently in hot pursuit of someone else who was—

Lane!

He gasped at the sight of her, straightened in his seat for a better view. Somehow, amidst the confusion, she'd managed to break outside and was already groping her way down the steps from the dock. Gabriel couldn't begin to fathom what she had in mind, was reassured to see the soldiers had nearly caught up.

"Damn it, Lane," he swore softly, though loud enough for Alex to hear.

"Least you know she's safe," the Maqlaq said, likewise sitting upright, "her bein' on this side."

Gabriel frowned at the remark, turned to catch the Maqlaq looking through the shattered window on his own side, then stare ahead with grim determination. The big-rig was quickly gathering momentum now, bouncing over the incoming rail tracks, beginning a wide arc through the northwest parking lot.

"You really think you can plow through those barricades outside the gate?"

"No way. Prob'ly make a good-size hole in the front a'the building, though." He cast a sideways glance, offered a twisted smile as his meaning sank in. "You got about ten seconds to jump, Healer, 'less you're plannin' to join me an' my brother."

It dawned on Gabriel the Maqlaq had no intention of trying to escape, maybe never did. And now Vincent's truck was a missile.

Apparently the U.S. Army had come to the same conclusion. The rifle fire resumed once more in deadly earnest, bullets pinging off the chrome bumper and grillwork, thudding into the cab's sheet metal, making a line of crisp ovals across the windshield before breaking out the window on Gabriel's side – without, incredibly, hitting either of them. The truck, meanwhile, was doing well over fifty now, tearing through the empty parking lot, pointed at the plant's metal façade just east of the employee entrance.

This is no way to end it, Gabriel thought – even if he *did* despise the life thrust on him by the universe. Besides, maybe there really *was* some truth to what Lane had said about his destiny, about something moving in and through his life, about there being a reason for everything that happened and everywhere he happened to be.

He let his consciousness fade to gray as he did whenever the power began to flow. Later, as if in another life, he would recall reaching past Alex to grab hold of the truck's steering wheel, then being surprised when the big Maqlaq abruptly stopped resisting him. He would also remember how, at one point, he seemed to be floating inside a ball of light he assumed was heaven but transformed into something more like hell.

And then he was running... running into darkness, running down into a cooling liquid embrace that took away the searing pain, that swathed and restored him like the waters of the River Jordan, and when he finally resurfaced it felt as if he'd been born again.

Lane couldn't explain how she'd freed herself from the two soldiers who tackled her only moments after she pushed off the railing, body-slamming her to the pavement just north of the loading dock. Maybe they'd knocked themselves senseless in the process, because neither of them so much as reached up to grab an ankle when she scrambled back to her feet and began limping, then loping, in the direction of the barreling big-rig. Not even Vincent, who'd managed to break outside seconds later, could call her off with his bellowed pleadings to let Gabriel go, saying she could do nothing more for him now and would only end up getting herself hurt.

And before she'd reached the front of the building, homing in on the sound of the diesel's engine, she *did* stumble, *did* fall, ripping the skin off the full length of one shin and portions of both palms. But she pushed herself up anyway, ignoring the pain, ignoring the fusillade of automatic weapons fire she could hear in the distance as she rounded the northwest corner of the ammo plant, running flat out again.

Until a blast of hot air pushed her backward like she'd met the front end of Amtrak's Starlite Express coming down from Chemult.

And it was precisely at that moment she saw it: A ball of the purest, blue-white luminescence, not unlike the light separating Stillwater's head and shoulders when she'd stood behind him on the grenade lines two years ago... a ball that slowly morphed into what she would later describe as a dazzling bouquet of mums that multiplied and roiled upward through her field of vision, along with streaks of brilliant gold, all of them ascending and curling in the most intricate spirals, then floating to the ground in a snowfall of fluorescent flower petals.

Perhaps a half-minute had elapsed when the same two soldiers, and then Vincent, finally found her on bloodied knees in the middle of the debris-strewn parking lot. She was facing eastward where the truck had crashed through the concrete and chain-link, and now sat half inside, half outside the perimeter fence, engulfed in the inferno sparked by a 50-caliber bullet that had found the mortar Alex left on the dashboard. The three men quickly lifted Lane to her feet, hustling her away as she now began to sob uncontrollably, while explosions from the trailer continued to shower hot metal all around them.

It wasn't until eight-thirty that morning, after Lane's parents had rushed in from Beatty to see her in the hospital, when Vincent was also allowed a brief visit. He came right to the point, reported what the forensics team had told him, explained how they'd waited until the fire in his disemboweled cab had burned itself out and the fuses in the trailer had stopped detonating. When at last it was safe to poke through the wreckage, they'd collected dozens of charred bone and tissue samples later identified as the remains of Alex Round Tree. But so far – and without any attempt to account for it – there was no trace of Gabriel's body.

"That's because he got away," Lane said when Vincent was done.

The mustachioed, stubble-faced truck driver didn't reply, was content to let her believe what she obviously wanted to, even as he found her steady gaze increasingly unnerving.

"He was already on the other side of the fence, heading for the river," she went on. "He must've climbed through the hole in the chain-link where the truck split it open. Or—I don't know—maybe he jumped out before the cab blew up."

"Lane..."

"Thing is, I can't believe no one else saw what—"

"*Laney!*"

She stopped, searched Vincent's face as he scowled back at her. It was only then he began to suspect the secret she hadn't yet revealed to anyone else, the miracle she did not share even with her own parents, perhaps because her father had neglected to bring along the one person she most wanted to see, and this was her way of punishing him.

At last she allowed the hint of a smile. "It's true, Vincent. I *did* see him. I saw Gabriel."

And Vincent thought back over all the events he'd witnessed since his arrival last night, and acknowledged that, yes, perhaps she had.

*T**he town of Sisters*** was little more than a rest stop. True, he might've stayed a month or two longer since there was plenty of work in the region, just as he'd been told some years ago, before the financial meltdown. And his carpentry skills were more than adequate to earn him a journeyman's job despite his lack of I.D. or tools, or anything other than the T-shirt, overalls and flip-flops he'd shown up in.

His temporary wardrobe, such as it was, had been cobbled together by two sympathetic fishermen he'd happened upon just north of Modoc Point, where the Sprague River empties into Upper Klamath Lake. The guileless retirees swallowed Gabriel's story about his clothing being stolen by locals when he doffed them for his "usual" brisk morning swim – including the part about the "really bad sunburn" he'd gotten from the resulting exposure. "My super-sensitive skin," he explained, prompting the pair to ferry him back to the highway so he could hitch a ride south, to the emergency clinic in Klamath Falls. Considering his appearance, it was a wonder anyone pulled over.

But someone *did,* only minutes after he'd positioned himself on the northbound side, and he arrived in the popular tourist town on his third big-rig. He stayed only long enough to earn enough money for a new duffle bag, fill it with a few changes of work clothes and buy several tubs of Bag Balm from the local Ace Hardware. The dressing for dairy cows, he'd learned through trial and error, was the only ointment capable of soothing the blistery rash extending upward from his left hip to his shoulder and across one side of his face.

Truth was, Gabriel might have expected far more severe – and more lasting – damage from the explosion. The change to his voice seemed permanent enough, after he'd sucked in a lung-full of the fireball that ripped open the roof of the cab and by all rights should have fried him like crisp bacon. Only the power flowing through his body at the time could have preserved him

But this same inexplicable energy had also apparently burned itself out in the process. The gift was gone. During his sojourn in Sisters, Gabriel had accidentally bumped into, or otherwise touched, no less than a dozen people. It was obvious he'd let his guard down during those final hours in Chiloquin, when keeping his secret didn't matter anymore. And the careless contact was utterly without effect each time, even in the case of a fellow construction worker who'd sliced himself with a Skillsaw and wouldn't stop bleeding despite Gabriel's best efforts.

The day he left Sisters he went so far as to test himself one last time on a golden retriever that had been hit by a car only moments earlier. While its owners – a mother and daughter out for an after-noon jog – stood by in tears, Gabriel gently lifted the dog's flaccid form off the asphalt and carried it over to a neighbor's lawn. And then he, too, broke into tears when it continued to lie on the grass without so much as a twitch.

Although he was crying more from relief than sorrow, Gabriel felt none of the redemption he'd experienced, if only temporarily, when he awoke beside Lane on their first morning together. And if his life had thereby returned to some kind of "normal," it now began to feel largely without purpose.

He found some solace in Warm Springs, an Indian reservation northwest of Redmond. He'd considered stopping in Redmond, actually, but decided against it when an electrician at one of its new subdivisions told him the city's former small-town ambience had long since disappeared in the growth spree now pushing its boundaries in every direction. More important, Gabriel was suddenly tired of hammers and circular saws and exterior-grade plywood. He couldn't face the same life as before.

Arriving in Warm Springs the following day, he took a job as a blackjack dealer at the confederated tribes' *Kah-Nee-Tah* casino, felt somehow comforted to find a place among the Wascos and the Paiutes despite his sadness that they, too, were forced to rely on Bustins for their livelihoods. He'd even passed himself off as part Maqlaq in order to get the job.

The story backfired when, two weeks later, the floor manager brought a guest to his table who was visiting relatives in the area. The full-blood Maqlaq was up from Chiloquin, and had recently lost his job at the ammo plant there. Though Gabriel was going by another name and kept his head shaved ever since his hair burned off in the explosion, he felt sure the visitor recognized him. And even if it was the Indian way to keep such secrets, to honor a man's right to start his life over with a brand new identity, Gabriel was back on the road the very next morning.

A few days later he found himself outside Yakima, Washington, where a sizeable Native American population was also entrenched, and he ended up spending the next two years in the area. He soon talked his way into a custodial-slash-handyman job at Providence Hospital in nearby Toppenish, signing on as Raphael Forrester, and in no time moved up to a job as orderly. He enjoyed working in the medical profession despite – or perhaps because of – the incredibly slow manner in which healing took place.

He also found new inspiration in the way *dying* took place. In fact he eventually befriended an outpatient at the hospital, a wheelchair-bound woman named Clarissa, not much older than he, who was bravely suffering through the final phases of cystic fibrosis, with only a trust fund from her deceased parents to care for her.

During his fifth month in Yakima, Clarissa invited him to move into her modest home on the outskirts of town. For nearly fifteen months he tended to her needs, exploring what he now looked upon as the "poetry" of her terminal illness, learning how to pleasure her in spite of her pain and to accept simple pleasures in return, growing in ways he never thought possible, and ultimately experiencing something very much like love. During her last six months he thought about Lane less and less, and rarely about who he'd been *before* Lane. And he considered all of this quite miraculous.

He quit his job at the hospital in Toppenish for the final seven weeks of Clarissa's life. To no one's surprise, she bequeathed him her house, a Ford Navigator with a built-in wheelchair lift, and the few shares of common stock remaining in her trust fund. Gabriel promptly sold the car and the stock and donated the proceeds to Clarissa's favorite charity, then continued to live in the house for a few more weeks until an ex-Microsoft exec from Issaquah offered to buy it for cash if he would sell it right then and there.

He took the out-of-the-blue offer as a sign, and the $40,000 profit from the house sale as an opportunity to begin the next phase of his life. He pondered going back to his roots, perhaps to attend the divinity school in Lynchburg where his mother had always hoped he would go. *But I've graduated from divinity school,* he reminded himself; and he decided to head back to California instead, maybe to Morro Bay, to rent a clapboard cottage with a view of the beach where he would listen for whatever divine guidance might whisper in the waves.

Taking only what he could fit into the duffle bag he'd kept since Sisters, Gabriel set out on a Thursday morning, thumbed a succession of short truck rides south, quickly tired of all the transfers. He spent most of that night and part of the following day at a *Flying J* truck stop in The Dalles until he found a trucker who was making a non-stop run all the way through Oregon to Redding, California, and would be leaving after lunch. The only route south, other than I-5 – which would've required a dog-leg to Portland – was Highway 97.

Gabriel knew that meant passing through a stretch of road rife with painful memories. But the trash-talking truck driver had assured him there would be no stops along the way other than the Black Bear Diner in Mt. Shasta City, and maybe a couple of short breaks to "gas up and take a piss." After Gabriel climbed into his cab and handed over a crisp hundred dollar bill for bus fare, he felt reasonably confident the driver would stick to his schedule.

The first sign of complications came just past Gilchrist, hardly more than a company-run mill town on the Little Deschutes River. Lining the eaves of a ranch house just south of town was a collection of sun-bleached antlers, a ghoulish reminder of Highway 97's reputation as a death-trap for deer. Gabriel had to smile when the trucker repeated the same speech he'd heard two years earlier – *Vincent;* hadn't thought of him in a while – about more deer dying from speeding cars than hunters' bullets. The smile disappeared when they too had to brake for a half dozen white-tails, narrowly avoiding their own contribution to the grim statistics.

By the time Gabriel spotted the faded green sign with the words *Chiloquin 6 MI,* he'd counted four deer carcasses along the roadside. He also felt his pulse quicken, and was able to relax, slightly, only after both of the exits heading east into town disappeared behind him like spent fire logs that flickered briefly before turning to ash.

A few more miles south, however, the trucker floated a proposal to stop at the Indian casino where he'd taken a break on several previous trips. "That thermos a' coffee I been nursin' is makin' me downright uncomfortable," he complained. "Sides, your C-note oughta buy us a good-sized bucket a' quarters. You wanna go pull on some one-arm Injun-givers?—my treat."

"One-armed what—?"

"Bandits, then. One-arm *bandits.* You know... slot machines."

"Isn't there some other rest stop between here and Klamath Falls?"

"Not where I could win fifty grand on one pull. You see that billboard back there?"

The trucker turned, squinted. Gabriel shifted uneasily, tried not to let on that stopping at the casino would be almost as distressing as a side trip to Chiloquin.

"You go ahead. I'll just hang out for a while, maybe stretch my legs."

Another sideways glance. "Uh huh. You got somethin' against Indians, maybe? Or else gambling?"

"Yeah, gambling." It was as good an excuse as any, and partly true, even when he was dealing blackjack. "Never had much luck at it."

The trucker shrugged as if to say, *Suit yourself,* let off the accelerator as the 30-foot sign flashing the name *Kla-Mo-Yah* appeared a half-mile ahead. Moments later, directly across from the casino entrance, a buck and two does scuffled down the highway embankment. Gabriel tensed, as did the trucker, both of them huffing with relief when the trio turned tail and broke for the lodgepoles.

"Come to think of it, you stay out with the rig, you might luck out and see what the locals use to make jerky."

He cackled at his own witticism – despite all the deer jokes having worn thin by now – waited for a cluster of oncoming cars to pass before turning into the truck parking area. Gabriel debated staying in the cab, finally decided chances were slim-to-none anyone could identify him, jumped down from the rig as the trucker hurried off with visions of triple arrowheads.

For ten minutes or so he paced the length of the gravel lot, silently chiding himself at how easily thoughts of the past seemed to roil up.

Another ten passed while he rested against the truck's front fender, arms crossed, soaking up some late-afternoon sun as he continued to ruminate, when the sound of screeching tires broke in.

He swirled to see a blur of chrome, blue metal and brown deer hide. The make of the car was the last thing on his mind as he bolted for the roadside where the driver skidded to a belated, dust-shrouded stop. But the instant he recognized it, he too skidded and stopped.

Thirty yards away was the same car he'd driven around southern Oregon two years ago. He was sure of it: 1965 sky-blue Mustang coupe, just as faded and pock-marked as when he'd last seen it, a dented rear fender now matched by freshly-crumpled metal in front.

And the occupant just now getting out: Shaggy blonde tresses haloed by sunlight, girlish silhouette implanted in his memory like one of the "mental snapshots" she once described as a legacy of her blindness. Odd thing was, she'd emerged from the *driver's* side of the car. And she was staring at him with a helpless, what-do-I-do-now expression even Clarissa's gentle, pleading eyes couldn't match.

Lane.

He remained frozen in place, finally remembered she couldn't possibly recognize him, hadn't regained her eyesight when they were together those few, life-altering days. Nor would she be likely to recognize his raspier voice, assuming he could unfreeze his limbs enough to go over and converse with her.

"Can you help me?"

She was calling him now, looking distractedly from Gabriel to the buck she'd just hit, to the front fender of the Mustang, then back. At last he forced himself to move, made his way across the parking lot, down the gully and up the embankment. He halted beside the splay-legged deer, knelt long enough to lay a hand on its ribcage and confirm neither breath nor heartbeat, then stood and looked up the highway toward Lane.

"You okay?"

"We're fine—just a little shaken up."

Gabriel nodded sympathetically, resumed walking, noticed for the first time another occupant in the car: Midnight brown hair, small face turned partway around, visible just above the windowsill of the passenger-side door.

"Do I just leave it there?" Lane was saying. "I mean, this has never..." Again the helpless expression. "I feel just terrible."

"It happens," Gabriel replied, avoiding the more colorful noun. "Guess bagging a deer is only a matter of time, you live around here." He shrugged, didn't know why he needed to ask; maybe it would seem more natural. "You, uh, *do* live around here?"

"Just up the road a bit, then east about ten miles." She squinted. "It *is* dead, right?"

"Yeah. I'm sure he didn't feel any pain."

She nodded thankfully for the partial reassurance, looked at the animal once more before glancing back at the Mustang. "You know anything about cars?"

Gabriel frowned, was surprised *she* didn't. His recollection of Lane was of a woman capable of doing pretty much everything for herself, even when she was blind.

"Don't wanna drive if it's not safe," she explained. "My daughter's with me."

He nodded approvingly at her caution, walked alongside the car as Lane gestured toward the front end. Gabriel stole a glance through the window when the child turned to look up – what was her name? *Jenna* – was pleased with himself for recalling another piece of the past. The thought briefly crossed his mind that she could recognize him, but Lane's daughter was barely three years old at the time, and they were together only a few hours. In any case, Gabriel was fairly certain he wouldn't have recognized *her*. She appeared far more Maqlaq than he remembered.

He stopped beside Lane, found it difficult to look at her, much less make eye contact, reached under the grill for the hood release. It popped open easily enough, but the edge of the sheet metal scraped loudly against the engine compartment as he strained to lift it.

"Ouch. Not a good sign, is it?" she ventured.

"Shouldn't be a problem, long as the radiator's not damaged," he said, businesslike, looking through the windshield before the hood stuck on its hinges. "So, did you adopt her?"

Again, he didn't know why he asked, kicked himself for seeming a bit too personal for the stranger he was supposed to be. "She's beautiful," he added quickly, hoping the compliment might clarify his query. Or was he now implying her mother *wasn't?* "I'm sorry. I didn't mean to be—"

"Don't apologize. I say whatever pops into my head, too. Can't exactly blame anybody else when *they* do."

That was the Lane he recalled. Gabriel turned toward her now, looked into her eyes as she stared back at him – right on target – felt his pulse quicken again. He hoped she wouldn't notice the arteries thumping in his neck, was suddenly struck by the effect she could still have on him, was all the more amazed to be standing here with her in the first place, with this woman who had changed his life in the course of three days, two years earlier almost to the day; how incredible the odds.

He also remembered how she'd once asked him to consider whether there might be larger forces operating in his life – and in hers, too – arranging events in some purposeful, even if enigmatic, way.

"And no, she's not adopted," she went on, now peering back with more than idle curiosity. "Her father lives with me, raises Appaloosas."

Father? *Appaloosas—?*

Buddy! She hadn't gone back to Richard, after all. Maybe Lane's vision had returned in more ways than one. He was grateful for the news, turned quickly away at the abrupt awareness his eyes were beginning to water.

He did his best to focus on what she'd asked him to do – inspect the radiator, check the hose fittings, look under the car for hidden leaks or other damage – tried to sound nonchalant as he tore off a piece of shredded insulation dangling alongside the oil pan.

"And you...? What do *you* do on your ranch?"

There was a pause. "Ranch?"

Damn! She never said—

"I never said we lived on a ranch."

"Oh. I just assumed you and your husband must live on a ranch... you know, if he raises Appaloosas."

"Didn't say we were married, either." She paused again, allowed a smile. "Not exactly the marrying type. It's some kind of miracle—" She nodded past the upraised hood at Jenna. "—her father is willing to live under the same roof with us, the way I am sometimes."

She waited while Gabriel pulled himself from beneath the front bumper and reached back inside the wheel well to make sure the crumpled metal wouldn't interfere with the tire.

"Anyway, to answer your question, I work at the ammo plant."

Gabriel practically beaned himself on the fender as he straightened. "There's still an ammo plant?"

Admittedly, he had no definitive knowledge either way, except for an article he'd seen in Yakima's weekly rag about some of the local Modocs' relatives losing jobs there. After another year without so much as a column-inch of newsprint, he'd basically forgotten about it.

"Well, we still refer to it that way around here, even though it was converted to civilian use about..."

Lane broke off eye contact, glanced skyward as if calculating the passage of time. Gabriel felt the lump in his throat grow still larger at the sight of her own tears welling up. She quickly blinked them away.

"...maybe two years ago, I'd guess. Army still owns the building, and they can go back into production if there's another war, or we invade somebody else." She brightened, turned back. "But there's almost a dozen private companies using the place now. Biggest one makes farm implements—the place I work for."

Gabriel ducked back under the fender. He toyed with the idea of just telling her, just admitting to her who he was; wasn't she beginning to suspect, anyway? How he wanted to throw his arms around her, go off somewhere and talk, fill in the last two years of each other's lives, let her know how happy he was that she had both her sight and her child back, not to mention a new life with a man who cared for her.

Which was exactly why he *couldn't* tell her. He fought more tears, remained beneath the car, hunched and unmoving, long enough for Lane to wonder why.

"Is there a problem? Did you find something?"

"No, no." He came up wiping an eye, hoped he could fool her once more. "Just some dirt blew in my face. *Damn* it." He immediately looked away at Jenna, shook his head ruefully. "Oh, sorry. I shouldn't—"

"Remember what I told you?" She cut him off, wagged a finger in mock disapproval. "Don't apologize. Besides, it's hardly the worst she's heard, believe me." A grin, then: "So the car's okay to drive?"

"Far as I can see. Too bad it's banged up, though. Maybe this'll be an excuse to finally get it fixed up the way it deserves."

He caught his second *faux pas* the instant she did. How would he know she'd had the car for some time *without* bothering to fix it up? The hole was beginning to get a little too deep.

"Are you... from around here?" she asked.

"No. Why?"

"I don't know. It just seems like..." She paused, blushed. "Nothing. You just... never mind—it's stupid."

He couldn't help feeling sorry for any painful memories he might be dredging up. It was enough *he* was suffering.

"I've passed through here once or twice, though. And I've been driving long enough..." Gabriel waved at the big-rig parked some distance away. The trucker he'd hitched a ride with was evidently losing quarters at a slow enough pace to keep him occupied. Then he turned, gazed even more conspicuously at the deer lying thirty yards south. "...long enough to have bagged a few myself."

He glanced sideways at Lane, watching as she peered down the highway at the buck, then gave the slightest nod to herself. Gabriel imagined the wheels turning: She'd seen him bend over, lay a hand on the downed deer. And it was still lying there, its long, shockingly-pink tongue dangling onto the asphalt. If the poor thing hadn't gotten up and run off by now, this couldn't be the man she suspected it might be.

"What did you say your name was?"

"Right. I don't think we've been properly introduced, have we?" He turned fully, put on a smile, held out his hand. "Friends call me Rafer."

"Rafer..."

She took his hand, repeated the name very deliberately, as if connecting the nickname with its original. Had he blundered again? Gabriel couldn't remember having told her anything but his middle name, though the police chief certainly knew.

At last she released his hand, stepped back around the front of her car to slam the hood. It scraped loudly again, but latched.

"Well, Rafer, *my* friends call me Laney. And I'm grateful you could have a look at—"

"How much do you think it would cost to get this thing restored?"

Gabriel interrupted her now, knew this too was crazy; but he couldn't let her just walk away. Not so soon. Not after two years.

"What?"

"Seriously. What would it take to get this thing back in mint condition?"

"Well, I..." She was obviously flustered, uncertain what he was getting at. "...I've had a couple of boyfriends do a little bodywork over the years." And then she stopped, scowled. "I don't know if I'd *want* to restore it—"

"Come on, Lane. Five thousand bucks? Six...? *Ten*—?"

"—'cause I kinda like it the way it—"

"Because you know what?—I just had a little luck, and I wouldn't mind sharing—"

"Luck? What do you—"

"—it with somebody."

"—mean you had a little luck?"

It was beginning to sound just like old times, insofar as three days was enough to qualify for the description. He laughed at the familiarity of their banter, which in turn made her laugh, bittersweet though it was.

Gabriel nodded toward the casino. "So happens I just hit a jackpot. Forty grand—can you believe it?" This, too, was partly true. And he was pleased when Lane glanced at the fieldstone-and-timber building nestled among the lodgepoles, raising an eyebrow as if she might believe him.

"Hell, I have no use for forty thousand dollars," he said flatly. "I'd give you ten of it right now, if you'll promise to use it—"

"Whoa—wait just a minute—"

And they were off again.

"—on your Mustang."

"I can't accept that kind of money—"

"Yes you can, Lane."

"—from a total stranger."

"You can because it was meant to be. You said yourself—"

He stopped as her eyes suddenly widened, realized he couldn't go there because it would give him completely away. He took a breath – and a different tack.

"You don't believe this could've happened by chance, do you? I luck into forty grand, and then I come out and stand here while this beautiful woman with her beautiful child bangs up the front of her classic car on some stray deer that just happens to cross the highway at that moment?"

She was still dumbstruck. The *beautiful woman* part didn't hurt, either.

"Look, Lane. I've got the cash back in my—" He caught himself as he was about to say *duffle bag;* one more clue he could ill afford. "—in the glove compartment of my truck. It'll take me thirty seconds to go over—"

"No, I told you—I can't. I mean, there's just no way I come home from my weekly appointment down at Klamath General with ten thousand—"

"Klamath General?"

They both stopped. *Weekly appointment?* Maybe she was still undergoing treatment for her eyes, Gabriel thought. But why would she drive herself on an undivided, mostly two-lane highway if her eyes weren't fully functional? And risk taking her daughter along if she—

Gabriel glanced at Jenna, knew when he turned back that Lane was already one step ahead of him. Which was also just like old times.

"It's not life-threatening or anything, only a constriction in some of her joints. I don't know—maybe I passed it on to her. My mother has bursitis pretty bad, even if she didn't get it this young."

He stepped closer to the passenger-side window, peered in, smiled. The little girl returned it easily, without hesitation.

And it was then he saw his Bible, lying on the hump between the bucket seats.

His Bible!

He all but gasped at the sight of the white, leatherette-bound volume, its ragged, gold-foil letters reflecting the waning sunlight. Lane thought at first it was Jenna who had caused his reaction, hurried over to see what could be wrong. Gabriel finally stopped gaping, but not before she'd spotted the real reason.

"My aunt had one just like it," he said hastily, without having to invent anything new. He'd used the story about the aunt so often he'd almost grown to believe that's where the Bible had come from, even though it bore his mother's inscription. "Looks like the same edition."

He noticed Lane out of the corner of his eyes, peering suspiciously again.

"You can take a closer look if you like," she said, now clearly testing him. "Jenna, honey, hand the Bible to Rafer, would you?"

"No, no—that's okay."

And yet, how he longed to touch it, to take the small brass cross between his fingertips, draw it along the zippered top, down the side and underneath, opening it to the elegantly-scripted words that would take him back across all those difficult years. And the treasures hidden beneath the title page... the brass pillbox, the ring, the key to the safety deposit box in Lawrence where there was even more cash than he had in his duffle bag, the photo of himself after he'd—

The photograph.

He was only eight at the time, but there might be enough of a resemblance, especially now that the side of his face had cleared up and he'd grown his hair back.

"Go ahead..."

Jenna was holding the Bible through the open window, still smiling up at him, blue eyes a breathtaking contrast to the dark brown hair riffling across her face as a breeze suddenly wafted through. Gabriel didn't know how or why the power returned just then, only that it *did.*

He let out a sigh, nodding to himself as if to admit he'd always known it would, finally accepted the Bible, glanced over it for only a few moments before handing it back. He took care to clasp Jenna's right hand against the cover before he released it, firmly, so there would be no spark, pretending he was only making sure she had a firm grip.

Lane was searching his face now. He pulled back from the window, turned to look at her, suddenly serene, suddenly aware as he met her eyes that he would mail the ten thousand dollars to her anyway. In fact he would send her the address of the safe deposit box in Lawrence and leave her the rest of his savings, too. He wouldn't need much money where he was going; and it comforted him knowing her dream of running a bed-and-breakfast might yet come true.

"Funny, the Bible's not anything like the one my aunt had," he lied. "I don't know what I was thinking."

"That *is* funny," Lane said dubiously. "It's also really weird, how I hardly ever take that Bible with me. It's not even mine."

Again she was searching him, hoping he might yet betray himself. And if anything, Gabriel was enjoying their little game, knowing his face would be burned into her memory now, as hers was in his, knowing it was all part of the same ongoing, unfolding miracle.

"For some reason I felt like I just had to bring it along today. And for a little while... I thought I knew why."

They continued to gaze at each other for several more moments, silently, even though Gabriel could have given her the reason – the same one she'd given him – until at last she nodded and repeated what she'd said earlier about being grateful for his help. And then she turned and walked around her car, got in and started the engine as Jenna waved happily; and after waiting for a big-rig to pass, she pulled back onto the highway.

Gabriel watched the Mustang ascend a small rise in the distance and disappear over the top, then turned back to see the deer still splayed across the shoulder. He knew his resurgent power wasn't because of the Bible, or because of anything hidden in its secret, hollowed-out holy of holies. It wasn't as if there was any magic in its pages, or some mystical force like that contained within the fictional, silvery orbs in the old movie he'd replayed a dozen times following his mother's death. The only efficacy the book bestowed was its persistent reminder of who he was, and what it was his lot to do and to be in life, whether he fought against it or not.

He allowed another smile, glad for what the universe had restored in this not-by-chance encounter, started walking back to the buck with a lightness of step he'd all but forgotten, with a renewed feeling of sheer boundlessness that made all things possible; and he knew the animal would not remain there for long.

EXTRAS

Study Guide 370

About the Author 373

Author Interview 374

Other Books by Mark Haskett 380

Pages for Notes 381

The following questions relate to the major themes and issues raised in GreaterMiracles. *They are provided by the publisher to fuel discussion in book clubs or other group settings, or simply to inspire further reflection by the individual reader. If you'd like to print out hardcopies of these questions for use in group settings, please download our PDF at www.IFMedia.org/GreaterMiracles/Guide.* If you wish to share any thoughts from your personal reflections or group discussions, please see the "Feedback" page on that website.

1   From the very beginning, Gabriel admits to a need for arranging periodic trysts with women whose health and fitness are more important than looks or personality. What do you think is the primary drive behind this need?

2   What are the circumstances that precipitate Gabriel's latest "journey" to the small town in Southern Oregon where he eventually meets Lane, and where most of our story takes place? Why does he feel like he's never able to stay in one location for very long?

3   If you were in possession of a gift such as Gabriel's, would you try to keep it secret, or make it public? Why or why not?

4   Gabriel recalls a mid-80s film, *Starman,* in which the leading character brings a deer back to life after a hunter has killed it. A decade later, the film *Powder* included a scene in which the death of a doe is a transformative event. What is the significance/symbolism of deer in these films? And why do you think Gabriel felt the need to save the two deer after they were hit by Vincent's truck?

5   Gabriel's character combines powers we normally think of as divine or supernatural – or even saintly – with sensuality and raw physicality. Do you think it is possible for men and women to reflect both a strong "physical" nature and a deeply spiritual side? Does one aspect diminish or complement the other?

6 Are there special gifts each of us possesses that others don't? How do we incorporate such gifts into our lives and still maintain balance with other personal needs and functions? Are these gifts related to what we think of as our purpose or "mission" in life? What happens if we focus solely on such gifts to the exclusion of others – or, on the other hand, we neglect or ignore them?

7 Who are the "Maqlaqs" and 'Bustins" in our story, and where did their names come from? While these are real names for real people, do they also represent other divisions or classes in our society?

8 Deputy Chino tells Gabriel about a Maqlaq legend depicting a kind of Prodigal Son figure who returns to the area to lead his people back to their Old Ways. How is Gabriel thought by some to fit this role? What are the "ways" the Maqlaq legend refers to, and how were they lost? What are the practices or ideals *we* have lost? And are there methods for recovering the essence of them, while accommodating the realities of today?

9 The ammunition plant near the real-life town of Chiloquin, Oregon, is only fictional. However, that industry *does* symbolize a very real presence in that town – and in communities throughout America. What is this "presence," and what does it say about us? About our future? How does our story resolve the issue, and is that solution realistic for our lives?

10 The title of our novel, *Greater Miracles*, is drawn from a term used in the Bible's New Testament. What is its meaning, theologically speaking, and how does it underscore a major theme in the book? How does Gabriel's analysis of Rev. D'Arcy's sermon on the "Loaves and Fishes" miracle relate to that theme?

(continued)

11　As the story unfolds, two issues arise which seem to complicate the growing relationship between Gabriel and Lane: The possibility that he may be a union activist, and the Termination/Restoration issue between America's Native American population and the federal government. How does this "complication" advance the plot? How is it relevant to the book's theme?

12　Lane's disability as a result of her accident at the munitions factory is a primary element in the story, and an ongoing challenge to Gabriel. Why does Gabriel view her disability a "miracle," both for himself and for Lane?

13　How do Lane's life choices in response to her accident illustrate the ways many of us deal with our own personal tragedies and challenges? How and why have her attitudes evolved? In what ways are her actions symbolic of our own spiritual journeys?

14　In literary parlance, Lane can be described as a "strong female protagonist." How is her strength illustrated as the story develops? What exemplifies her strength at the conclusion?

15　The book's apparent climax at the ammo plant isn't really "the end of the story." The narrative continues with a single chapter that takes us through another two years of Gabriel's life, and brings us to one last, bittersweet scene between Lane and Gabriel... and another deer. How does this chapter tie up any "loose ends" – or *does* it?

16　*(Optional)* Is the conclusion of *Greater Miracles* satisfying, or does it leave you wanting more... or both? Please tell the publisher if you'd like to be notified if/when a sequel comes out. You may also share your thoughts with the author, or send a brief review of the book, by going to: www.IFMedia.org/GreaterMiracles/Comments.

MARK HASKETT is a working artist, writer and musician, and has been a student of philosophy and religion for most of his adult life. He has authored articles, novels and non-fiction books, each of which invites his readers to explore the deeper dimensions of everyday life that provide meaning and enhance mutual understanding. (For brief synopses of his other books, turn to page 380.)

Active in his local interfaith community, Mark is a frequent guest speaker and moderator on matters of practical faith and spirituality. He occasionally tours with his "Song of The Prophet" concert/service drawn from Kahlil Gibran's poetic masterwork, The Prophet.

Mark resides with his wife Nancy in California's Central Valley, and may be contacted directly by going to: www.IFMedia.org/Feedback.

IF MEDIA: *A story featuring some kind of "miracle man" with healing powers isn't exactly new. But I see you've given it a "novel" twist, you'll pardon the pun.*

Mark: A couple of twists, actually. First, Gabriel can't help it. Just brushing up against someone on a bus, or accidentally knocking into a wheelchair-bound vet... any physical contact will get the job done. And the problem is – the second twist – is that Gabriel doesn't want that job.

Why would anybody not want miraculous powers?

Mark: Because, for one thing, once our protagonist has been discovered, people won't leave him alone. Ever since Gabriel was given his so-called "gift," he's simply unable to live anything approaching a normal life, which he wants back desperately. Instead, he's always on guard, and almost always on the run.

...Until a trucker who abets his most recent "escape" drops him off in a small half-Anglo, half-Indian town in southern Oregon.

Mark: "Drops him off" is probably not the best way to put it. In any case, this is just one more temporary stopover in Gabriel's vagabond existence. But it's where my novel spends most of its time.

Because Gabriel thinks he's found the solution to his "problem."

Mark: Right – in the form of Lane D'Arcy, a woman with a physical disability that, for some unknown reason, doesn't respond to his miraculous touch. For Gabriel, this is kind of a miracle in itself. Lane lives on a secluded ranch, she seems to like having him around...

... And then things get complicated.

Mark: As they always do, right? To quote John Lennon, "Life is what happens when you're busy making other plans." Besides which, we can't keep running away from who we are forever.

One of the themes in your novel, I'm presuming.

Mark: A minor one. The main theme has to do with what we think a "miracle" is in the first place. Gabriel's powers are the kind most of us traditionally associate with the word – the thing that happens in the Bible or in religious lore, or maybe in super-hero comic books. I'll let readers decide for themselves what the real miracle is, or miracles *are*, in the book. Or in our lives.

And that explains your book's title, **Greater Miracles...**

Mark: Yes, although that wasn't the original title.

Which was...?

Mark: Funny story. For several years the manuscript had the working title, "Lesser Miracles," after a term in the New Testament where Jesus' followers were instructed to go out and perform their own signs and wonders. Maybe not the show-stoppers a Son of God might perform, but the little, everyday ones that tend to restore your faith in life and your fellow human beings. Anyhow, as I'm working on my final draft, some really creepy B-movie comes out with that title, which I really didn't want my novel to be associated with. So *Greater Miracles* it is.

Okay then, sticking with the religious theme—

Mark: I'd avoid labeling this a "religious book," by the way. In fact, if *Greater Miracles* were a movie, there are a couple of scenes that might earn it a solid "R" rating. And, like I've

(continued on next page)

said elsewhere, I prefer to describe my writing as "spiritual, not religious."

But you do get into religion.

Mark: All of my books do. Faith and religion are major components of our lives, even if you're not what people think of as "religious."

Which is a topic for discussion in one of your other books, FaithSpeak.

Mark: Yeah, and I've actually written a lot more *non*-fiction than fiction concerning that subject. But I also believe that a good, old-fashioned work of pure fiction can sometimes reveal a lot more about truth and faith and the meaning of life than a sacred text or sermon. Or a seminar on how to be a good Catholic or Jew or whatever.

Okay, staying on topic then... Most of your story takes place in the little burg of Chiloquin, Oregon. Is that a real place?

Mark: Chill-oh-*keen*, by the way. Not *kwin*, like "The Mighty Quinn." At least that's how the name is spoken according to the elder Native Americans I interviewed there. And yes, it's a real town, with a struggling economy and mixed population that includes members of the Maqlaq tribe among others – pronounced less like "mac-lack" than those slippers some of us grew up with. Think *muk-luks*.

So why Chiloquin?

Mark: Well, it's a town just off Highway 97 my wife and kids and I would drive by on our yearly vacations to Oregon where my in-laws lived. One day I decided to pull off and see what was there. The fact that my "miracle man" storyline was rumbling around in my brain at the time turned out to be serendipitous.

Is it pretty much as you describe it, physically and demographically?

Mark: The town itself is. I've taken a few liberties with some of the surrounding geography and the Army ammunition plant that plays a major role in the story. The plant isn't really located just outside of town there, although it *does* symbolize the heavy hand our federal government has played in the region, at least with the local tribes.

There's a Vietnam-era ammo plant about ten miles from my home in Central California, however, that served as my inspiration for the fictional one in Chiloquin. I was given several tours of the facility and asked to take photos for a national company that was contracted by the Army to convert it to civilian use. I did the brochure for them, not realizing at the time I was actually doing research for a future novel!

Then again, everything we do is "research" for our future lives, whether we're writers or teachers... or interviewers.

Mark: Well said.

What else inspired you about Chiloquin, or at least the general area?

Mark: That so many possible themes and subplots come together there. Like Native American and Anglo culture clash... well, not necessarily "clash," but differences in lifestyles and values. And the idea of an ammunition factory in an otherwise pastoral setting, as if to remind us that we all participate in a war economy, even if we try to distance ourselves from that ugly reality. Plus the fact that life's

(concluded on following pages)

biggest issues often play out in small, intimate settings – which is why authors love small towns.

There's a scene in the book where Gabriel gets into an argument with a church pastor in another small town, over the New Testament story Christians know as the Miracle of the Loaves and Fishes...

Mark: Let's not go there, if you don't mind. That little episode pretty much summarizes what I see as the biggest mistake we all make when thinking about miracles. I could simply tell you what I think, but I'd rather the story say it for me.

Fair enough. So let's talk about the nice little surprise that comes right after that scene...

Mark: Uh, let's not go there either, since I'd rather not have this interview turn out like one of those movie trailers where you basically see all the high points and now there's no reason to go and spend money on a ticket.

Or now that you've read the book, you don't need to go see the movie.

Mark: Now there's a thought. Of all the published and unpublished manuscripts I've written – including a half dozen screenplays... out of all those works, this is the one I'd most love to see made into a feature film. Even with all the other subplots complicating things, it's such a beautiful little story about two people coming to own who they are. And I'd love to hear if my readers agree with me.

And I feel like we could end this little interview right there... except that I'd really like to ask you about the book's ending.

Mark: Which one?

Well, that's right. There's the climax that takes place at the ammo plant. Then there's the final chapter that compresses the next two years in Gabriel's life, culminating in what I can only describe as a bittersweet scene where Gabriel unexpectedly crosses paths with Lane one more time.

Mark: And she doesn't recognize him. Yeah, that whole sequence came to me in a sort of waking dream, literally in the middle of the night. I had to get out of bed so I wouldn't wake up my wife, then go lie down in another room while this scene played out in my mind almost like I was watching a movie. And I, well... this is going to make me sound kind of pathetic... I cried at the end.

Ah, but it's not really the end, is it?

Mark: No, frankly, it might easily be the beginning of a sequel or two. But whether any of us will get to see what comes next in Gabriel's life – me included – is another question I'd like my readers to weigh in on.

Well, here's hoping they do.

When evangelist Jimmy Talbot opens a Gospel-themed casino in downtown Las Vegas, estranged half-brother Levi is assigned to lead an investigation into the bomb threat and the string of grisly murders connected to it. Both a crime novel and social commentary, **CALVARY CASINO** is ultimately a page-turning parable on the subject of reconciliation and redemption.

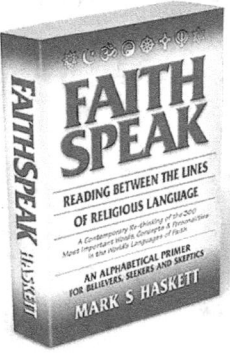

This book will change the way you think about "faith" and "religion" – and about the loaded words we too often use without knowing what they really mean. While masquerading as a down-to-earth lexicon of inter-religious terminology, **FAITHSPEAK** is an adventure in comparative religion, and a handy resource for the reader's ongoing spiritual journeys.

The timeless wisdom of Kahlil Gibran's poetic masterwork, The Prophet, is showcased in these insightful reflections on 101 of the book's most compelling passages. Divided into nine even-more-fundamental themes that underlie Gibran's 26 "counsels," **A DEEPER SONG** infuses the full breadth of human experience with fresh meaning and significance.

Whether you're a devoted fan of Star Trek® or not, you'll find a treasury of inspiration and insight in **BOLDLY GOING ON YOUR INNER VOYAGE**. Each daily reading begins with a quotation from one of the franchise's fascinating characters, then offers thought-provoking meditations and practical affirmations on themes ranging from Inner Conflict to Forgiveness, from Accepting Oneself to Serving Others.*

NOTES